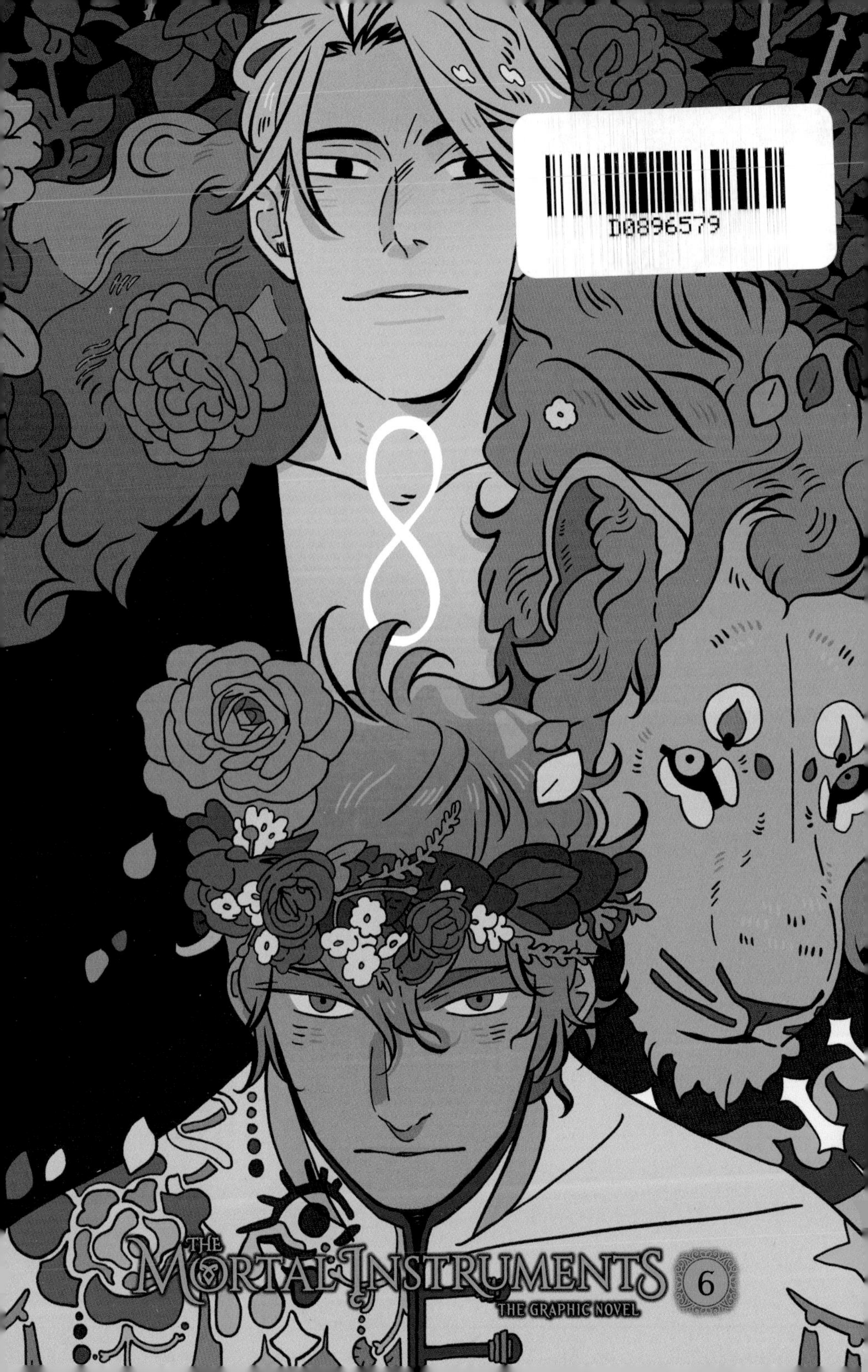
THE MORTAL INSTRUMENTS
6
THE GRAPHIC NOVEL
D0896579

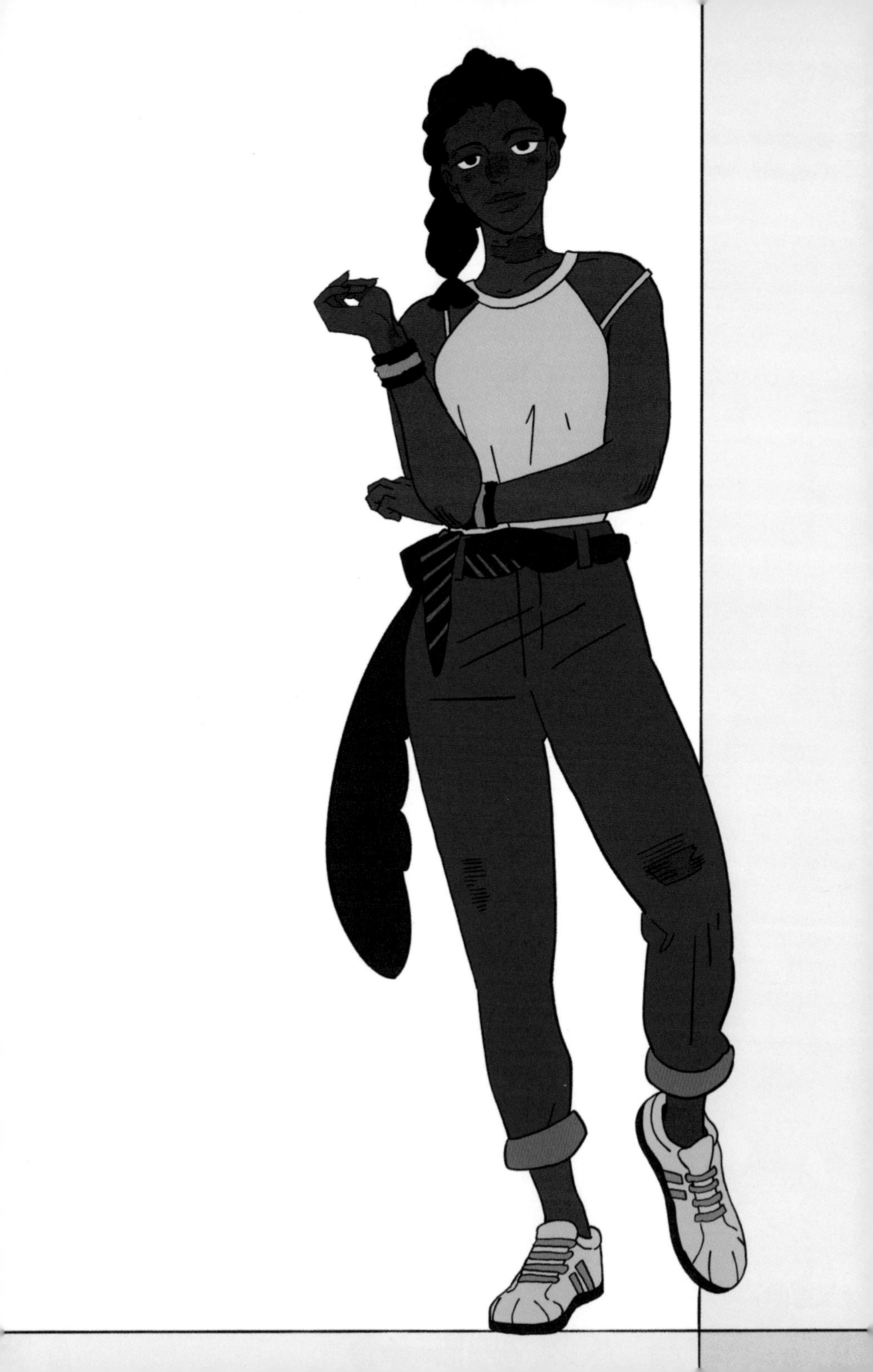

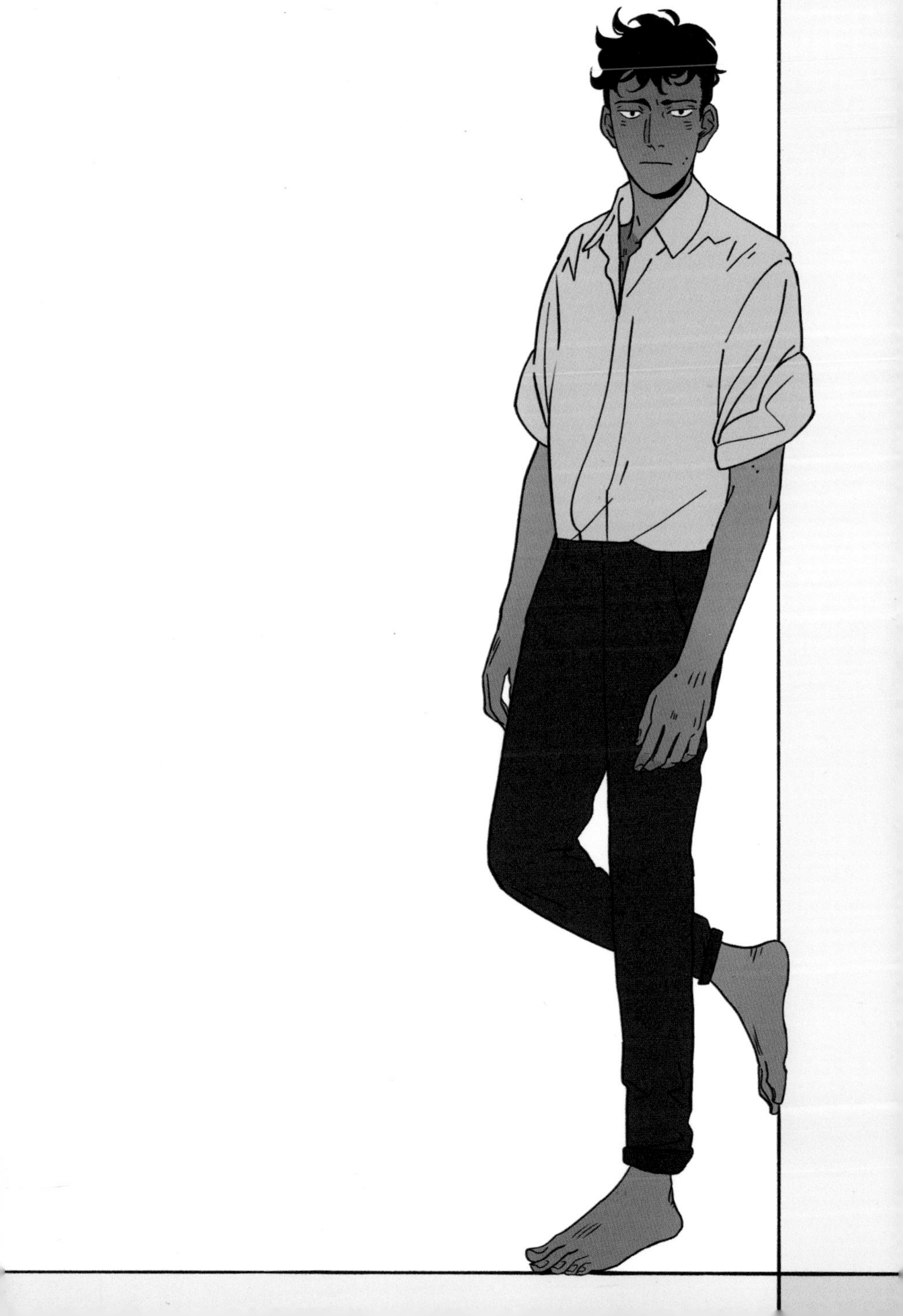

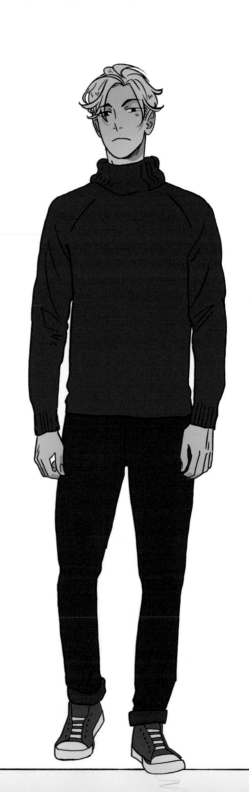

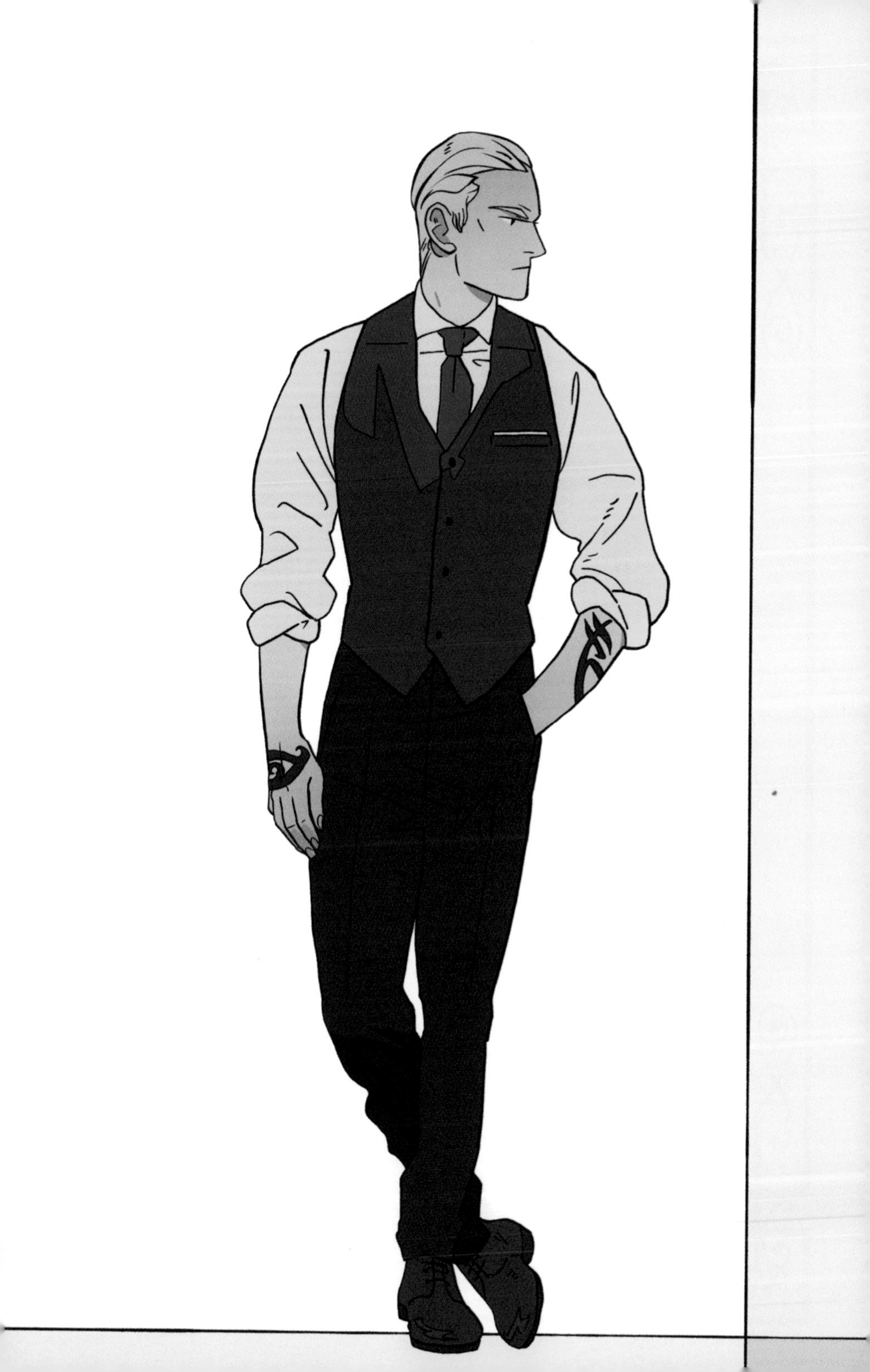

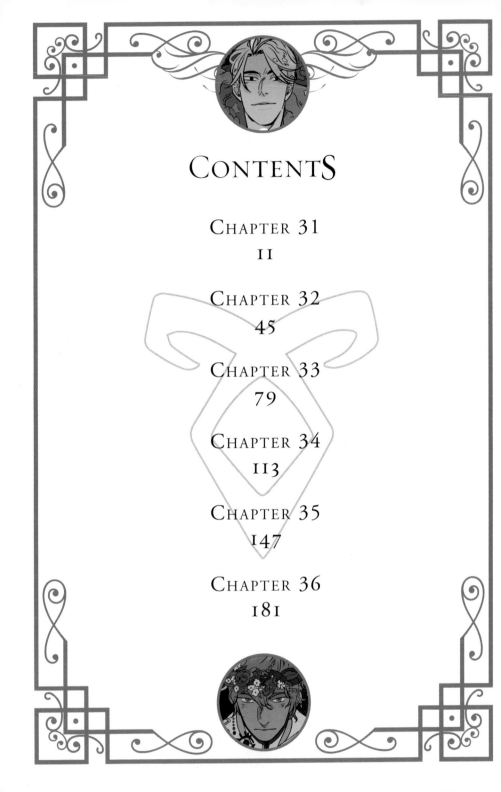

CONTENTS

THE MORTAL INSTRUMENTS

THE GRAPHIC NOVEL

STORY BY
CASSANDRA CLARE

6

ART BY
CASSANDRA JEAN

THE MORTAL INSTRUMENTS 6
THE GRAPHIC NOVEL

CASSANDRA CLARE
CASSANDRA JEAN

ART AND ADAPTATION: CASSANDRA JEAN
LETTERING: ABIGAIL BLACKMAN

Text copyright © 2009 by Cassandra Clare, LLC

Illustrations © 2022 by Yen Press, LLC

Yen Press, LLC supports the right to free expression and the value of copyright. The purpose of copyright is to encourage writers and artists to produce the creative works that enrich our culture.

The scanning, uploading, and distribution of this book without permission is a theft of the author's intellectual property. If you would like permission to use material from the book (other than for review purposes), please contact the publisher. Thank you for your support of the author's rights.

Yen Press
150 West 30th Street, 19th Floor
New York, NY 10001

Visit us at yenpress.com
facebook.com/yenpress
twitter.com/yenpress
yenpress.tumblr.com
instagram.com/yenpress

First Yen Press Edition: December 2022
Edited by Abigail Blackman & Yen Press Editorial: JuYoun Lee
Designed by Yen Press Design: Wendy Chan

Yen Press is an imprint of Yen Press, LLC.
The Yen Press name and logo are trademarks of Yen Press, LLC.

The publisher is not responsible for websites (or their content) that are not owned by the publisher.

Library of Congress Control Number: 2017945496

ISBNs: 978-1-9753-4128-2 (paperback)
978-1-9753-4129-9 (ebook)

1 3 5 7 9 10 8 6 4 2

WOR

Printed in the United States of America

Chapter 31

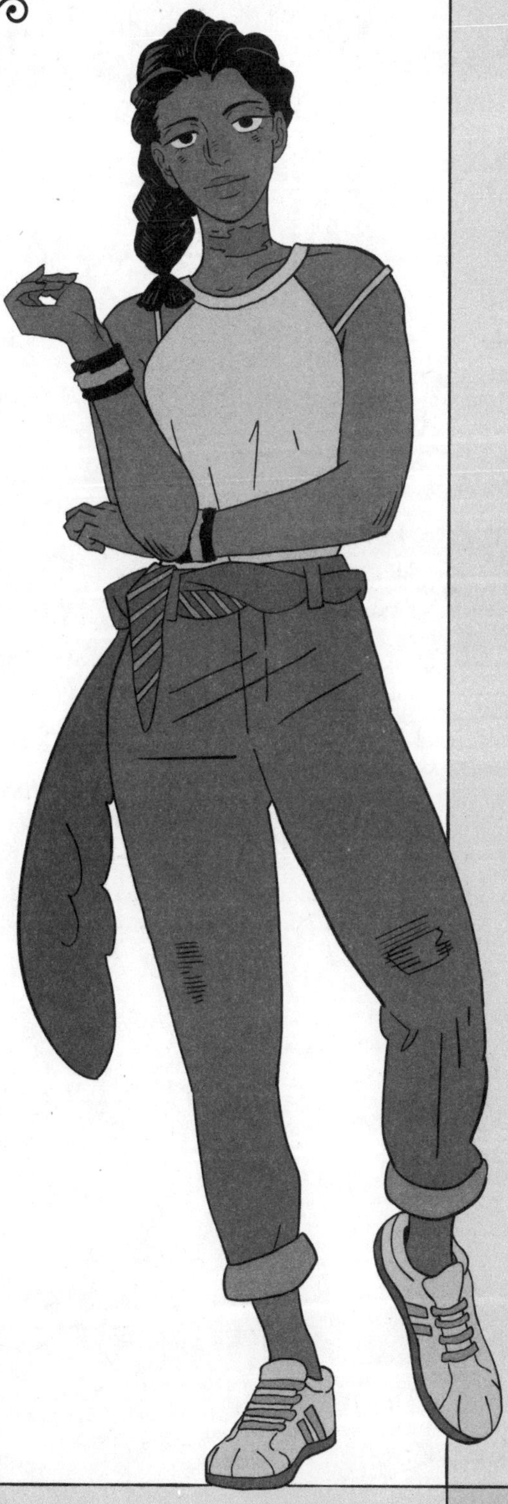

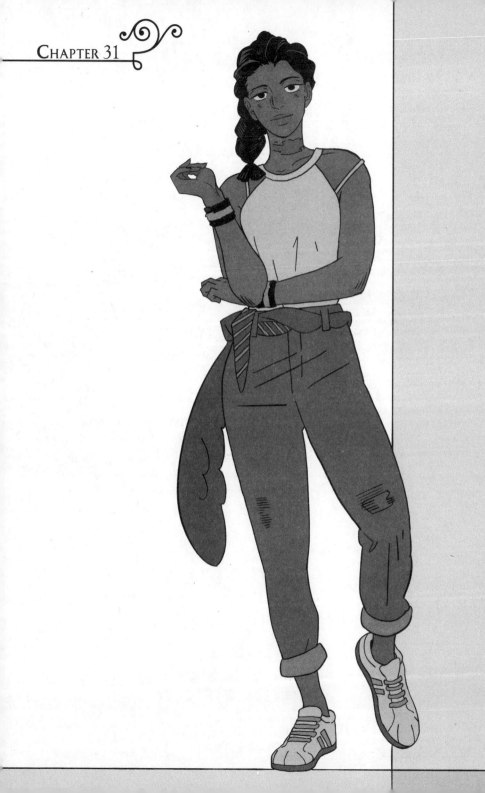

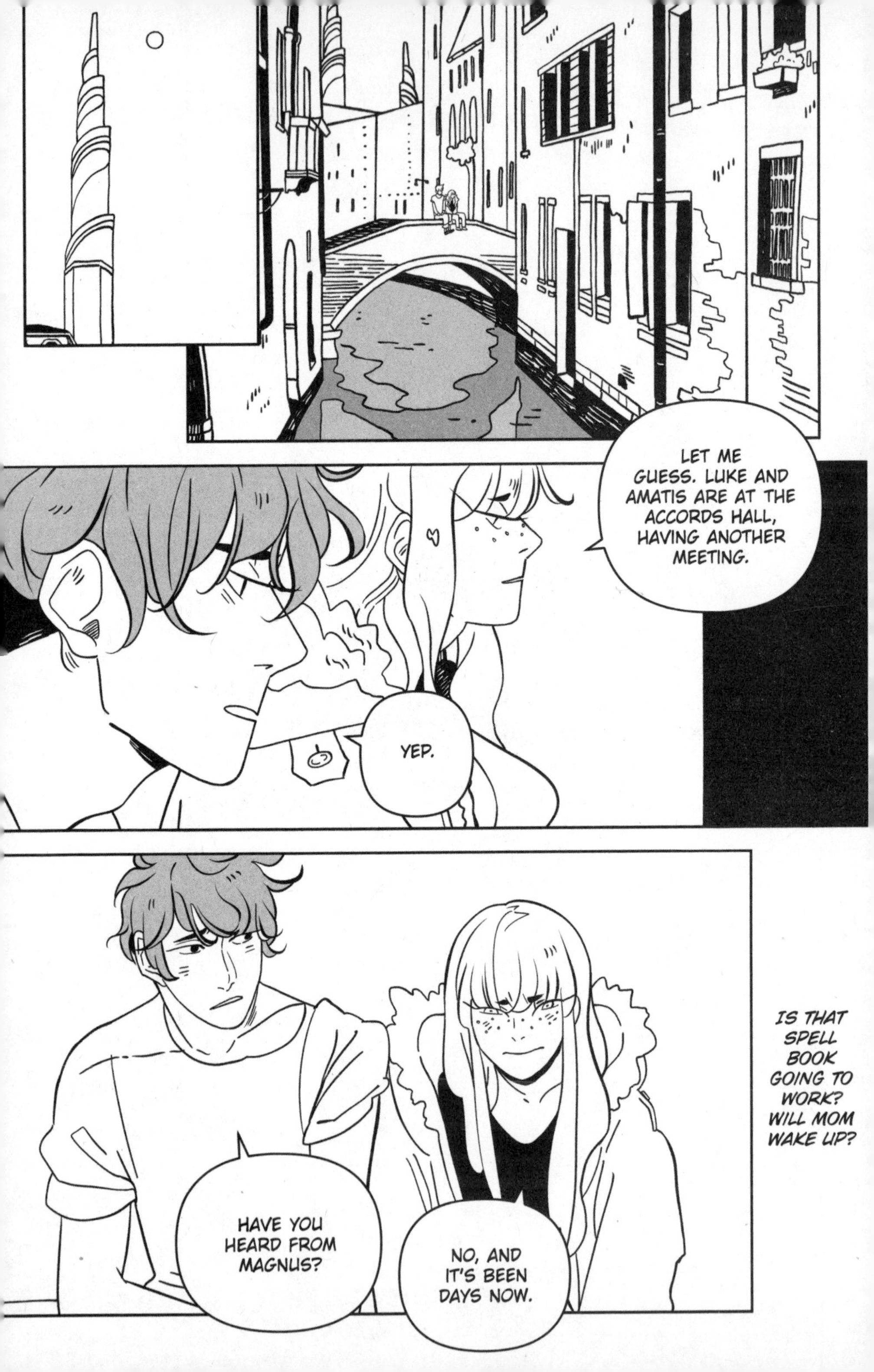
LET ME GUESS. LUKE AND AMATIS ARE AT THE ACCORDS HALL, HAVING ANOTHER MEETING.
YEP.
IS THAT SPELL BOOK GOING TO WORK? WILL MOM WAKE UP?
HAVE YOU HEARD FROM MAGNUS?
NO, AND IT'S BEEN DAYS NOW.

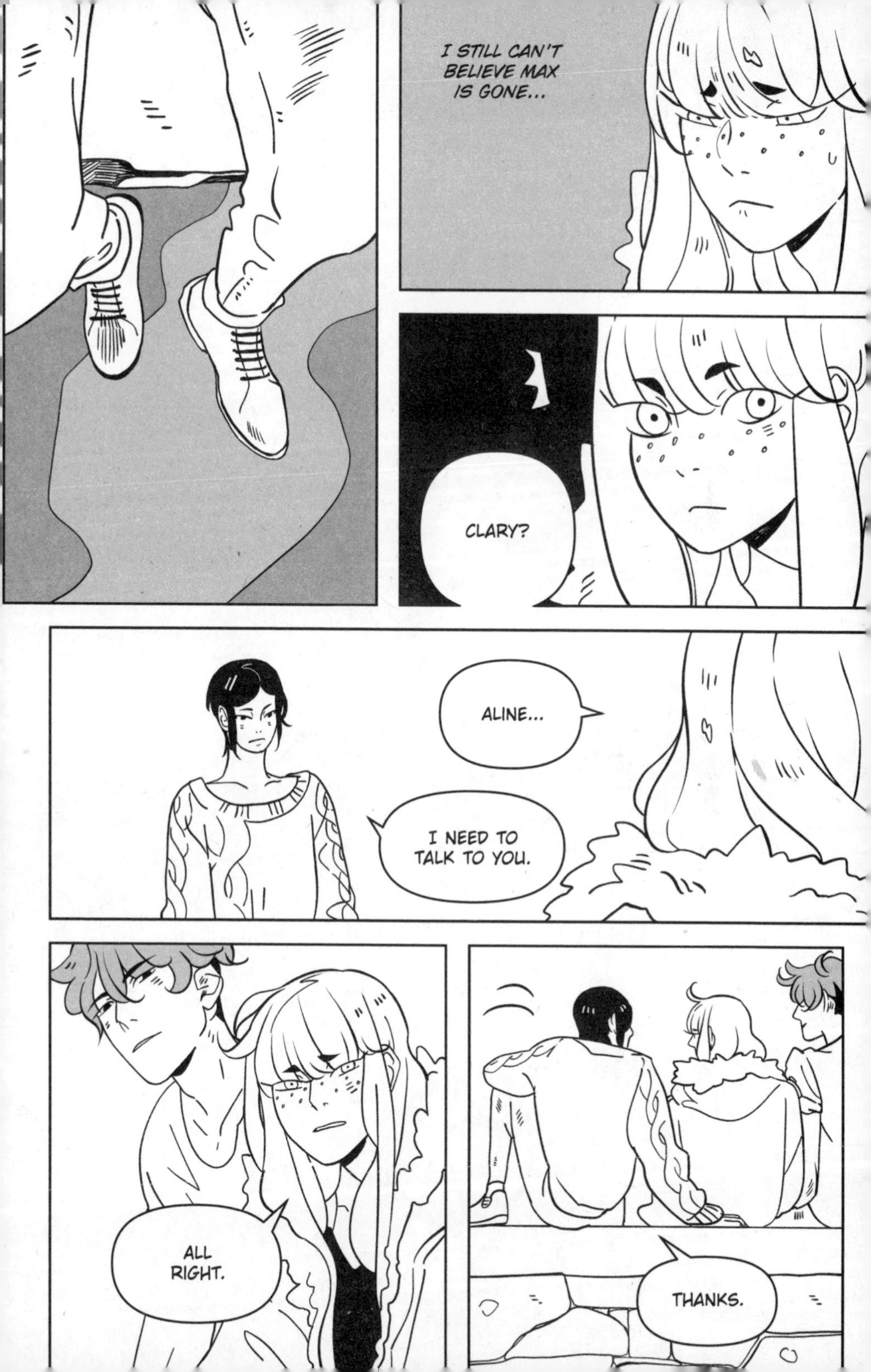
I STILL CAN'T
BELIEVE MAX
IS GONE...
CLARY?
ALINE...
I NEED TO
TALK TO YOU.
ALL
RIGHT.
THANKS.

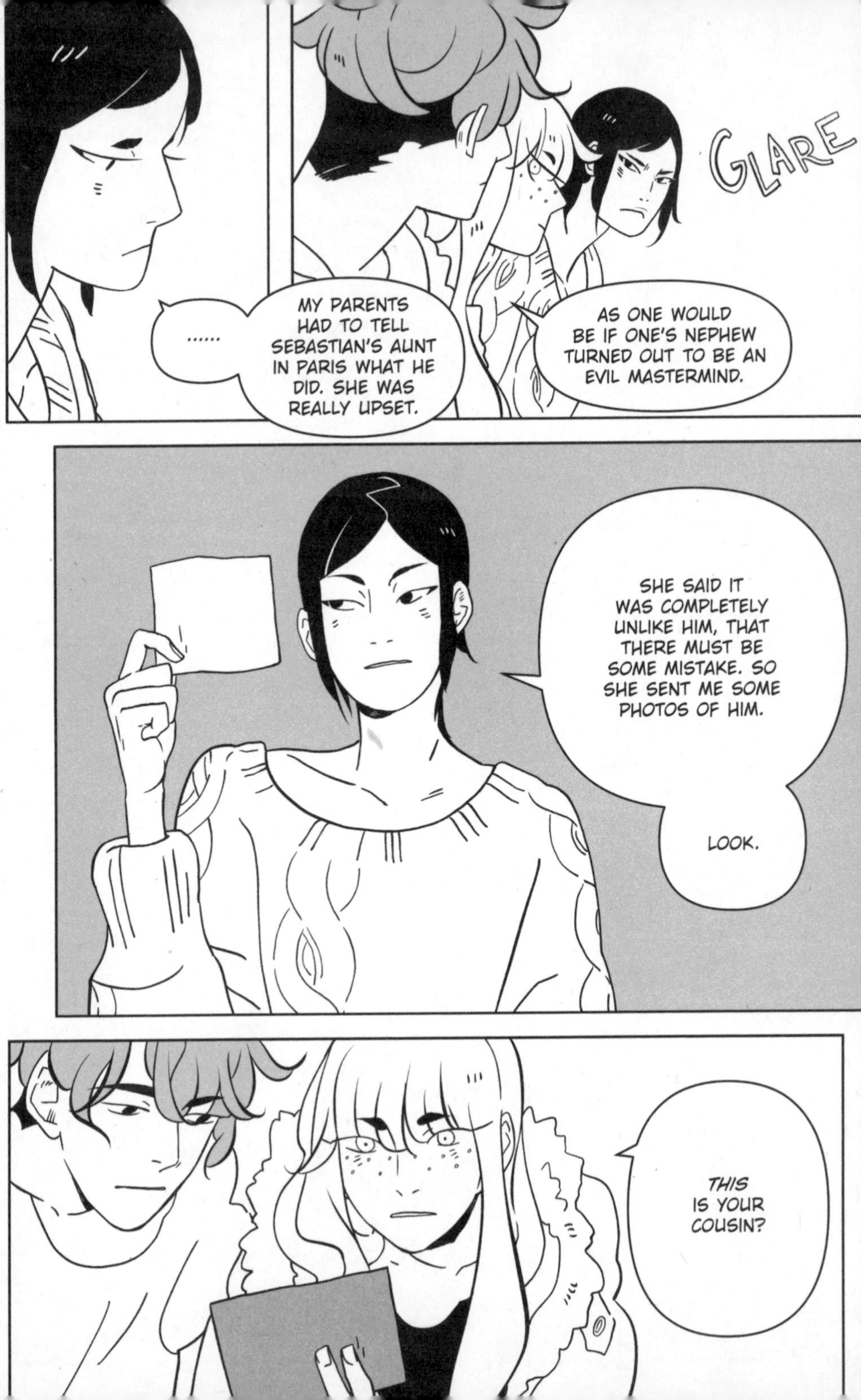
......
MY PARENTS HAD TO TELL SEBASTIAN'S AUNT IN PARIS WHAT HE DID. SHE WAS REALLY UPSET.
AS ONE WOULD BE IF ONE'S NEPHEW TURNED OUT TO BE AN EVIL MASTERMIND.
GLARE
SHE SAID IT WAS COMPLETELY UNLIKE HIM, THAT THERE MUST BE SOME MISTAKE. SO SHE SENT ME SOME PHOTOS OF HIM.
LOOK.
THIS IS YOUR COUSIN?

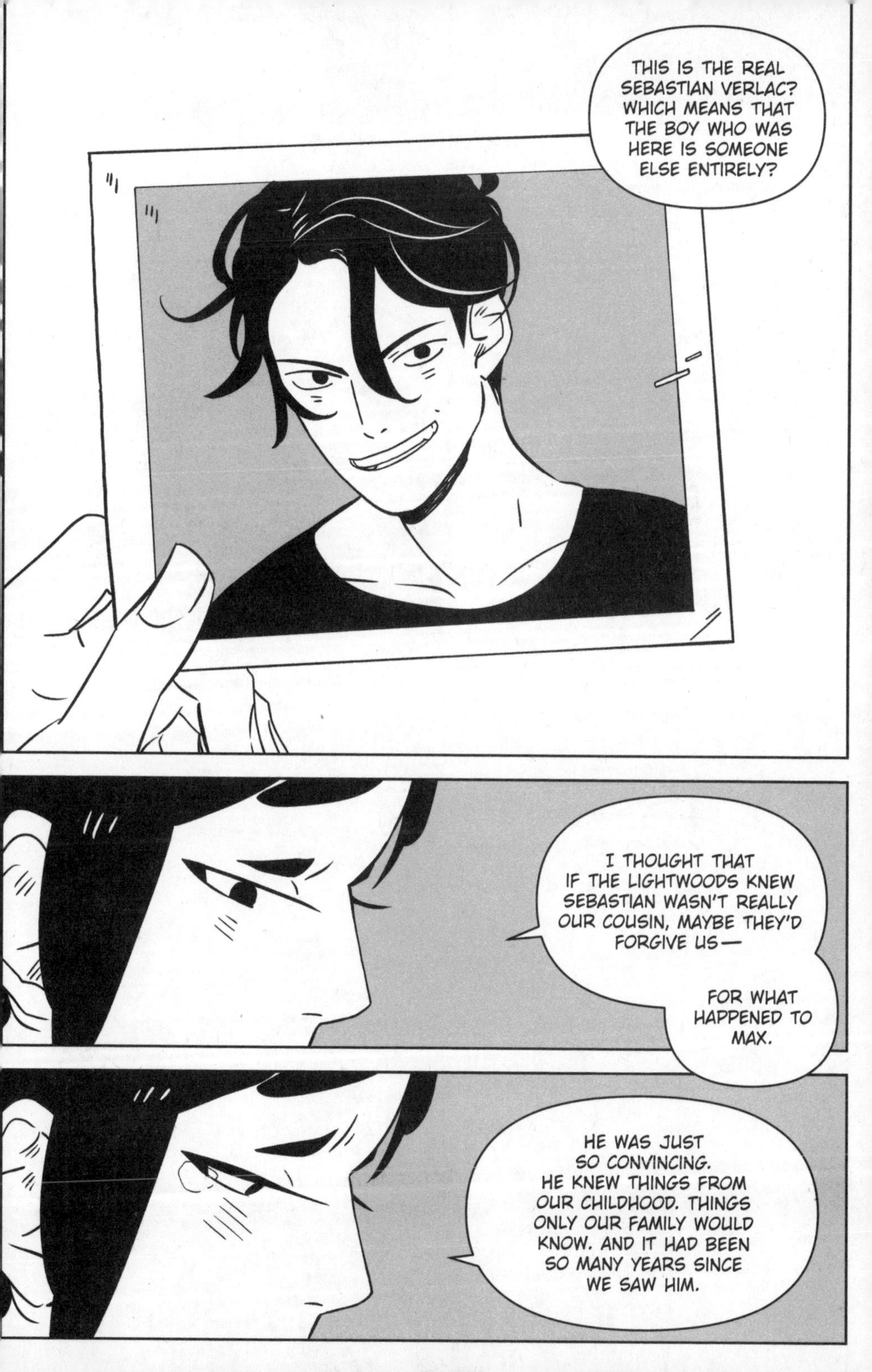
THIS IS THE REAL SEBASTIAN VERLAC? WHICH MEANS THAT THE BOY WHO WAS HERE IS SOMEONE ELSE ENTIRELY?
I THOUGHT THAT IF THE LIGHTWOODS KNEW SEBASTIAN WASN'T REALLY OUR COUSIN, MAYBE THEY'D FORGIVE US—
FOR WHAT HAPPENED TO MAX.
HE WAS JUST SO CONVINCING. HE KNEW THINGS FROM OUR CHILDHOOD. THINGS ONLY OUR FAMILY WOULD KNOW. AND IT HAD BEEN SO MANY YEARS SINCE WE SAW HIM.

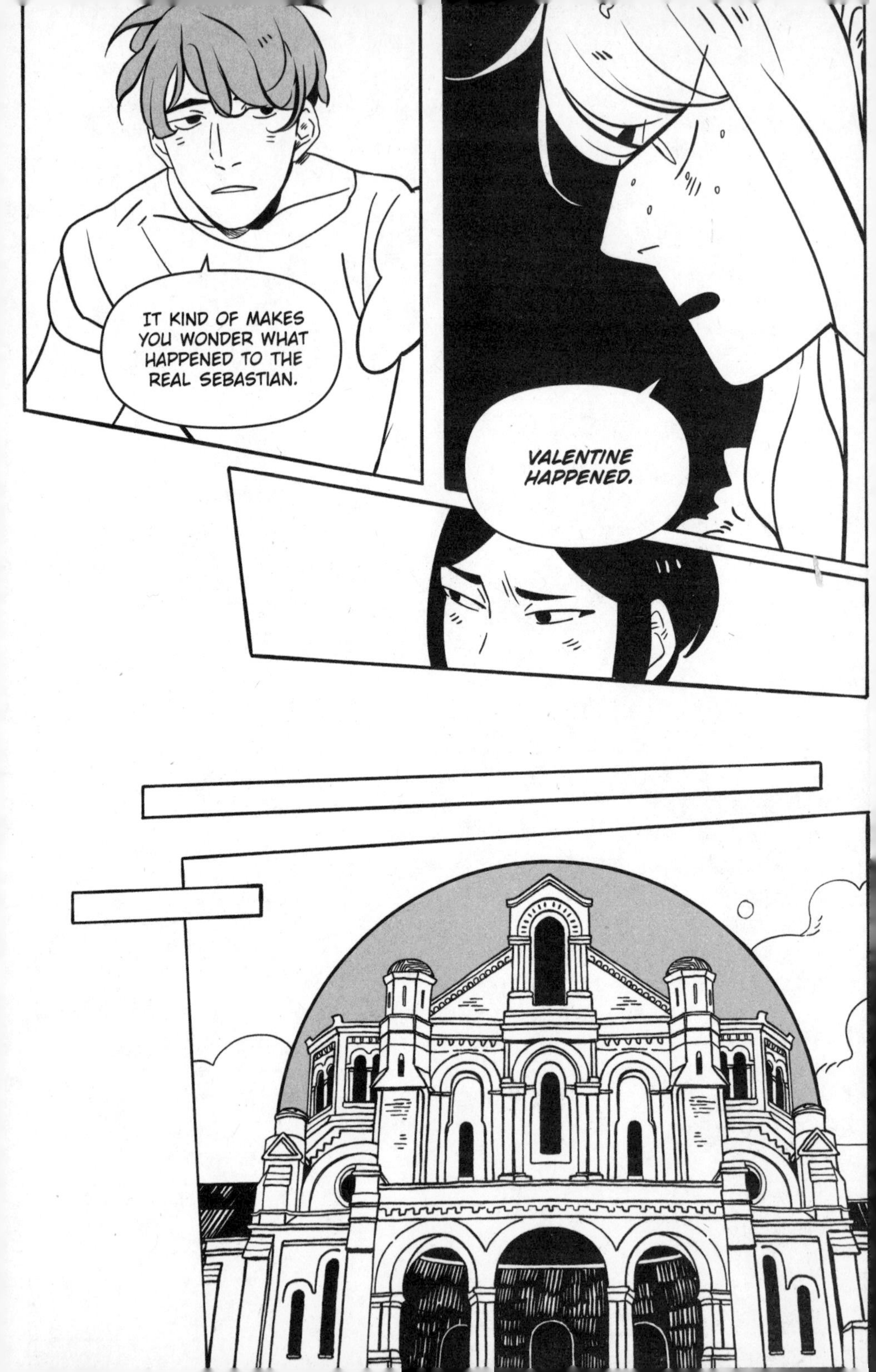
IT KIND OF MAKES YOU WONDER WHAT HAPPENED TO THE REAL SEBASTIAN.
VALENTINE HAPPENED.

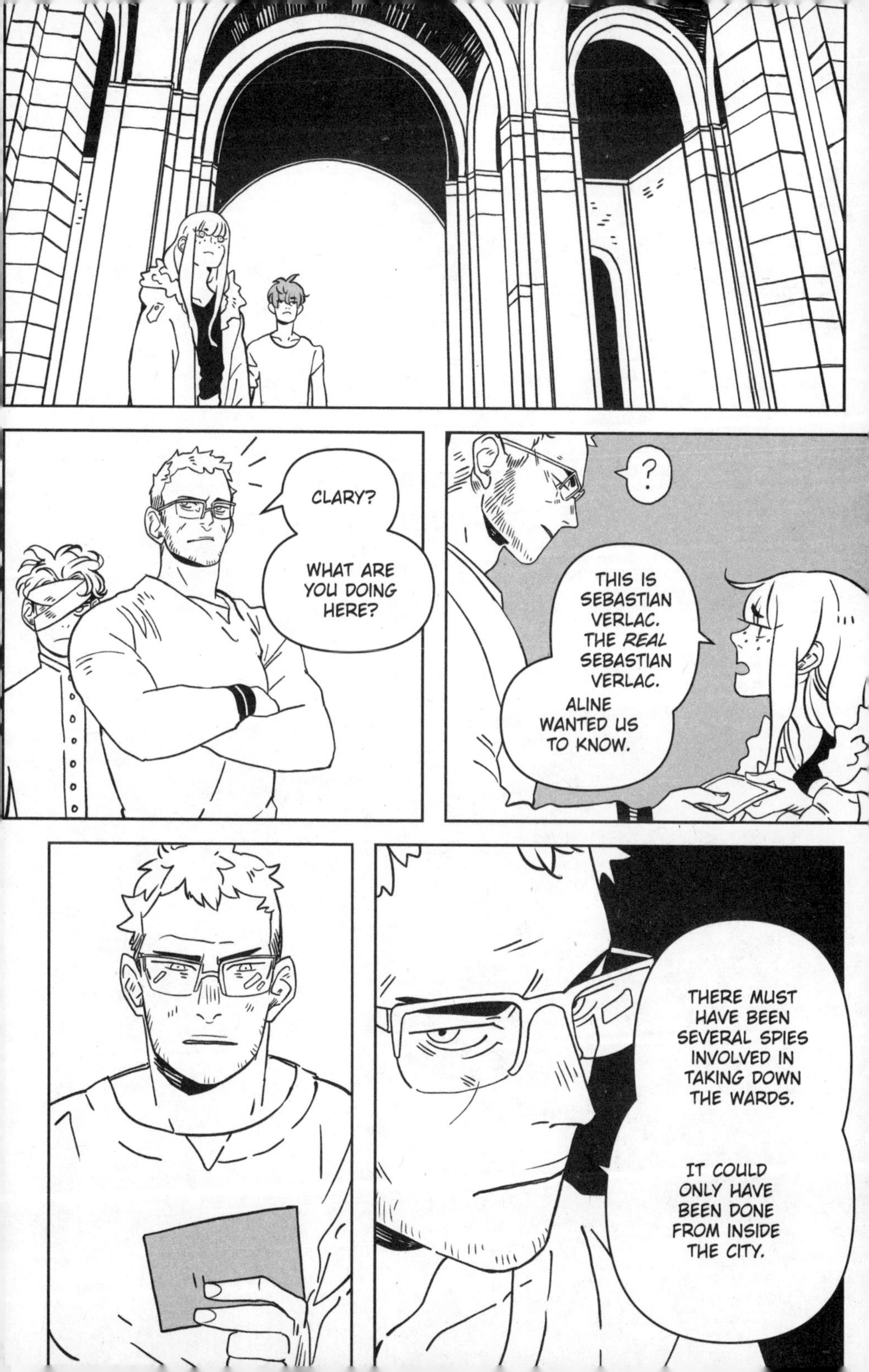

CLARY?
WHAT ARE YOU DOING HERE?
?
THIS IS SEBASTIAN VERLAC. THE *REAL* SEBASTIAN VERLAC.
ALINE WANTED US TO KNOW.
THERE MUST HAVE BEEN SEVERAL SPIES INVOLVED IN TAKING DOWN THE WARDS.
IT COULD ONLY HAVE BEEN DONE FROM INSIDE THE CITY.

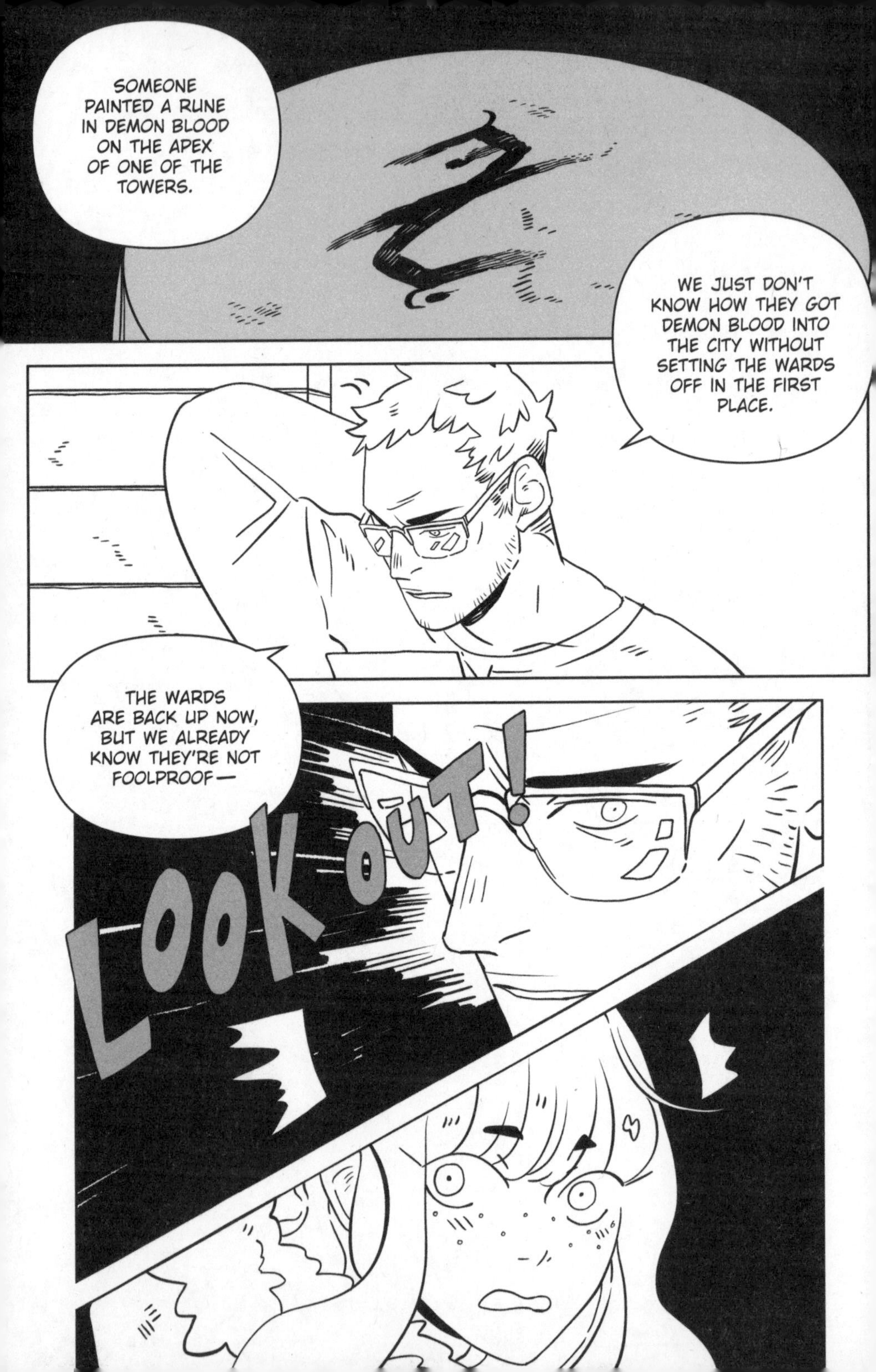
SOMEONE PAINTED A RUNE IN DEMON BLOOD ON THE APEX OF ONE OF THE TOWERS.
WE JUST DON'T KNOW HOW THEY GOT DEMON BLOOD INTO THE CITY WITHOUT SETTING THE WARDS OFF IN THE FIRST PLACE.
THE WARDS ARE BACK UP NOW, BUT WE ALREADY KNOW THEY'RE NOT FOOLPROOF—
LOOK OUT!

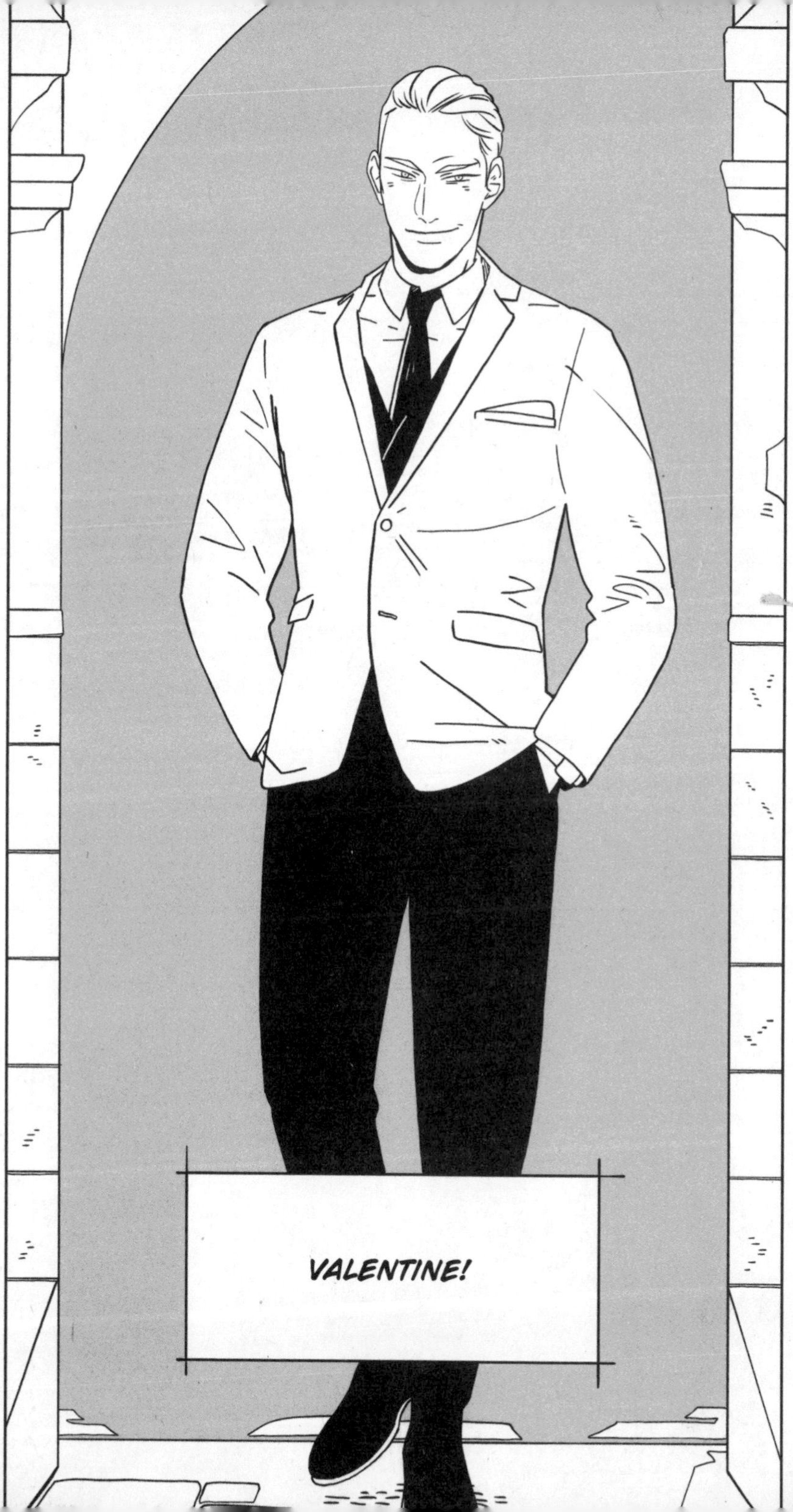
VALENTINE!

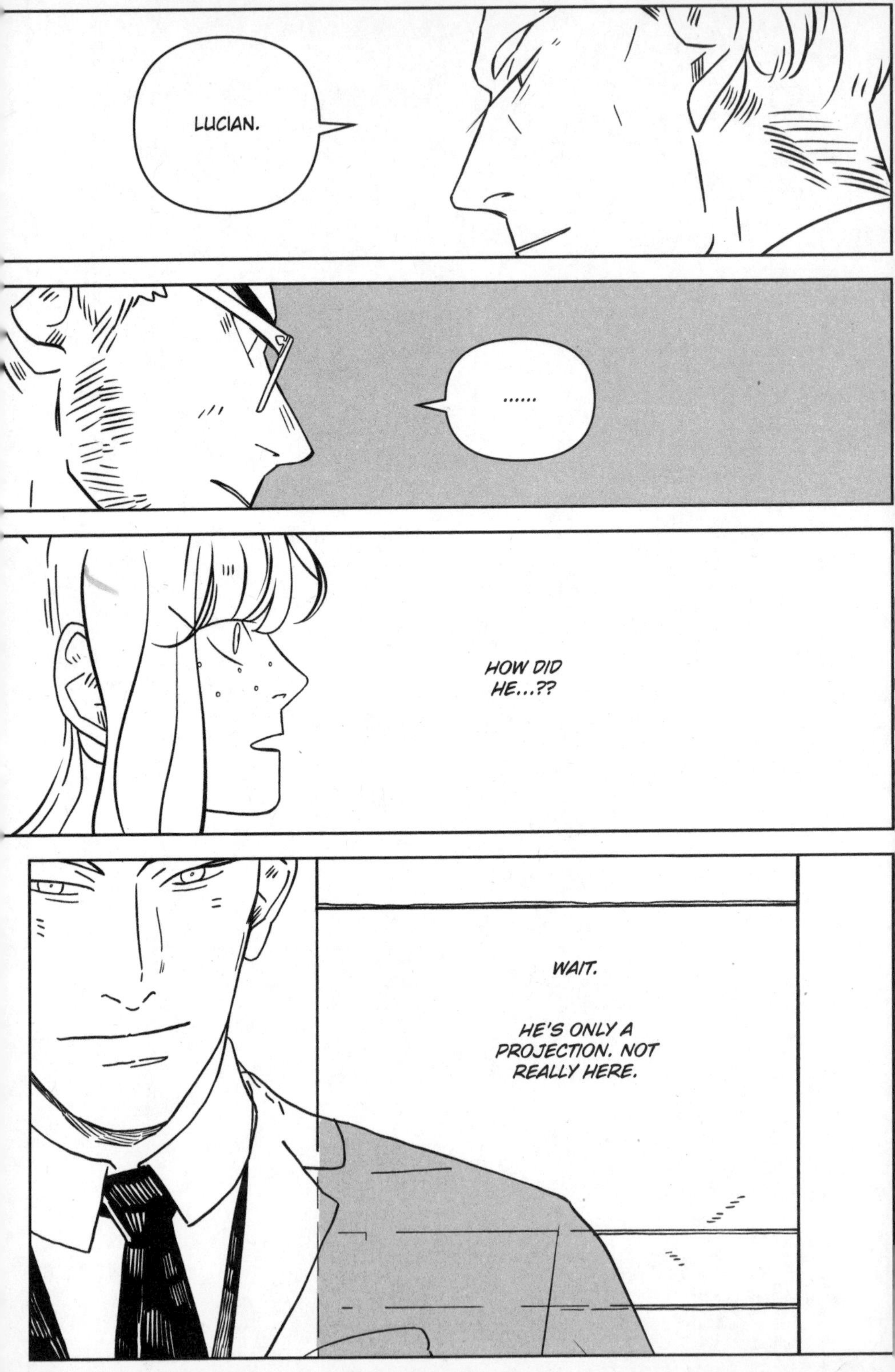
LUCIAN.
......
HOW DID HE...??
WAIT.
HE'S ONLY A PROJECTION. NOT REALLY HERE.

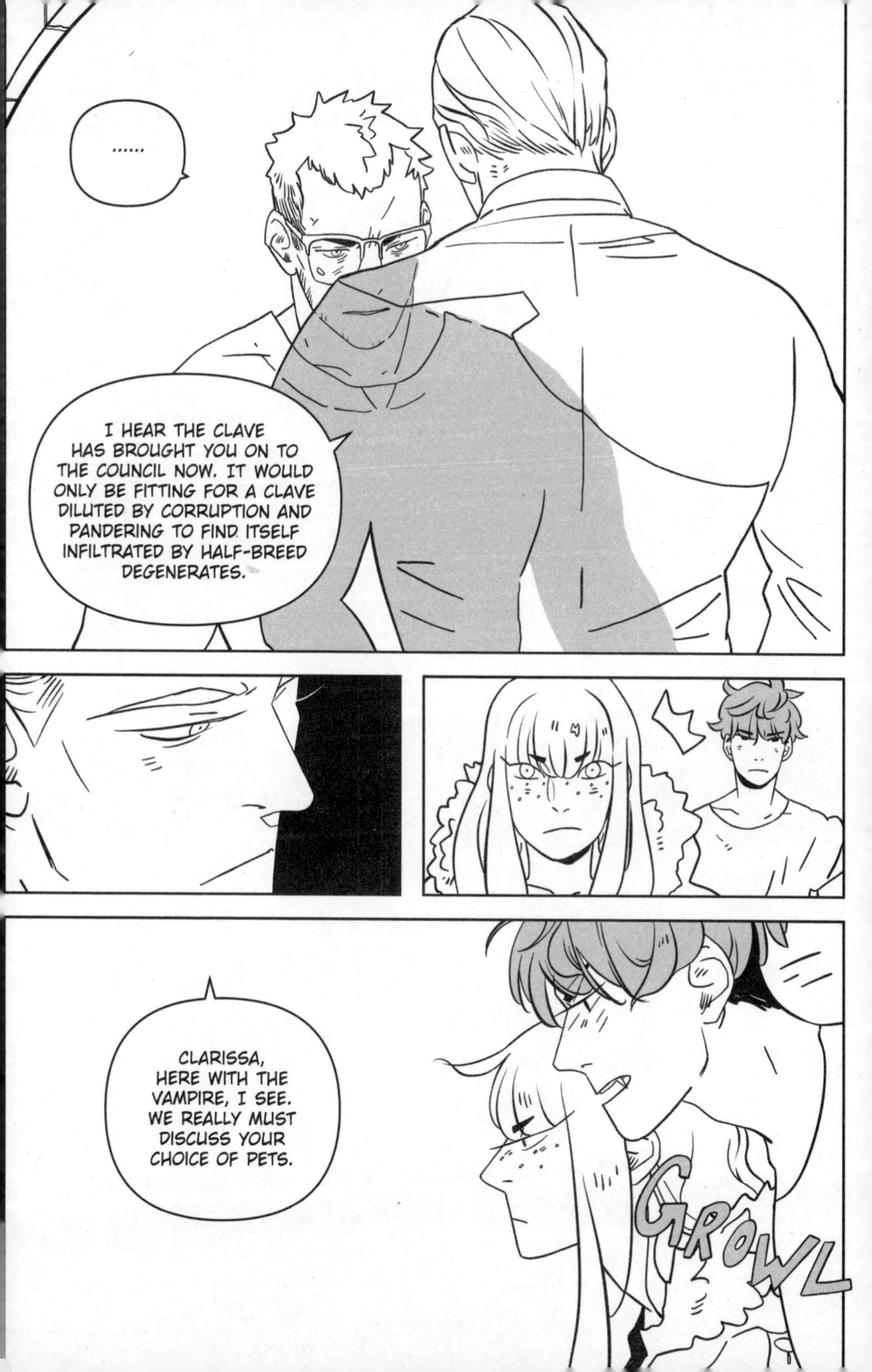
......
I HEAR THE CLAVE HAS BROUGHT YOU ON TO THE COUNCIL NOW. IT WOULD ONLY BE FITTING FOR A CLAVE DILUTED BY CORRUPTION AND PANDERING TO FIND ITSELF INFILTRATED BY HALF-BREED DEGENERATES.
CLARISSA, HERE WITH THE VAMPIRE, I SEE. WE REALLY MUST DISCUSS YOUR CHOICE OF PETS.
GROWL

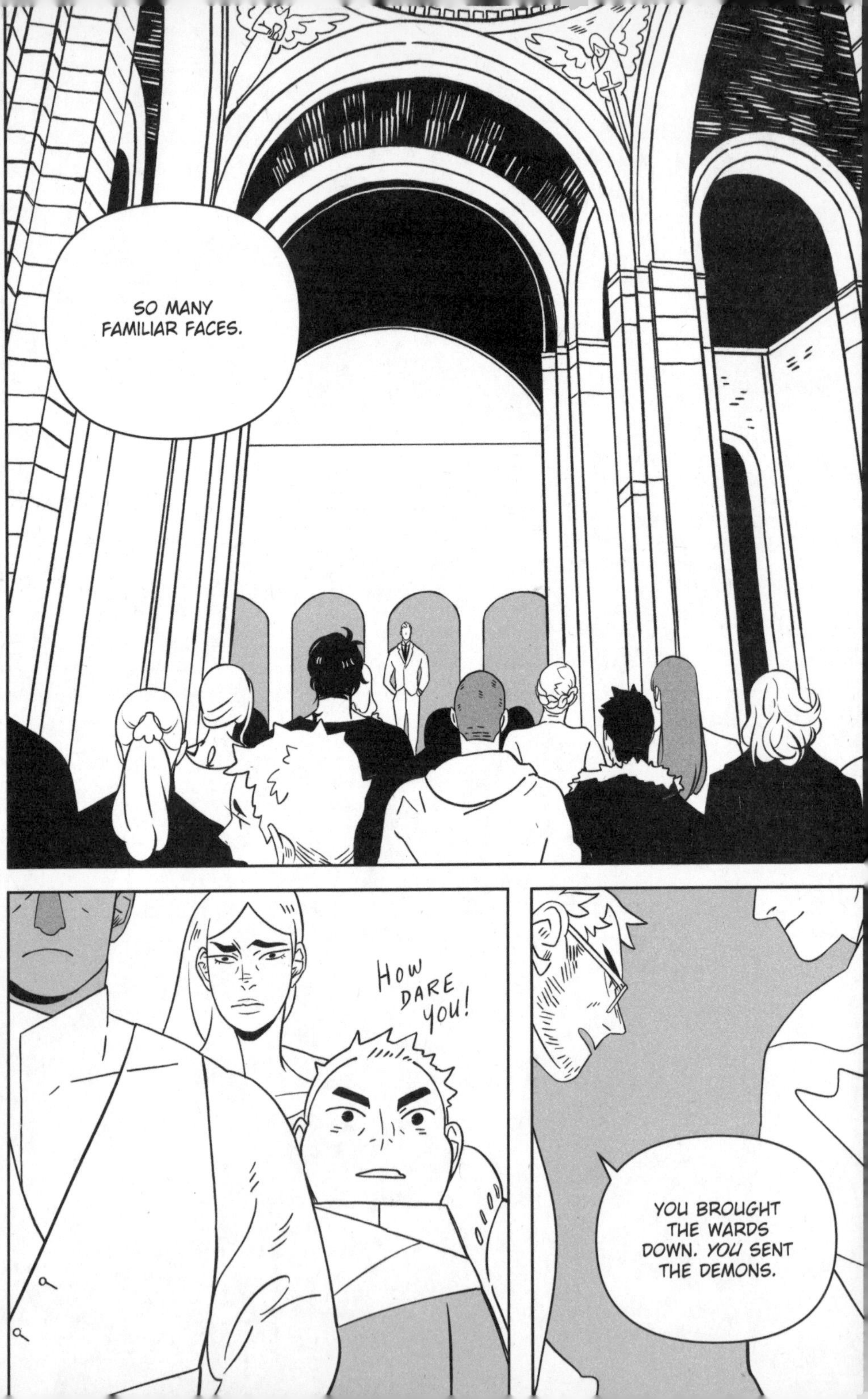
SO MANY FAMILIAR FACES.
HOW DARE YOU!
YOU BROUGHT THE WARDS DOWN. *YOU* SENT THE DEMONS.

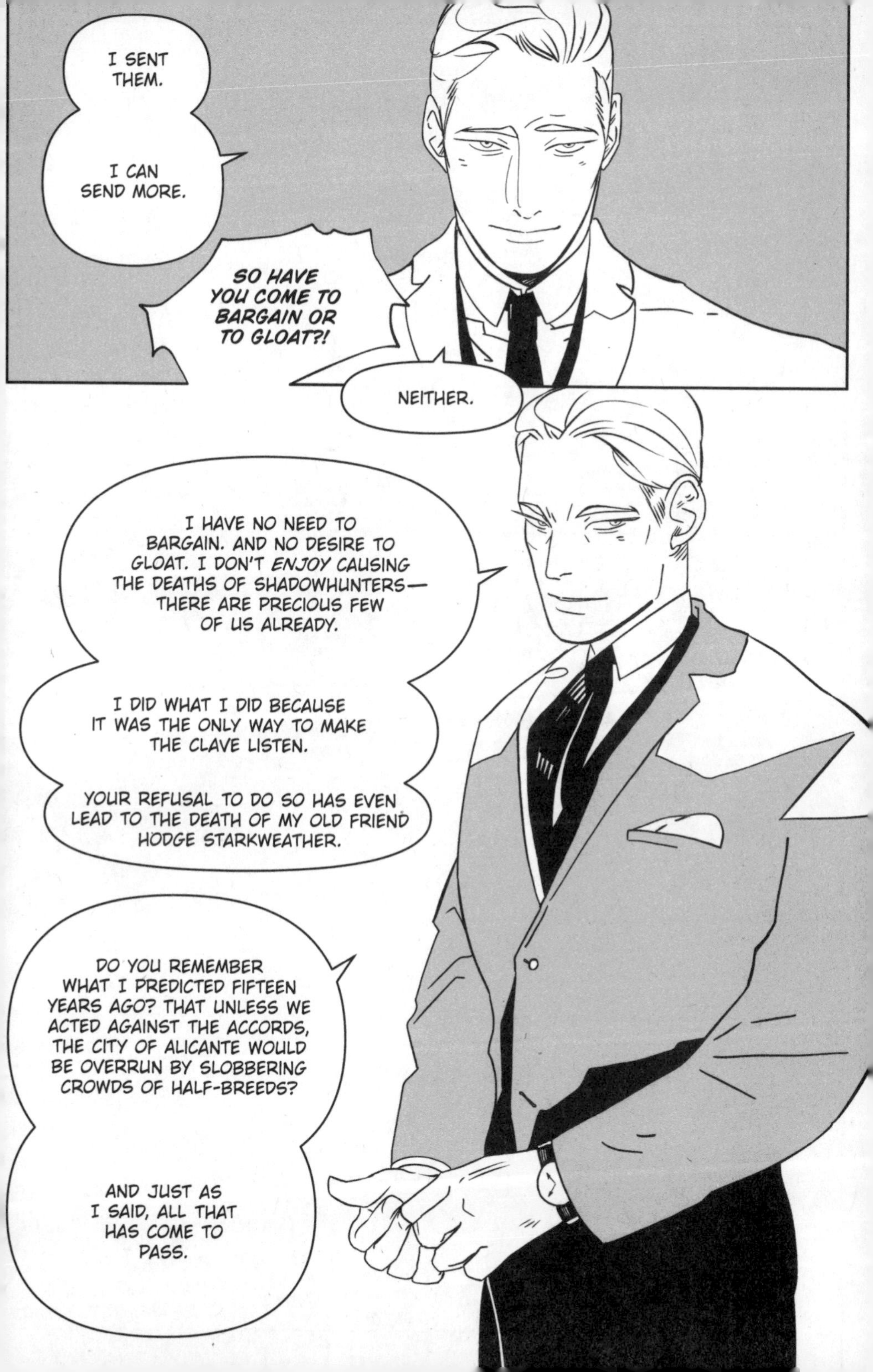
I SENT THEM.
I CAN SEND MORE.
SO HAVE YOU COME TO BARGAIN OR TO GLOAT?!
NEITHER.
I HAVE NO NEED TO BARGAIN. AND NO DESIRE TO GLOAT. I DON'T *ENJOY* CAUSING THE DEATHS OF SHADOWHUNTERS— THERE ARE PRECIOUS FEW OF US ALREADY.
I DID WHAT I DID BECAUSE IT WAS THE ONLY WAY TO MAKE THE CLAVE LISTEN.
YOUR REFUSAL TO DO SO HAS EVEN LEAD TO THE DEATH OF MY OLD FRIEND HODGE STARKWEATHER.
DO YOU REMEMBER WHAT I PREDICTED FIFTEEN YEARS AGO? THAT UNLESS WE ACTED AGAINST THE ACCORDS, THE CITY OF ALICANTE WOULD BE OVERRUN BY SLOBBERING CROWDS OF HALF-BREEDS?
AND JUST AS I SAID, ALL THAT HAS COME TO PASS.

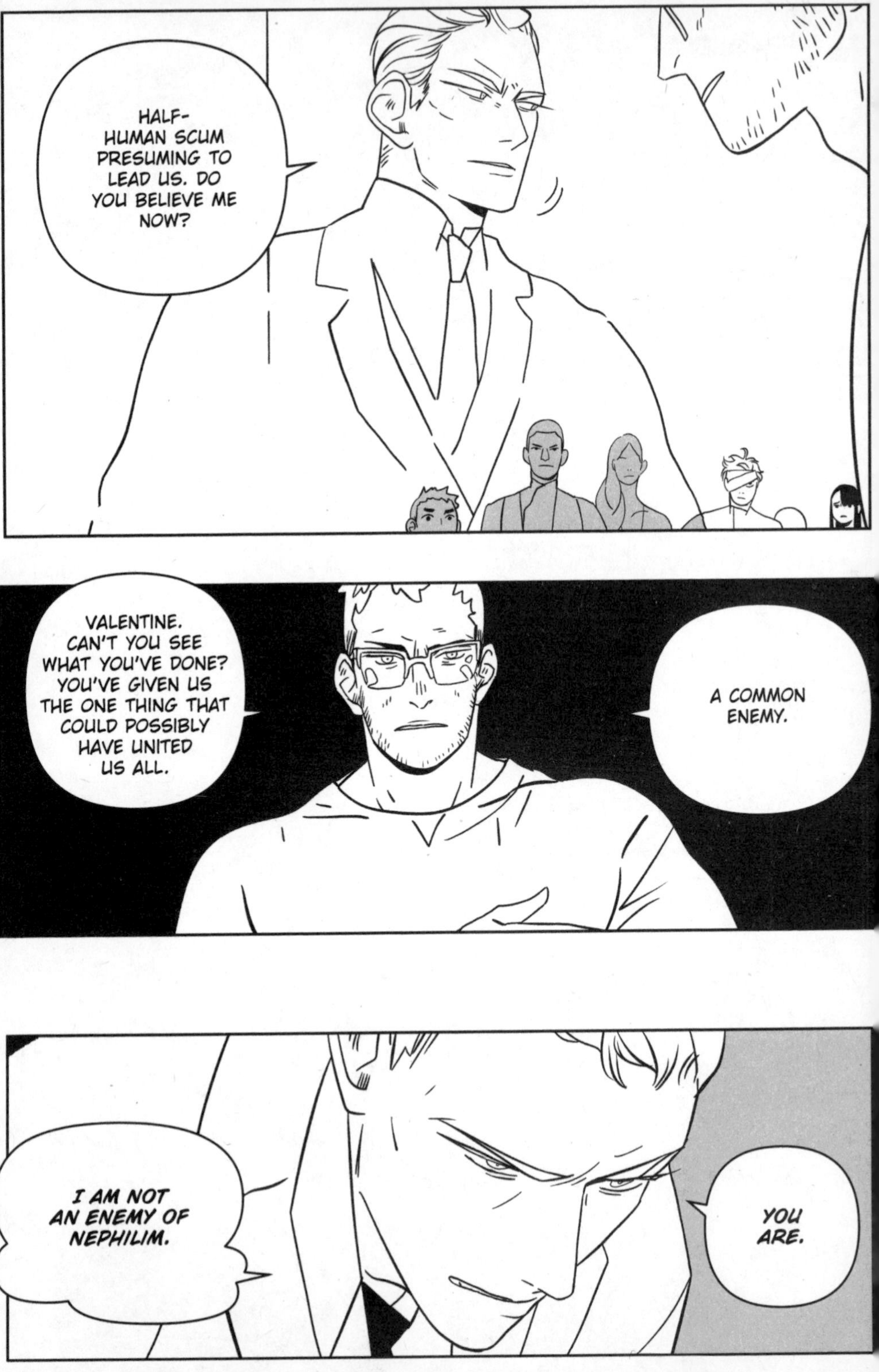
HALF-HUMAN SCUM PRESUMING TO LEAD US. DO YOU BELIEVE ME NOW?
VALENTINE. CAN'T YOU SEE WHAT YOU'VE DONE? YOU'VE GIVEN US THE ONE THING THAT COULD POSSIBLY HAVE UNITED US ALL.
A COMMON ENEMY.
I AM NOT AN ENEMY OF NEPHILIM.
YOU ARE.

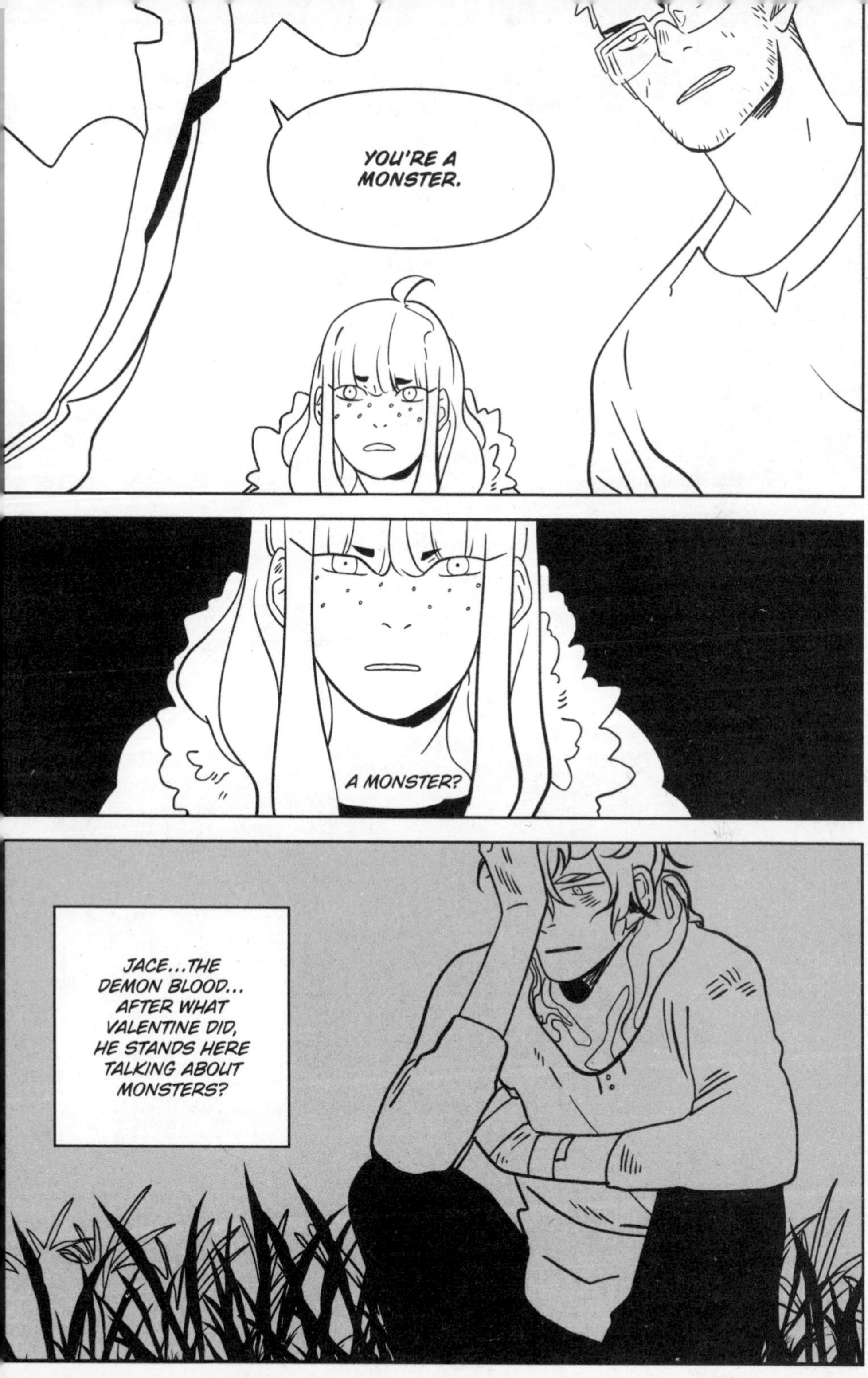
YOU'RE A MONSTER.
A MONSTER?
JACE...THE DEMON BLOOD... AFTER WHAT VALENTINE DID, HE STANDS HERE TALKING ABOUT MONSTERS?

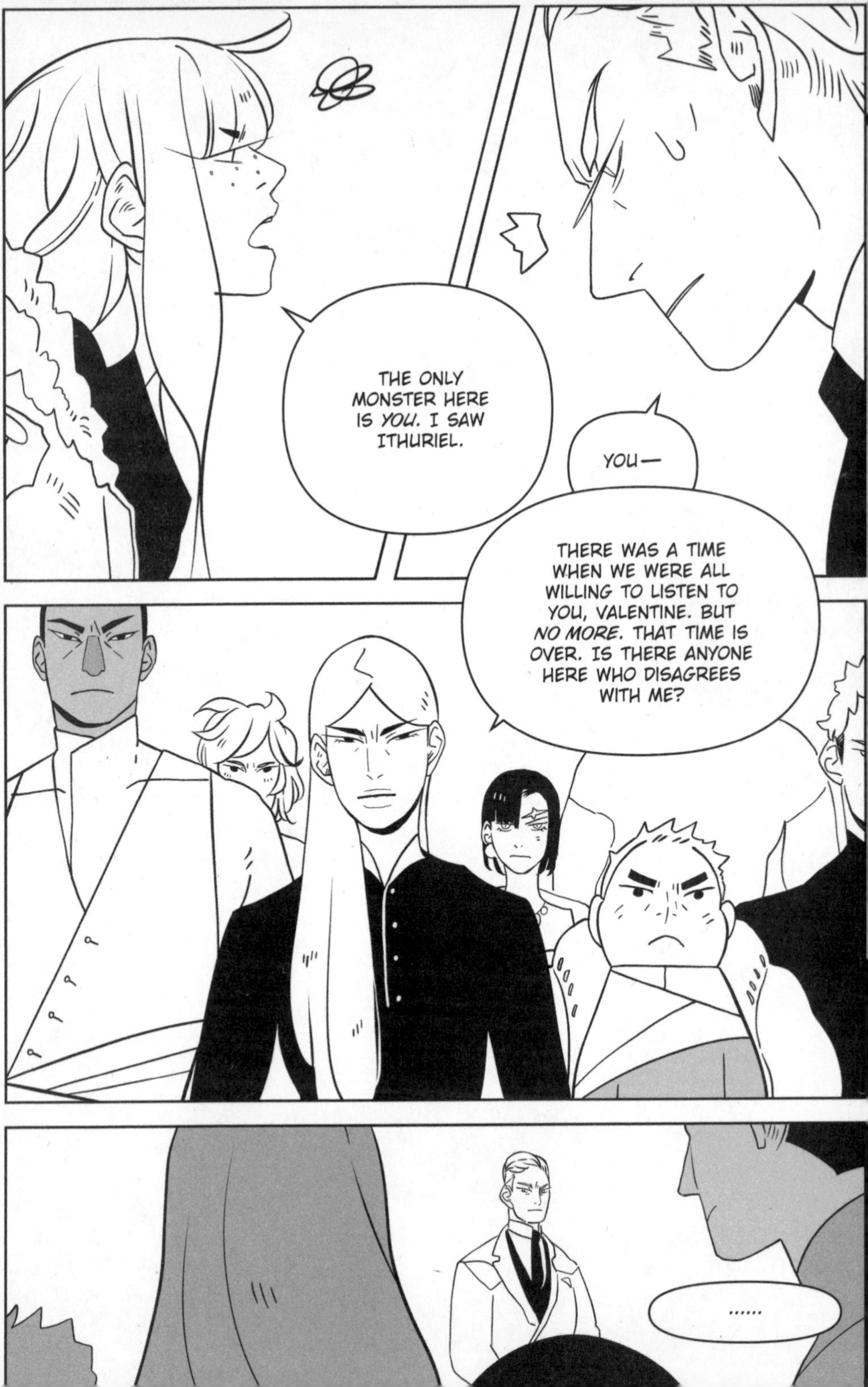
THE ONLY MONSTER HERE IS *YOU*. I SAW ITHURIEL.
YOU—
THERE WAS A TIME WHEN WE WERE ALL WILLING TO LISTEN TO YOU, VALENTINE. BUT *NO MORE*. THAT TIME IS OVER. IS THERE ANYONE HERE WHO DISAGREES WITH ME?
......

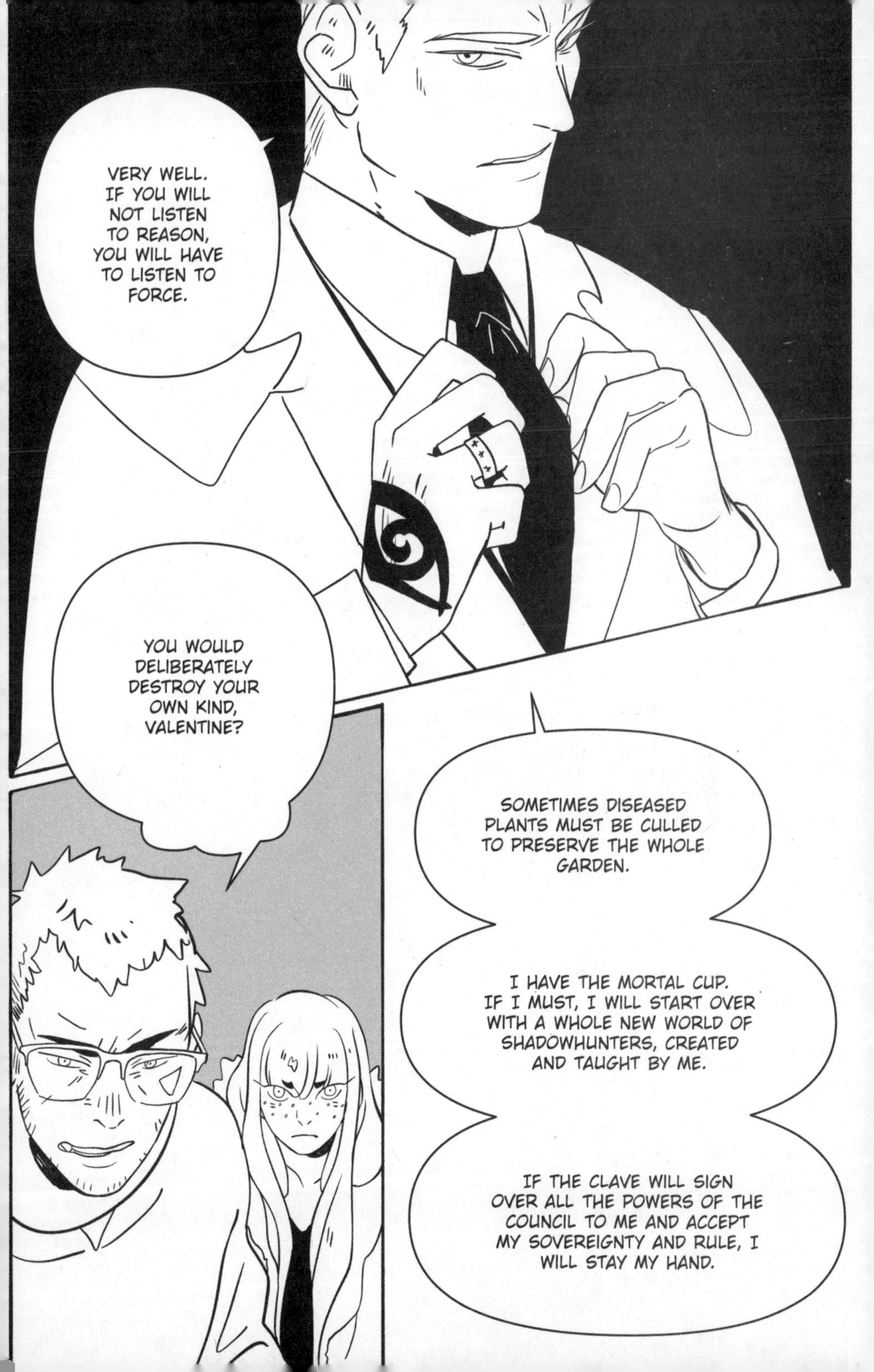
VERY WELL. IF YOU WILL NOT LISTEN TO REASON, YOU WILL HAVE TO LISTEN TO FORCE.
YOU WOULD DELIBERATELY DESTROY YOUR OWN KIND, VALENTINE?
SOMETIMES DISEASED PLANTS MUST BE CULLED TO PRESERVE THE WHOLE GARDEN.
I HAVE THE MORTAL CUP. IF I MUST, I WILL START OVER WITH A WHOLE NEW WORLD OF SHADOWHUNTERS, CREATED AND TAUGHT BY ME.
IF THE CLAVE WILL SIGN OVER ALL THE POWERS OF THE COUNCIL TO ME AND ACCEPT MY SOVEREIGNTY AND RULE, I WILL STAY MY HAND.

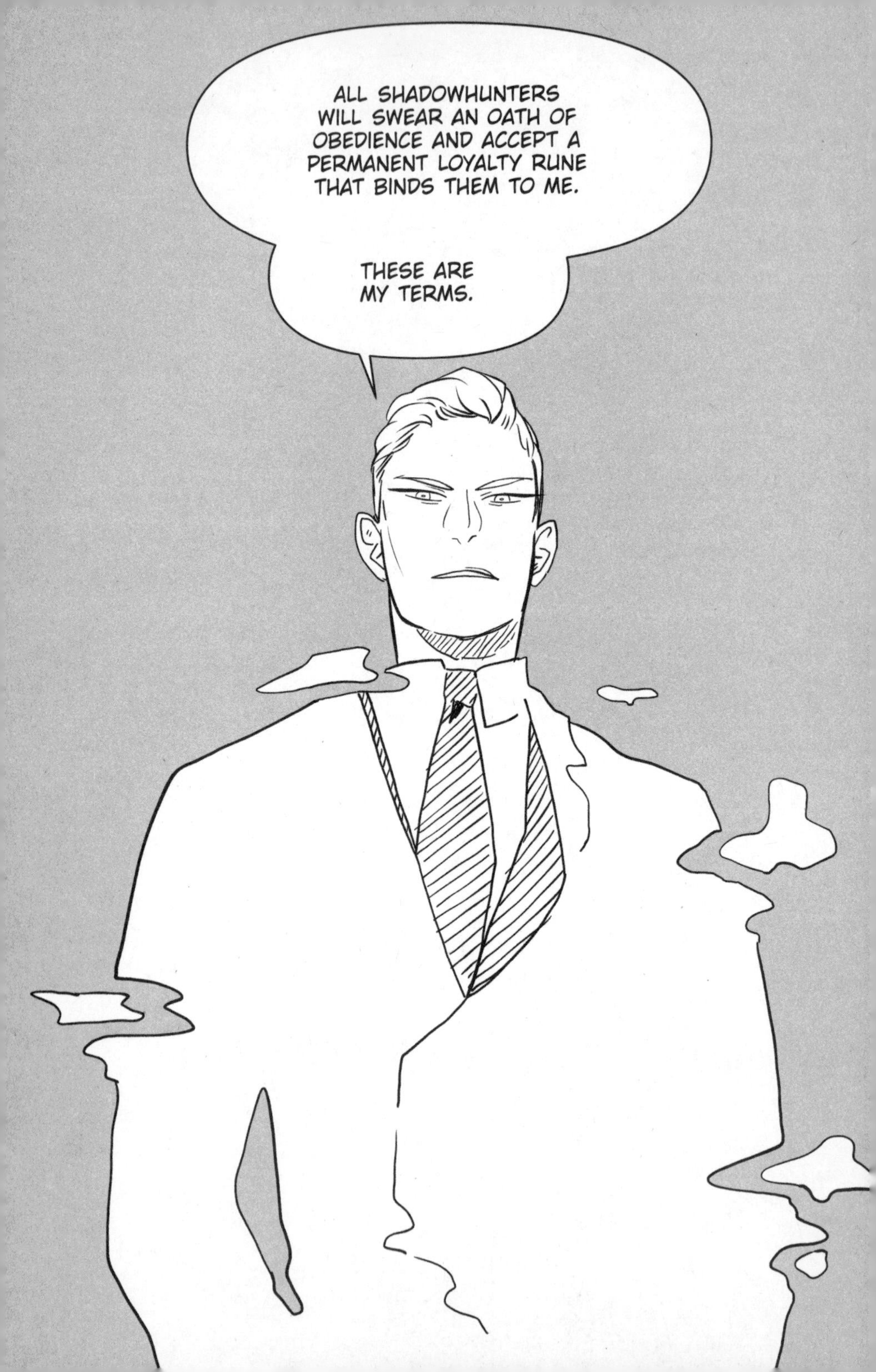
ALL SHADOWHUNTERS WILL SWEAR AN OATH OF OBEDIENCE AND ACCEPT A PERMANENT LOYALTY RUNE THAT BINDS THEM TO ME.
THESE ARE MY TERMS.

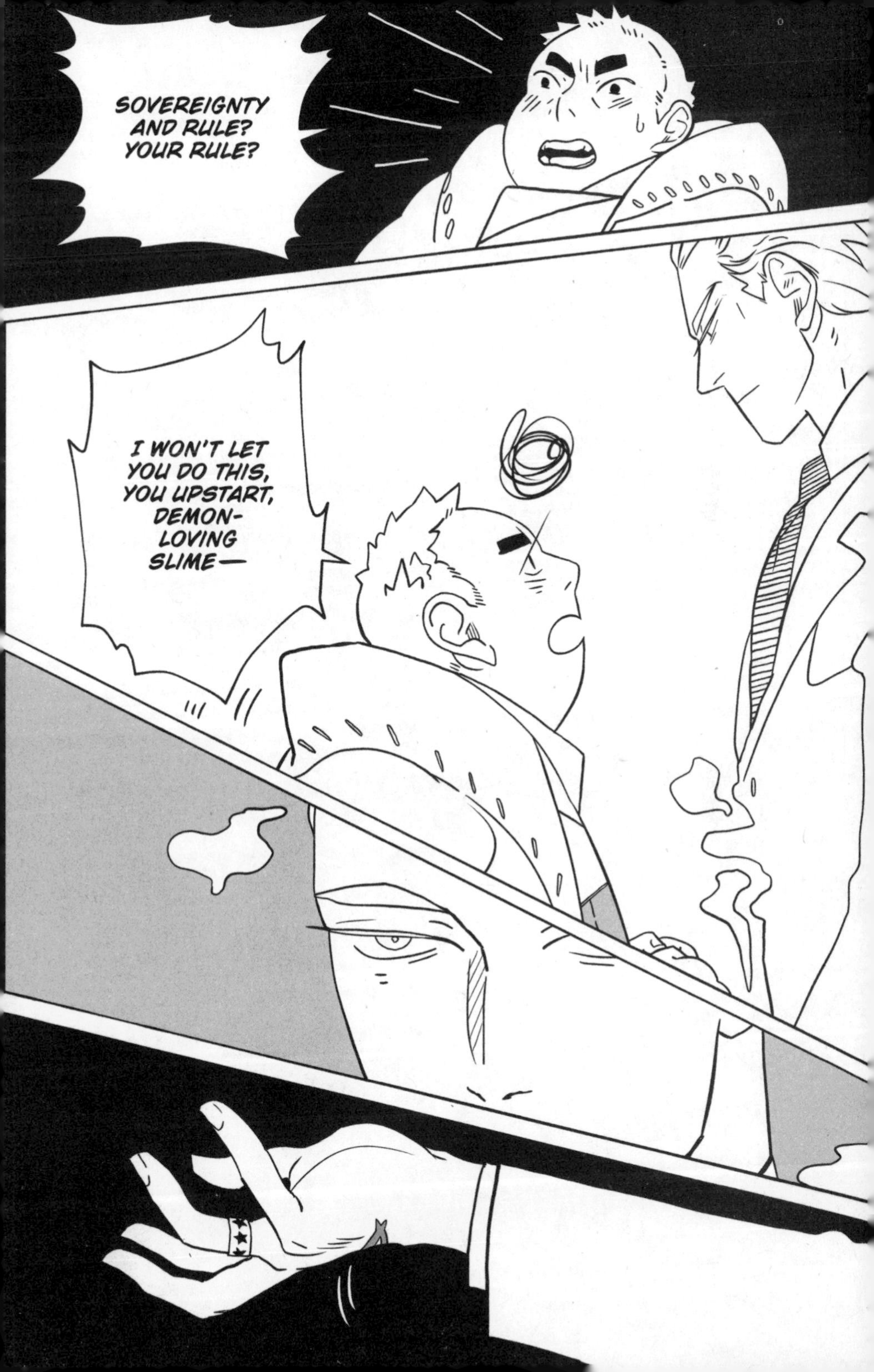
SOVEREIGNTY AND RULE? YOUR RULE?
I WON'T LET YOU DO THIS, YOU UPSTART, DEMON-LOVING SLIME—

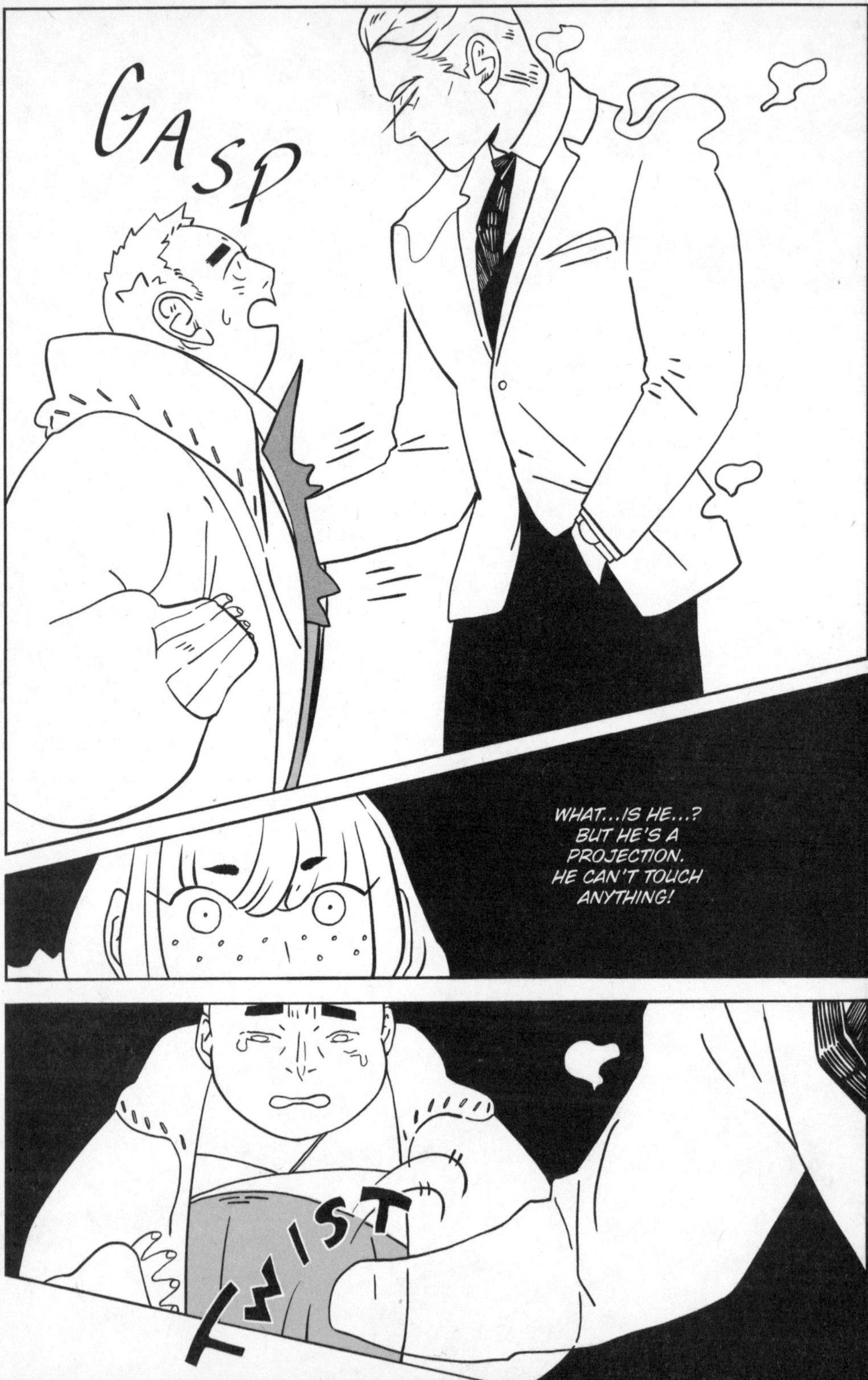
GASP
WHAT...IS HE...? BUT HE'S A PROJECTION. HE CAN'T TOUCH ANYTHING!
TWIST

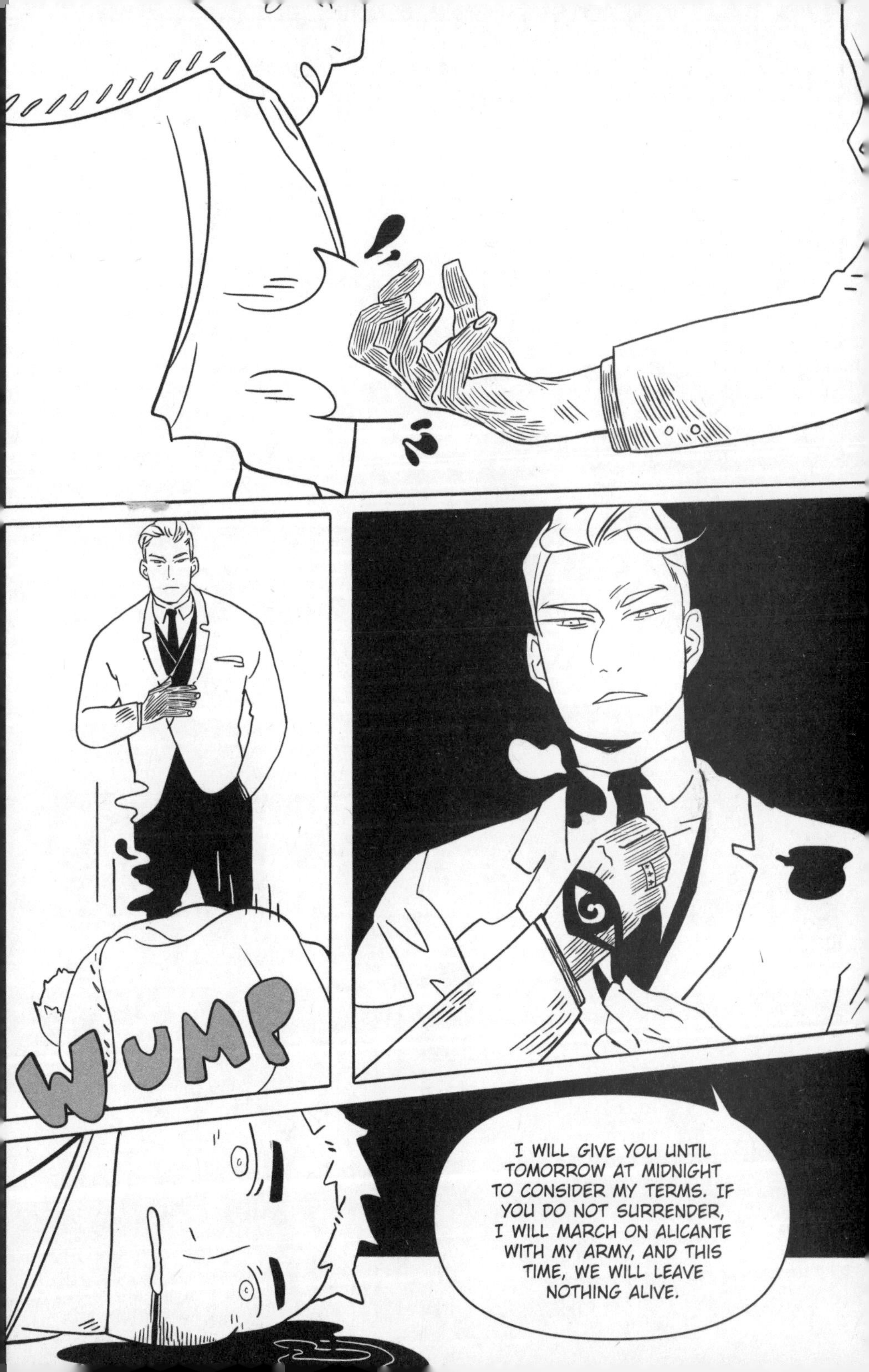
WUMP
I WILL GIVE YOU UNTIL TOMORROW AT MIDNIGHT TO CONSIDER MY TERMS. IF YOU DO NOT SURRENDER, I WILL MARCH ON ALICANTE WITH MY ARMY, AND THIS TIME, WE WILL LEAVE NOTHING ALIVE.

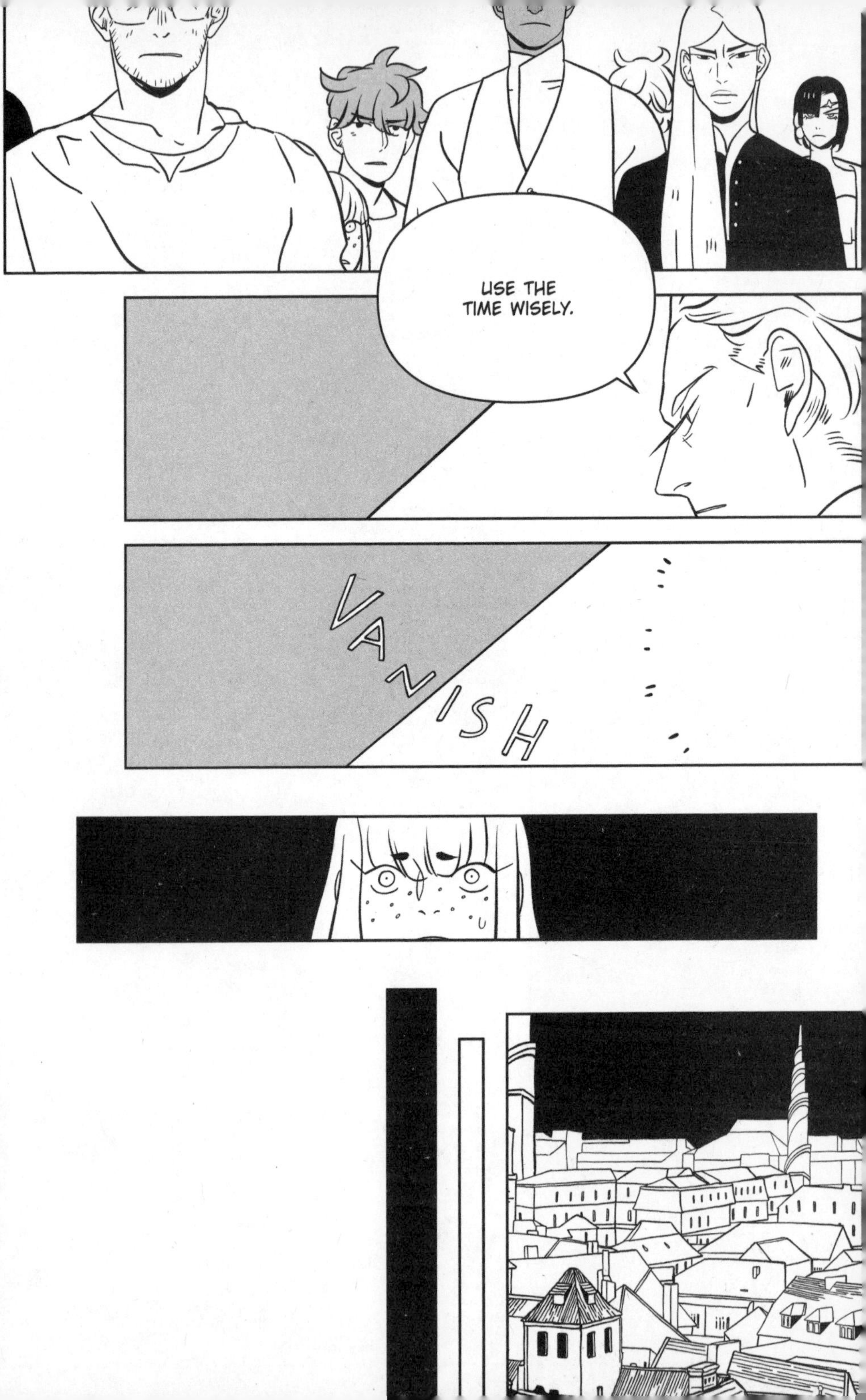
USE THE TIME WISELY.
VANISH

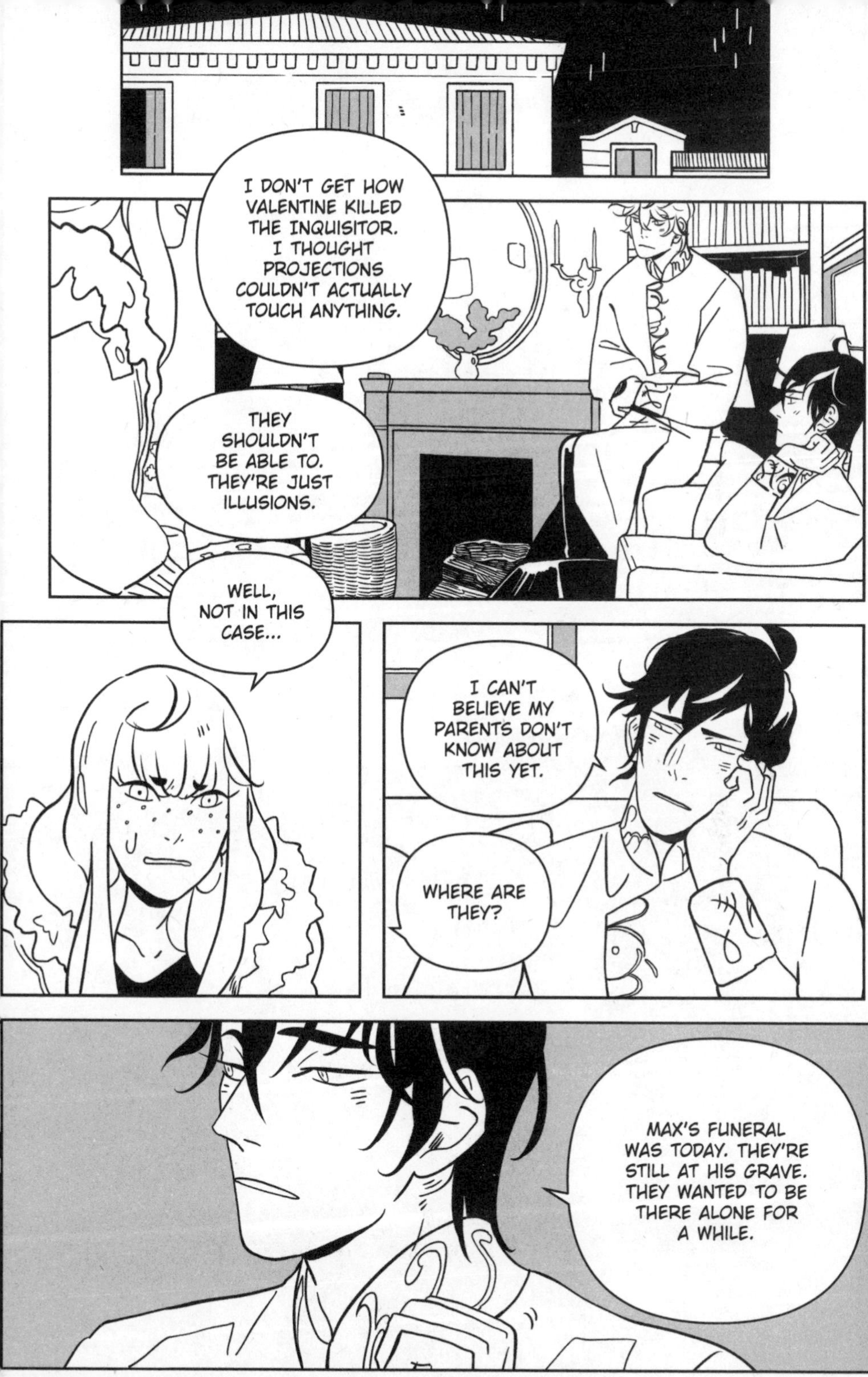
I DON'T GET HOW VALENTINE KILLED THE INQUISITOR. I THOUGHT PROJECTIONS COULDN'T ACTUALLY TOUCH ANYTHING.
THEY SHOULDN'T BE ABLE TO. THEY'RE JUST ILLUSIONS.
WELL, NOT IN THIS CASE...
I CAN'T BELIEVE MY PARENTS DON'T KNOW ABOUT THIS YET.
WHERE ARE THEY?
MAX'S FUNERAL WAS TODAY. THEY'RE STILL AT HIS GRAVE. THEY WANTED TO BE THERE ALONE FOR A WHILE.

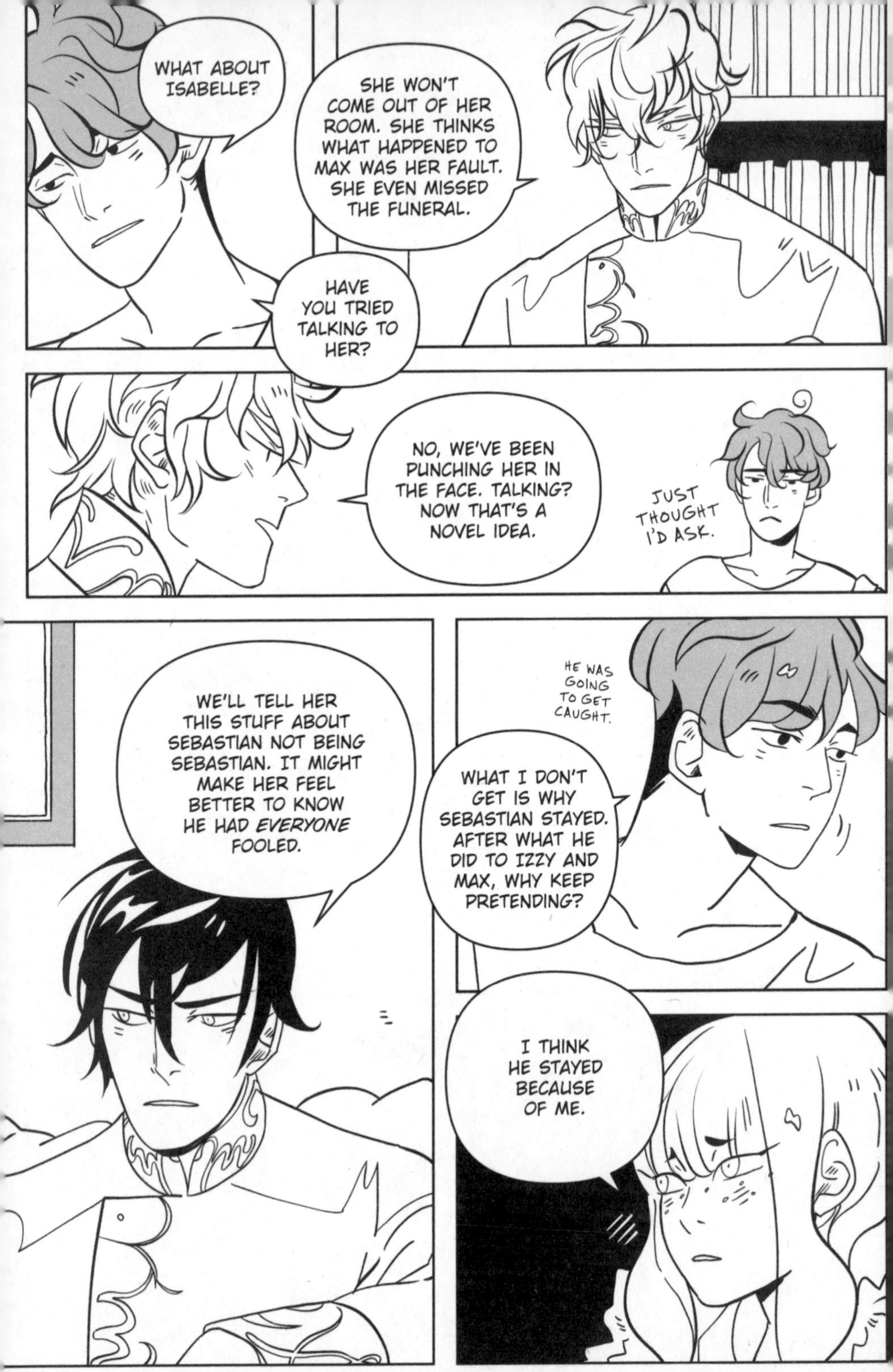
WHAT ABOUT ISABELLE?
SHE WON'T COME OUT OF HER ROOM. SHE THINKS WHAT HAPPENED TO MAX WAS HER FAULT. SHE EVEN MISSED THE FUNERAL.
HAVE YOU TRIED TALKING TO HER?
NO, WE'VE BEEN PUNCHING HER IN THE FACE. TALKING? NOW THAT'S A NOVEL IDEA.
JUST THOUGHT I'D ASK.
WE'LL TELL HER THIS STUFF ABOUT SEBASTIAN NOT BEING SEBASTIAN. IT MIGHT MAKE HER FEEL BETTER TO KNOW HE HAD *EVERYONE* FOOLED.
HE WAS GOING TO GET CAUGHT.
WHAT I DON'T GET IS WHY SEBASTIAN STAYED. AFTER WHAT HE DID TO IZZY AND MAX, WHY KEEP PRETENDING?
I THINK HE STAYED BECAUSE OF ME.

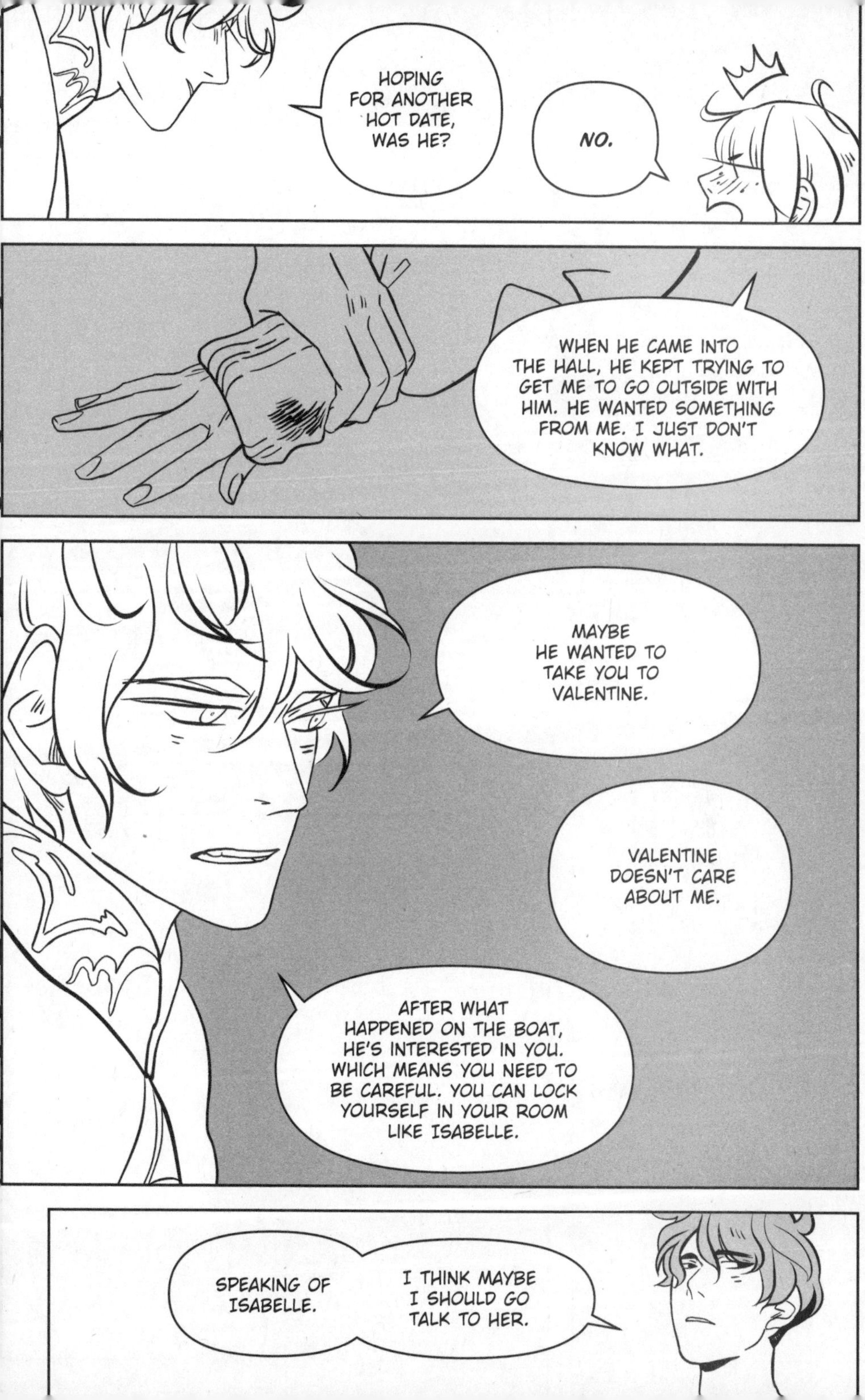
HOPING FOR ANOTHER HOT DATE, WAS HE?
NO.
WHEN HE CAME INTO THE HALL, HE KEPT TRYING TO GET ME TO GO OUTSIDE WITH HIM. HE WANTED SOMETHING FROM ME. I JUST DON'T KNOW WHAT.
MAYBE HE WANTED TO TAKE YOU TO VALENTINE.
VALENTINE DOESN'T CARE ABOUT ME.
AFTER WHAT HAPPENED ON THE BOAT, HE'S INTERESTED IN YOU. WHICH MEANS YOU NEED TO BE CAREFUL. YOU CAN LOCK YOURSELF IN YOUR ROOM LIKE ISABELLE.
SPEAKING OF ISABELLE.
I THINK MAYBE I SHOULD GO TALK TO HER.

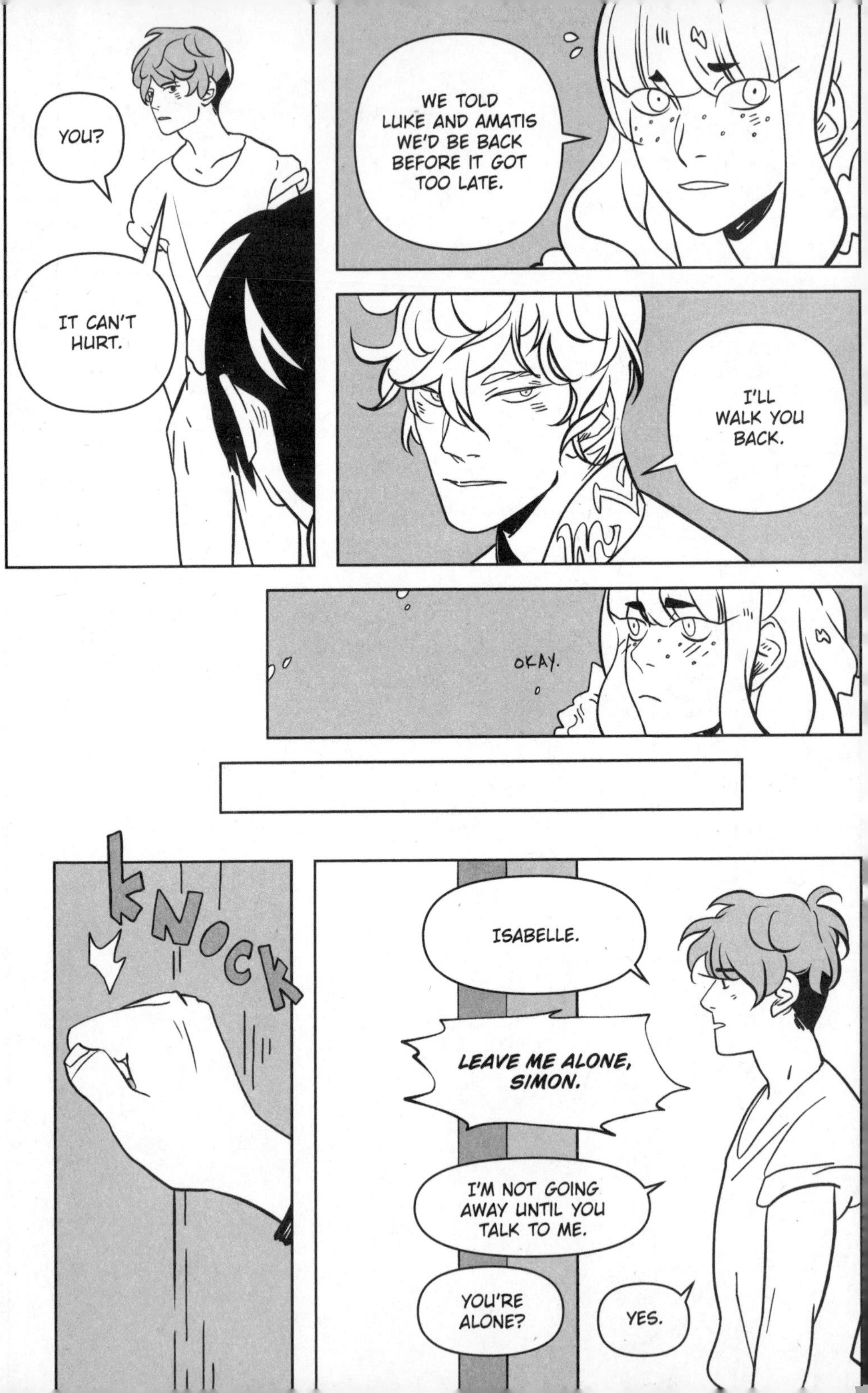
YOU?
IT CAN'T HURT.
WE TOLD LUKE AND AMATIS WE'D BE BACK BEFORE IT GOT TOO LATE.
I'LL WALK YOU BACK.
OKAY.
KNOCK
ISABELLE.
LEAVE ME ALONE, SIMON.
I'M NOT GOING AWAY UNTIL YOU TALK TO ME.
YOU'RE ALONE?
YES.

WHAT DO YOU WANT?

WHAT HAPPENED TO MAX. IT WASN'T YOUR FAULT.

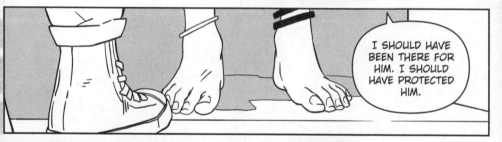

I SHOULD HAVE BEEN THERE FOR HIM. I SHOULD HAVE PROTECTED HIM.

YOU WERE UNCONSCIOUS. YOU NEARLY DIED, IZZY.

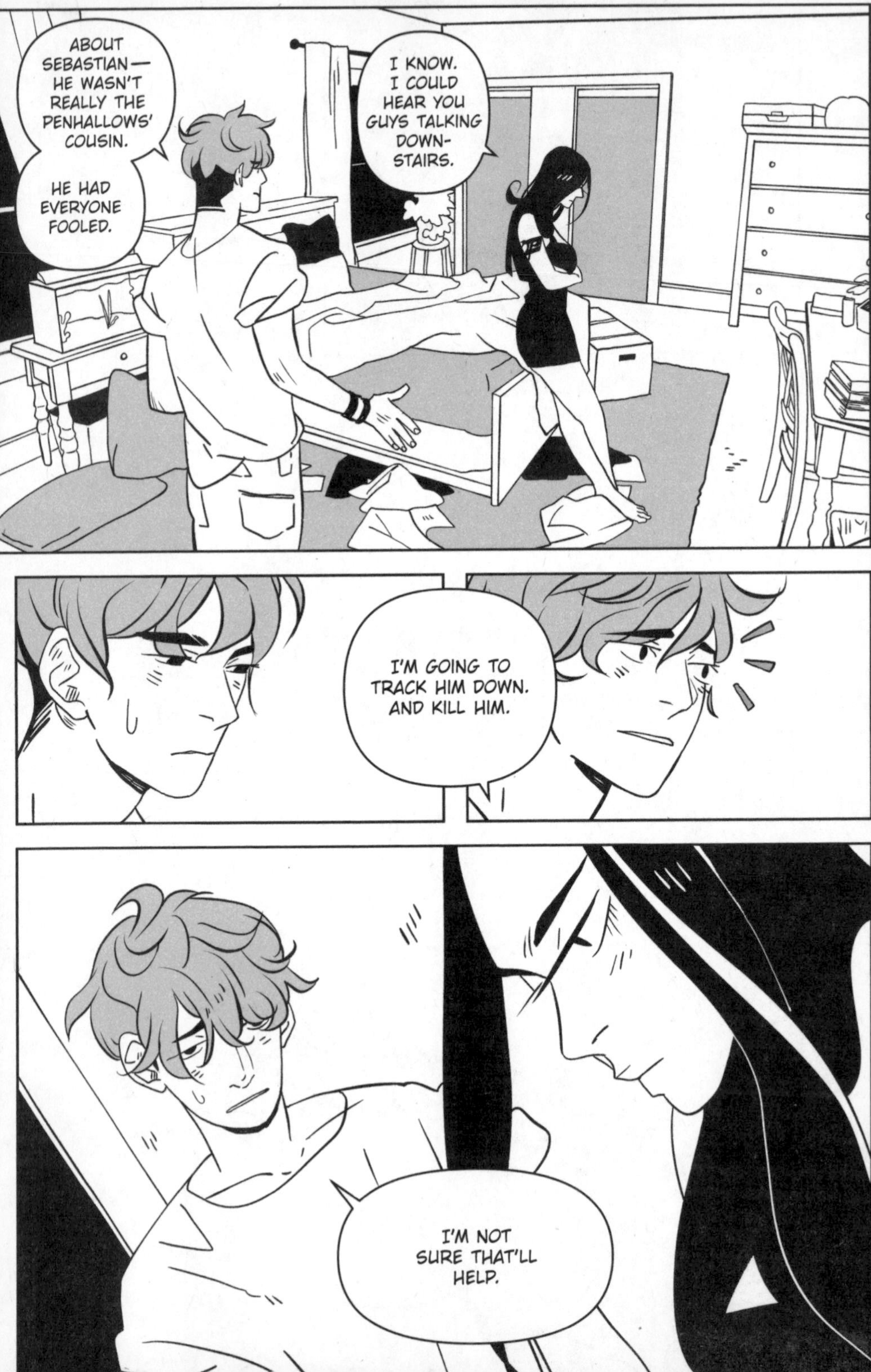
ABOUT SEBASTIAN— HE WASN'T REALLY THE PENHALLOWS' COUSIN.
HE HAD EVERYONE FOOLED.
I KNOW. I COULD HEAR YOU GUYS TALKING DOWN-STAIRS.
I'M GOING TO TRACK HIM DOWN. AND KILL HIM.
I'M NOT SURE THAT'LL HELP.

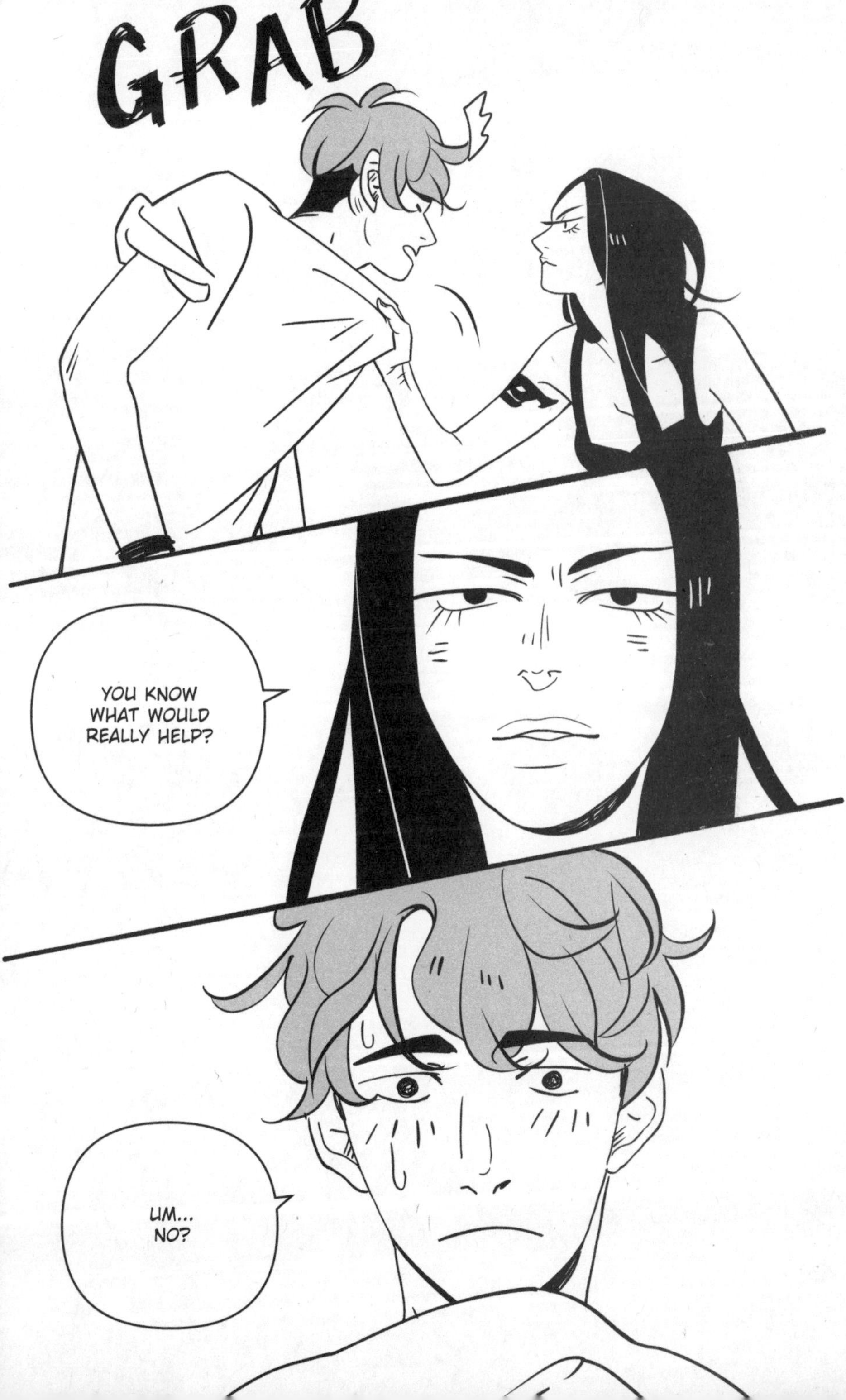
GRAB
YOU KNOW WHAT WOULD REALLY HELP?
UM... NO?

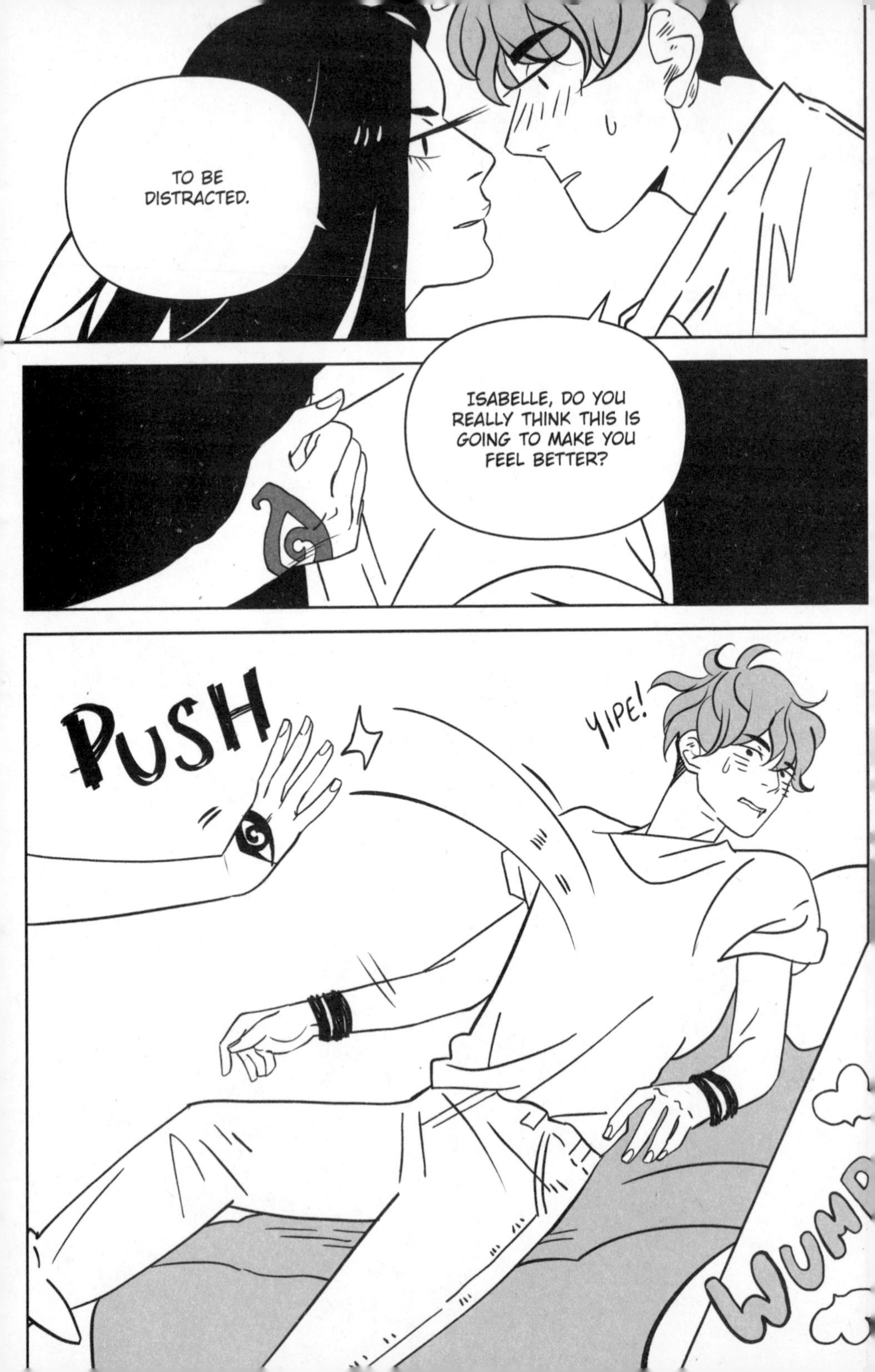
TO BE DISTRACTED.
ISABELLE, DO YOU REALLY THINK THIS IS GOING TO MAKE YOU FEEL BETTER?
PUSH
YIPE!

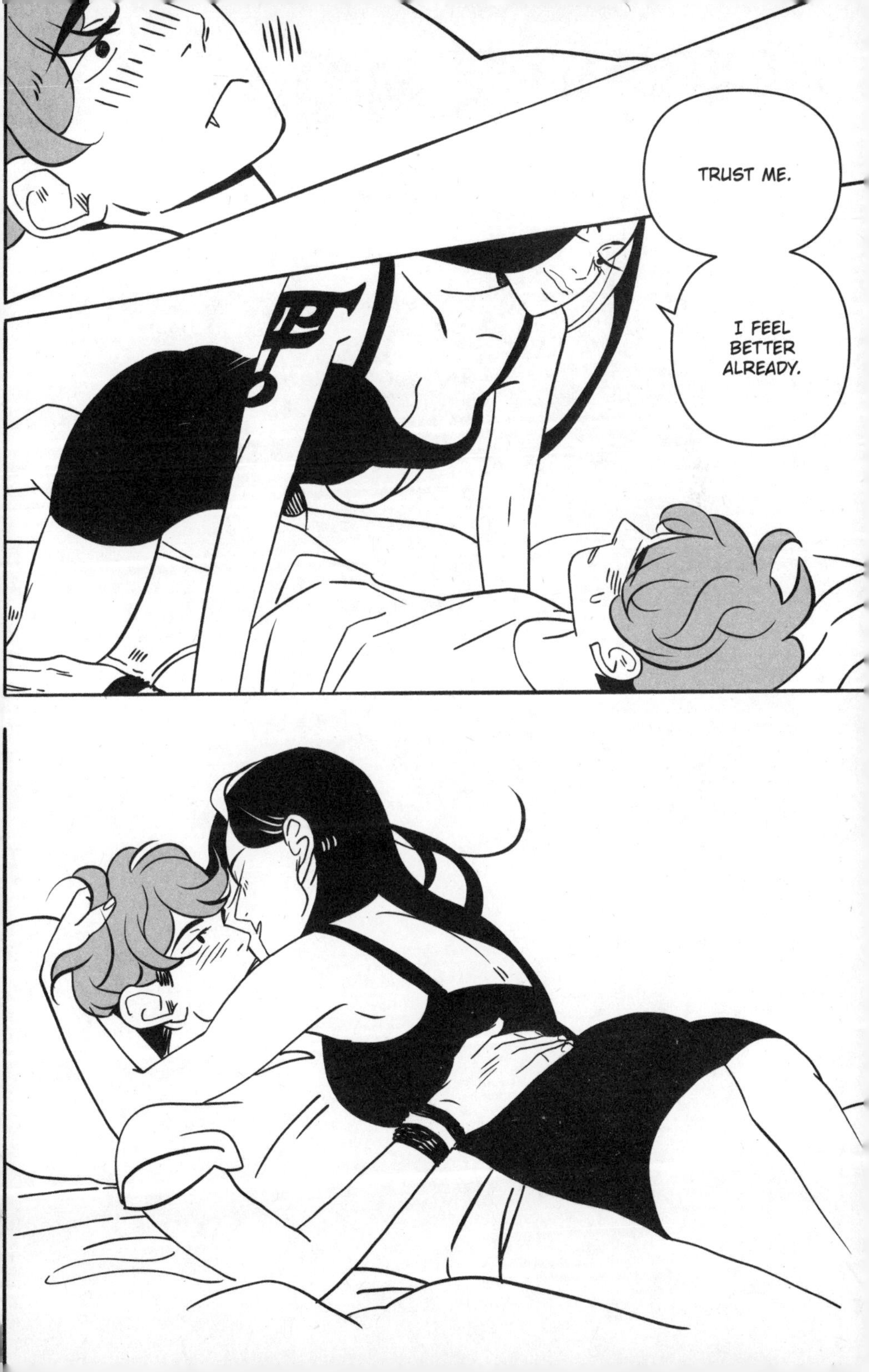
TRUST ME.
I FEEL BETTER ALREADY.

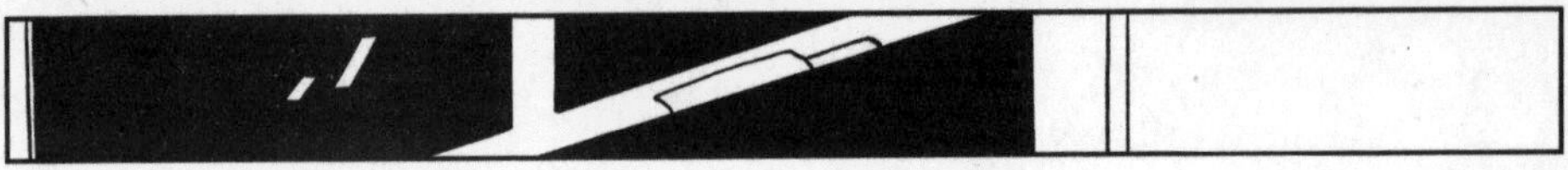

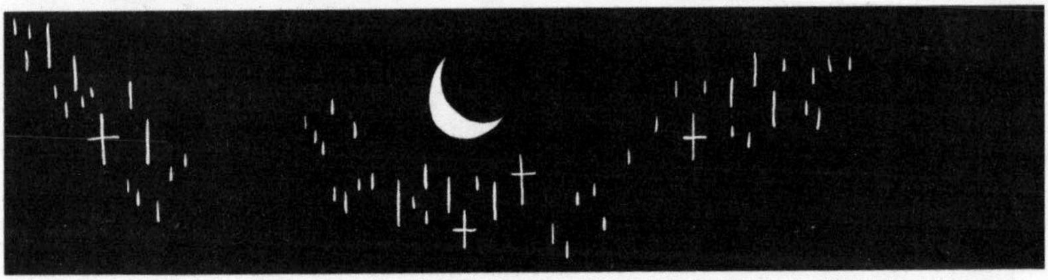

THE MORTAL INSTRUMENTS

THE GRAPHIC NOVEL

THE MORTAL INSTRUMENTS

THE GRAPHIC NOVEL

Chapter 32

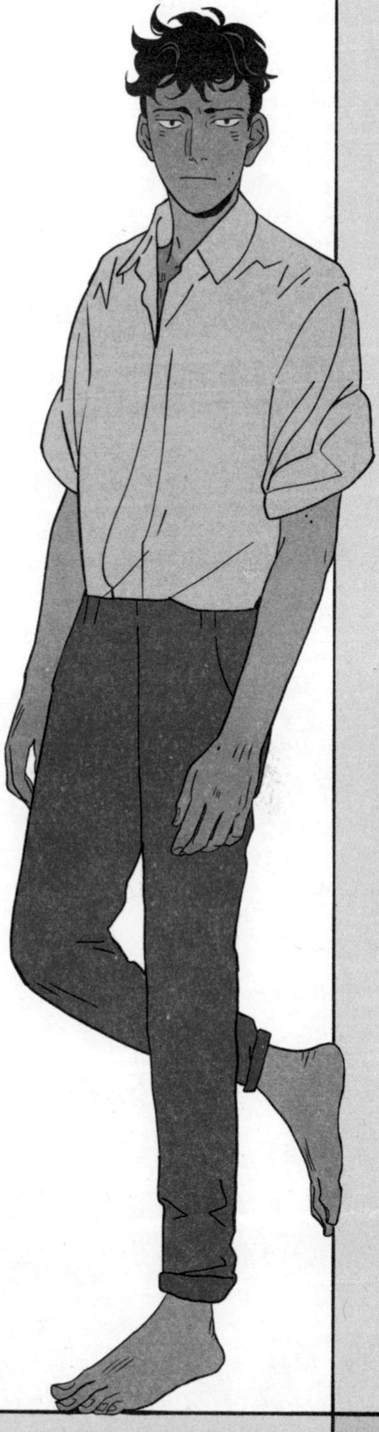

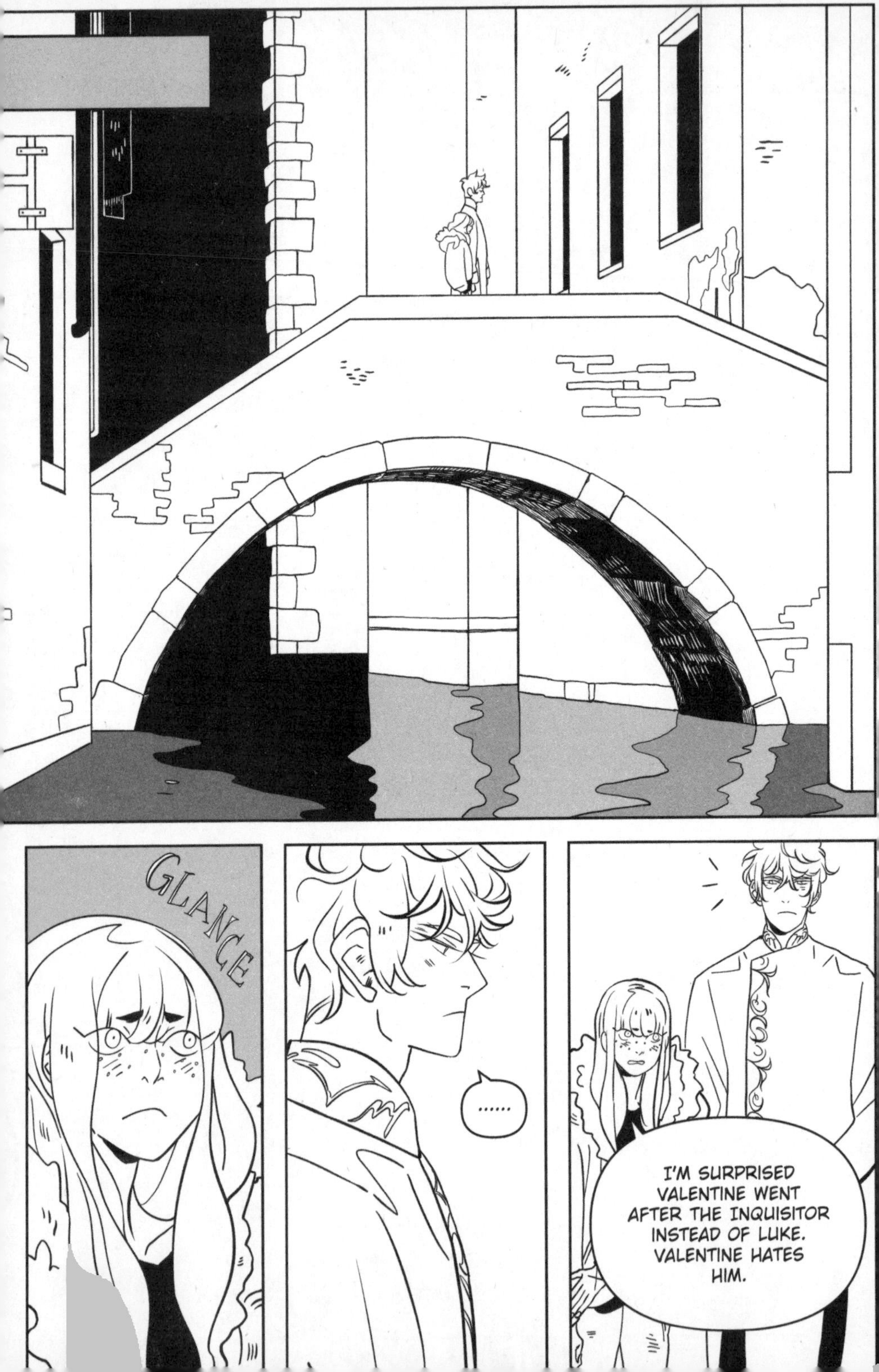
GLANCE
......
I'M SURPRISED VALENTINE WENT AFTER THE INQUISITOR INSTEAD OF LUKE. VALENTINE HATES HIM.

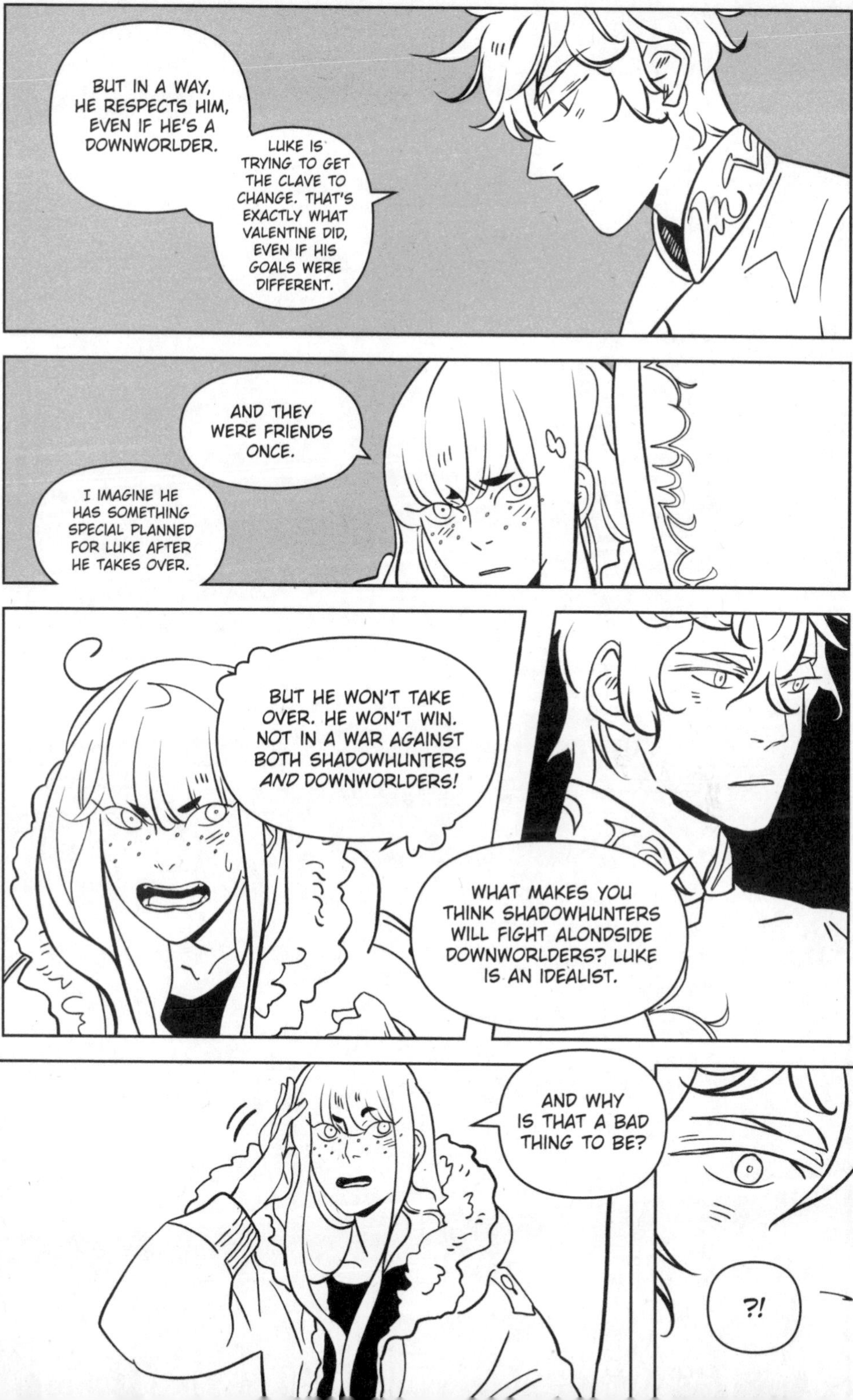
BUT IN A WAY, HE RESPECTS HIM, EVEN IF HE'S A DOWNWORLDER.
LUKE IS TRYING TO GET THE CLAVE TO CHANGE. THAT'S EXACTLY WHAT VALENTINE DID, EVEN IF HIS GOALS WERE DIFFERENT.
AND THEY WERE FRIENDS ONCE.
I IMAGINE HE HAS SOMETHING SPECIAL PLANNED FOR LUKE AFTER HE TAKES OVER.
BUT HE WON'T TAKE OVER. HE WON'T WIN. NOT IN A WAR AGAINST BOTH SHADOWHUNTERS AND DOWNWORLDERS!
WHAT MAKES YOU THINK SHADOWHUNTERS WILL FIGHT ALONDSIDE DOWNWORLDERS? LUKE IS AN IDEALIST.
AND WHY IS THAT A BAD THING TO BE?
?!

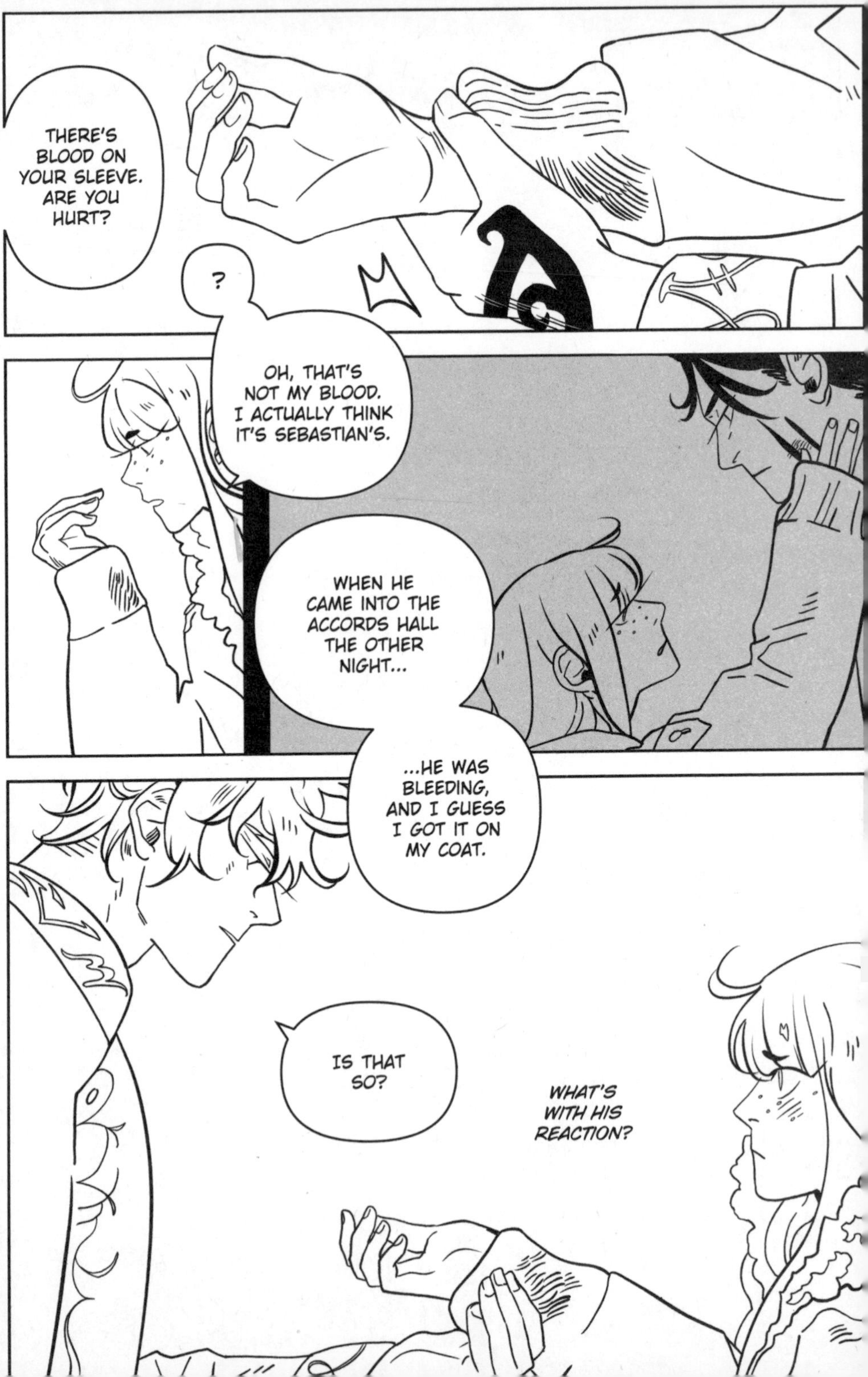
THERE'S BLOOD ON YOUR SLEEVE. ARE YOU HURT?
?
OH, THAT'S NOT MY BLOOD. I ACTUALLY THINK IT'S SEBASTIAN'S.
WHEN HE CAME INTO THE ACCORDS HALL THE OTHER NIGHT...
...HE WAS BLEEDING, AND I GUESS I GOT IT ON MY COAT.
IS THAT SO?
WHAT'S WITH HIS REACTION?

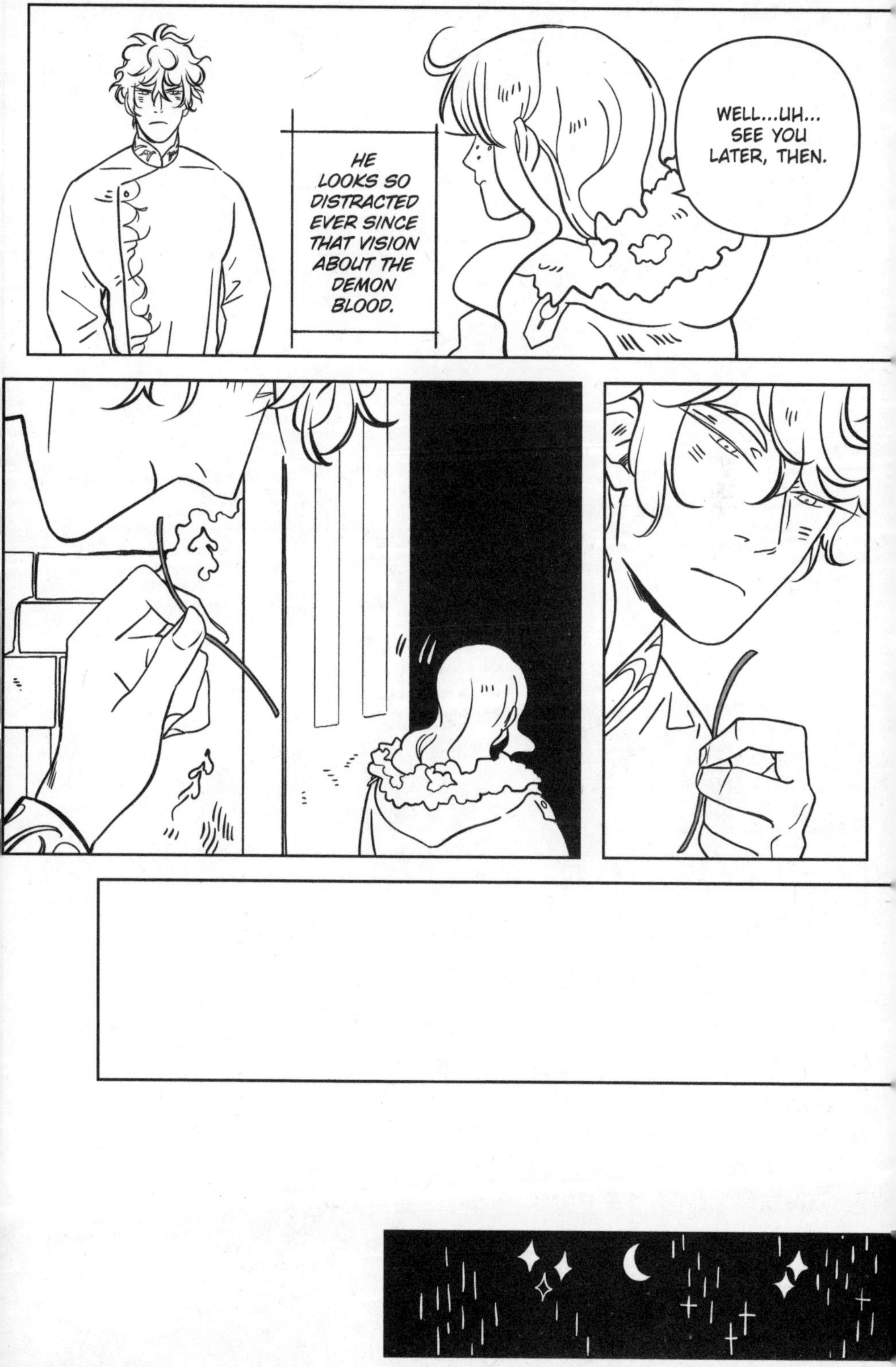
HE LOOKS SO DISTRACTED EVER SINCE THAT VISION ABOUT THE DEMON BLOOD.
WELL...UH... SEE YOU LATER, THEN.

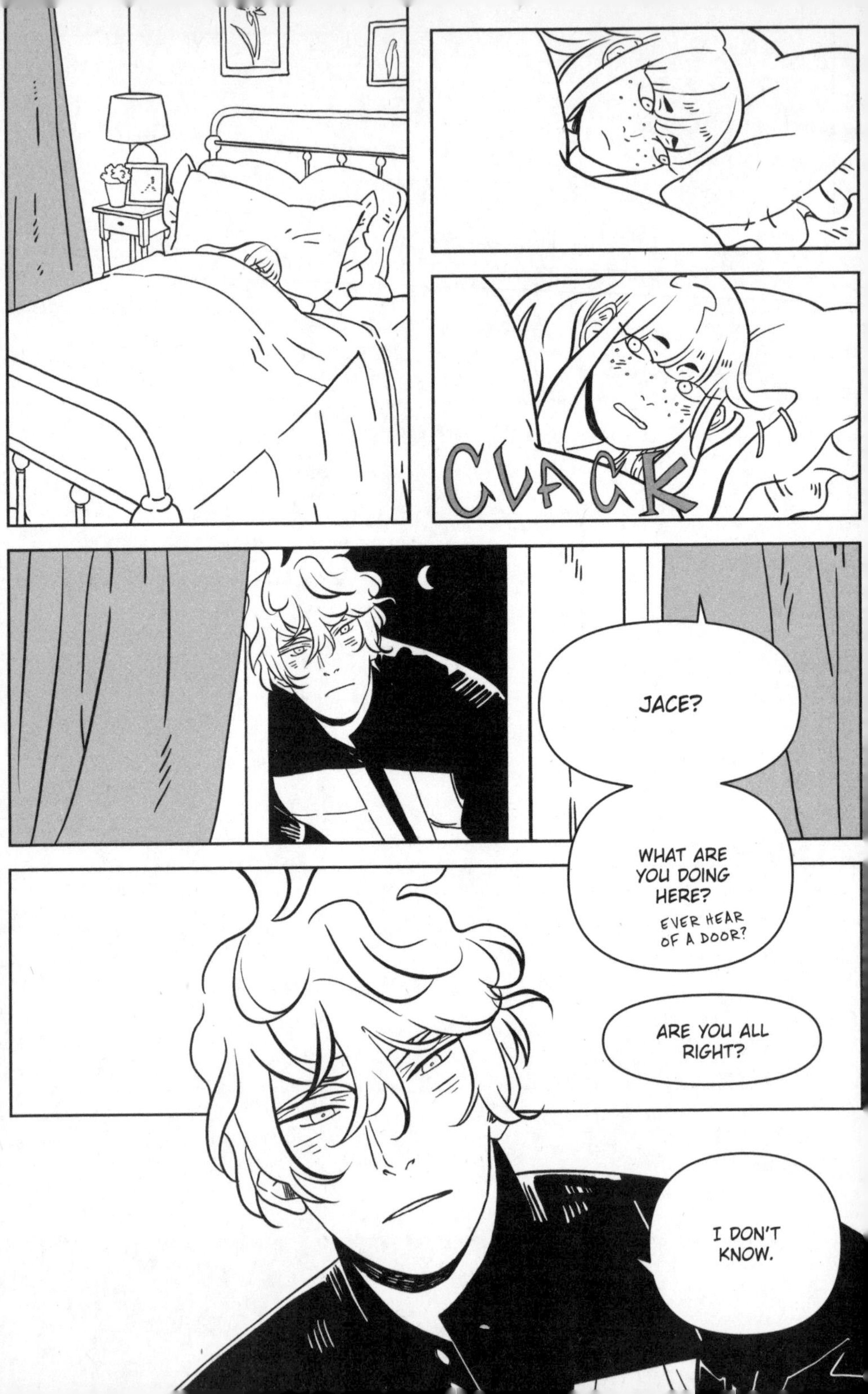
CLACK
JACE?
WHAT ARE YOU DOING HERE?
EVER HEAR OF A DOOR?
ARE YOU ALL RIGHT?
I DON'T KNOW.

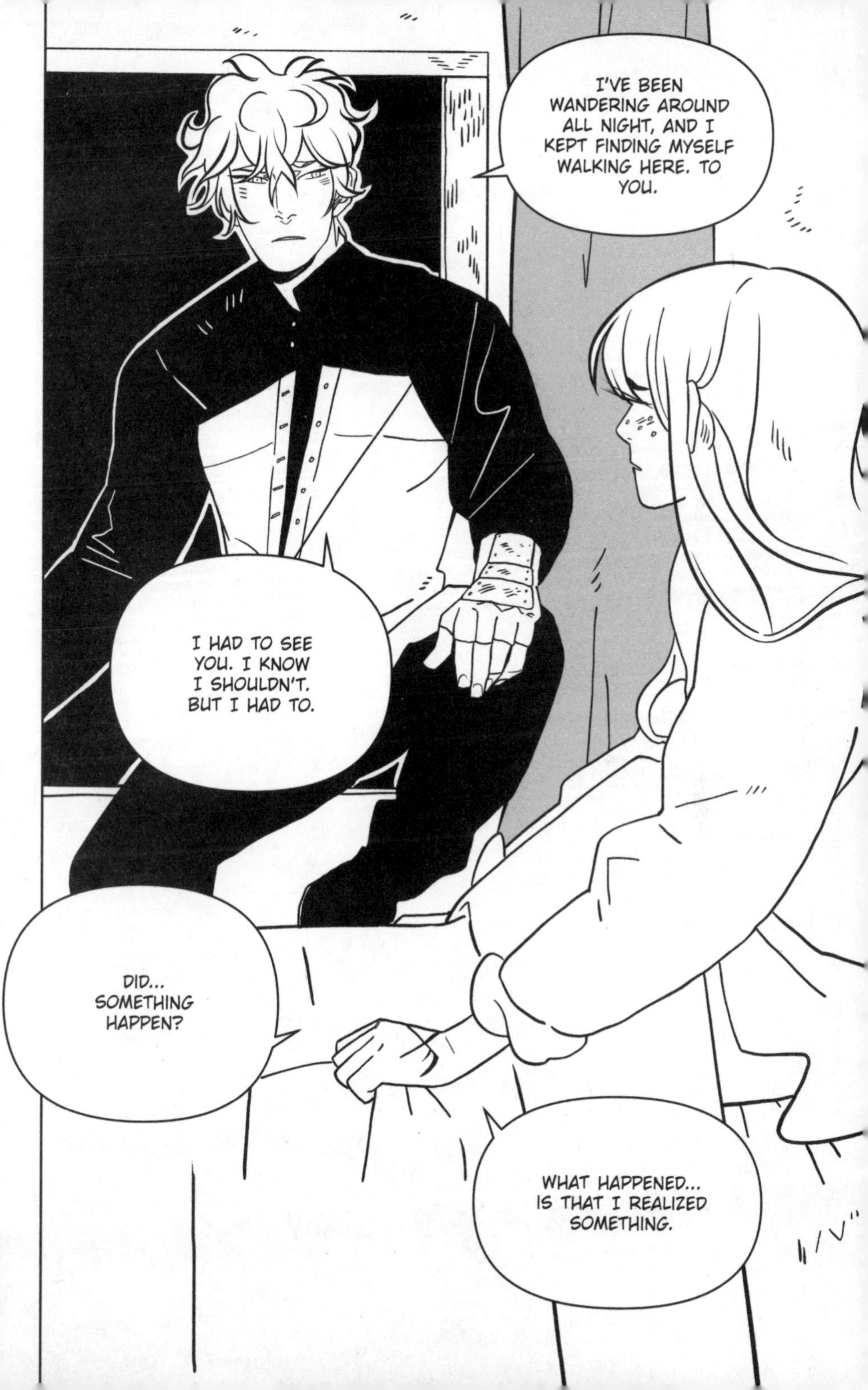
I'VE BEEN WANDERING AROUND ALL NIGHT, AND I KEPT FINDING MYSELF WALKING HERE. TO YOU.
I HAD TO SEE YOU. I KNOW I SHOULDN'T. BUT I HAD TO.
DID... SOMETHING HAPPEN?
WHAT HAPPENED... IS THAT I REALIZED SOMETHING.

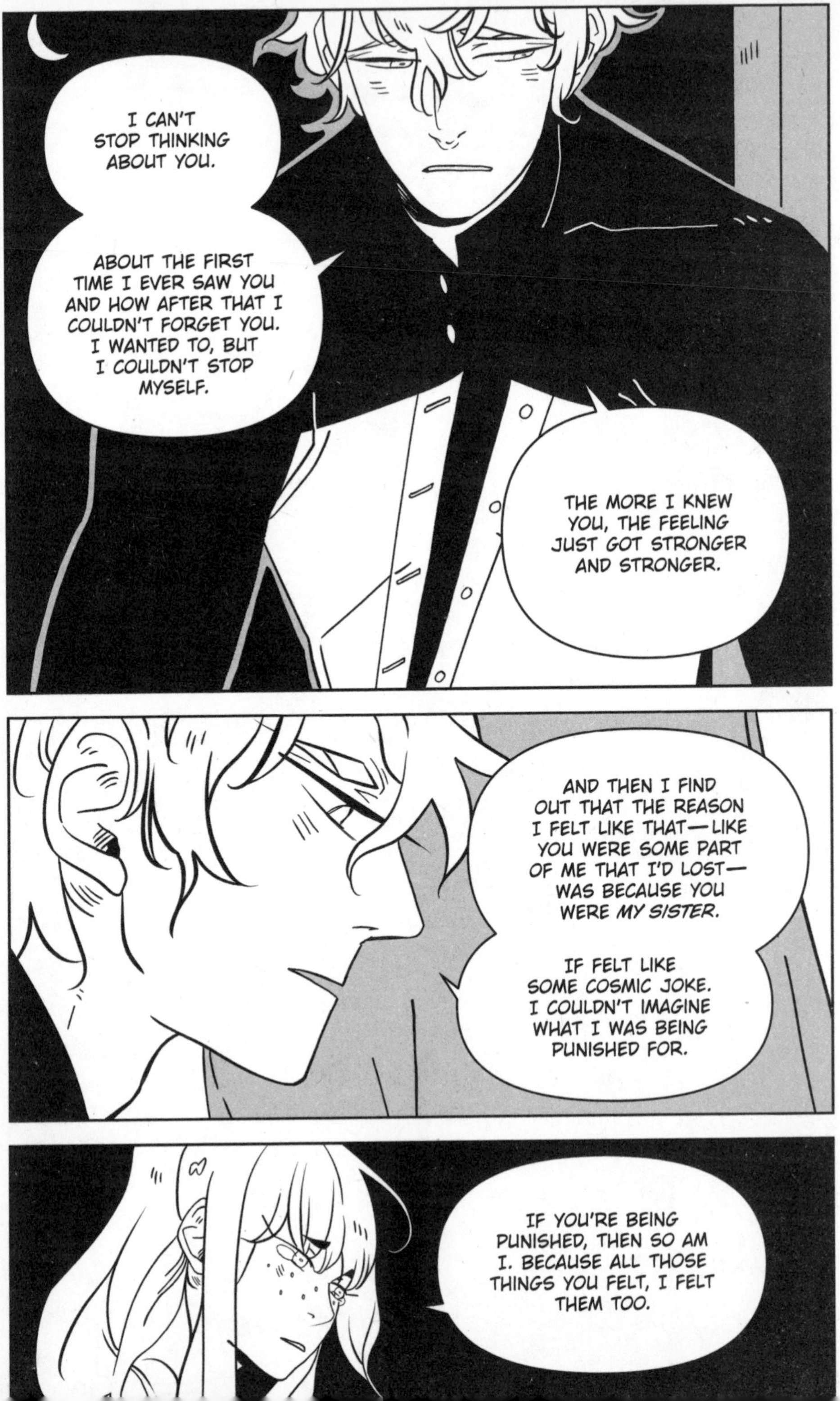
I CAN'T STOP THINKING ABOUT YOU.
ABOUT THE FIRST TIME I EVER SAW YOU AND HOW AFTER THAT I COULDN'T FORGET YOU. I WANTED TO, BUT I COULDN'T STOP MYSELF.
THE MORE I KNEW YOU, THE FEELING JUST GOT STRONGER AND STRONGER.
AND THEN I FIND OUT THAT THE REASON I FELT LIKE THAT—LIKE YOU WERE SOME PART OF ME THAT I'D LOST—WAS BECAUSE YOU WERE *MY SISTER*.
IF FELT LIKE SOME COSMIC JOKE. I COULDN'T IMAGINE WHAT I WAS BEING PUNISHED FOR.
IF YOU'RE BEING PUNISHED, THEN SO AM I. BECAUSE ALL THOSE THINGS YOU FELT, I FELT THEM TOO.

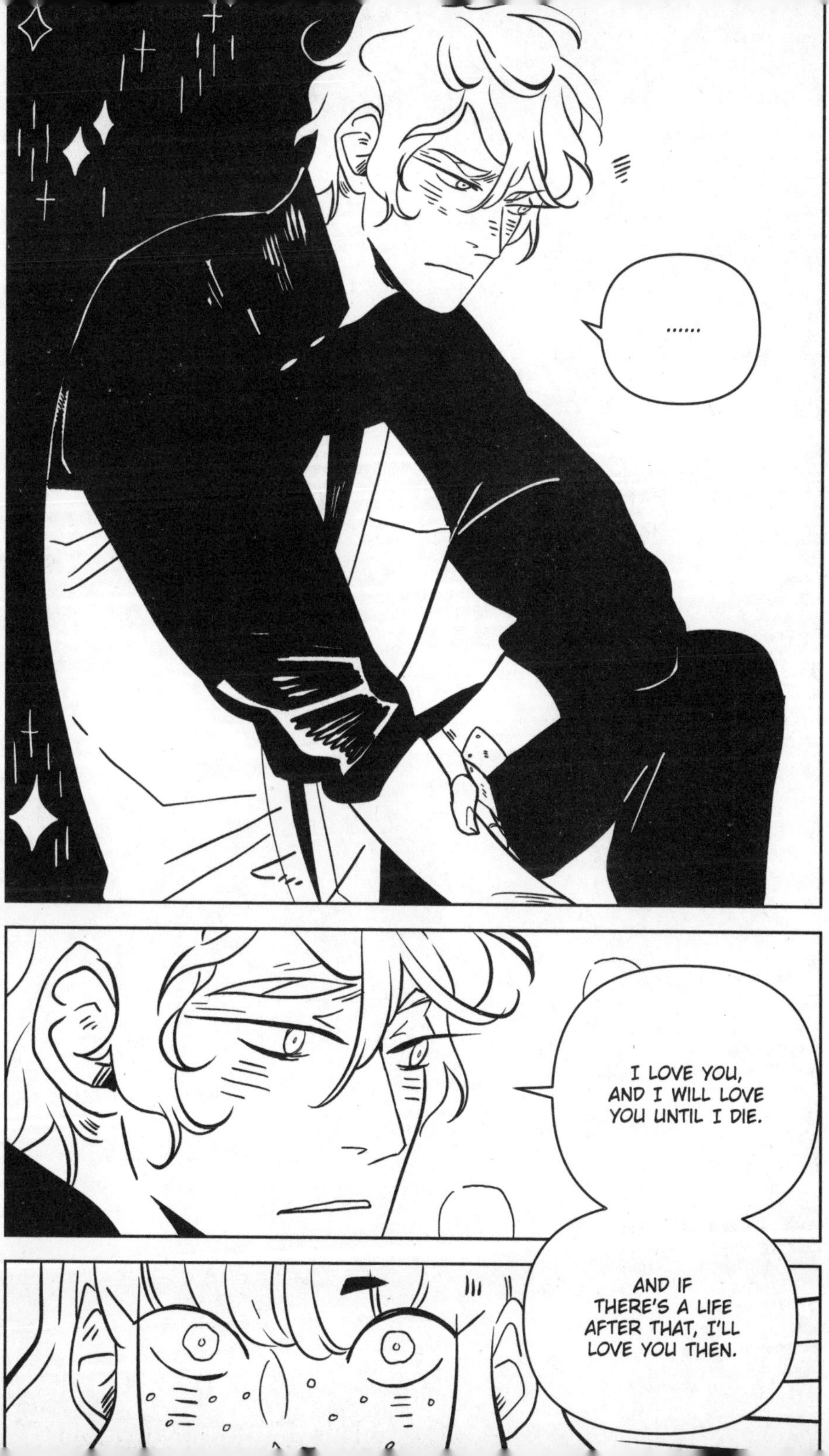
......
I LOVE YOU, AND I WILL LOVE YOU UNTIL I DIE.
AND IF THERE'S A LIFE AFTER THAT, I'LL LOVE YOU THEN.

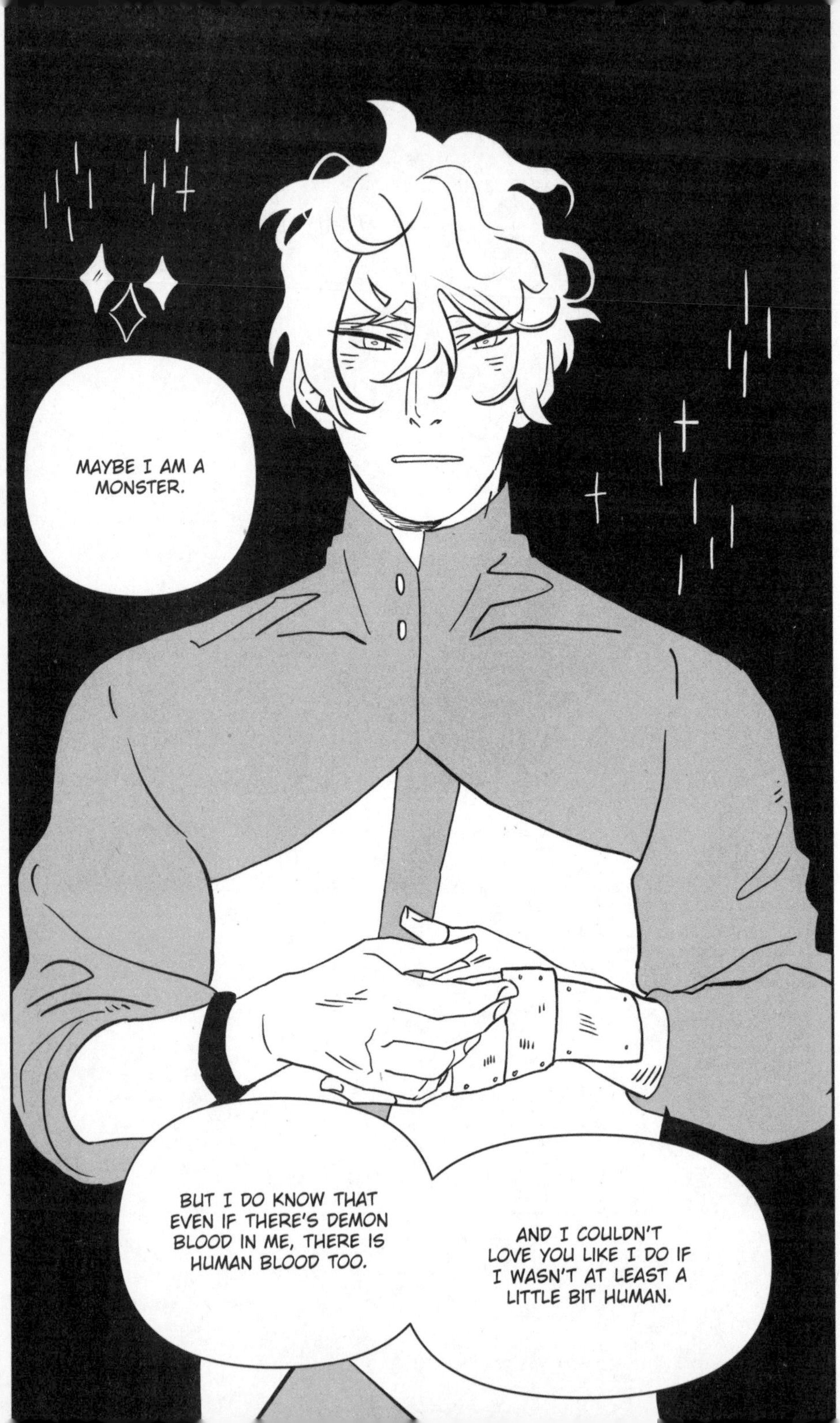
MAYBE I AM A MONSTER.
BUT I DO KNOW THAT EVEN IF THERE'S DEMON BLOOD IN ME, THERE IS HUMAN BLOOD TOO.
AND I COULDN'T LOVE YOU LIKE I DO IF I WASN'T AT LEAST A LITTLE BIT HUMAN.

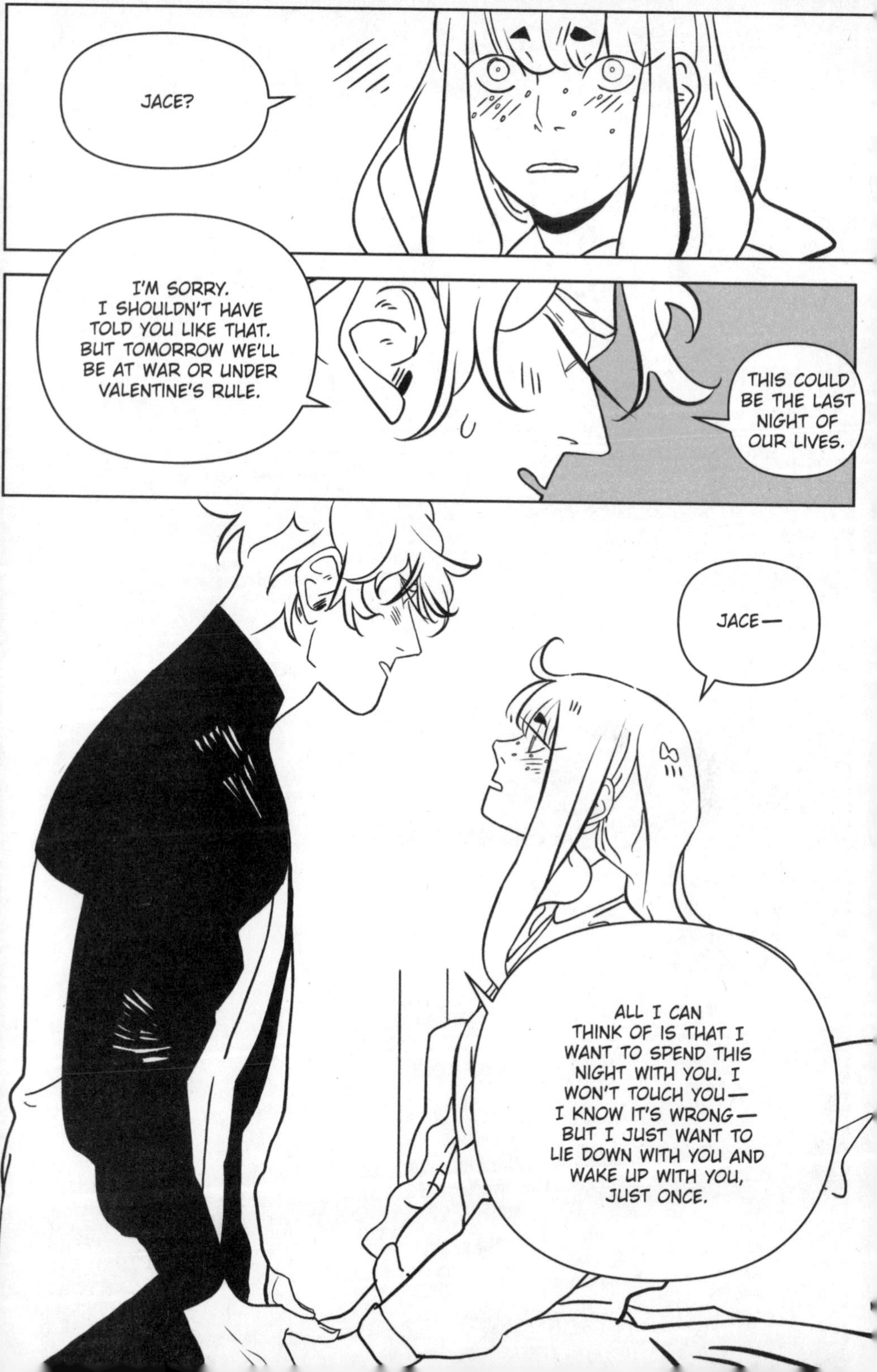
JACE?
I'M SORRY. I SHOULDN'T HAVE TOLD YOU LIKE THAT. BUT TOMORROW WE'LL BE AT WAR OR UNDER VALENTINE'S RULE.
THIS COULD BE THE LAST NIGHT OF OUR LIVES.
JACE—
ALL I CAN THINK OF IS THAT I WANT TO SPEND THIS NIGHT WITH YOU. I WON'T TOUCH YOU— I KNOW IT'S WRONG— BUT I JUST WANT TO LIE DOWN WITH YOU AND WAKE UP WITH YOU, JUST ONCE.

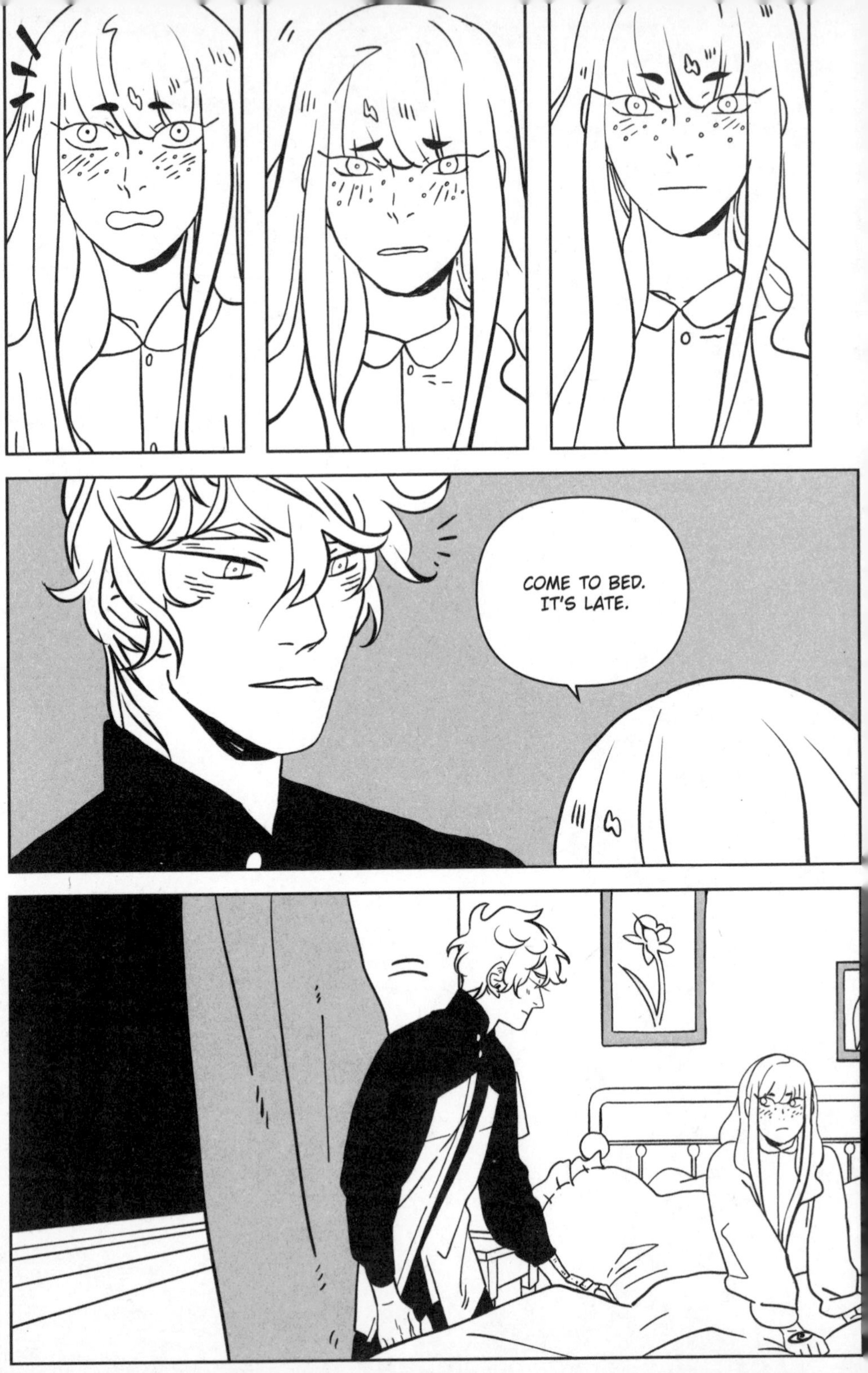
COME TO BED. IT'S LATE.

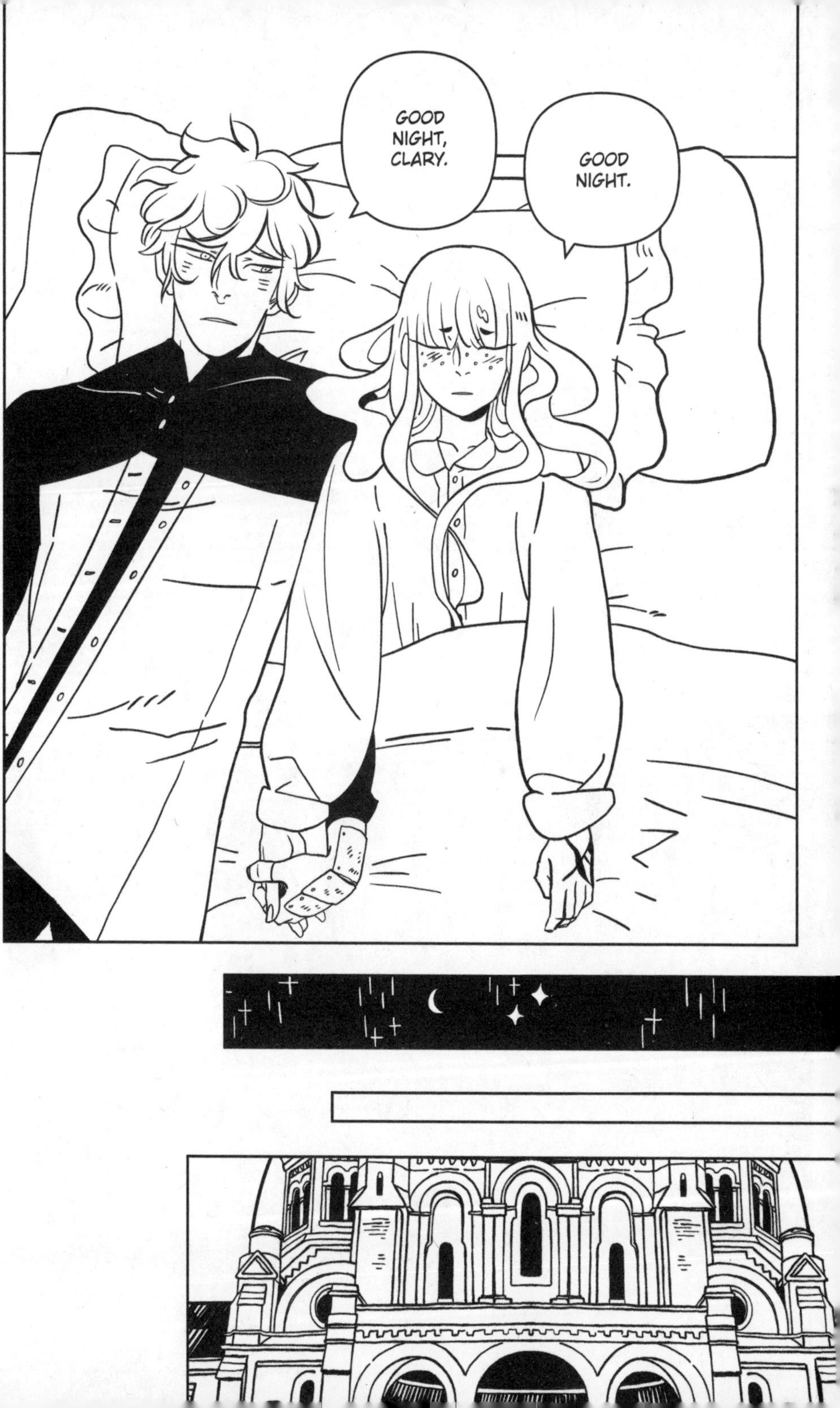
GOOD NIGHT, CLARY.
GOOD NIGHT.

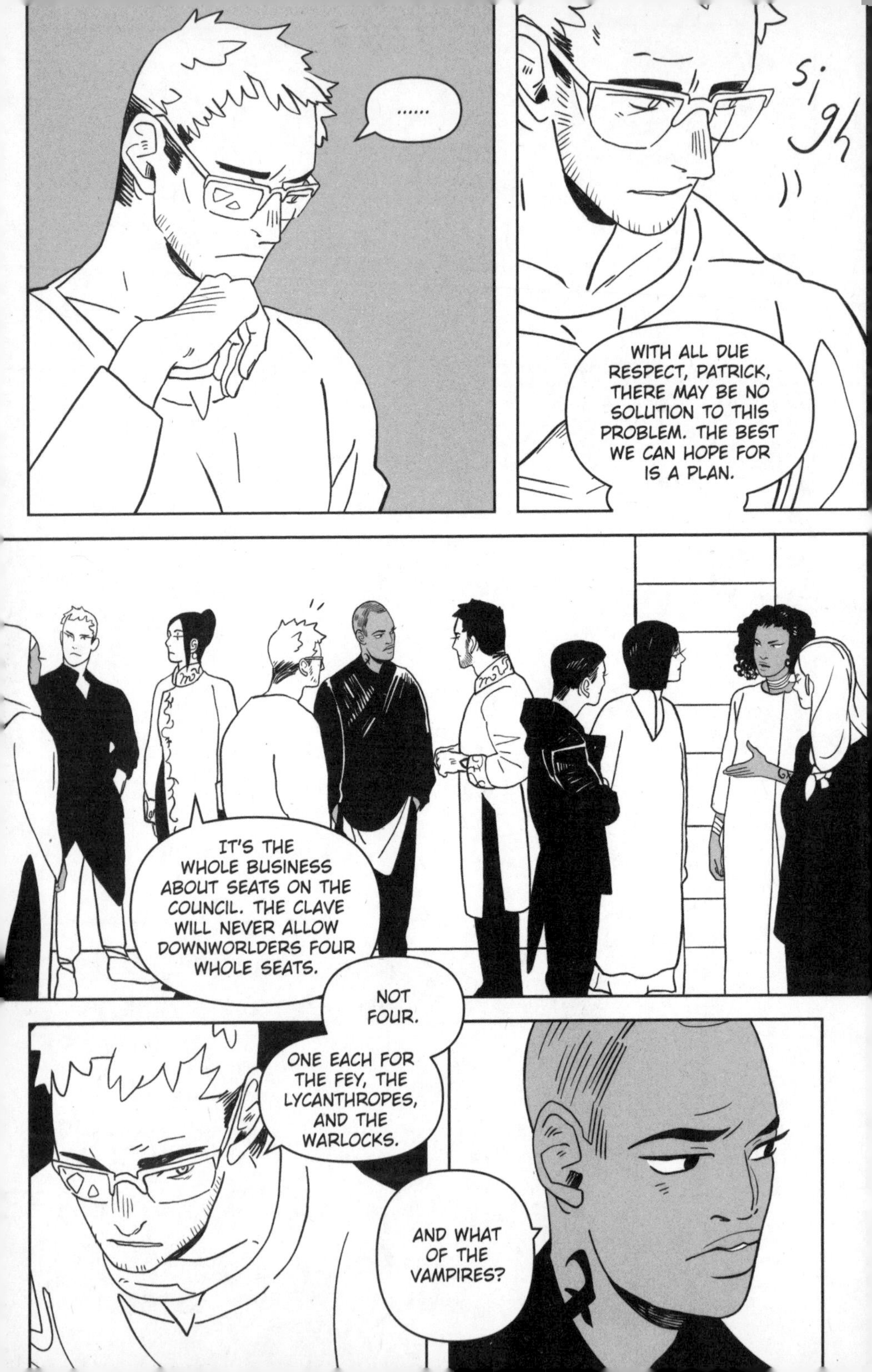
......
sigh
WITH ALL DUE RESPECT, PATRICK, THERE MAY BE NO SOLUTION TO THIS PROBLEM. THE BEST WE CAN HOPE FOR IS A PLAN.
IT'S THE WHOLE BUSINESS ABOUT SEATS ON THE COUNCIL. THE CLAVE WILL NEVER ALLOW DOWNWORLDERS FOUR WHOLE SEATS.
NOT FOUR.
ONE EACH FOR THE FEY, THE LYCANTHROPES, AND THE WARLOCKS.
AND WHAT OF THE VAMPIRES?

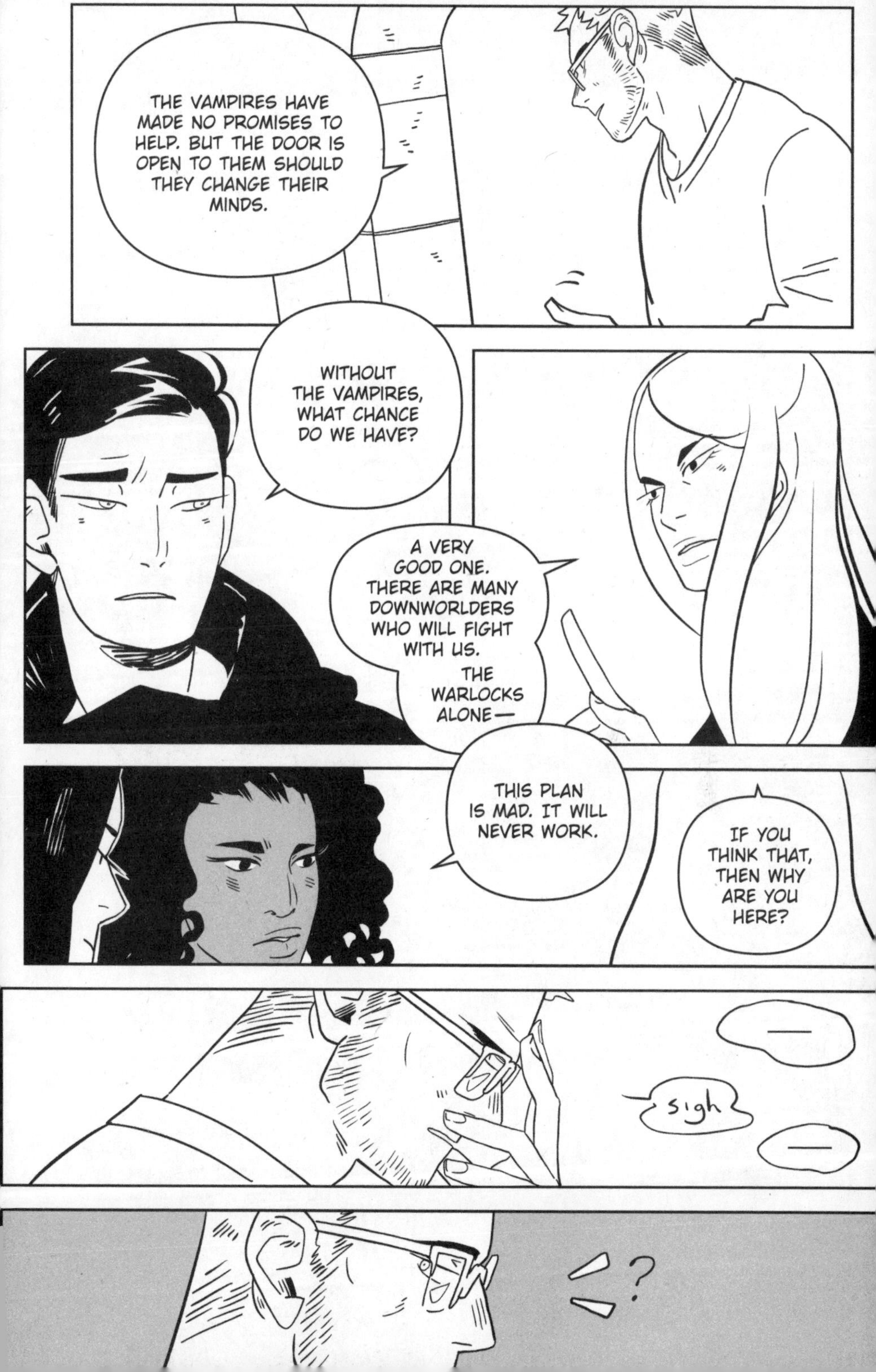
THE VAMPIRES HAVE MADE NO PROMISES TO HELP. BUT THE DOOR IS OPEN TO THEM SHOULD THEY CHANGE THEIR MINDS.
WITHOUT THE VAMPIRES, WHAT CHANCE DO WE HAVE?
A VERY GOOD ONE. THERE ARE MANY DOWNWORLDERS WHO WILL FIGHT WITH US.
THE WARLOCKS ALONE—
THIS PLAN IS MAD. IT WILL NEVER WORK.
IF YOU THINK THAT, THEN WHY ARE YOU HERE?
—
sigh
—
?

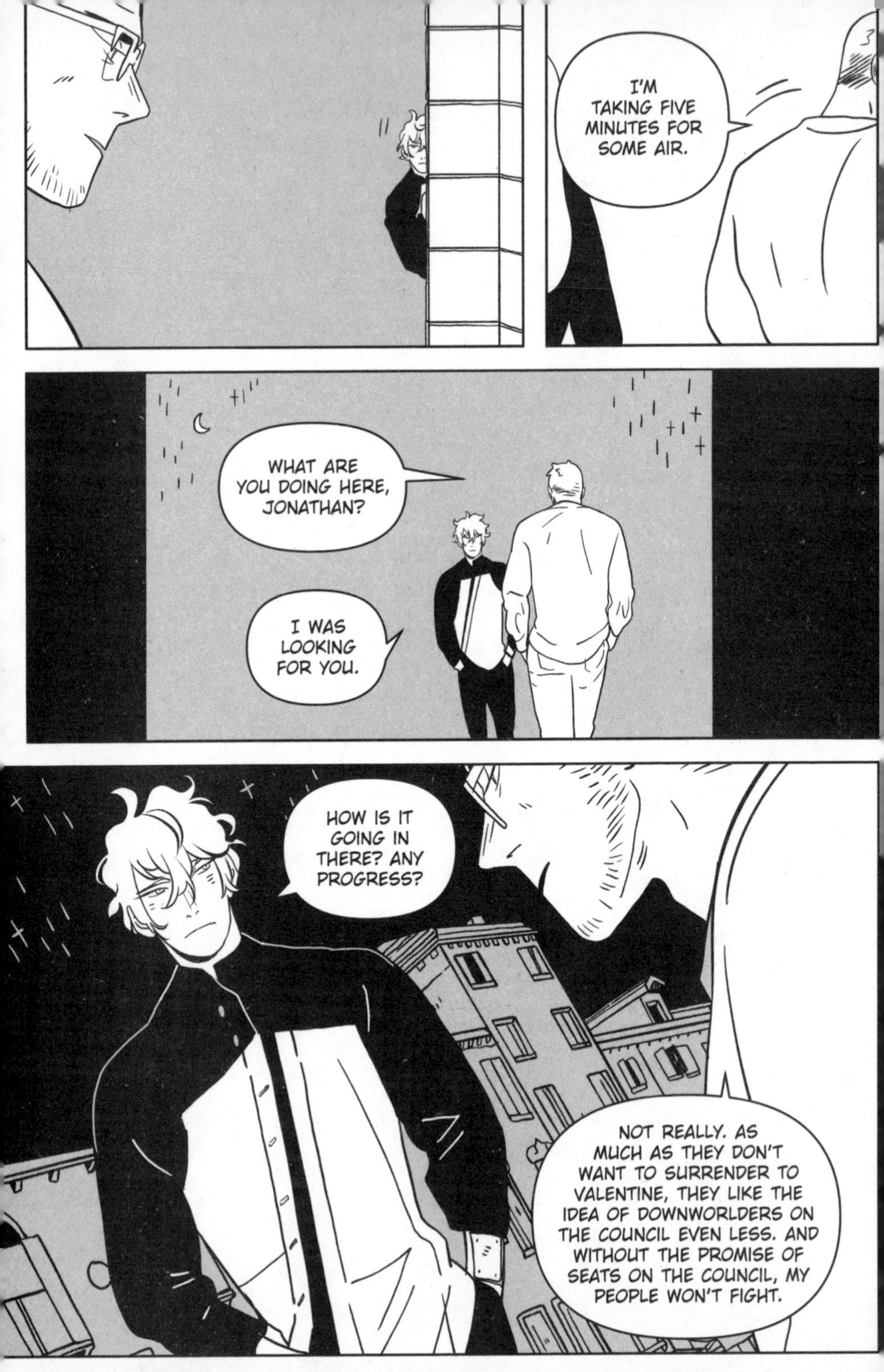
I'M TAKING FIVE MINUTES FOR SOME AIR.
WHAT ARE YOU DOING HERE, JONATHAN?
I WAS LOOKING FOR YOU.
HOW IS IT GOING IN THERE? ANY PROGRESS?
NOT REALLY. AS MUCH AS THEY DON'T WANT TO SURRENDER TO VALENTINE, THEY LIKE THE IDEA OF DOWNWORLDERS ON THE COUNCIL EVEN LESS. AND WITHOUT THE PROMISE OF SEATS ON THE COUNCIL, MY PEOPLE WON'T FIGHT.

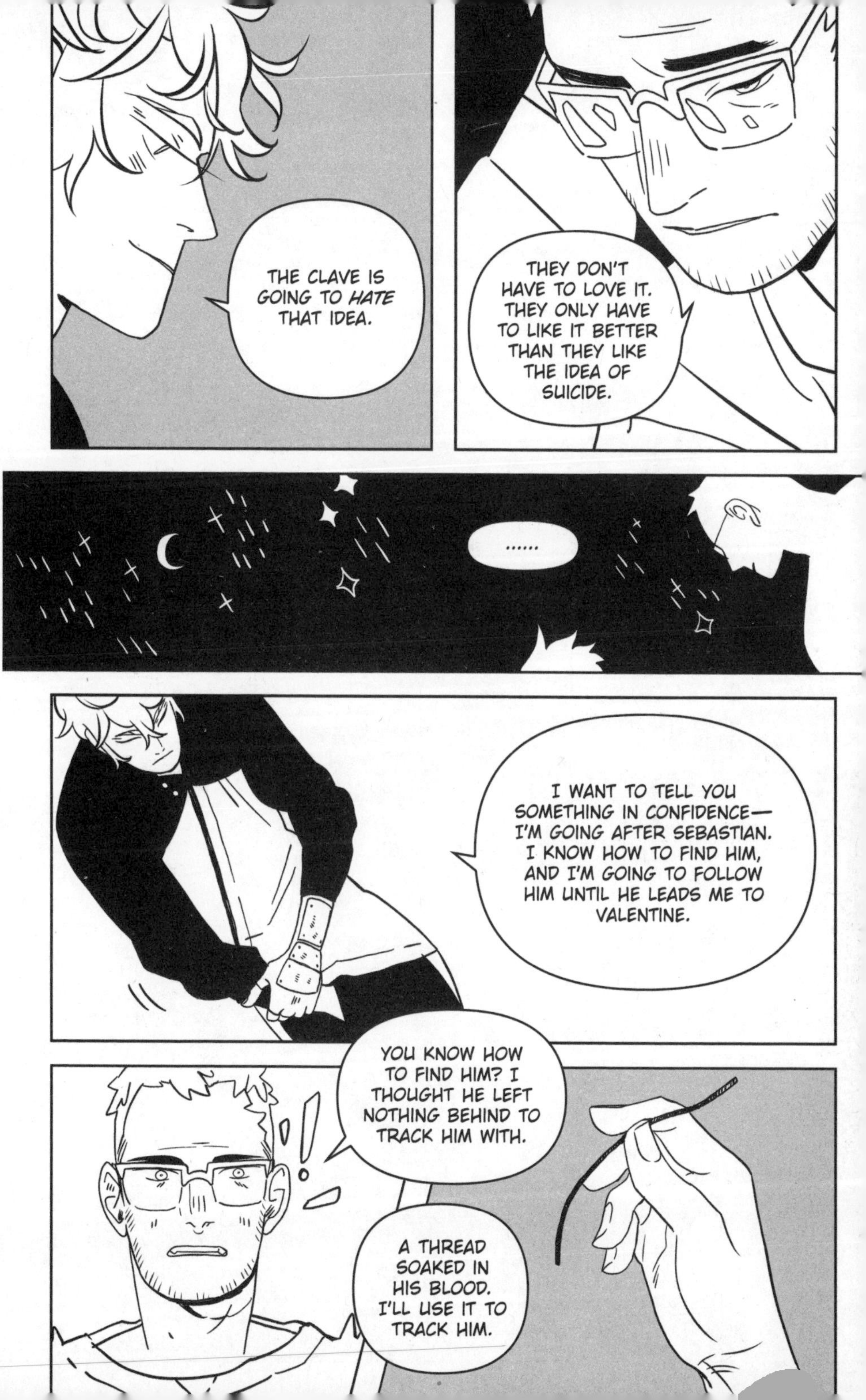
THE CLAVE IS GOING TO *HATE* THAT IDEA.
THEY DON'T HAVE TO LOVE IT. THEY ONLY HAVE TO LIKE IT BETTER THAN THEY LIKE THE IDEA OF SUICIDE.
......
I WANT TO TELL YOU SOMETHING IN CONFIDENCE— I'M GOING AFTER SEBASTIAN. I KNOW HOW TO FIND HIM, AND I'M GOING TO FOLLOW HIM UNTIL HE LEADS ME TO VALENTINE.
YOU KNOW HOW TO FIND HIM? I THOUGHT HE LEFT NOTHING BEHIND TO TRACK HIM WITH.
A THREAD SOAKED IN HIS BLOOD. I'LL USE IT TO TRACK HIM.

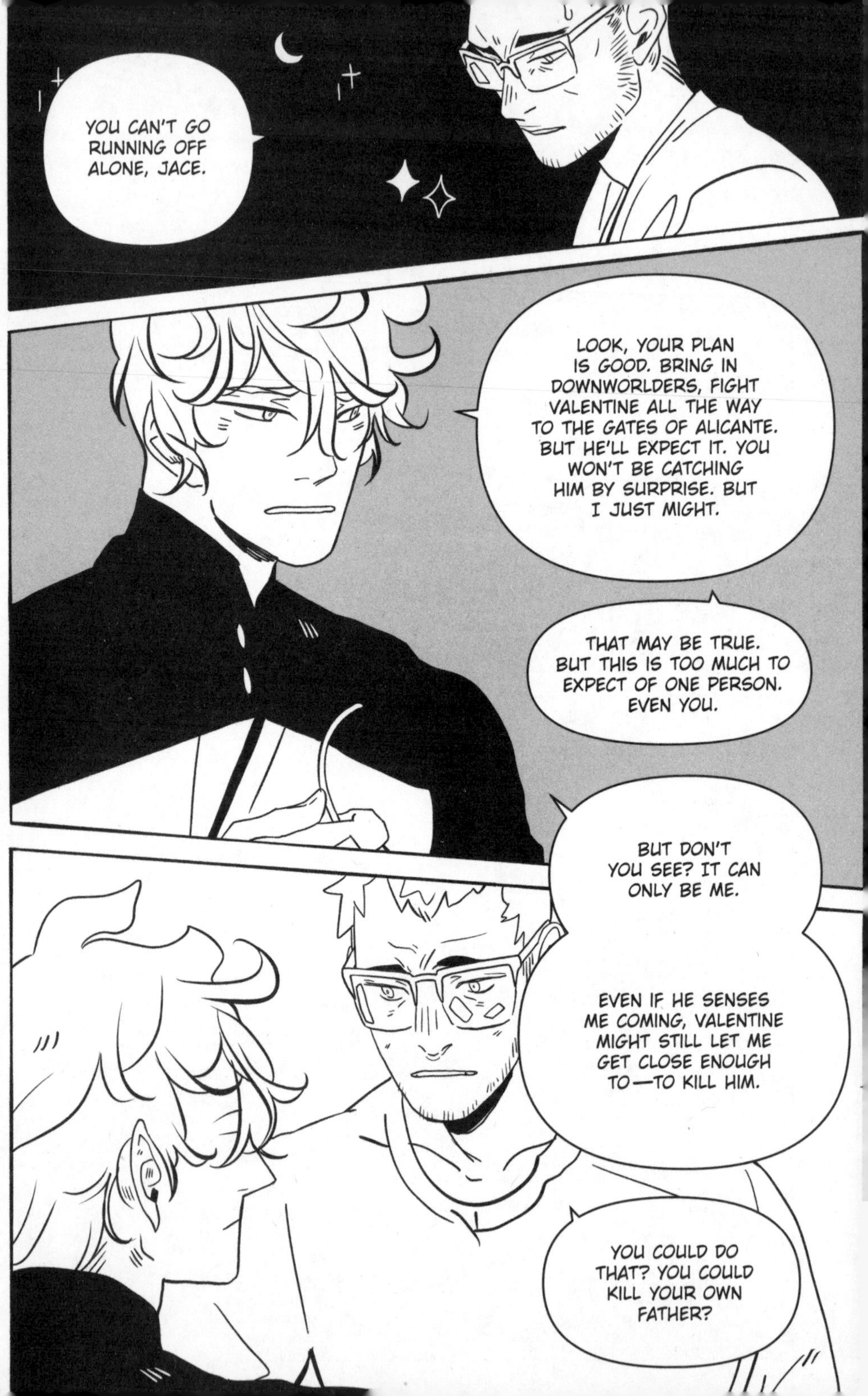
YOU CAN'T GO RUNNING OFF ALONE, JACE.
LOOK, YOUR PLAN IS GOOD. BRING IN DOWNWORLDERS, FIGHT VALENTINE ALL THE WAY TO THE GATES OF ALICANTE. BUT HE'LL EXPECT IT. YOU WON'T BE CATCHING HIM BY SURPRISE. BUT I JUST MIGHT.
THAT MAY BE TRUE. BUT THIS IS TOO MUCH TO EXPECT OF ONE PERSON. EVEN YOU.
BUT DON'T YOU SEE? IT CAN ONLY BE ME.
EVEN IF HE SENSES ME COMING, VALENTINE MIGHT STILL LET ME GET CLOSE ENOUGH TO—TO KILL HIM.
YOU COULD DO THAT? YOU COULD KILL YOUR OWN FATHER?

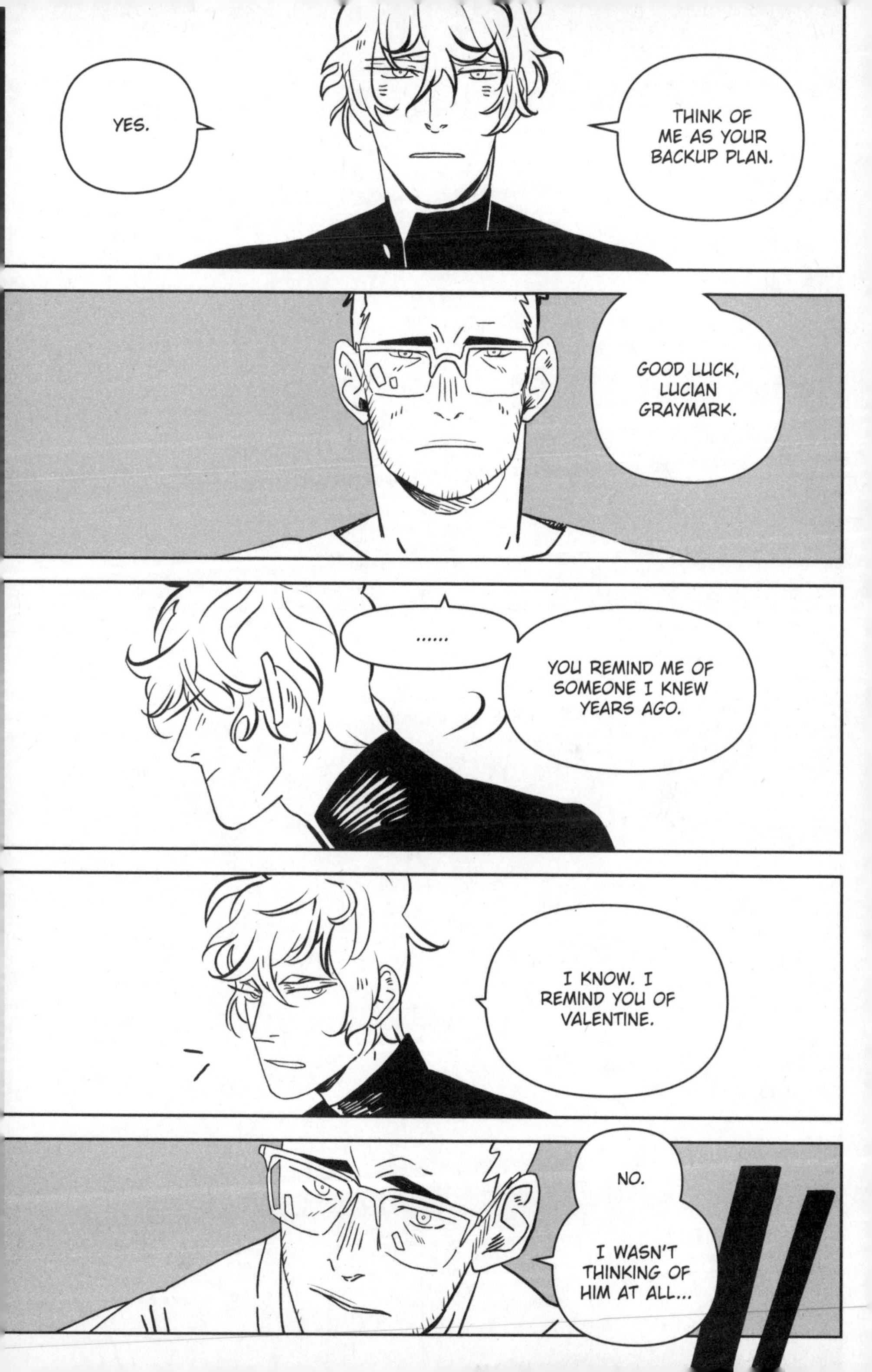
YES.
THINK OF ME AS YOUR BACKUP PLAN.
GOOD LUCK, LUCIAN GRAYMARK.
......
YOU REMIND ME OF SOMEONE I KNEW YEARS AGO.
I KNOW. I REMIND YOU OF VALENTINE.
NO.
I WASN'T THINKING OF HIM AT ALL...

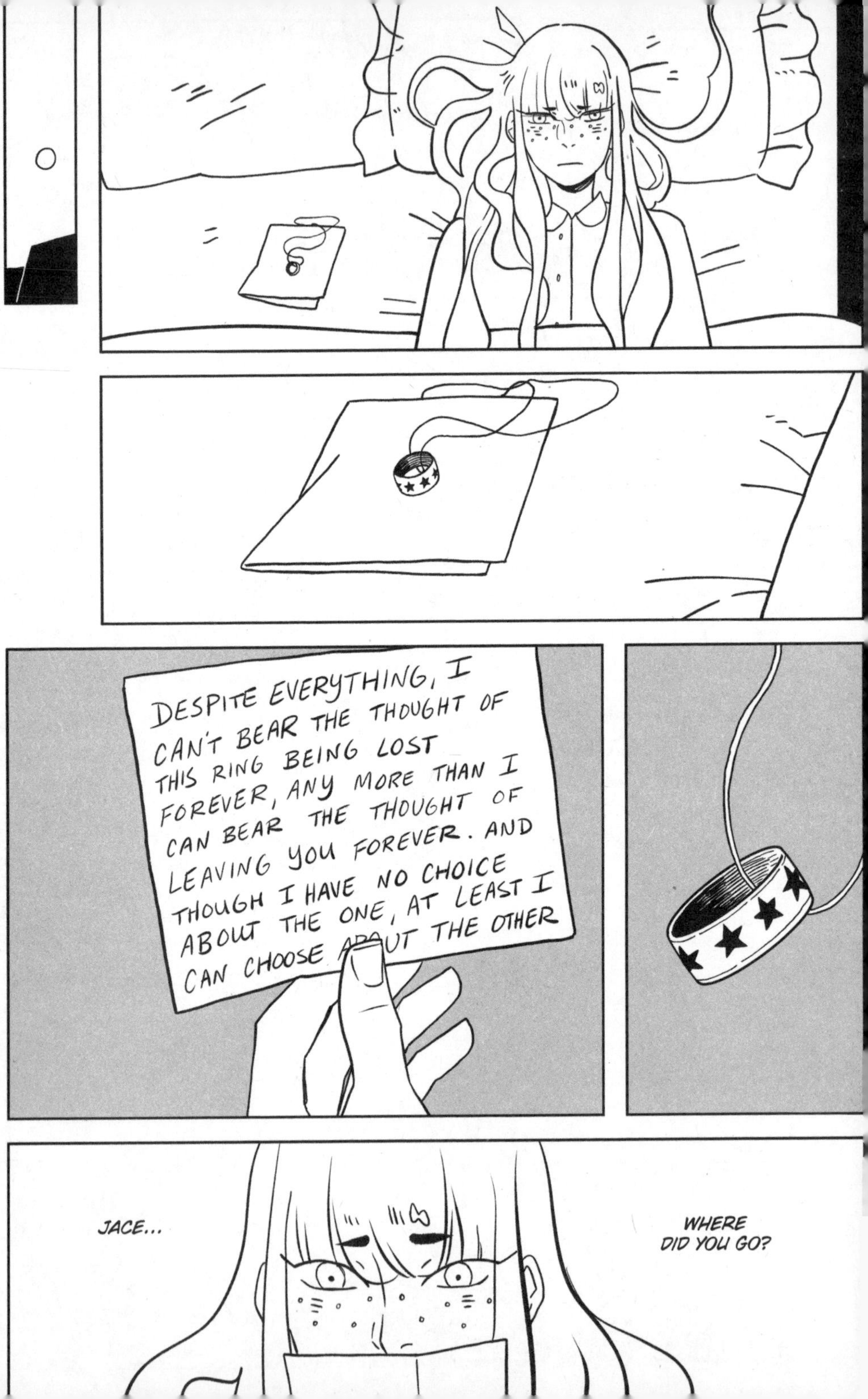
DESPITE EVERYTHING, I CAN'T BEAR THE THOUGHT OF THIS RING BEING LOST FOREVER, ANY MORE THAN I CAN BEAR THE THOUGHT OF LEAVING YOU FOREVER. AND THOUGH I HAVE NO CHOICE ABOUT THE ONE, AT LEAST I CAN CHOOSE ABOUT THE OTHER
JACE...
WHERE DID YOU GO?

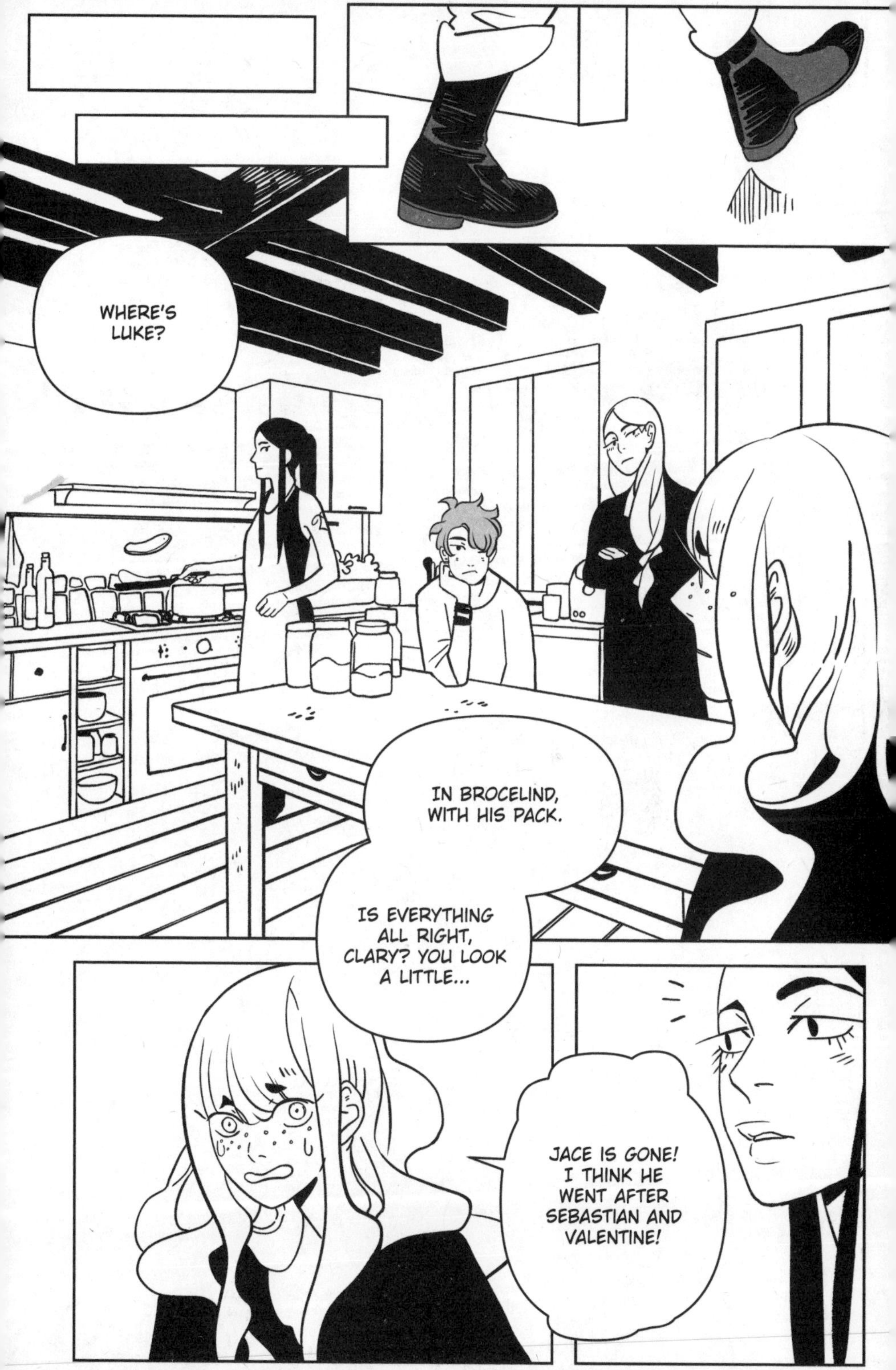
WHERE'S LUKE?
IN BROCELIND, WITH HIS PACK.
IS EVERYTHING ALL RIGHT, CLARY? YOU LOOK A LITTLE...
JACE IS GONE! I THINK HE WENT AFTER SEBASTIAN AND VALENTINE!

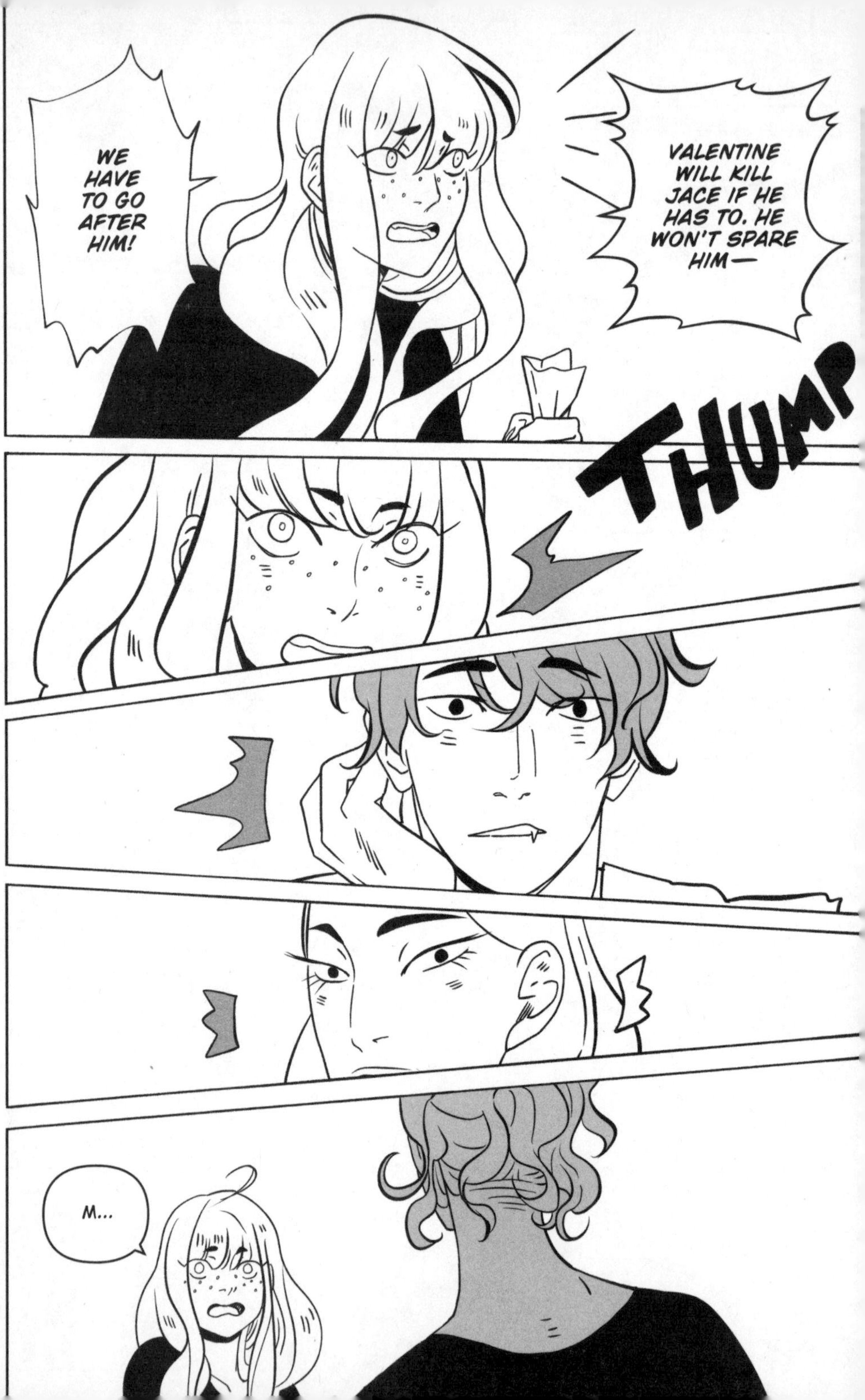
WE HAVE TO GO AFTER HIM!
VALENTINE WILL KILL JACE IF HE HAS TO. HE WON'T SPARE HIM—
THUMP
M...

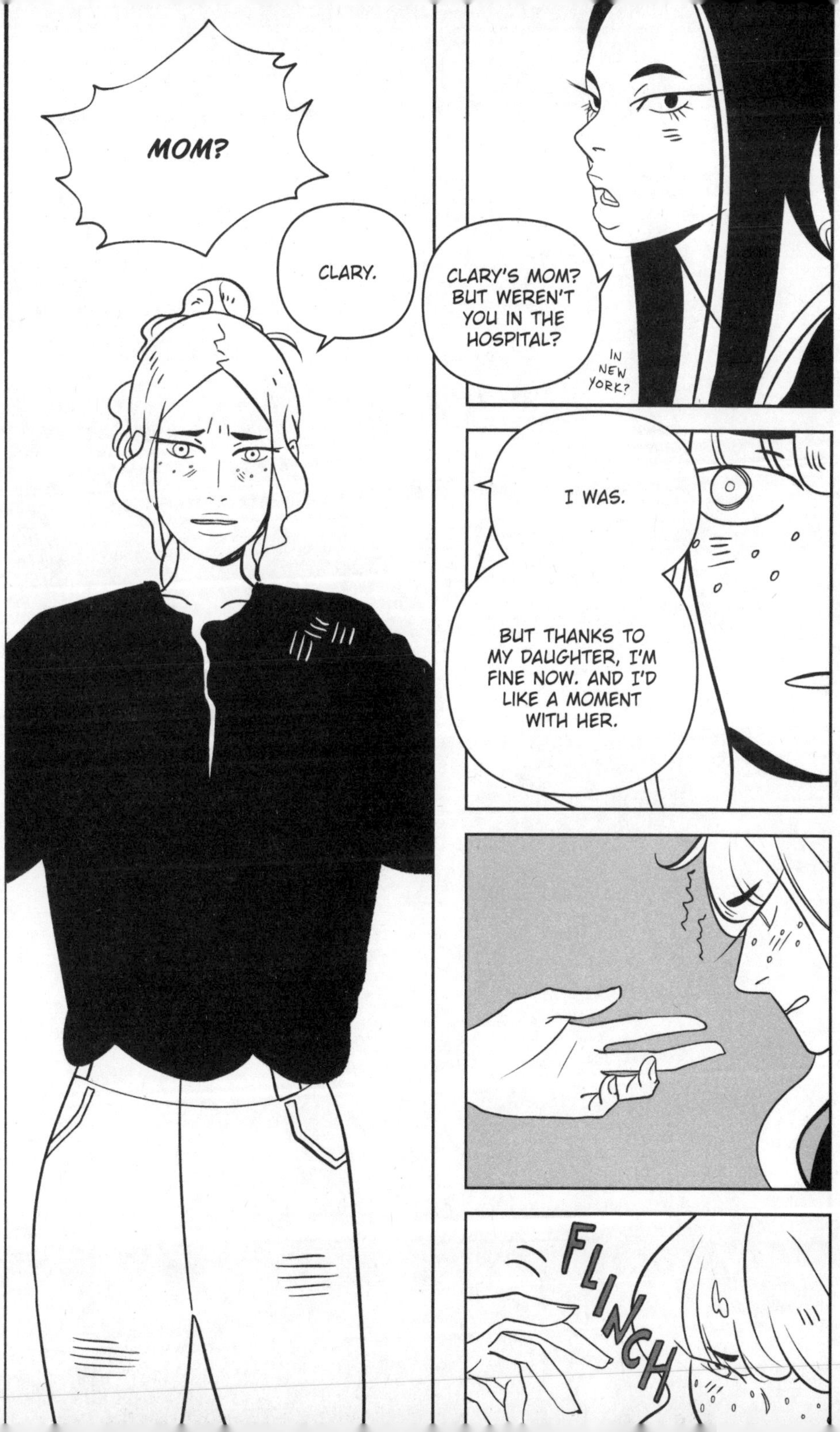
MOM?
CLARY.
CLARY'S MOM? BUT WEREN'T YOU IN THE HOSPITAL?
IN NEW YORK?
I WAS.
BUT THANKS TO MY DAUGHTER, I'M FINE NOW. AND I'D LIKE A MOMENT WITH HER.
FLINCH

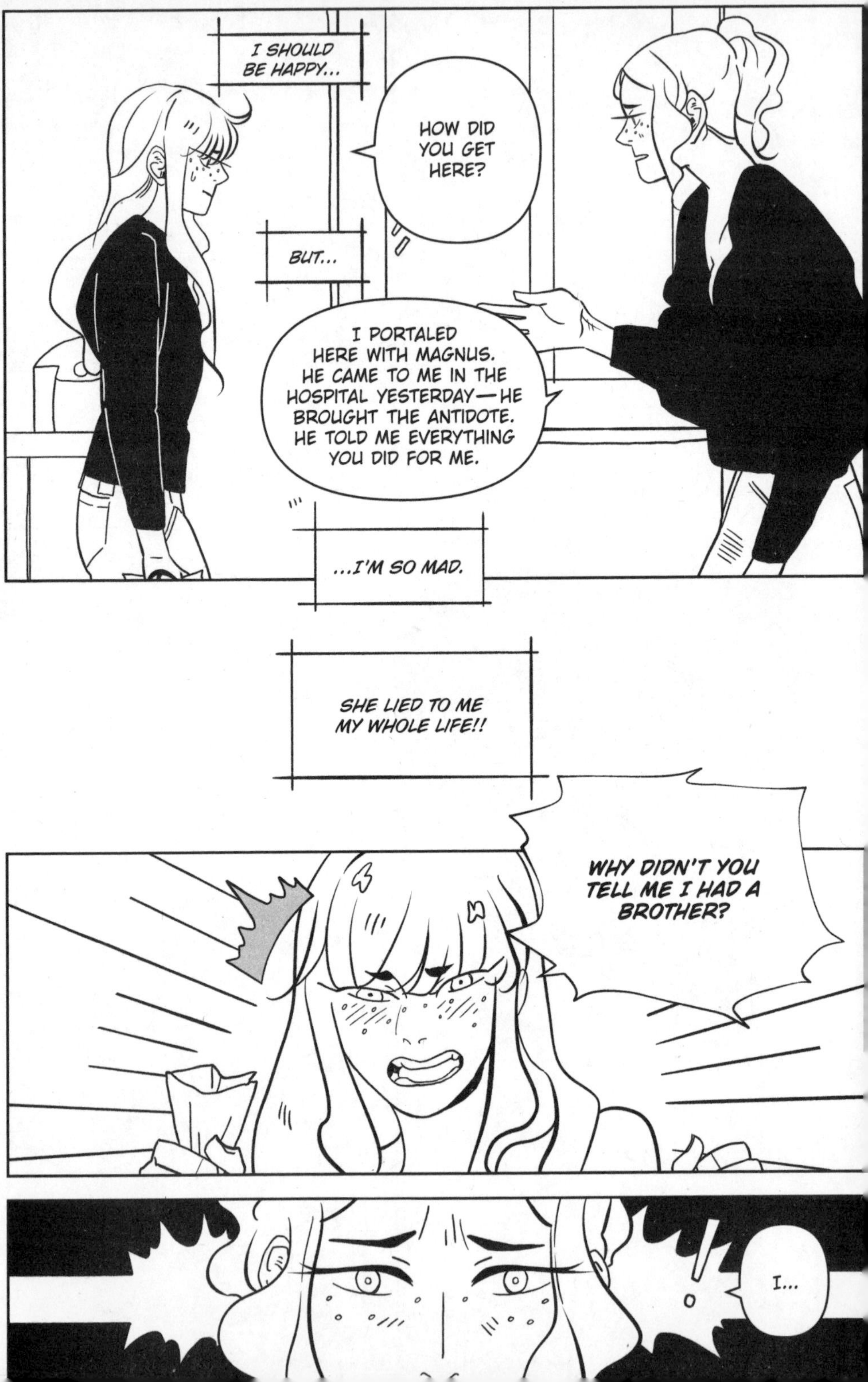
I SHOULD BE HAPPY...
HOW DID YOU GET HERE?
BUT...
I PORTALED HERE WITH MAGNUS. HE CAME TO ME IN THE HOSPITAL YESTERDAY—HE BROUGHT THE ANTIDOTE. HE TOLD ME EVERYTHING YOU DID FOR ME.
...I'M SO MAD.
SHE LIED TO ME MY WHOLE LIFE!!
WHY DIDN'T YOU TELL ME I HAD A BROTHER?
I...

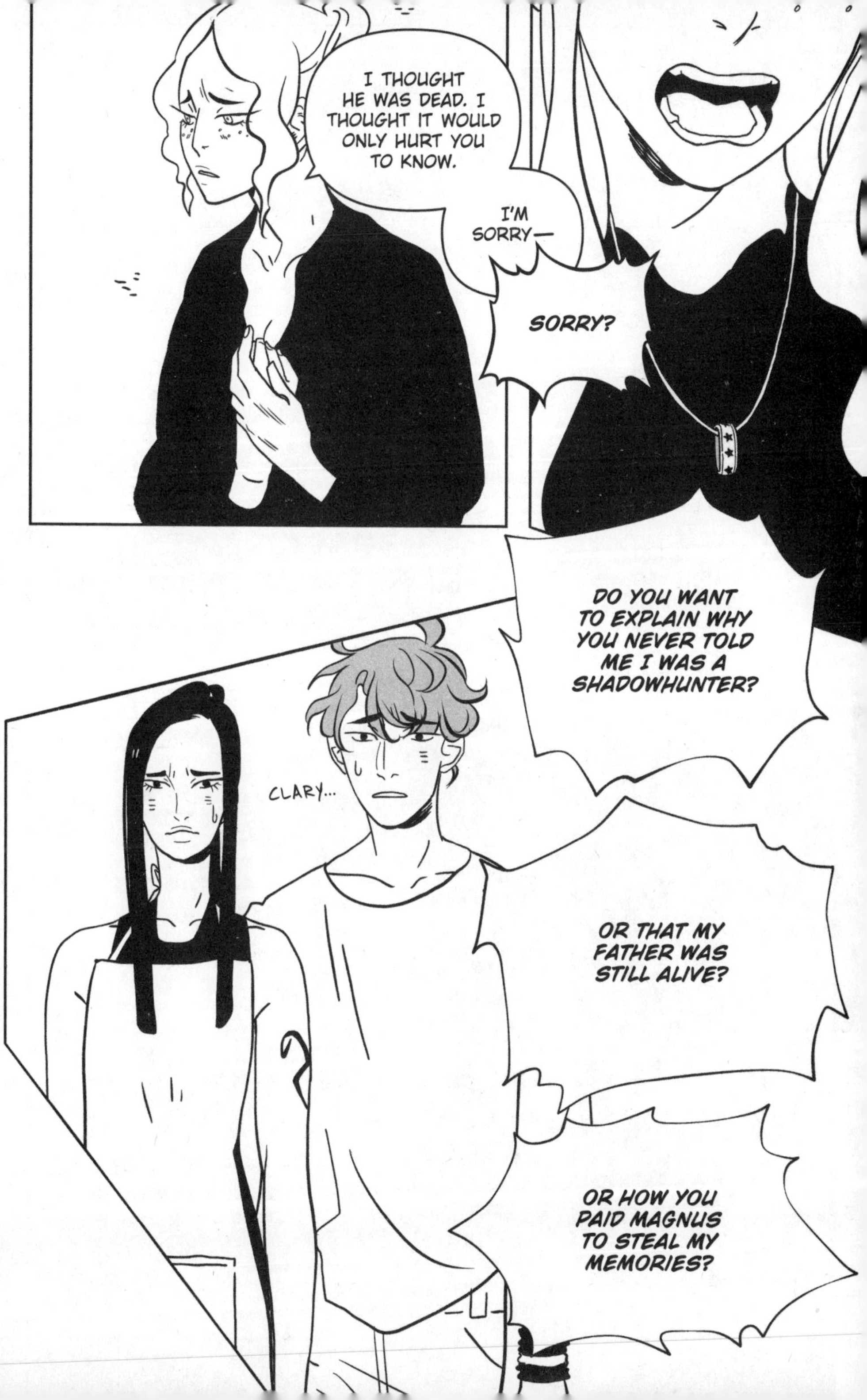
I THOUGHT HE WAS DEAD. I THOUGHT IT WOULD ONLY HURT YOU TO KNOW.
I'M SORRY—
SORRY?
DO YOU WANT TO EXPLAIN WHY YOU NEVER TOLD ME I WAS A SHADOWHUNTER?
CLARY...
OR THAT MY FATHER WAS STILL ALIVE?
OR HOW YOU PAID MAGNUS TO STEAL MY MEMORIES?

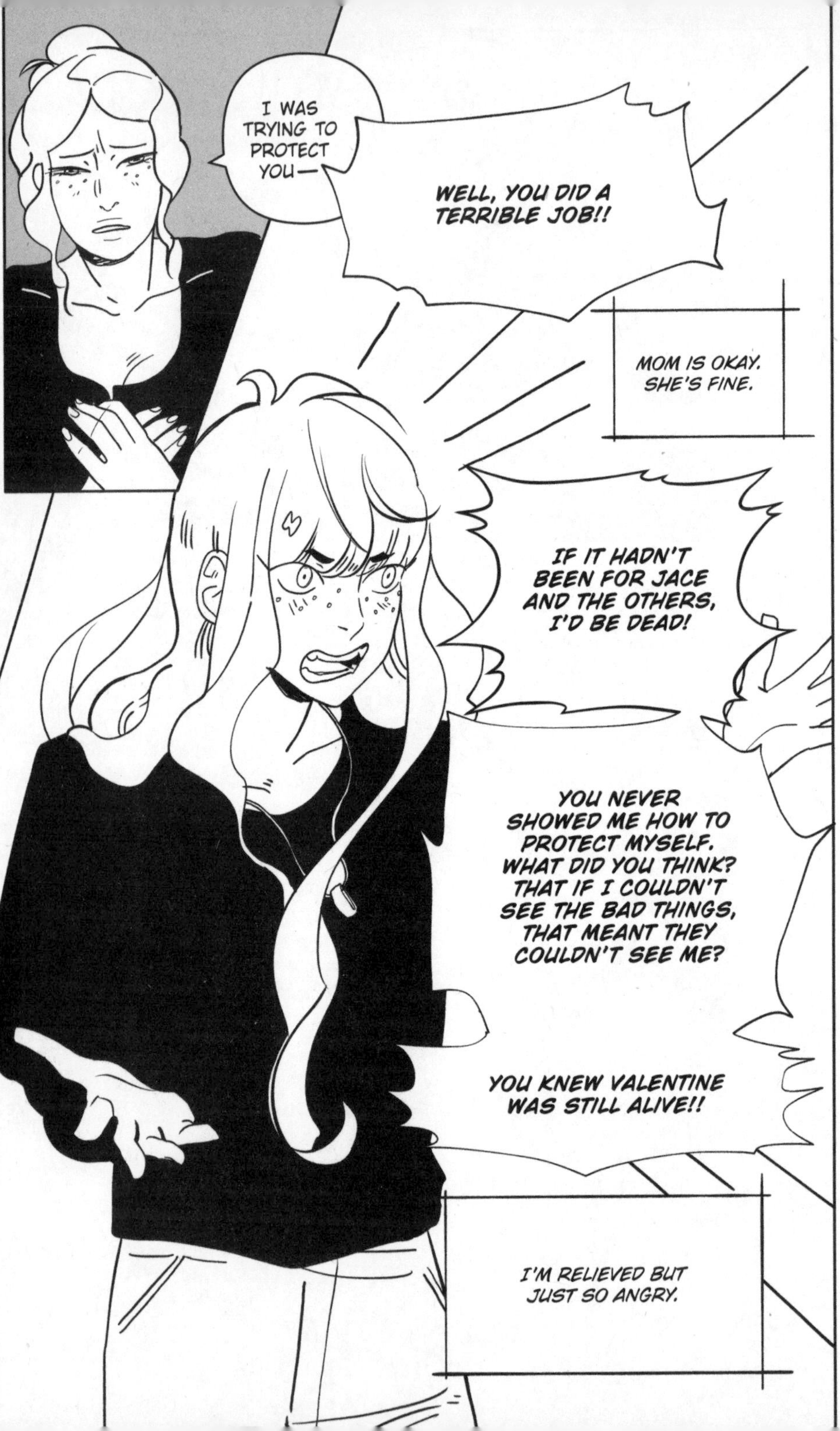

I WAS TRYING TO PROTECT YOU—
WELL, YOU DID A TERRIBLE JOB!!
MOM IS OKAY. SHE'S FINE.
IF IT HADN'T BEEN FOR JACE AND THE OTHERS, I'D BE DEAD!
YOU NEVER SHOWED ME HOW TO PROTECT MYSELF. WHAT DID YOU THINK? THAT IF I COULDN'T SEE THE BAD THINGS, THAT MEANT THEY COULDN'T SEE ME?
YOU KNEW VALENTINE WAS STILL ALIVE!!
I'M RELIEVED BUT JUST SO ANGRY.

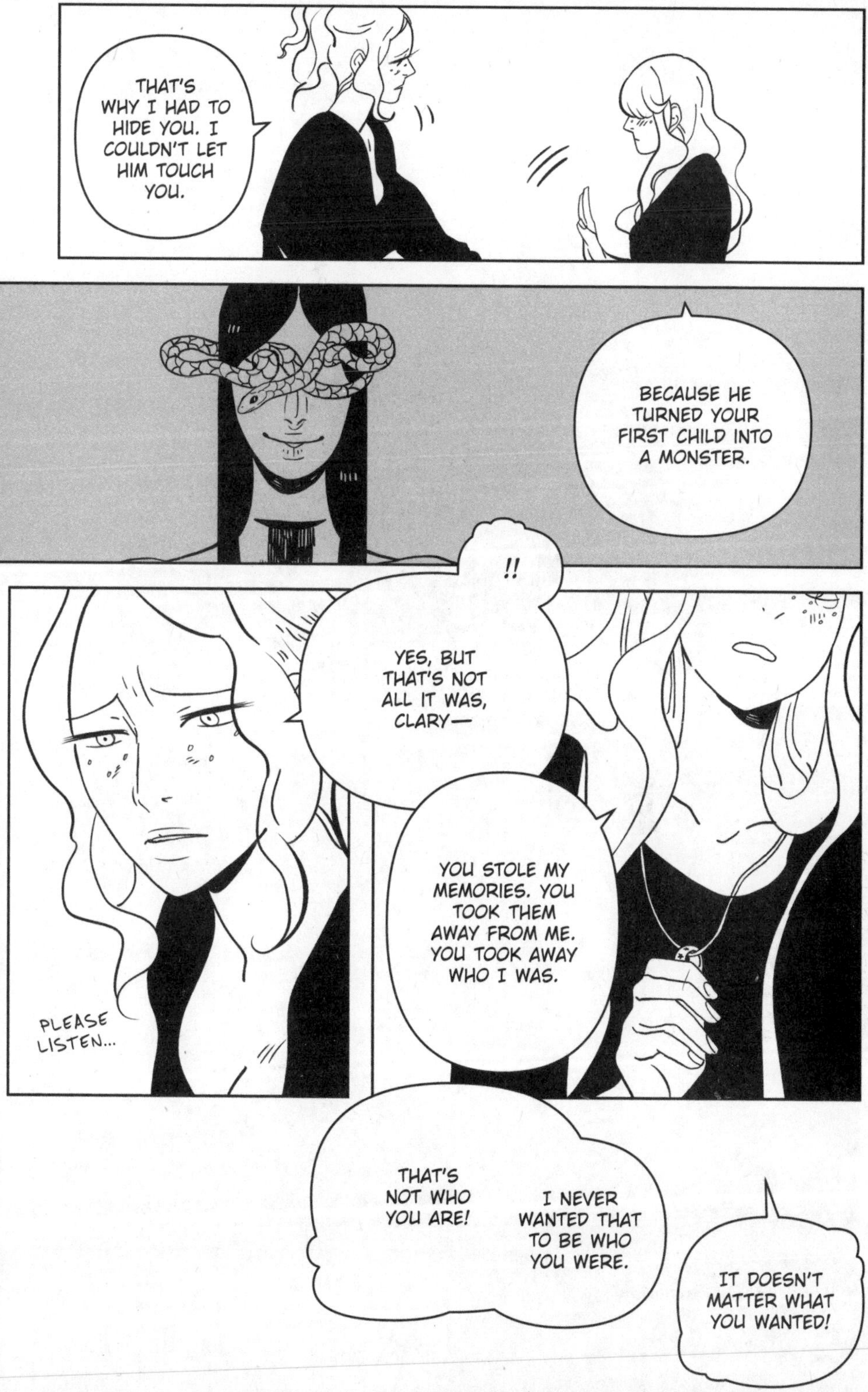
THAT'S WHY I HAD TO HIDE YOU. I COULDN'T LET HIM TOUCH YOU.
BECAUSE HE TURNED YOUR FIRST CHILD INTO A MONSTER.
!!
YES, BUT THAT'S NOT ALL IT WAS, CLARY—
PLEASE LISTEN...
YOU STOLE MY MEMORIES. YOU TOOK THEM AWAY FROM ME. YOU TOOK AWAY WHO I WAS.
THAT'S NOT WHO YOU ARE!
I NEVER WANTED THAT TO BE WHO YOU WERE.
IT DOESN'T MATTER WHAT YOU WANTED!

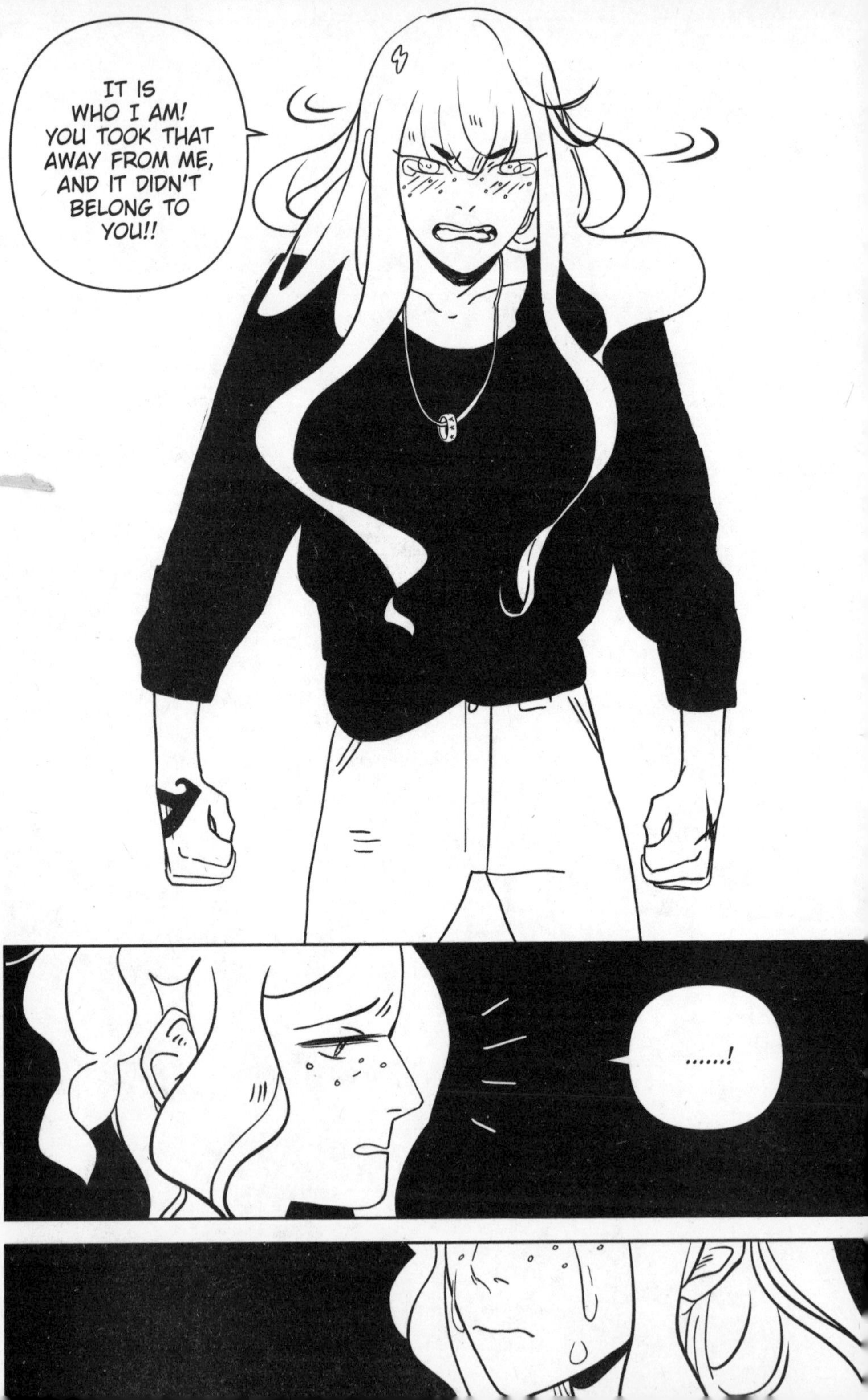
IT IS WHO I AM! YOU TOOK THAT AWAY FROM ME, AND IT DIDN'T BELONG TO YOU!!
......!

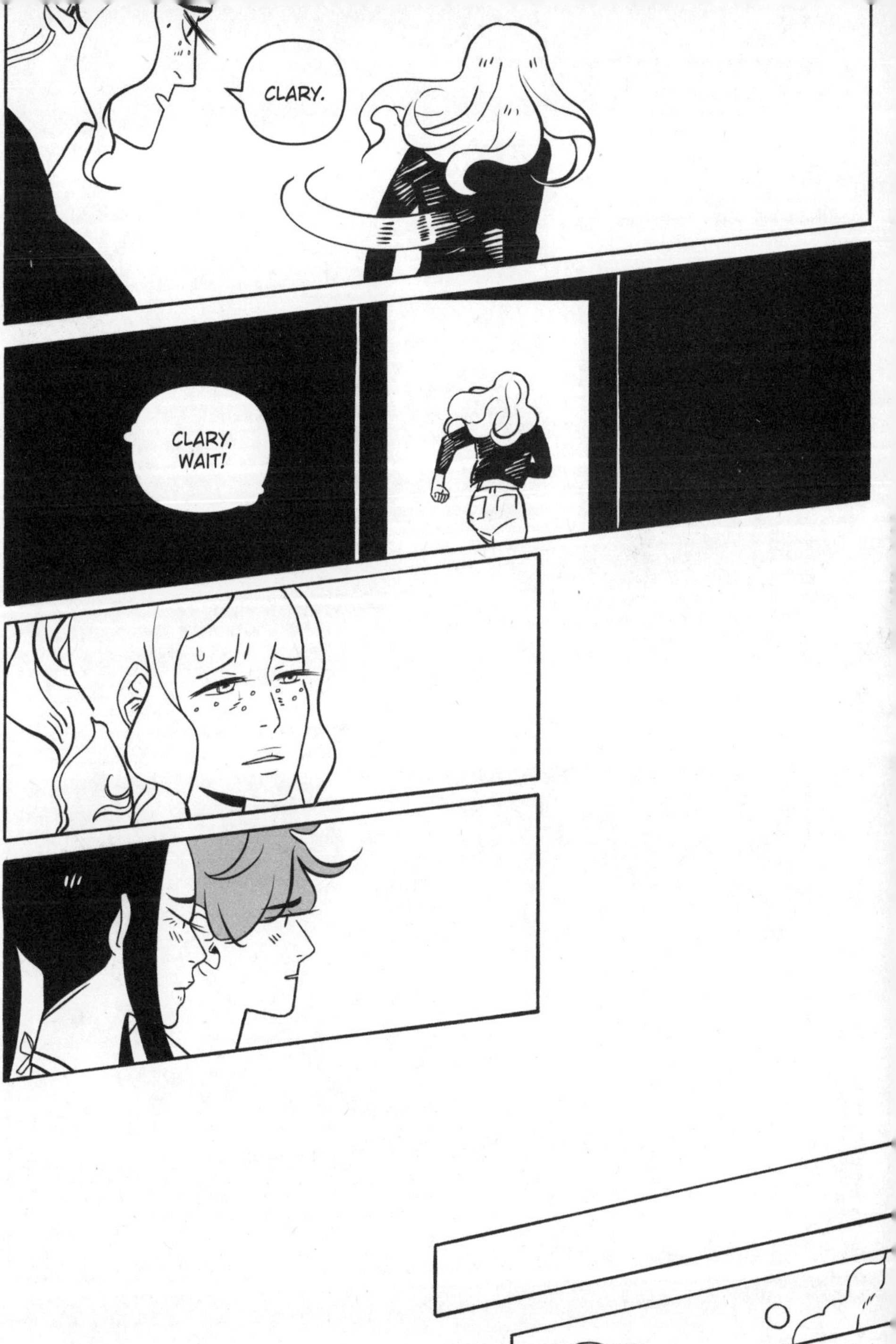
CLARY.
CLARY, WAIT!

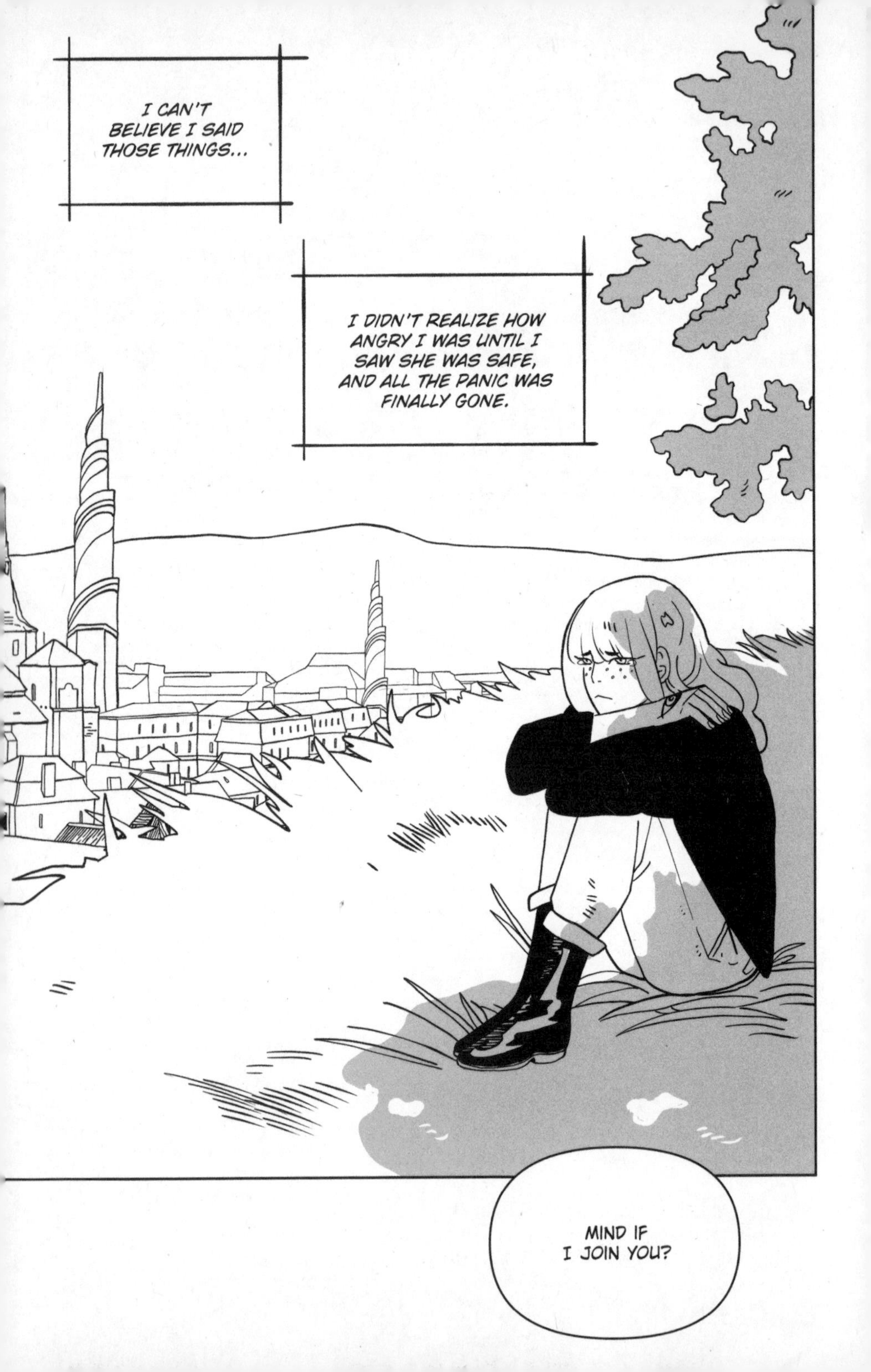
I CAN'T BELIEVE I SAID THOSE THINGS...
I DIDN'T REALIZE HOW ANGRY I WAS UNTIL I SAW SHE WAS SAFE, AND ALL THE PANIC WAS FINALLY GONE.
MIND IF I JOIN YOU?

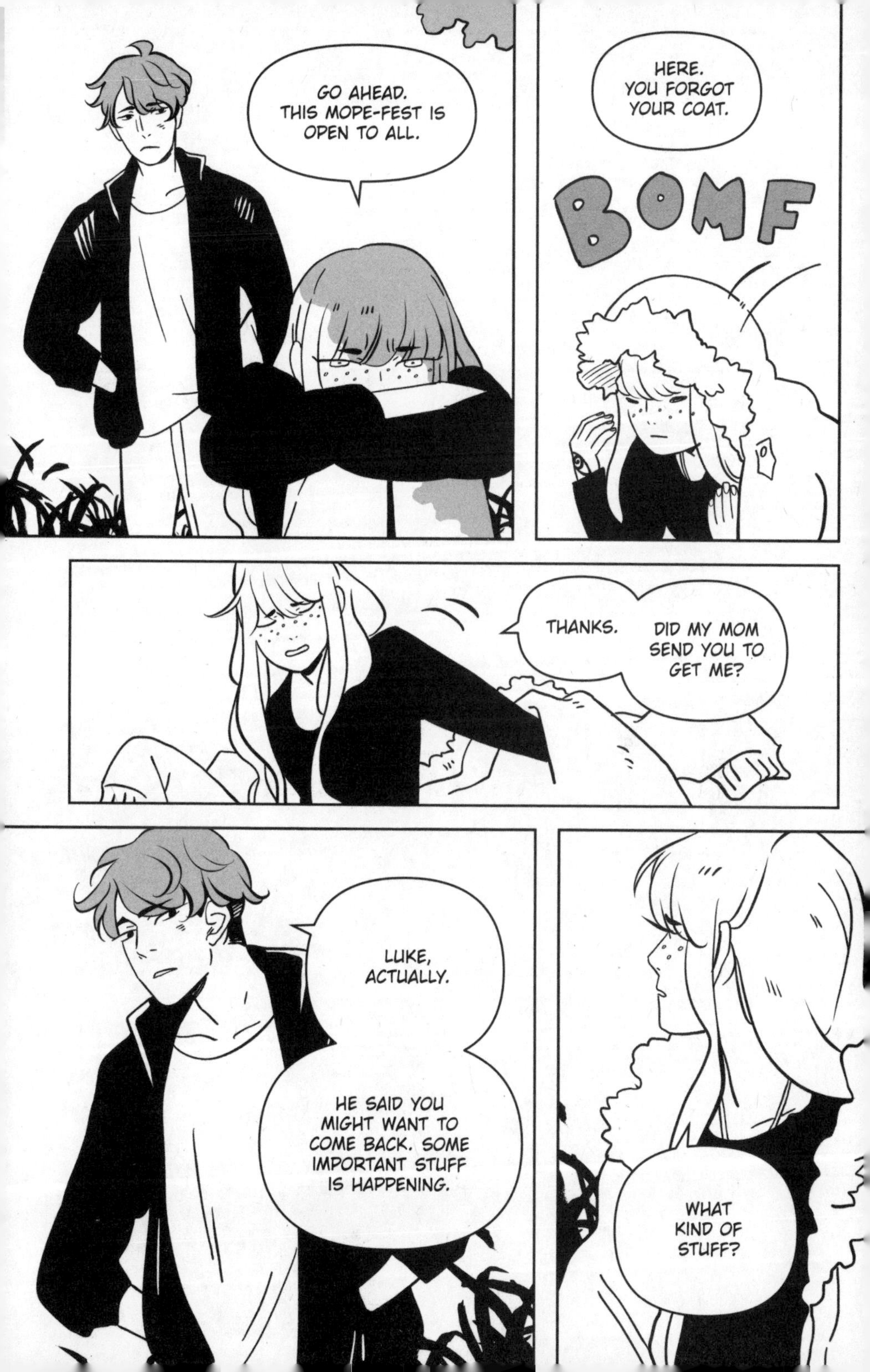
GO AHEAD. THIS MOPE-FEST IS OPEN TO ALL.
HERE. YOU FORGOT YOUR COAT.
BOMF
THANKS.
DID MY MOM SEND YOU TO GET ME?
LUKE, ACTUALLY.
HE SAID YOU MIGHT WANT TO COME BACK. SOME IMPORTANT STUFF IS HAPPENING.
WHAT KIND OF STUFF?

LUKE GAVE THE CLAVE UNTIL SUNSET TO DECIDE WHETHER THEY'D AGREE TO GIVE THE DOWNWORLDERS SEATS ON THE COUNCIL.

THEY'LL AGREE. THEY HAVE TO.

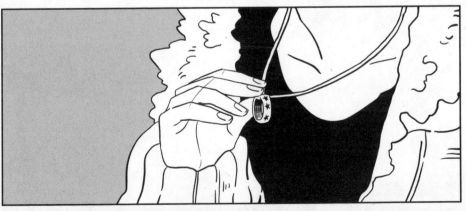

THE MORTAL INSTRUMENTS

THE GRAPHIC NOVEL

THE MORTAL INSTRUMENTS

THE GRAPHIC NOVEL

Chapter 33

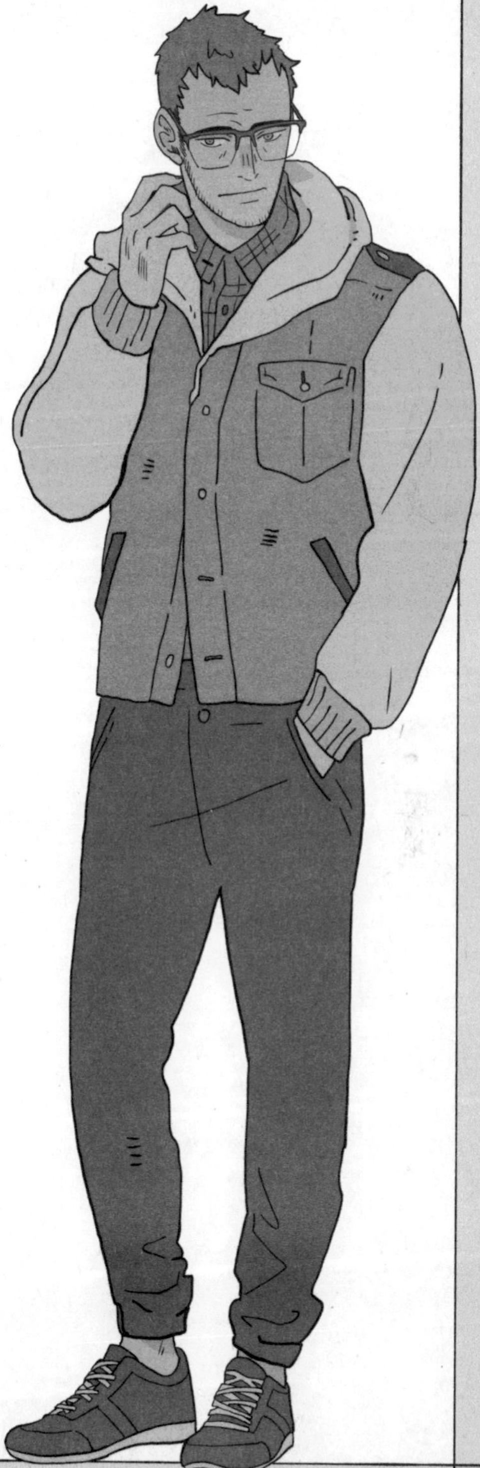

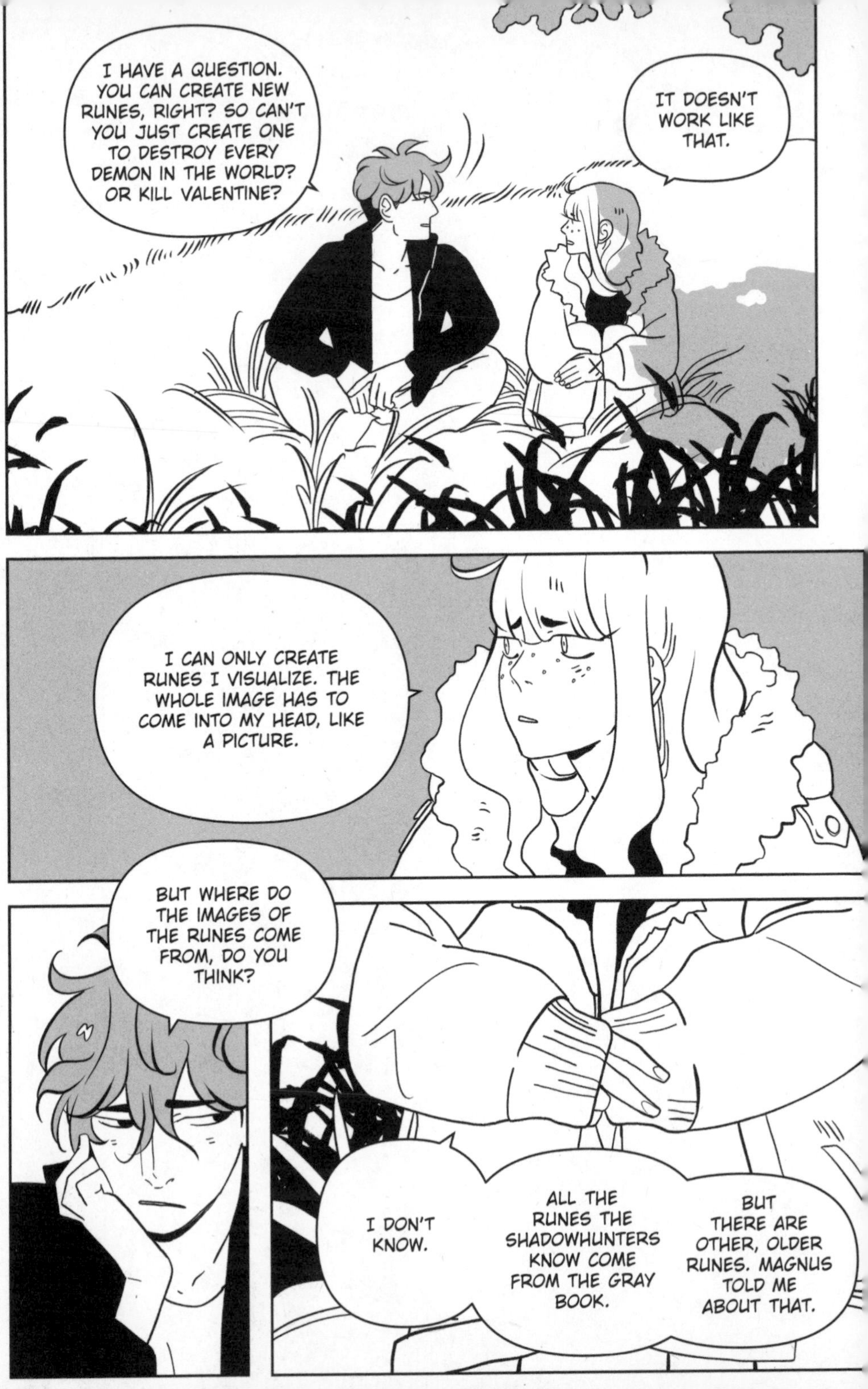
I HAVE A QUESTION. YOU CAN CREATE NEW RUNES, RIGHT? SO CAN'T YOU JUST CREATE ONE TO DESTROY EVERY DEMON IN THE WORLD? OR KILL VALENTINE?
IT DOESN'T WORK LIKE THAT.
I CAN ONLY CREATE RUNES I VISUALIZE. THE WHOLE IMAGE HAS TO COME INTO MY HEAD, LIKE A PICTURE.
BUT WHERE DO THE IMAGES OF THE RUNES COME FROM, DO YOU THINK?
I DON'T KNOW.
ALL THE RUNES THE SHADOWHUNTERS KNOW COME FROM THE GRAY BOOK.
BUT THERE ARE OTHER, OLDER RUNES. MAGNUS TOLD ME ABOUT THAT.

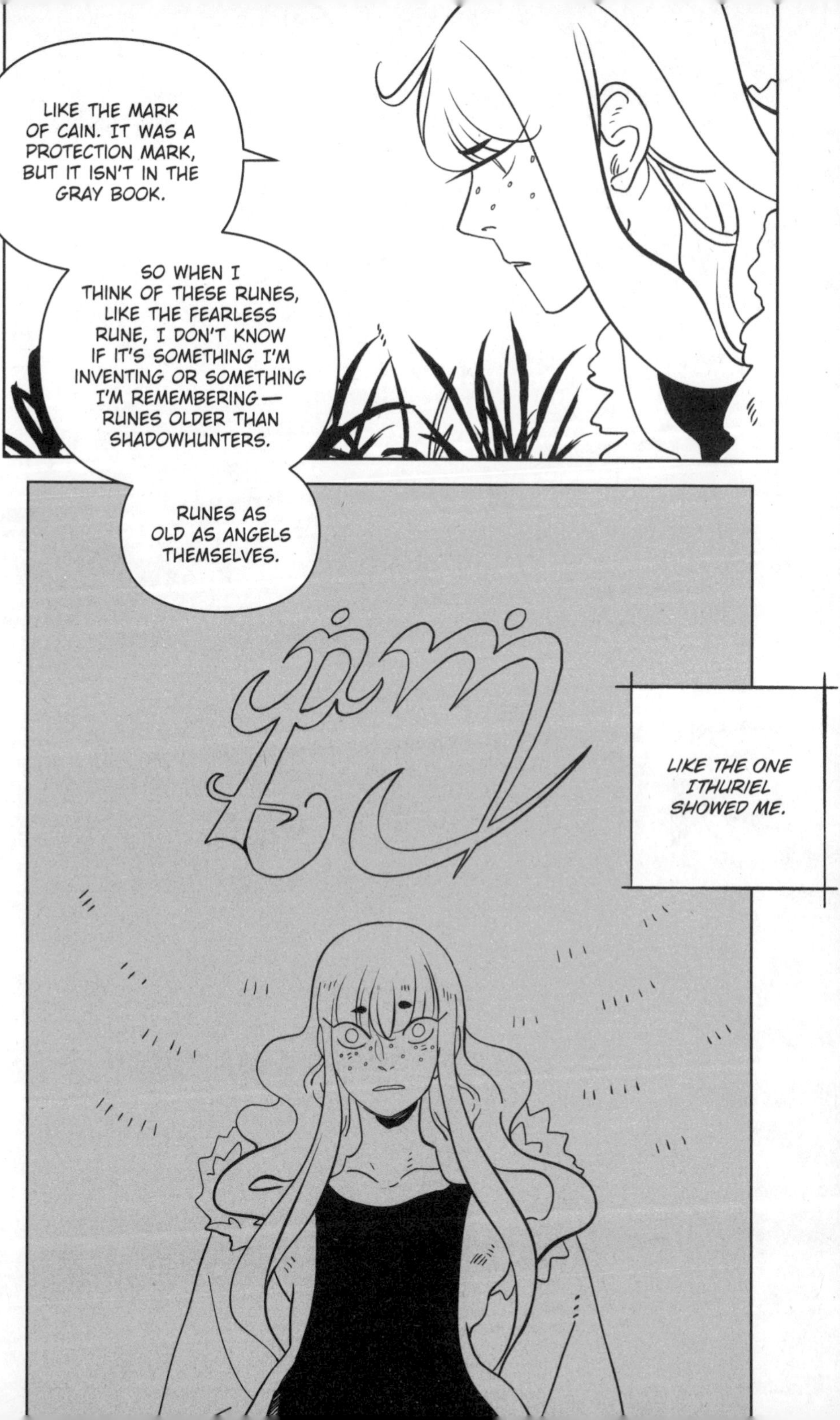
LIKE THE MARK OF CAIN. IT WAS A PROTECTION MARK, BUT IT ISN'T IN THE GRAY BOOK.
SO WHEN I THINK OF THESE RUNES, LIKE THE FEARLESS RUNE, I DON'T KNOW IF IT'S SOMETHING I'M INVENTING OR SOMETHING I'M REMEMBERING— RUNES OLDER THAN SHADOWHUNTERS.
RUNES AS OLD AS ANGELS THEMSELVES.
LIKE THE ONE ITHURIEL SHOWED ME.

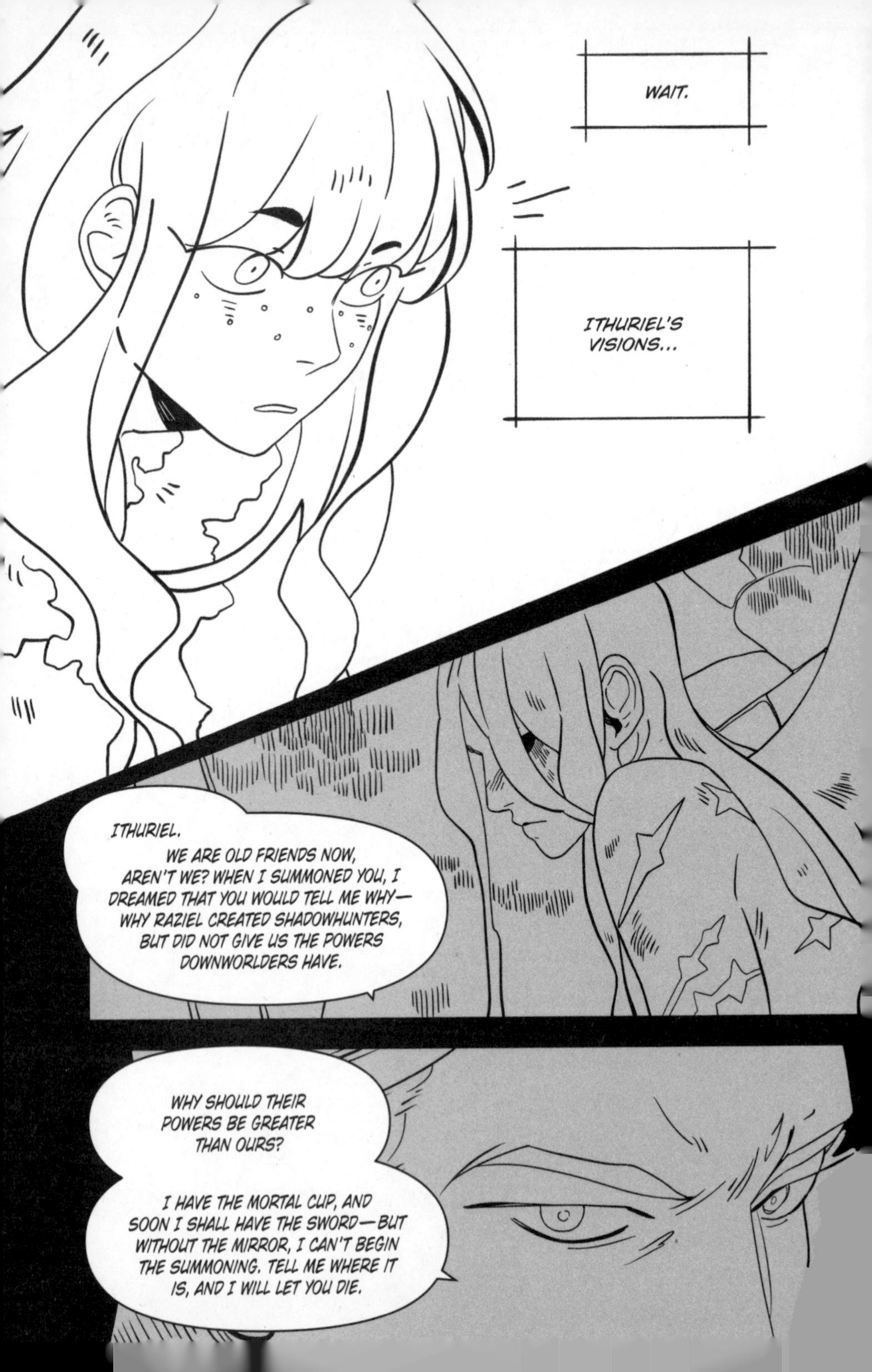
WAIT.
ITHURIEL'S VISIONS...
ITHURIEL. WE ARE OLD FRIENDS NOW, AREN'T WE? WHEN I SUMMONED YOU, I DREAMED THAT YOU WOULD TELL ME WHY—WHY RAZIEL CREATED SHADOWHUNTERS, BUT DID NOT GIVE US THE POWERS DOWNWORLDERS HAVE.
WHY SHOULD THEIR POWERS BE GREATER THAN OURS?
I HAVE THE MORTAL CUP, AND SOON I SHALL HAVE THE SWORD—BUT WITHOUT THE MIRROR, I CAN'T BEGIN THE SUMMONING. TELL ME WHERE IT IS, AND I WILL LET YOU DIE.

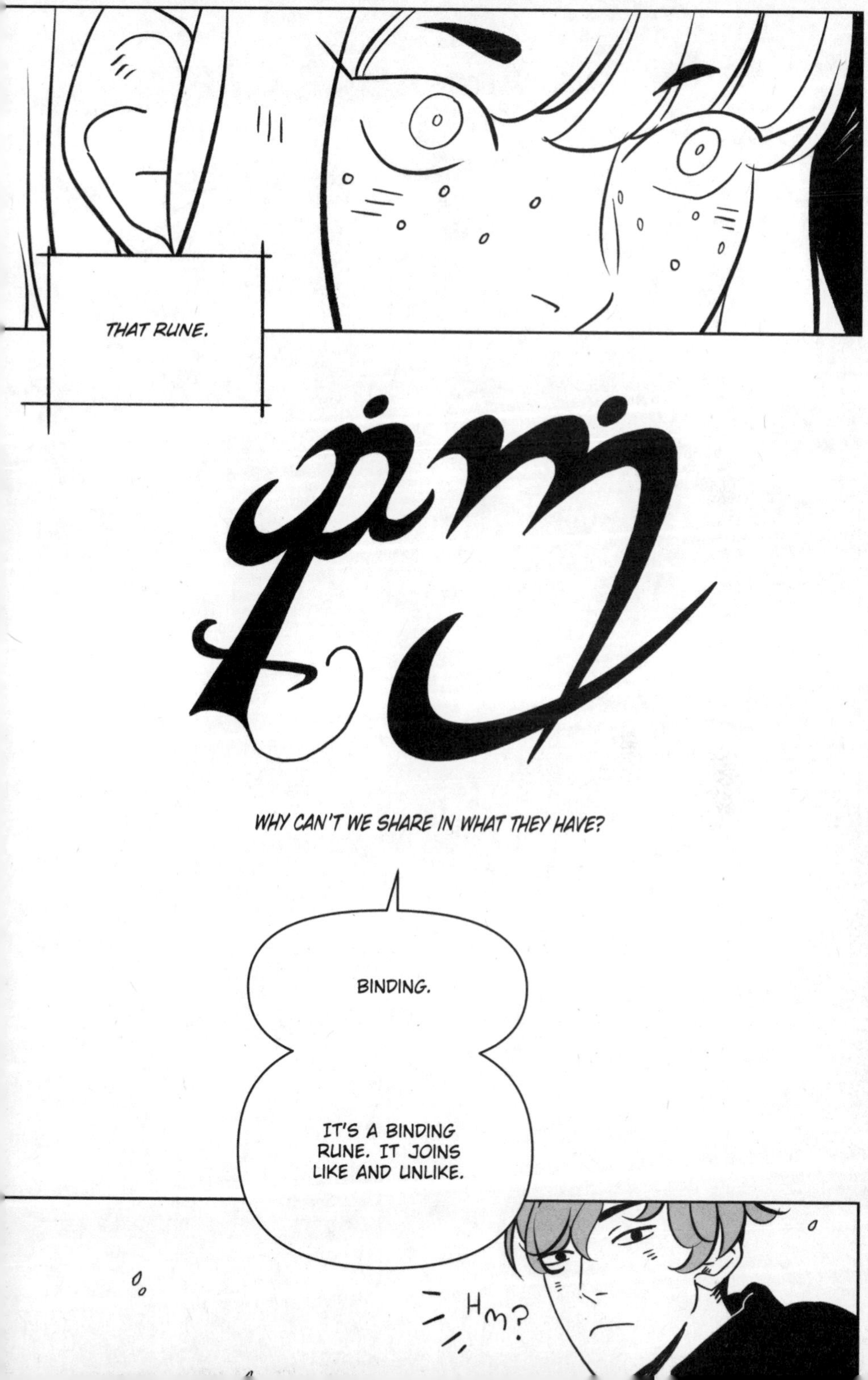
THAT RUNE.
WHY CAN'T WE SHARE IN WHAT THEY HAVE?
BINDING.
IT'S A BINDING RUNE. IT JOINS LIKE AND UNLIKE.
HM?

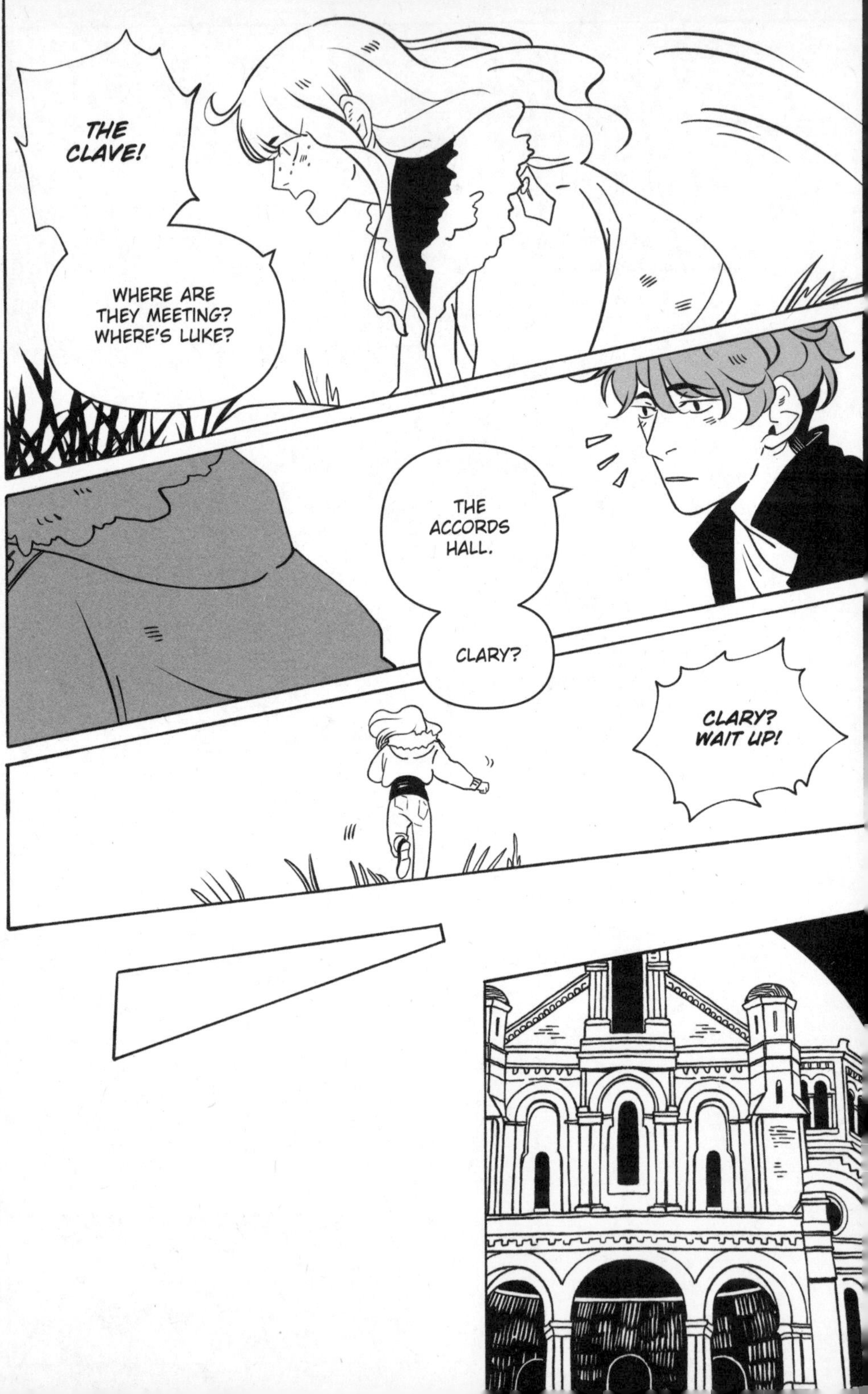
THE CLAVE!
WHERE ARE THEY MEETING? WHERE'S LUKE?
THE ACCORDS HALL.
CLARY?
CLARY? WAIT UP!

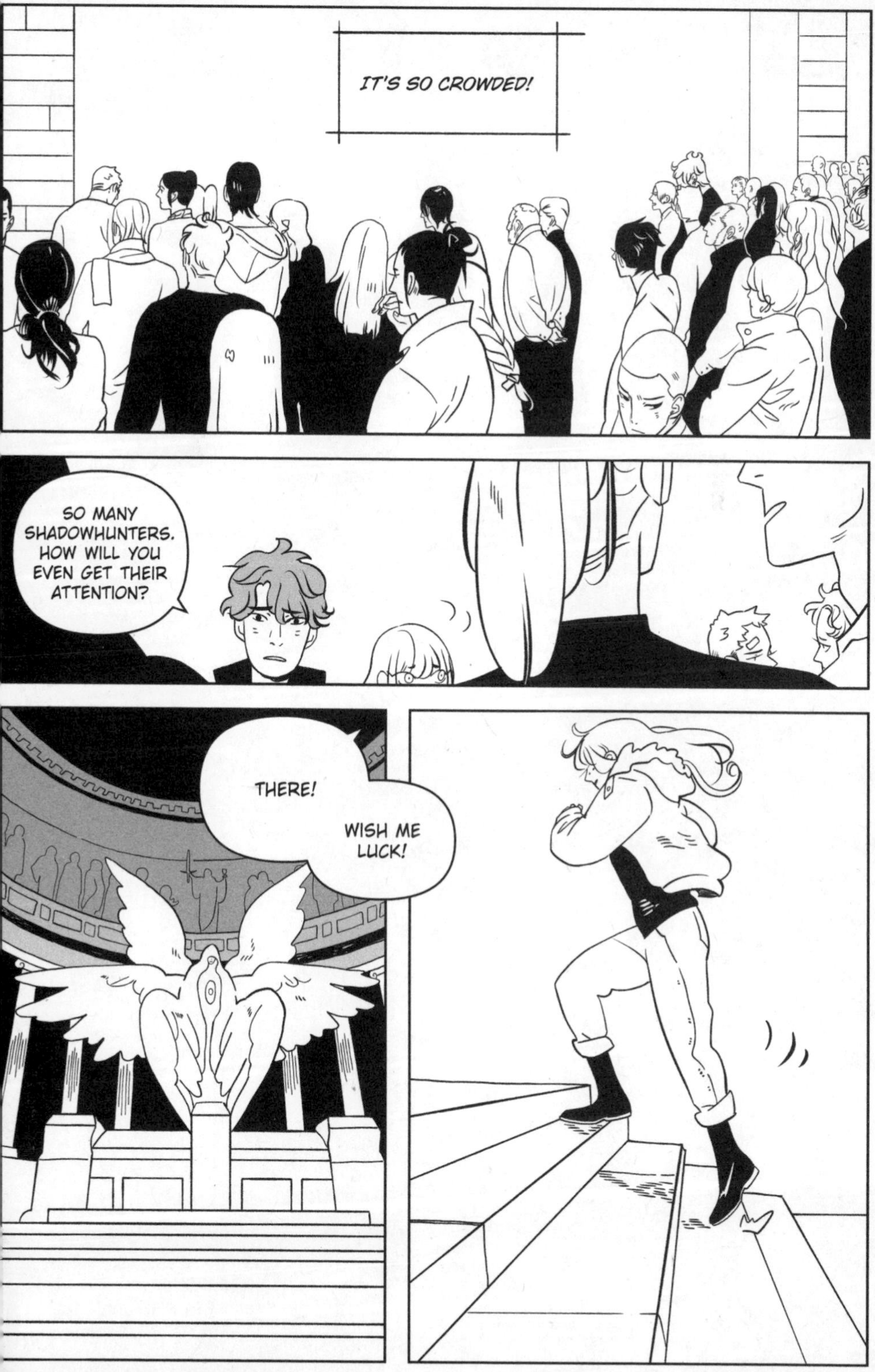
IT'S SO CROWDED!
SO MANY SHADOWHUNTERS. HOW WILL YOU EVEN GET THEIR ATTENTION?
THERE!
WISH ME LUCK!

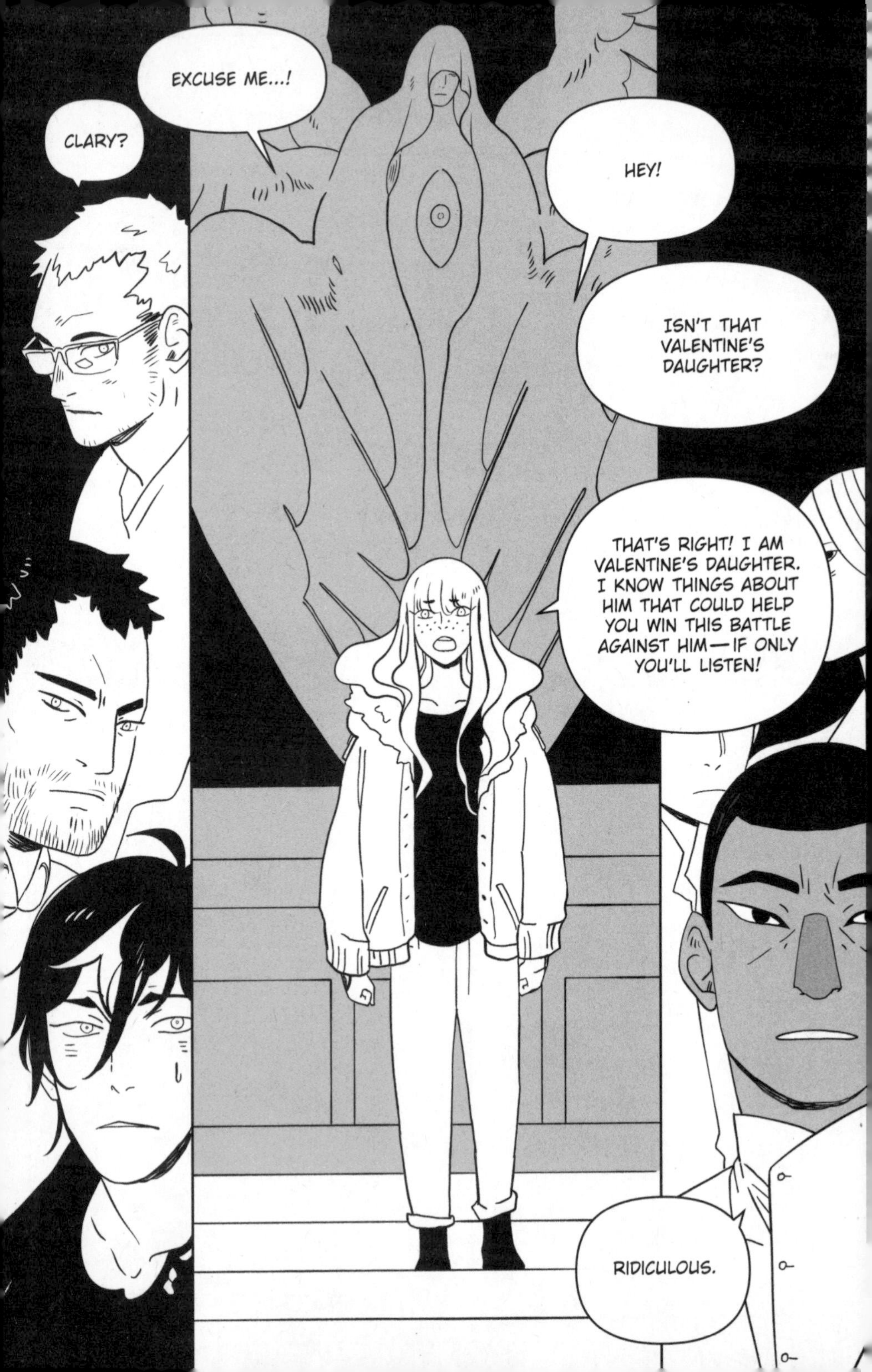
EXCUSE ME...!
CLARY?
HEY!
ISN'T THAT VALENTINE'S DAUGHTER?
THAT'S RIGHT! I AM VALENTINE'S DAUGHTER. I KNOW THINGS ABOUT HIM THAT COULD HELP YOU WIN THIS BATTLE AGAINST HIM—IF ONLY YOU'LL LISTEN!
RIDICULOUS.

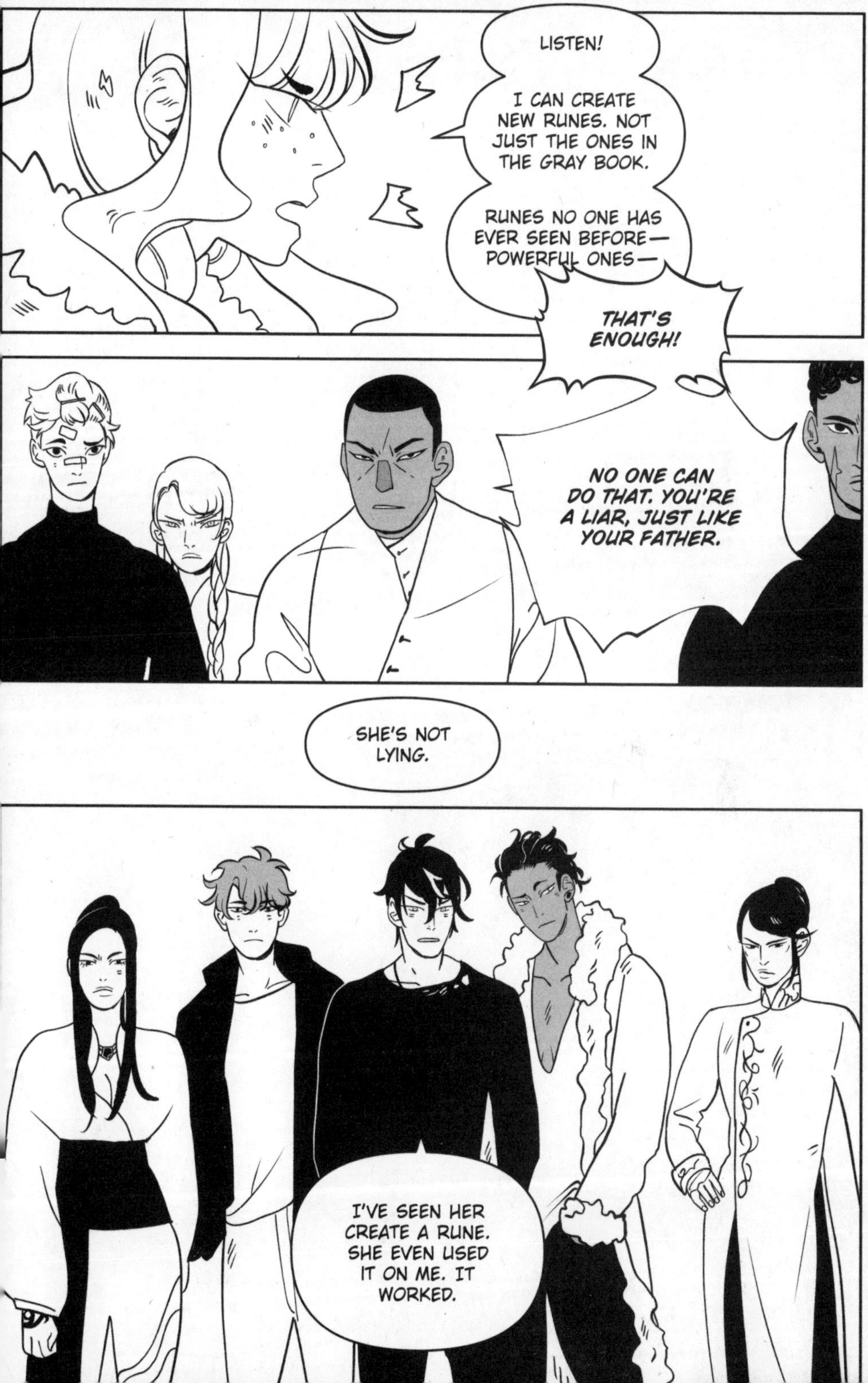
LISTEN!
I CAN CREATE NEW RUNES. NOT JUST THE ONES IN THE GRAY BOOK.
RUNES NO ONE HAS EVER SEEN BEFORE—POWERFUL ONES—
THAT'S ENOUGH!
NO ONE CAN DO THAT. YOU'RE A LIAR, JUST LIKE YOUR FATHER.
SHE'S NOT LYING.
I'VE SEEN HER CREATE A RUNE. SHE EVEN USED IT ON ME. IT WORKED.

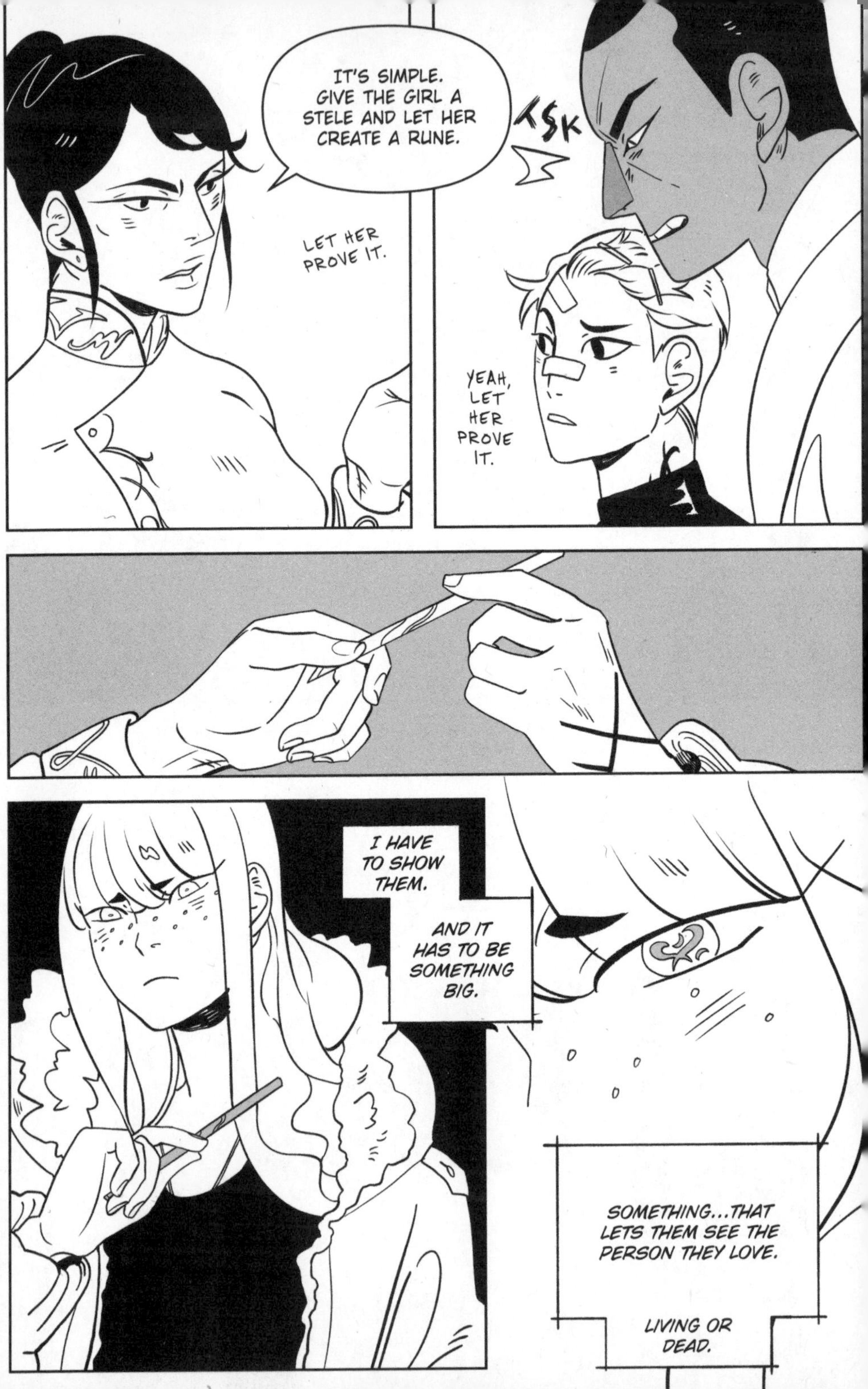
IT'S SIMPLE. GIVE THE GIRL A STELE AND LET HER CREATE A RUNE.
LET HER PROVE IT.
TSK
YEAH, LET HER PROVE IT.
I HAVE TO SHOW THEM.
AND IT HAS TO BE SOMETHING BIG.
SOMETHING...THAT LETS THEM SEE THE PERSON THEY LOVE.
LIVING OR DEAD.

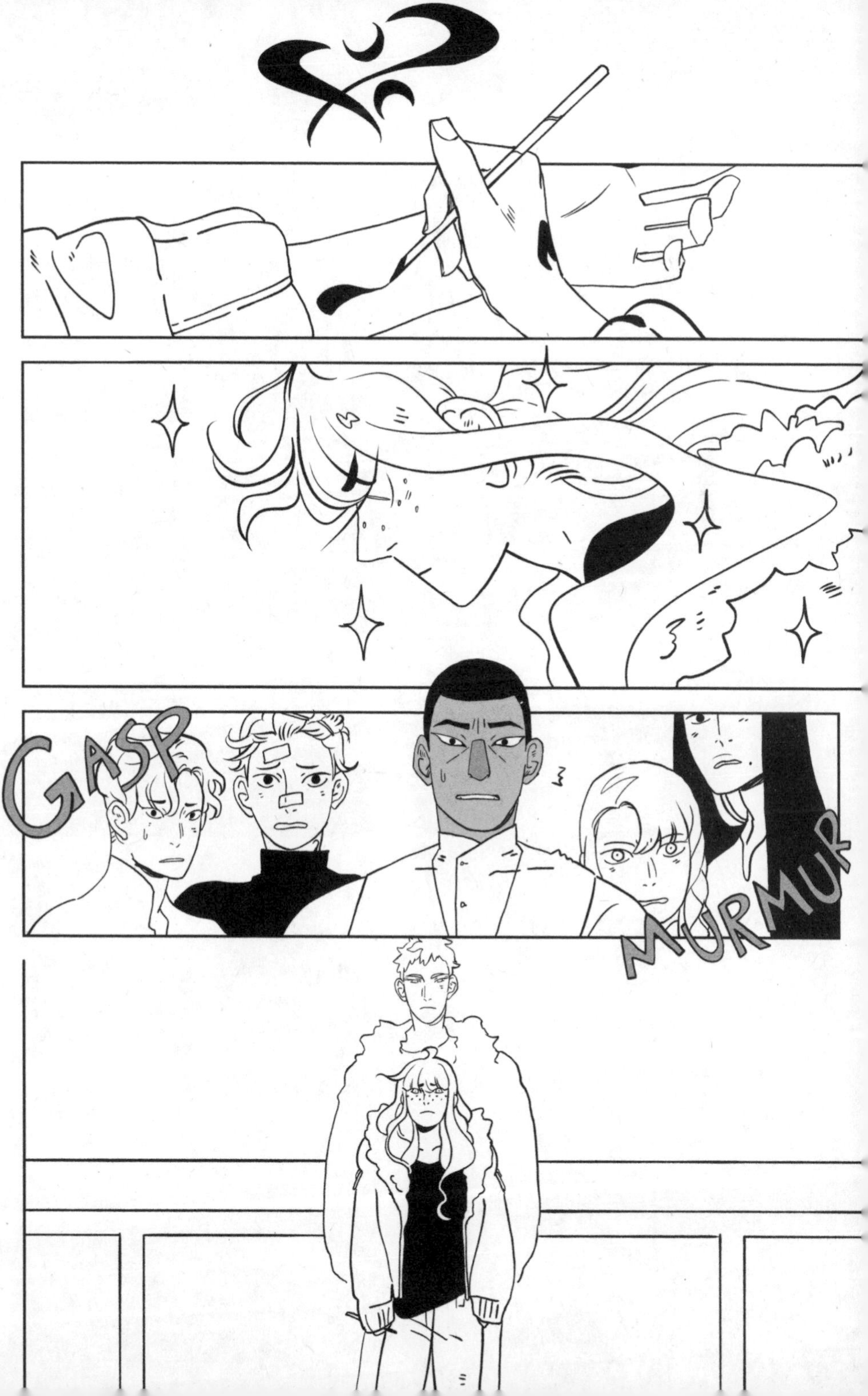
GASP
MURMUR

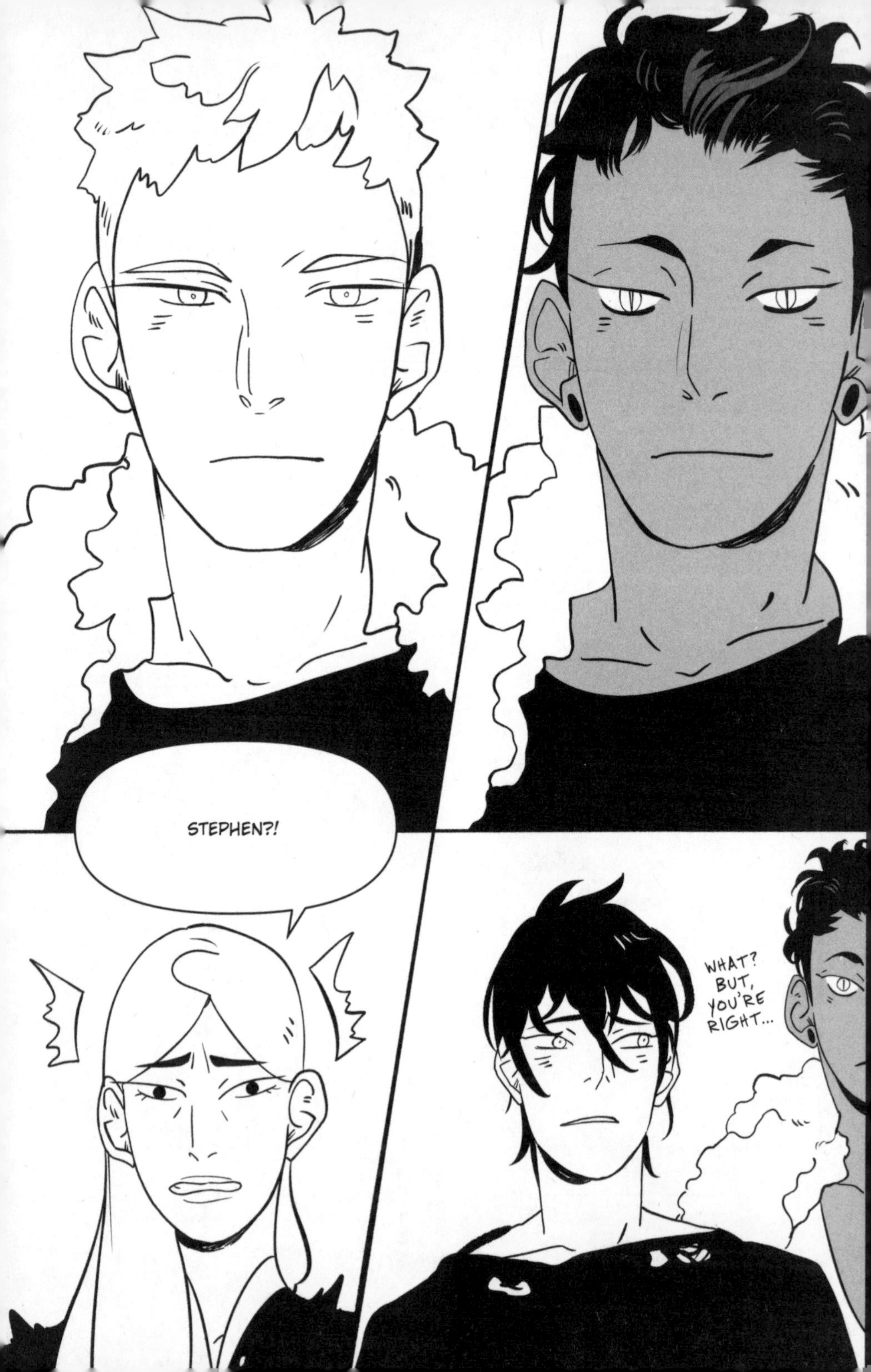
STEPHEN?!
WHAT? BUT, YOU'RE RIGHT...

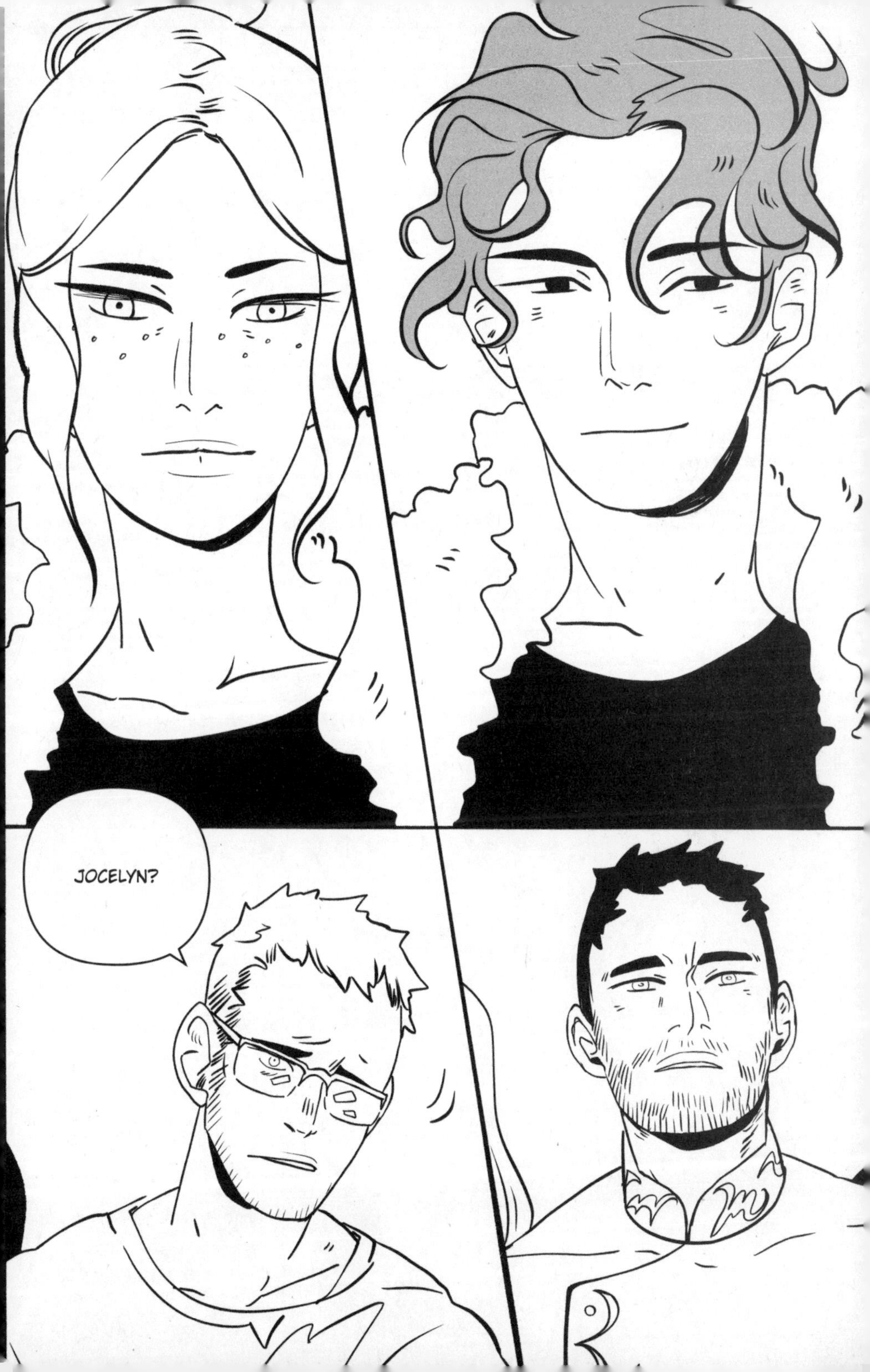
JOCELYN?

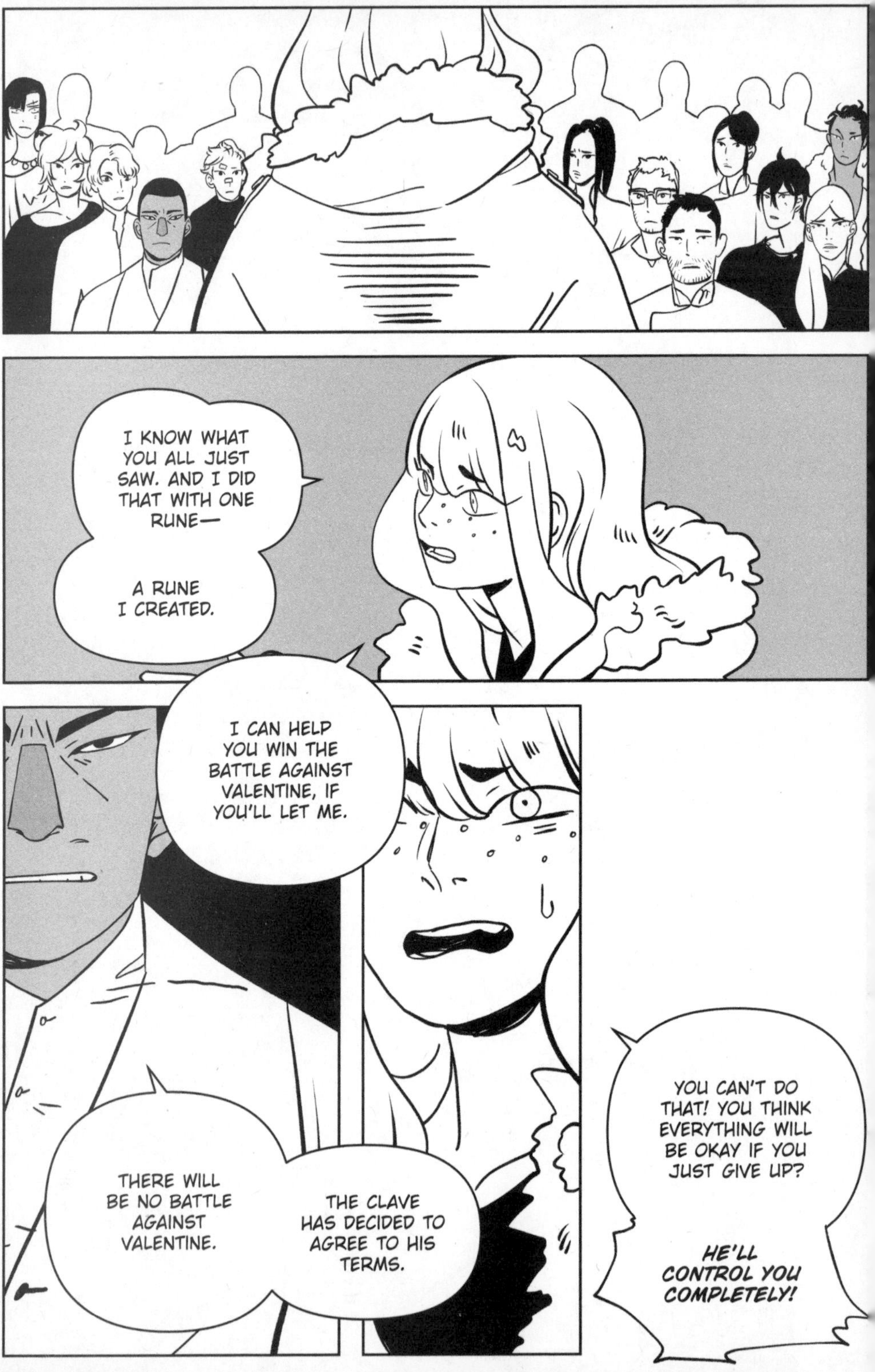
I KNOW WHAT YOU ALL JUST SAW. AND I DID THAT WITH ONE RUNE—
A RUNE I CREATED.
I CAN HELP YOU WIN THE BATTLE AGAINST VALENTINE, IF YOU'LL LET ME.
THERE WILL BE NO BATTLE AGAINST VALENTINE.
THE CLAVE HAS DECIDED TO AGREE TO HIS TERMS.
YOU CAN'T DO THAT! YOU THINK EVERYTHING WILL BE OKAY IF YOU JUST GIVE UP?
HE'LL CONTROL YOU COMPLETELY!

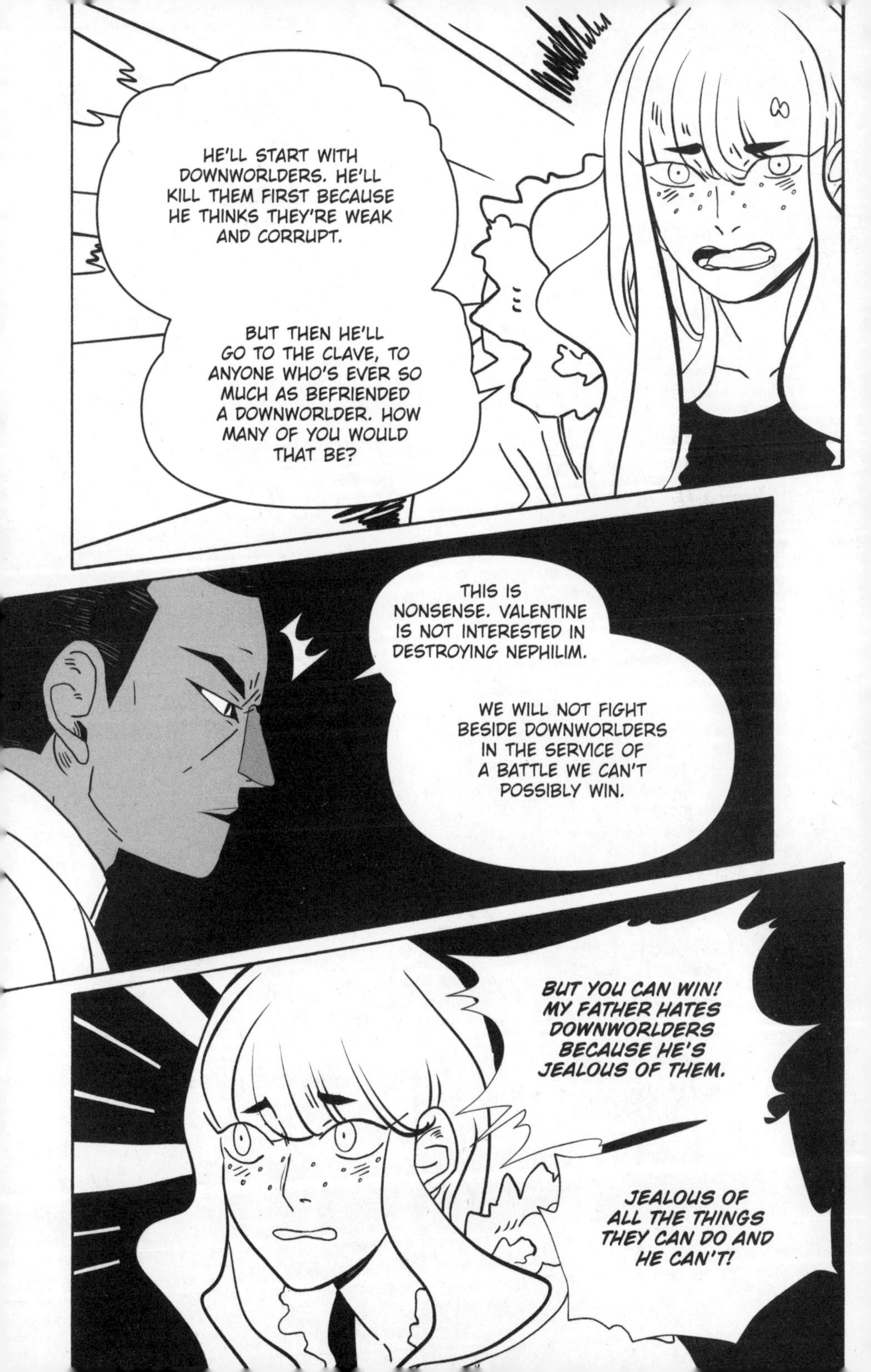
HE'LL START WITH DOWNWORLDERS. HE'LL KILL THEM FIRST BECAUSE HE THINKS THEY'RE WEAK AND CORRUPT.
BUT THEN HE'LL GO TO THE CLAVE, TO ANYONE WHO'S EVER SO MUCH AS BEFRIENDED A DOWNWORLDER. HOW MANY OF YOU WOULD THAT BE?
THIS IS NONSENSE. VALENTINE IS NOT INTERESTED IN DESTROYING NEPHILIM.
WE WILL NOT FIGHT BESIDE DOWNWORLDERS IN THE SERVICE OF A BATTLE WE CAN'T POSSIBLY WIN.
BUT YOU CAN WIN! MY FATHER HATES DOWNWORLDERS BECAUSE HE'S JEALOUS OF THEM.
JEALOUS OF ALL THE THINGS THEY CAN DO AND HE CAN'T!

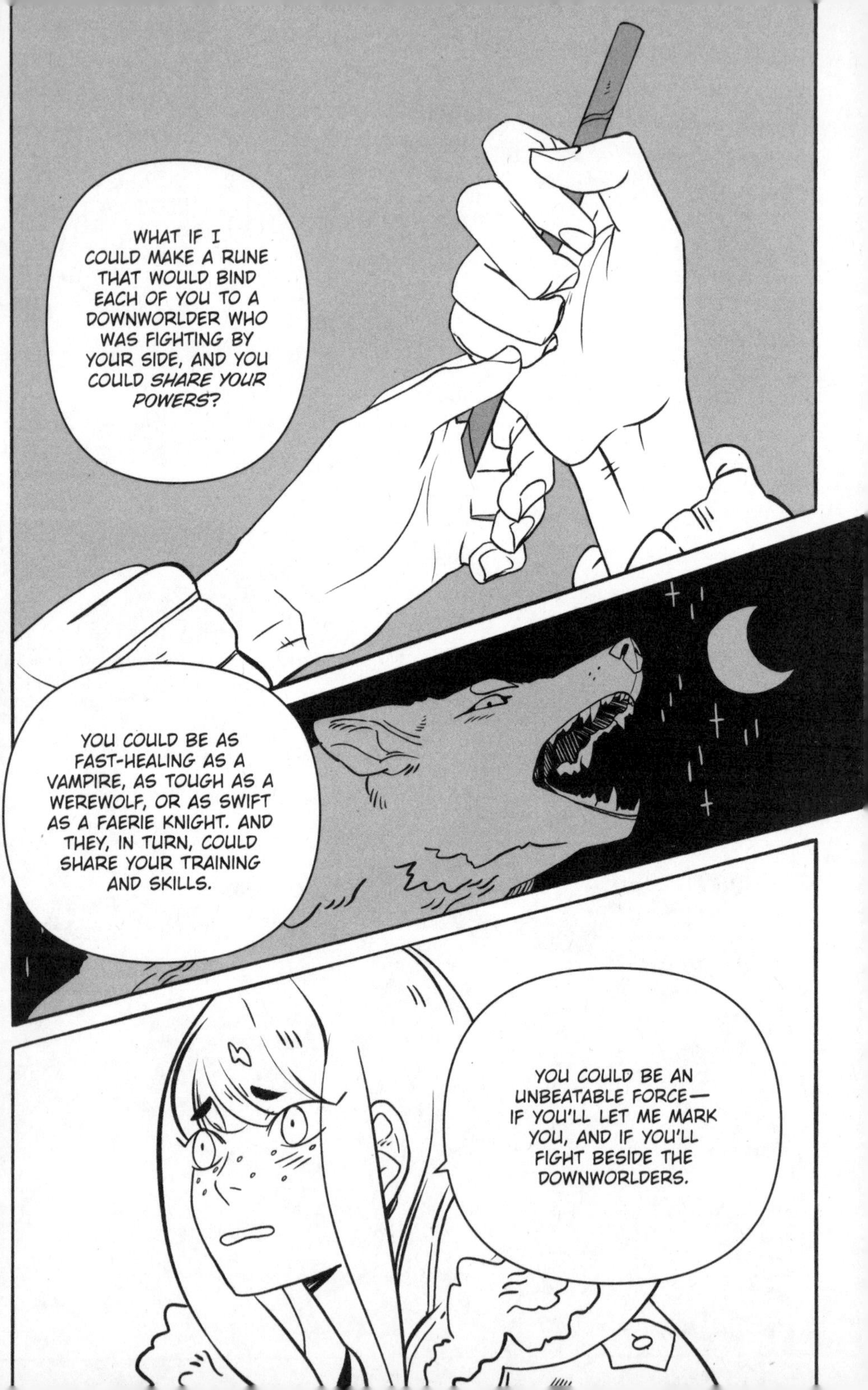
WHAT IF I COULD MAKE A RUNE THAT WOULD BIND EACH OF YOU TO A DOWNWORLDER WHO WAS FIGHTING BY YOUR SIDE, AND YOU COULD *SHARE YOUR POWERS?*
YOU COULD BE AS FAST-HEALING AS A VAMPIRE, AS TOUGH AS A WEREWOLF, OR AS SWIFT AS A FAERIE KNIGHT. AND THEY, IN TURN, COULD SHARE YOUR TRAINING AND SKILLS.
YOU COULD BE AN UNBEATABLE FORCE— IF YOU'LL LET ME MARK YOU, AND IF YOU'LL FIGHT BESIDE THE DOWNWORLDERS.

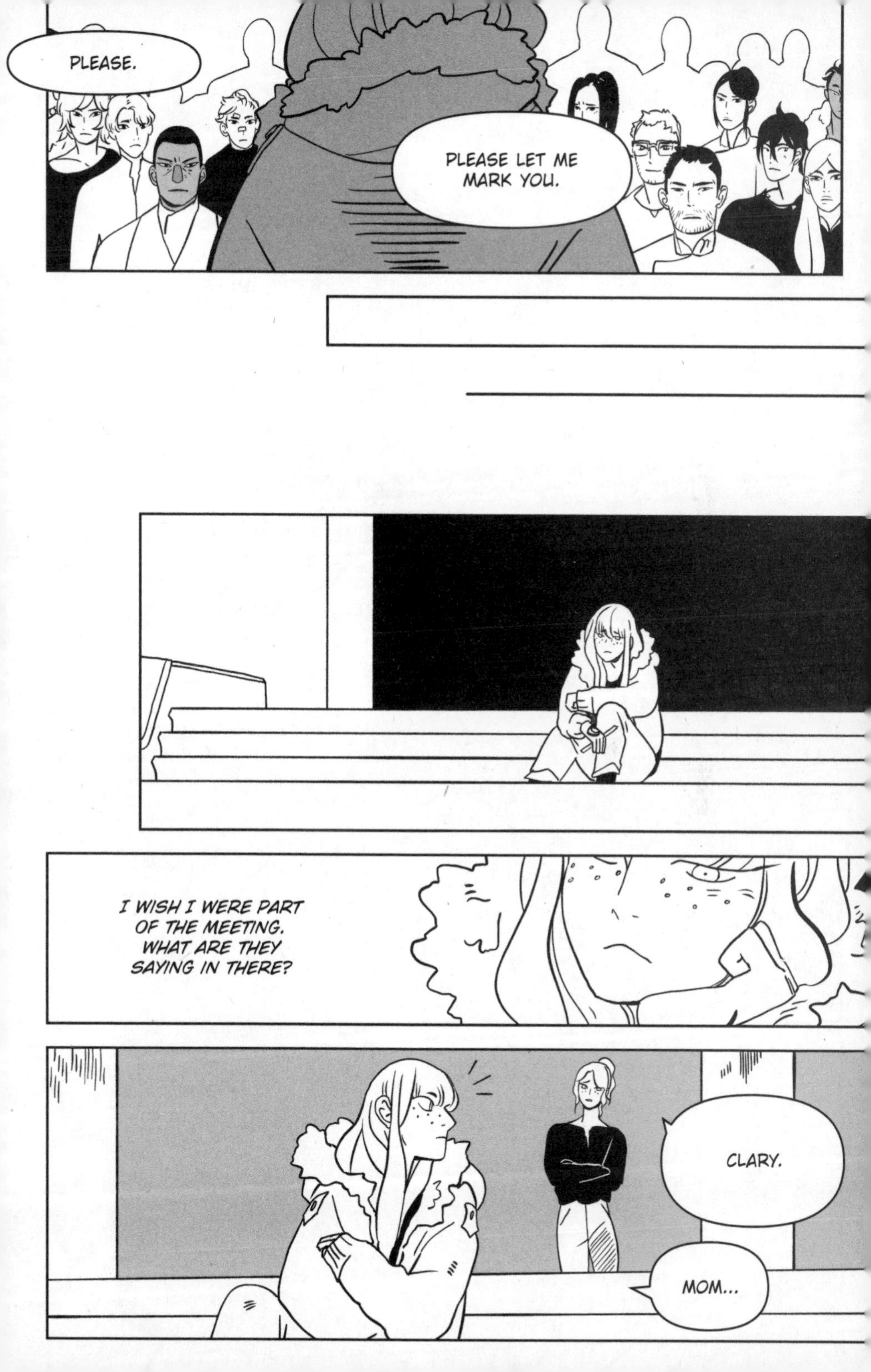

PLEASE.
PLEASE LET ME MARK YOU.
I WISH I WERE PART OF THE MEETING. WHAT ARE THEY SAYING IN THERE?
CLARY.
MOM...

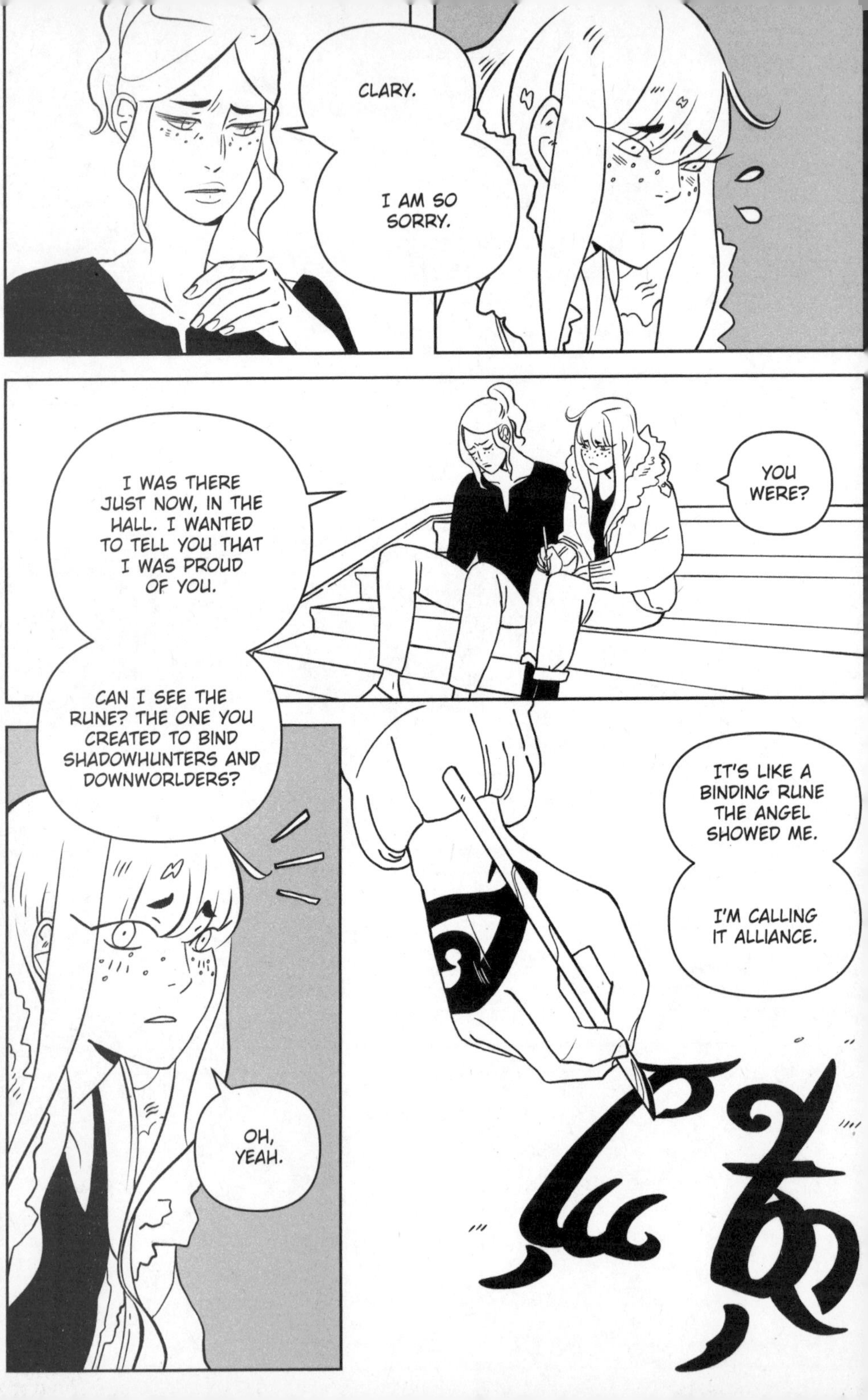
CLARY.
I AM SO SORRY.
I WAS THERE JUST NOW, IN THE HALL. I WANTED TO TELL YOU THAT I WAS PROUD OF YOU.
YOU WERE?
CAN I SEE THE RUNE? THE ONE YOU CREATED TO BIND SHADOWHUNTERS AND DOWNWORLDERS?
OH, YEAH.
IT'S LIKE A BINDING RUNE THE ANGEL SHOWED ME.
I'M CALLING IT ALLIANCE.

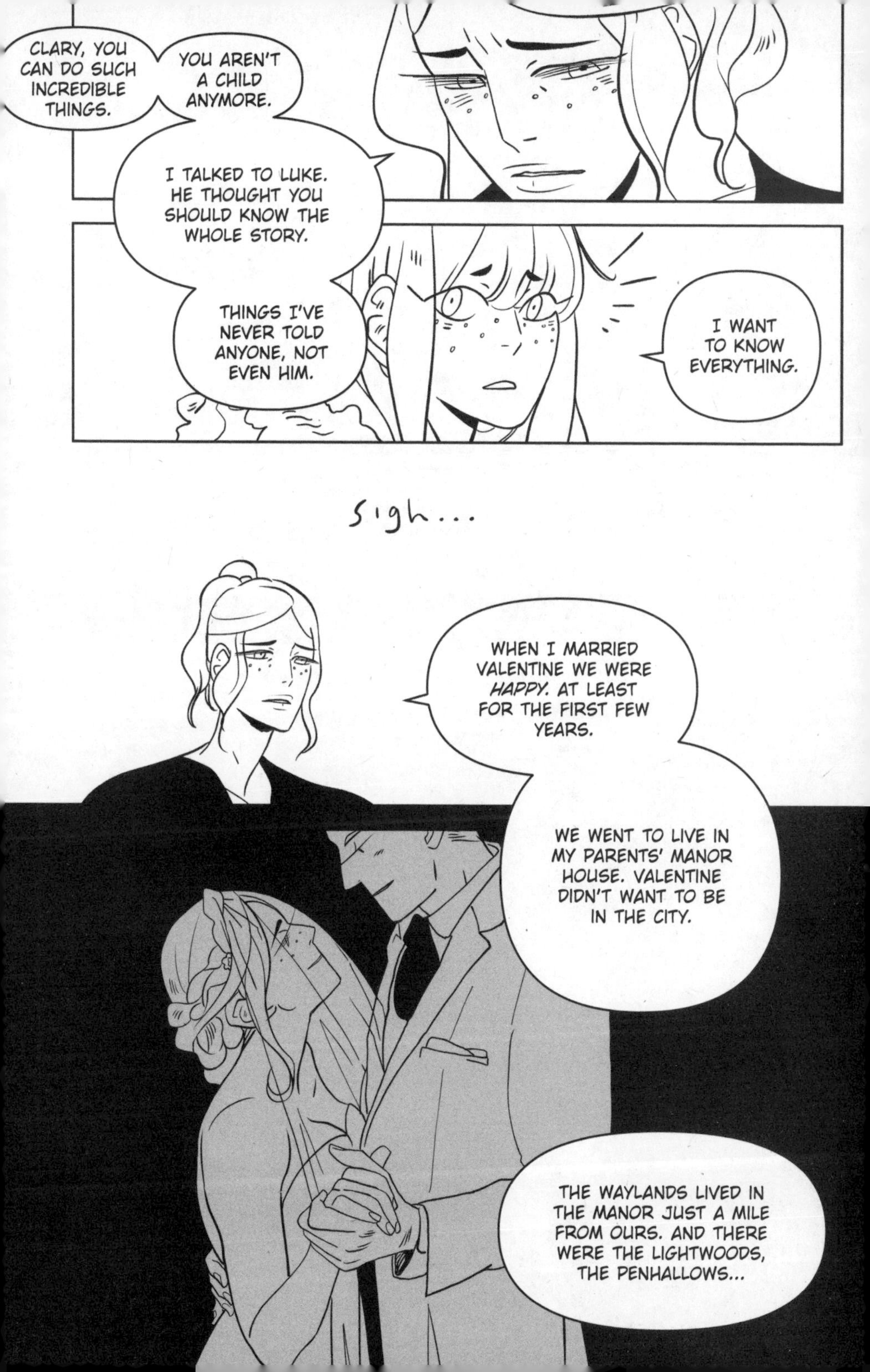
CLARY, YOU CAN DO SUCH INCREDIBLE THINGS.
YOU AREN'T A CHILD ANYMORE.
I TALKED TO LUKE. HE THOUGHT YOU SHOULD KNOW THE WHOLE STORY.
THINGS I'VE NEVER TOLD ANYONE, NOT EVEN HIM.
I WANT TO KNOW EVERYTHING.
sigh...
WHEN I MARRIED VALENTINE WE WERE *HAPPY*. AT LEAST FOR THE FIRST FEW YEARS.
WE WENT TO LIVE IN MY PARENTS' MANOR HOUSE. VALENTINE DIDN'T WANT TO BE IN THE CITY.
THE WAYLANDS LIVED IN THE MANOR JUST A MILE FROM OURS. AND THERE WERE THE LIGHTWOODS, THE PENHALLOWS...

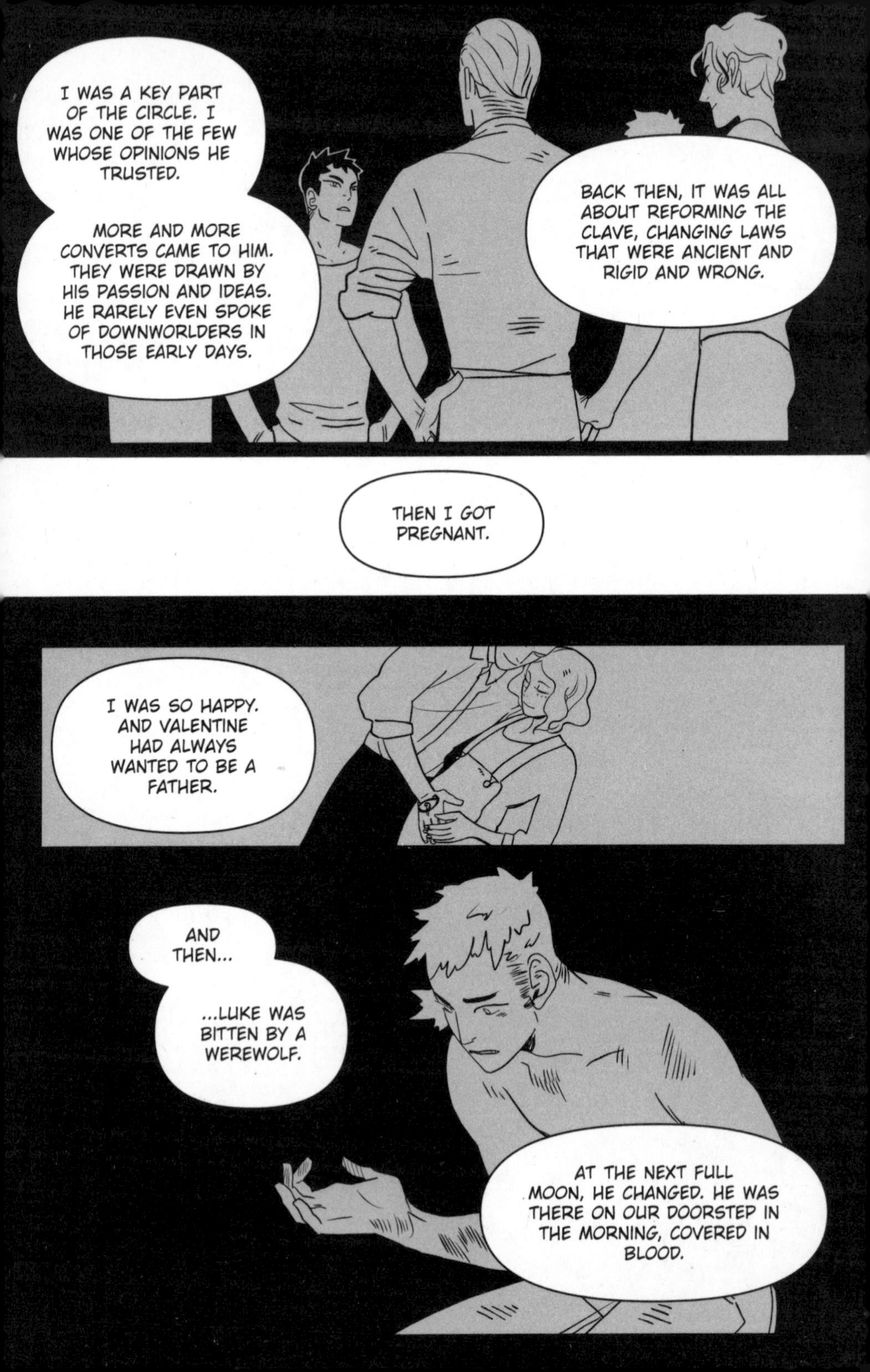
I WAS A KEY PART OF THE CIRCLE. I WAS ONE OF THE FEW WHOSE OPINIONS HE TRUSTED.
MORE AND MORE CONVERTS CAME TO HIM. THEY WERE DRAWN BY HIS PASSION AND IDEAS. HE RARELY EVEN SPOKE OF DOWNWORLDERS IN THOSE EARLY DAYS.
BACK THEN, IT WAS ALL ABOUT REFORMING THE CLAVE, CHANGING LAWS THAT WERE ANCIENT AND RIGID AND WRONG.
THEN I GOT PREGNANT.
I WAS SO HAPPY. AND VALENTINE HAD ALWAYS WANTED TO BE A FATHER.
AND THEN...
...LUKE WAS BITTEN BY A WEREWOLF.
AT THE NEXT FULL MOON, HE CHANGED. HE WAS THERE ON OUR DOORSTEP IN THE MORNING, COVERED IN BLOOD.

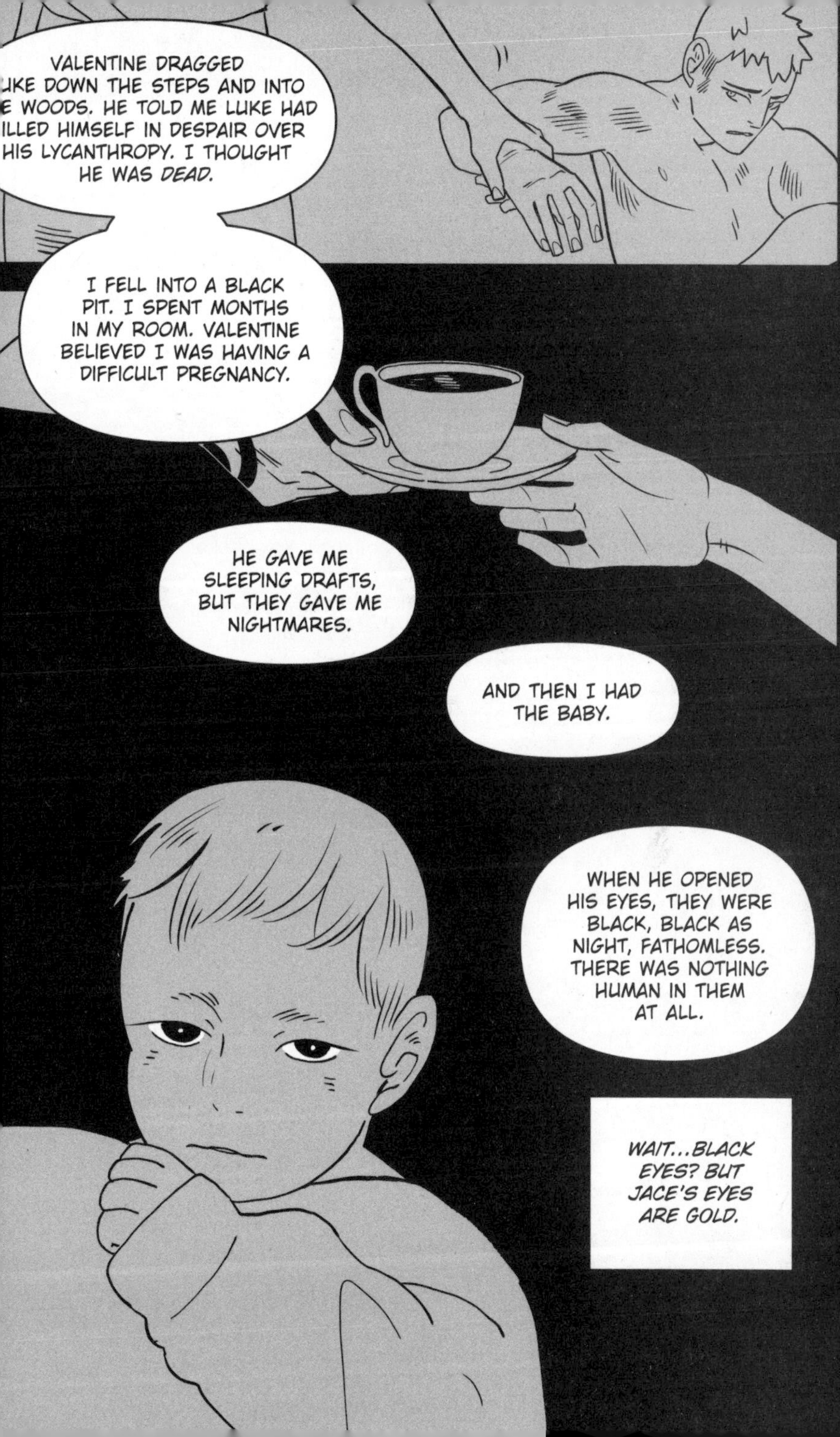
VALENTINE DRAGGED
UKE DOWN THE STEPS AND INTO
E WOODS. HE TOLD ME LUKE HAD
ILLED HIMSELF IN DESPAIR OVER
HIS LYCANTHROPY. I THOUGHT
HE WAS DEAD.
I FELL INTO A BLACK PIT. I SPENT MONTHS IN MY ROOM. VALENTINE BELIEVED I WAS HAVING A DIFFICULT PREGNANCY.
HE GAVE ME SLEEPING DRAFTS, BUT THEY GAVE ME NIGHTMARES.
AND THEN I HAD THE BABY.
WHEN HE OPENED HIS EYES, THEY WERE BLACK, BLACK AS NIGHT, FATHOMLESS. THERE WAS NOTHING HUMAN IN THEM AT ALL.
WAIT...BLACK EYES? BUT JACE'S EYES ARE GOLD.

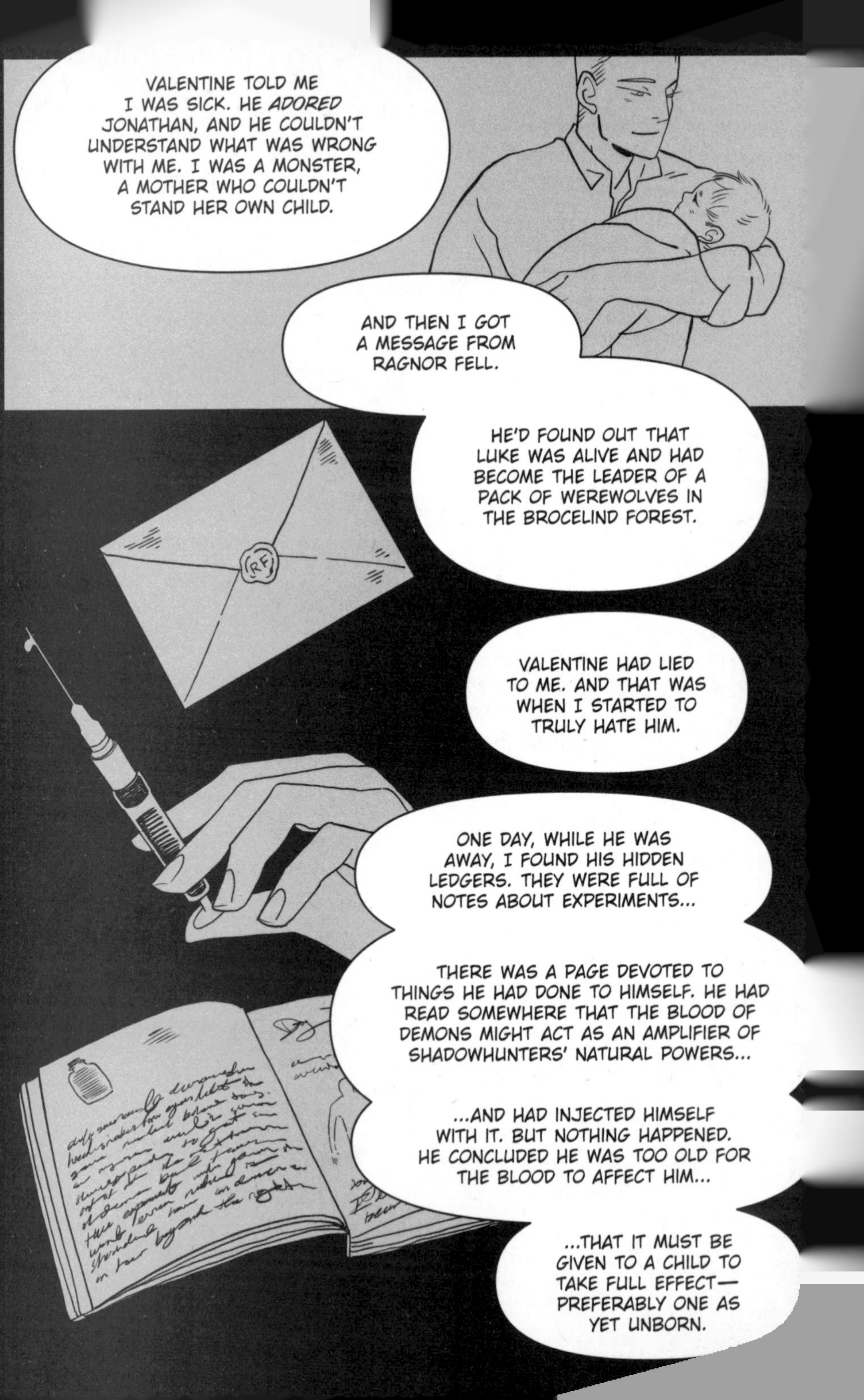
VALENTINE TOLD ME I WAS SICK. HE *ADORED* JONATHAN, AND HE COULDN'T UNDERSTAND WHAT WAS WRONG WITH ME. I WAS A MONSTER, A MOTHER WHO COULDN'T STAND HER OWN CHILD.
AND THEN I GOT A MESSAGE FROM RAGNOR FELL.
HE'D FOUND OUT THAT LUKE WAS ALIVE AND HAD BECOME THE LEADER OF A PACK OF WEREWOLVES IN THE BROCELIND FOREST.
RF
VALENTINE HAD LIED TO ME. AND THAT WAS WHEN I STARTED TO TRULY HATE HIM.
ONE DAY, WHILE HE WAS AWAY, I FOUND HIS HIDDEN LEDGERS. THEY WERE FULL OF NOTES ABOUT EXPERIMENTS...
THERE WAS A PAGE DEVOTED TO THINGS HE HAD DONE TO HIMSELF. HE HAD READ SOMEWHERE THAT THE BLOOD OF DEMONS MIGHT ACT AS AN AMPLIFIER OF SHADOWHUNTERS' NATURAL POWERS...
...AND HAD INJECTED HIMSELF WITH IT. BUT NOTHING HAPPENED. HE CONCLUDED HE WAS TOO OLD FOR THE BLOOD TO AFFECT HIM...
...THAT IT MUST BE GIVEN TO A CHILD TO TAKE FULL EFFECT— PREFERABLY ONE AS YET UNBORN.

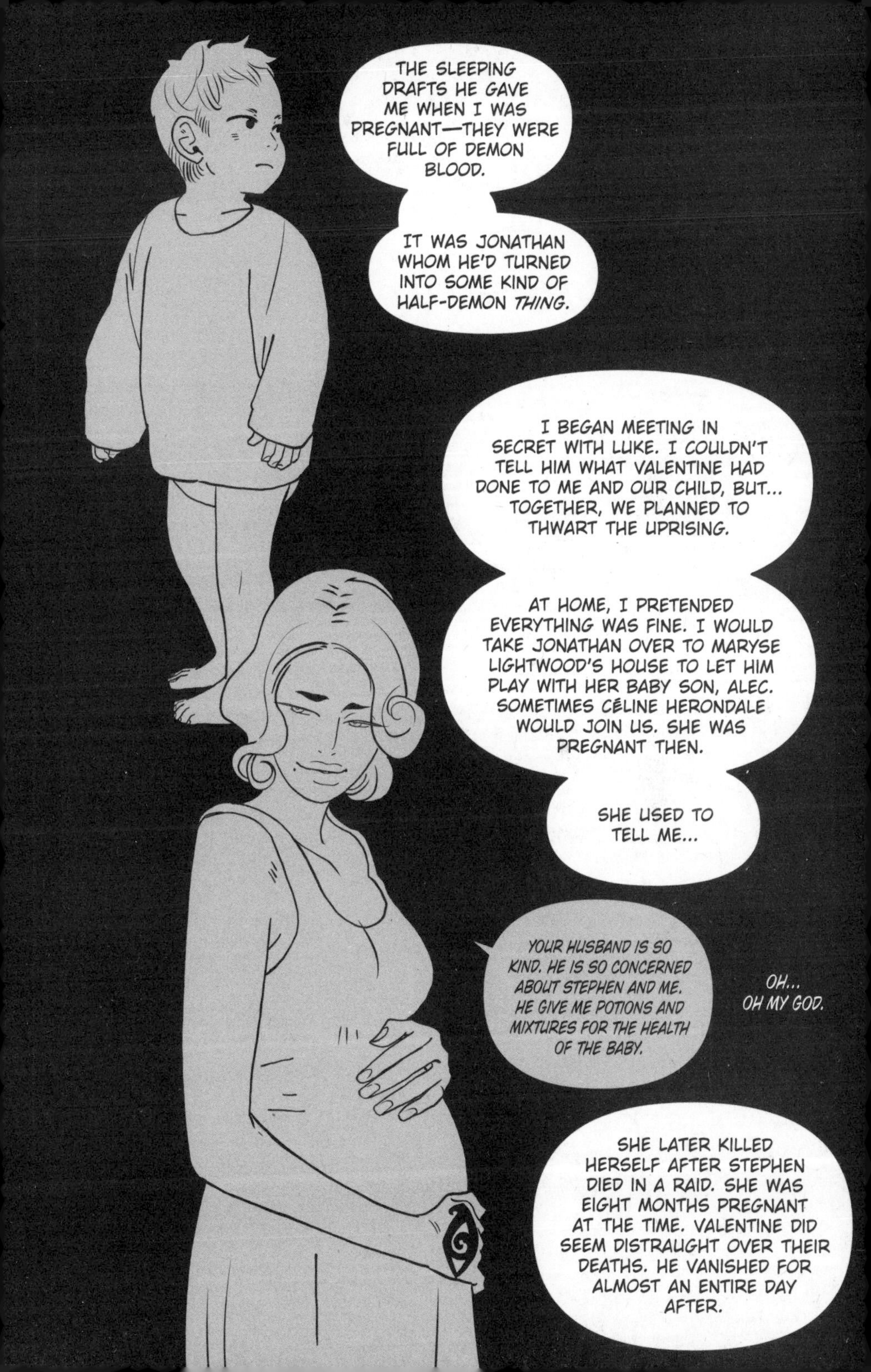
THE SLEEPING DRAFTS HE GAVE ME WHEN I WAS PREGNANT—THEY WERE FULL OF DEMON BLOOD.
IT WAS JONATHAN WHOM HE'D TURNED INTO SOME KIND OF HALF-DEMON *THING*.
I BEGAN MEETING IN SECRET WITH LUKE. I COULDN'T TELL HIM WHAT VALENTINE HAD DONE TO ME AND OUR CHILD, BUT... TOGETHER, WE PLANNED TO THWART THE UPRISING.
AT HOME, I PRETENDED EVERYTHING WAS FINE. I WOULD TAKE JONATHAN OVER TO MARYSE LIGHTWOOD'S HOUSE TO LET HIM PLAY WITH HER BABY SON, ALEC. SOMETIMES CÉLINE HERONDALE WOULD JOIN US. SHE WAS PREGNANT THEN.
SHE USED TO TELL ME...
YOUR HUSBAND IS SO KIND. HE IS SO CONCERNED ABOUT STEPHEN AND ME. HE GIVE ME POTIONS AND MIXTURES FOR THE HEALTH OF THE BABY.
OH... OH MY GOD.
SHE LATER KILLED HERSELF AFTER STEPHEN DIED IN A RAID. SHE WAS EIGHT MONTHS PREGNANT AT THE TIME. VALENTINE DID SEEM DISTRAUGHT OVER THEIR DEATHS. HE VANISHED FOR ALMOST AN ENTIRE DAY AFTER.

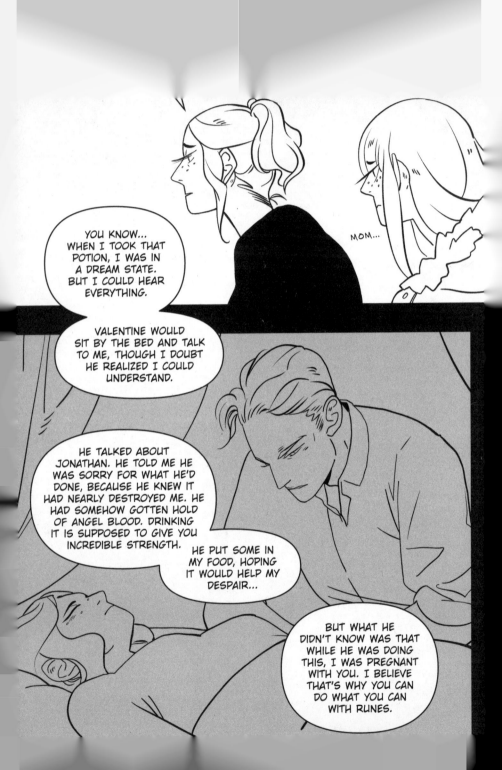

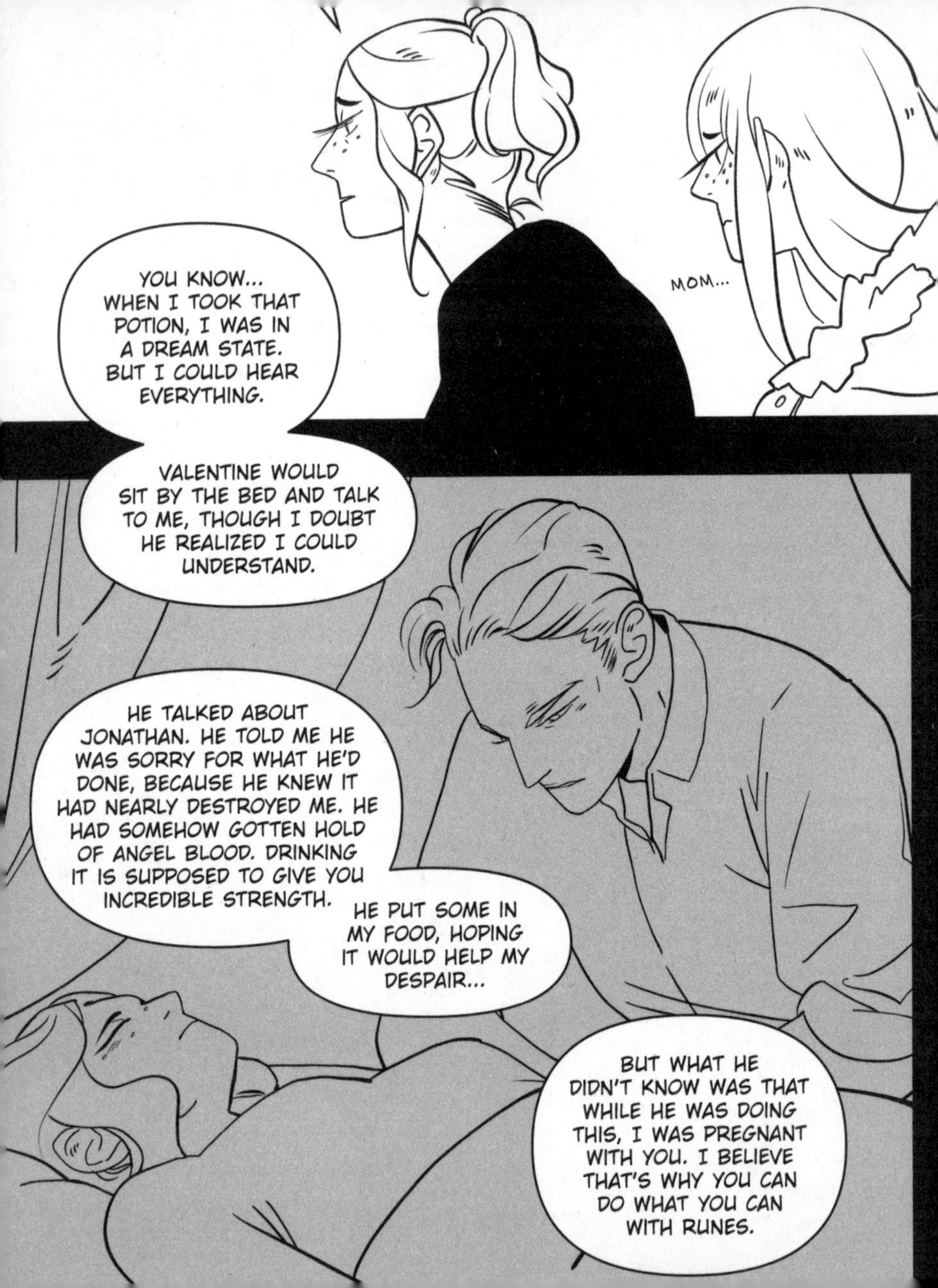
YOU KNOW... WHEN I TOOK THAT POTION, I WAS IN A DREAM STATE. BUT I COULD HEAR EVERYTHING.
MOM...
VALENTINE WOULD SIT BY THE BED AND TALK TO ME, THOUGH I DOUBT HE REALIZED I COULD UNDERSTAND.
HE TALKED ABOUT JONATHAN. HE TOLD ME HE WAS SORRY FOR WHAT HE'D DONE, BECAUSE HE KNEW IT HAD NEARLY DESTROYED ME. HE HAD SOMEHOW GOTTEN HOLD OF ANGEL BLOOD. DRINKING IT IS SUPPOSED TO GIVE YOU INCREDIBLE STRENGTH.
HE PUT SOME IN MY FOOD, HOPING IT WOULD HELP MY DESPAIR...
BUT WHAT HE DIDN'T KNOW WAS THAT WHILE HE WAS DOING THIS, I WAS PREGNANT WITH YOU. I BELIEVE THAT'S WHY YOU CAN DO WHAT YOU CAN WITH RUNES.

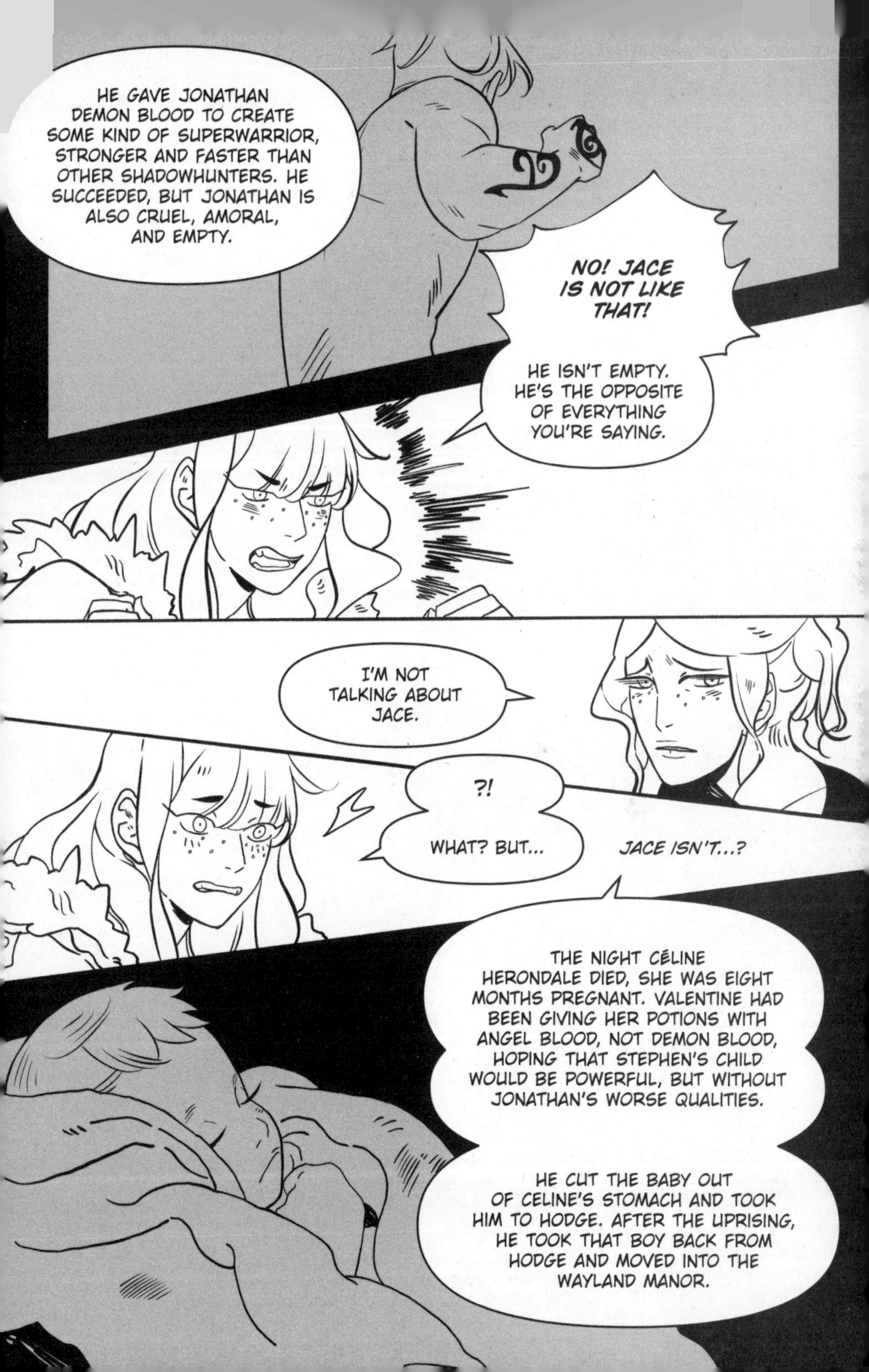
HE GAVE JONATHAN DEMON BLOOD TO CREATE SOME KIND OF SUPERWARRIOR, STRONGER AND FASTER THAN OTHER SHADOWHUNTERS. HE SUCCEEDED, BUT JONATHAN IS ALSO CRUEL, AMORAL, AND EMPTY.
NO! JACE IS NOT LIKE THAT!
HE ISN'T EMPTY. HE'S THE OPPOSITE OF EVERYTHING YOU'RE SAYING.
I'M NOT TALKING ABOUT JACE.
?!
WHAT? BUT...
JACE ISN'T...?
THE NIGHT CÉLINE HERONDALE DIED, SHE WAS EIGHT MONTHS PREGNANT. VALENTINE HAD BEEN GIVING HER POTIONS WITH ANGEL BLOOD, NOT DEMON BLOOD, HOPING THAT STEPHEN'S CHILD WOULD BE POWERFUL, BUT WITHOUT JONATHAN'S WORSE QUALITIES.
HE CUT THE BABY OUT OF CELINE'S STOMACH AND TOOK HIM TO HODGE. AFTER THE UPRISING, HE TOOK THAT BOY BACK FROM HODGE AND MOVED INTO THE WAYLAND MANOR.

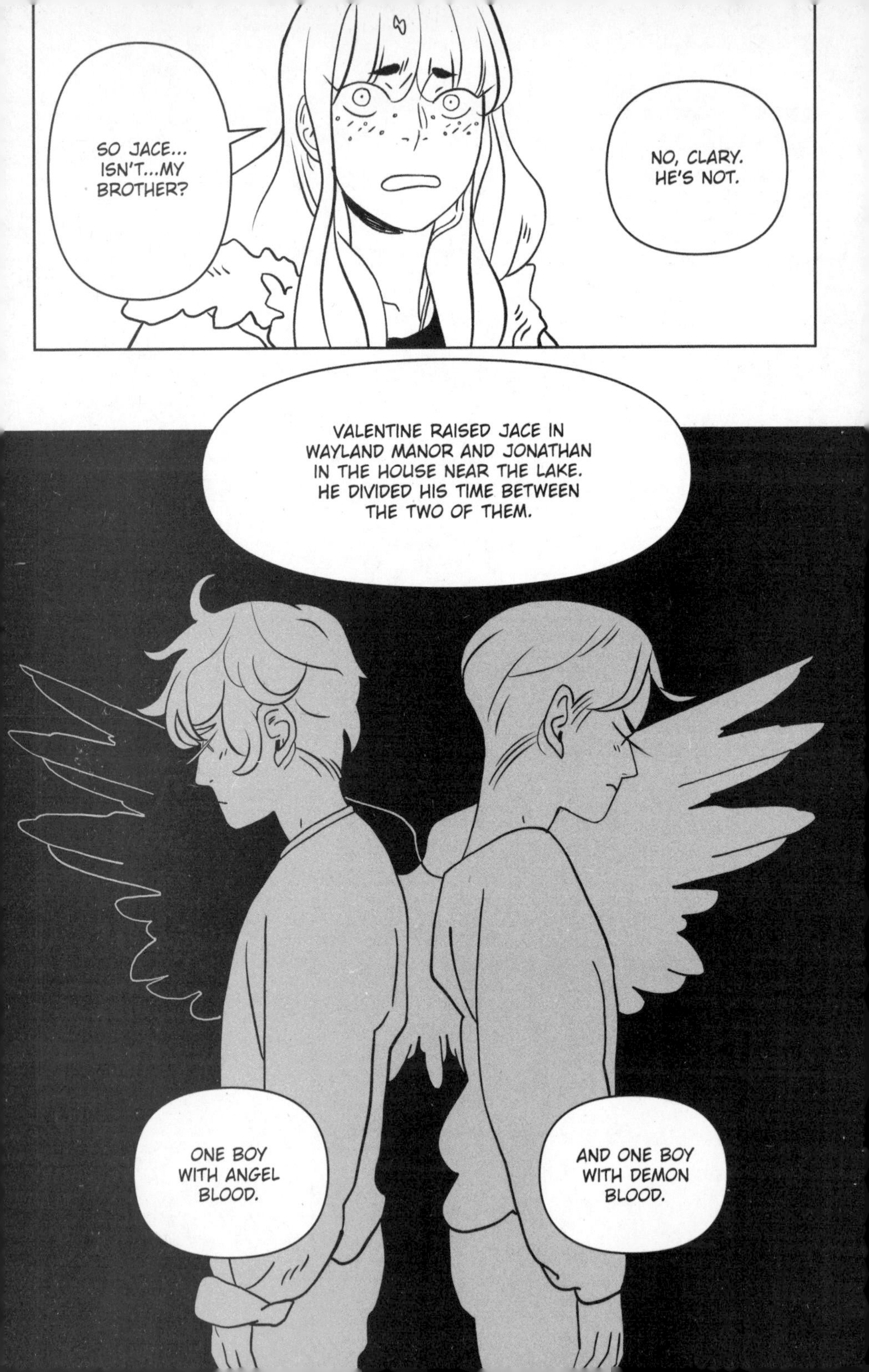
SO JACE... ISN'T...MY BROTHER?
NO, CLARY. HE'S NOT.
VALENTINE RAISED JACE IN WAYLAND MANOR AND JONATHAN IN THE HOUSE NEAR THE LAKE. HE DIVIDED HIS TIME BETWEEN THE TWO OF THEM.
ONE BOY WITH ANGEL BLOOD.
AND ONE BOY WITH DEMON BLOOD.

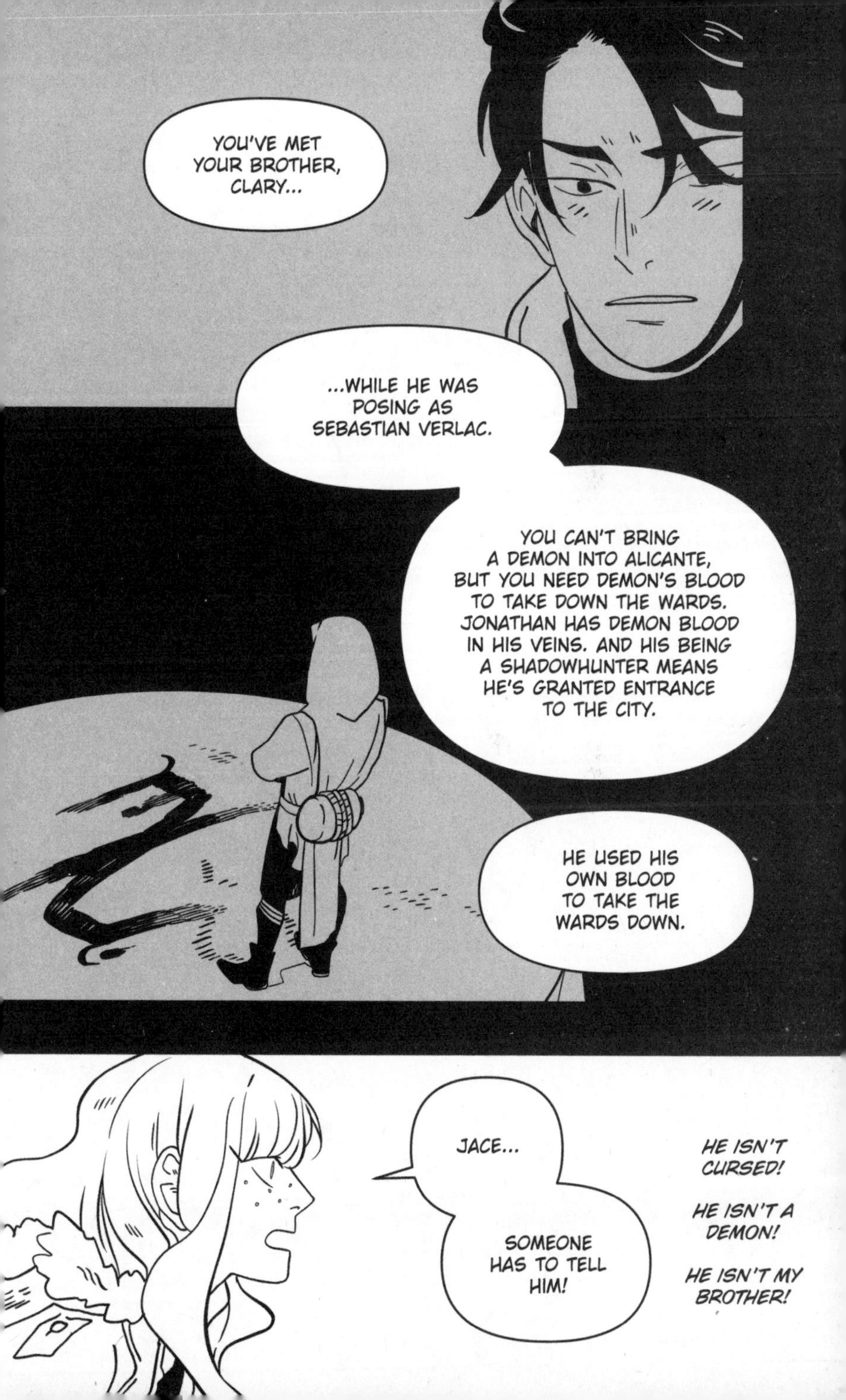
YOU'VE MET YOUR BROTHER, CLARY...
...WHILE HE WAS POSING AS SEBASTIAN VERLAC.
YOU CAN'T BRING A DEMON INTO ALICANTE, BUT YOU NEED DEMON'S BLOOD TO TAKE DOWN THE WARDS. JONATHAN HAS DEMON BLOOD IN HIS VEINS. AND HIS BEING A SHADOWHUNTER MEANS HE'S GRANTED ENTRANCE TO THE CITY.
HE USED HIS OWN BLOOD TO TAKE THE WARDS DOWN.
HE ISN'T CURSED!
HE ISN'T A DEMON!
HE ISN'T MY BROTHER!
JACE...
SOMEONE HAS TO TELL HIM!

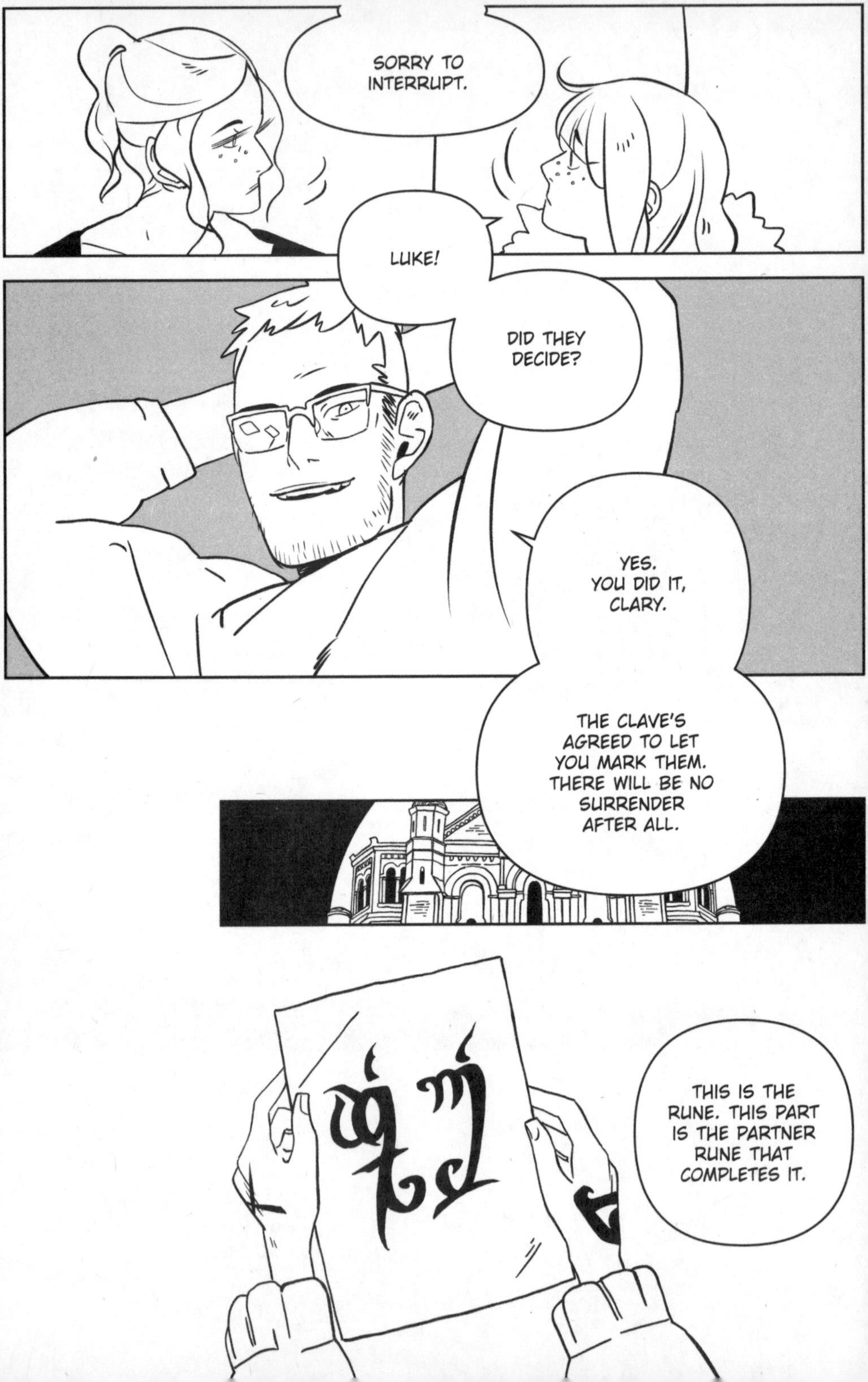
SORRY TO INTERRUPT.
LUKE!
DID THEY DECIDE?
YES. YOU DID IT, CLARY.
THE CLAVE'S AGREED TO LET YOU MARK THEM. THERE WILL BE NO SURRENDER AFTER ALL.
THIS IS THE RUNE. THIS PART IS THE PARTNER RUNE THAT COMPLETES IT.

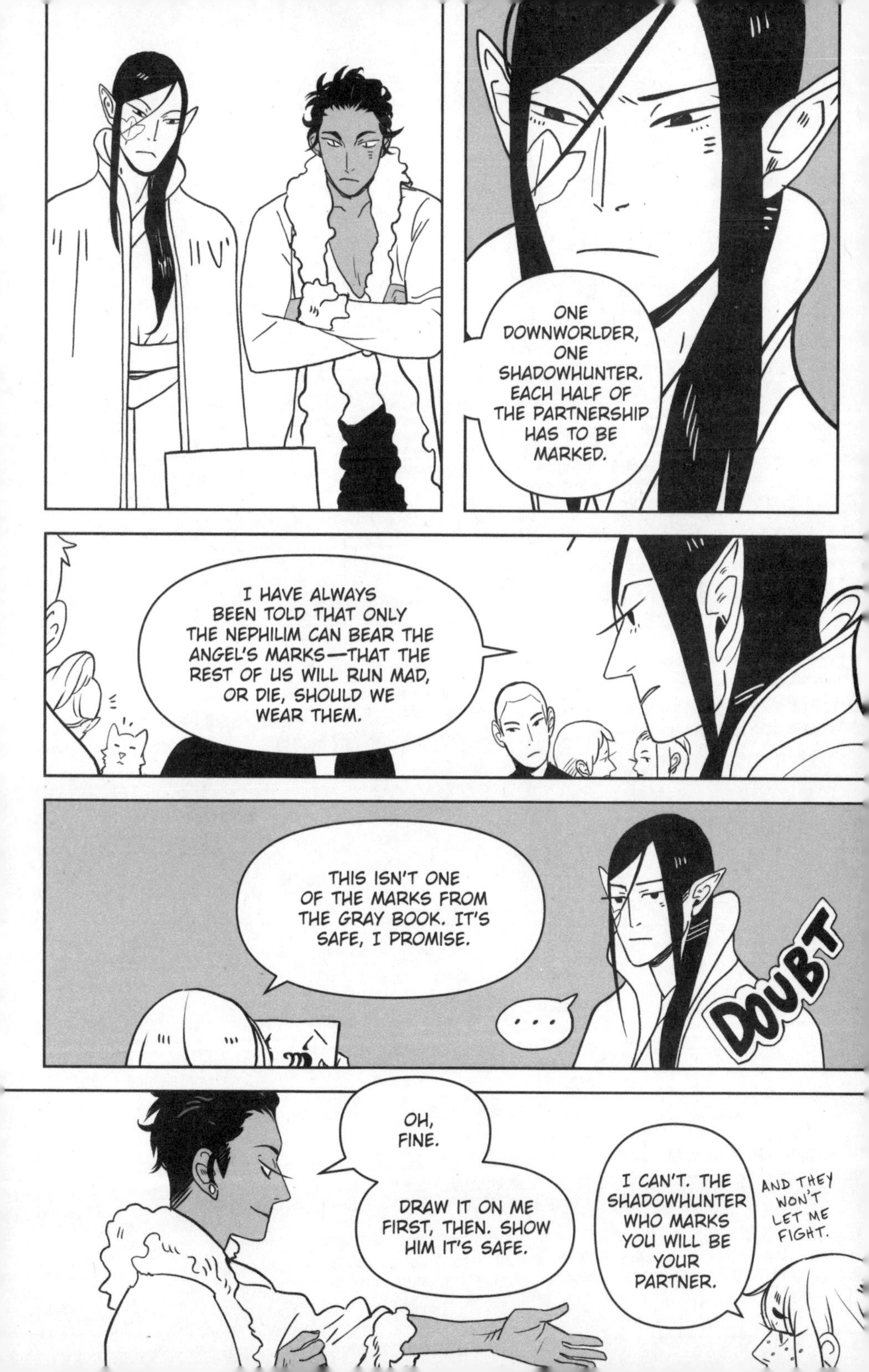

ONE DOWNWORLDER, ONE SHADOWHUNTER. EACH HALF OF THE PARTNERSHIP HAS TO BE MARKED.
I HAVE ALWAYS BEEN TOLD THAT ONLY THE NEPHILIM CAN BEAR THE ANGEL'S MARKS—THAT THE REST OF US WILL RUN MAD, OR DIE, SHOULD WE WEAR THEM.
THIS ISN'T ONE OF THE MARKS FROM THE GRAY BOOK. IT'S SAFE, I PROMISE.
...
DOUBT
OH, FINE.
DRAW IT ON ME FIRST, THEN. SHOW HIM IT'S SAFE.
I CAN'T. THE SHADOWHUNTER WHO MARKS YOU WILL BE YOUR PARTNER.
AND THEY WON'T LET ME FIGHT.

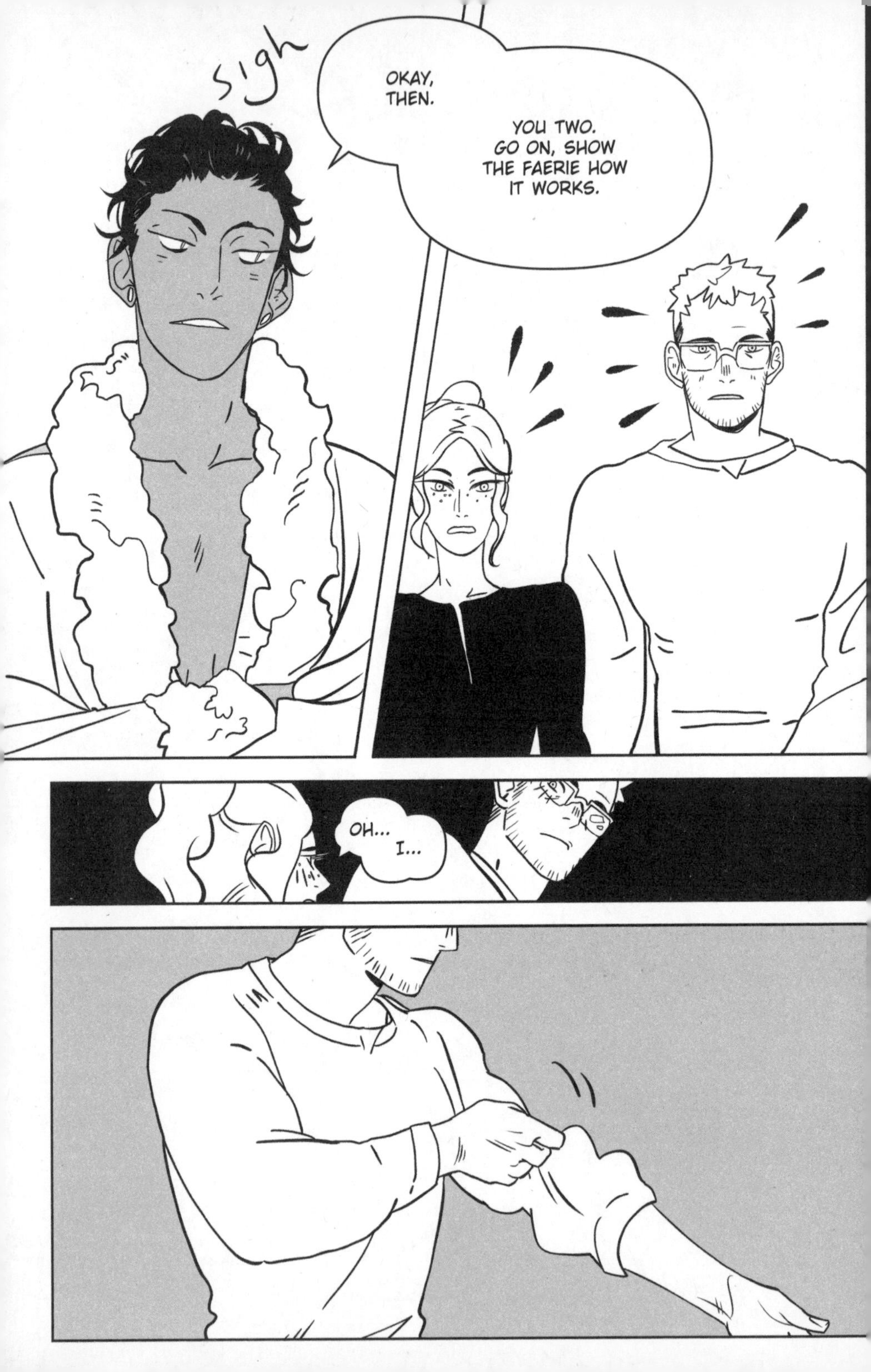
sigh
OKAY, THEN.
YOU TWO. GO ON, SHOW THE FAERIE HOW IT WORKS.
OH... I...

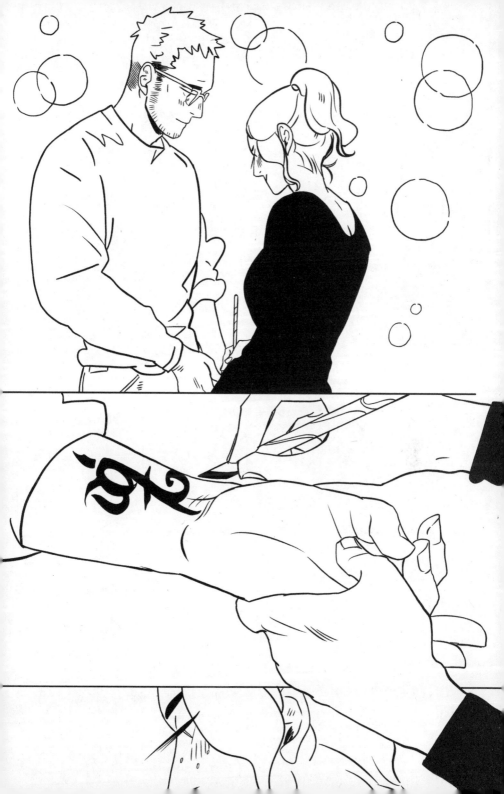

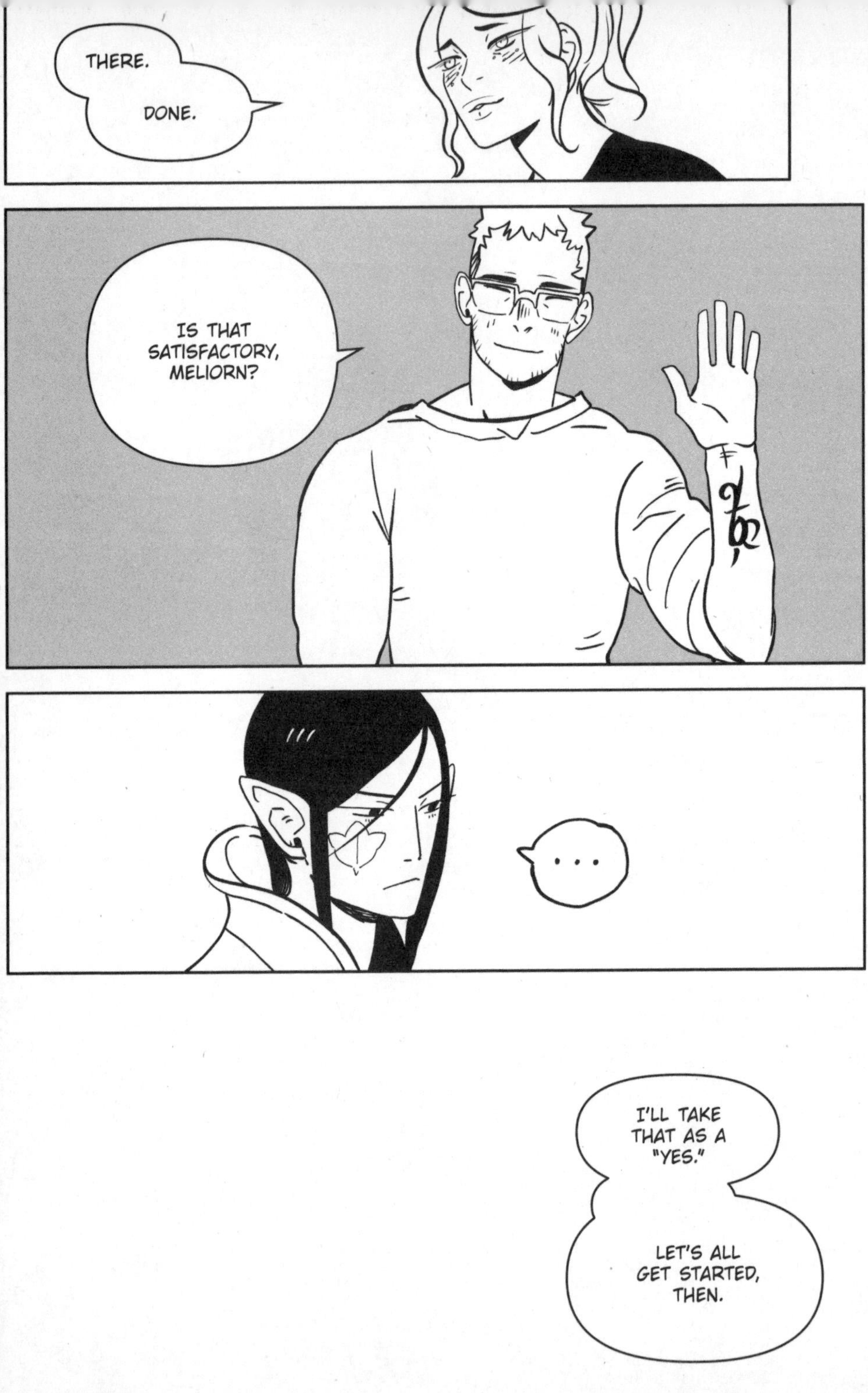
THERE.
DONE.
IS THAT SATISFACTORY, MELIORN?
...
I'LL TAKE THAT AS A "YES."
LET'S ALL GET STARTED, THEN.

THE MORTAL INSTRUMENTS

THE GRAPHIC NOVEL

THE MORTAL INSTRUMENTS

THE GRAPHIC NOVEL

Chapter 34

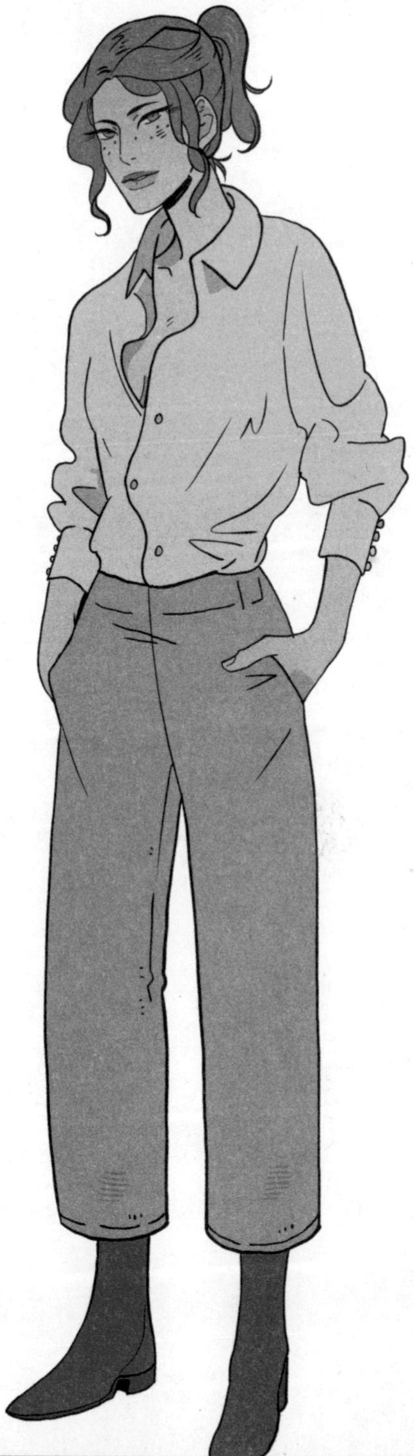

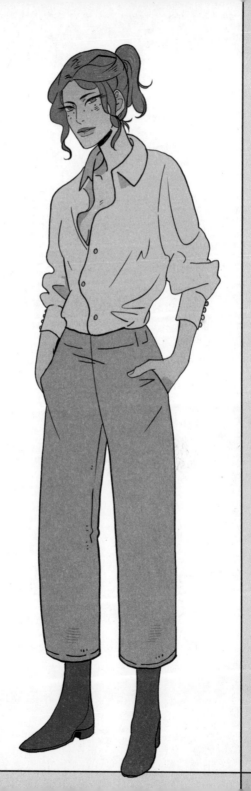

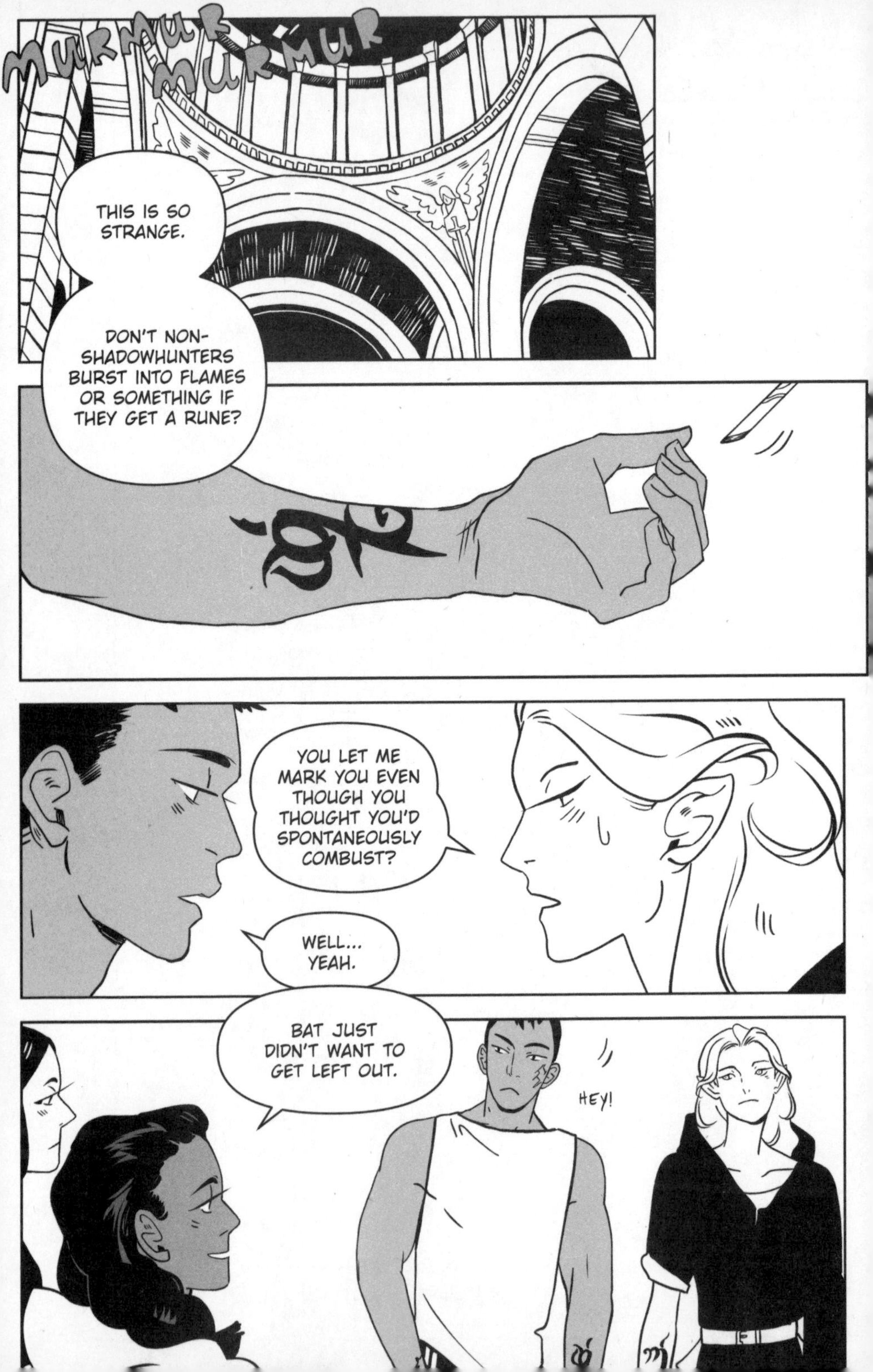
MURMUR MURMUR
THIS IS SO STRANGE.
DON'T NON-SHADOWHUNTERS BURST INTO FLAMES OR SOMETHING IF THEY GET A RUNE?
YOU LET ME MARK YOU EVEN THOUGH YOU THOUGHT YOU'D SPONTANEOUSLY COMBUST?
WELL... YEAH.
BAT JUST DIDN'T WANT TO GET LEFT OUT.
HEY!

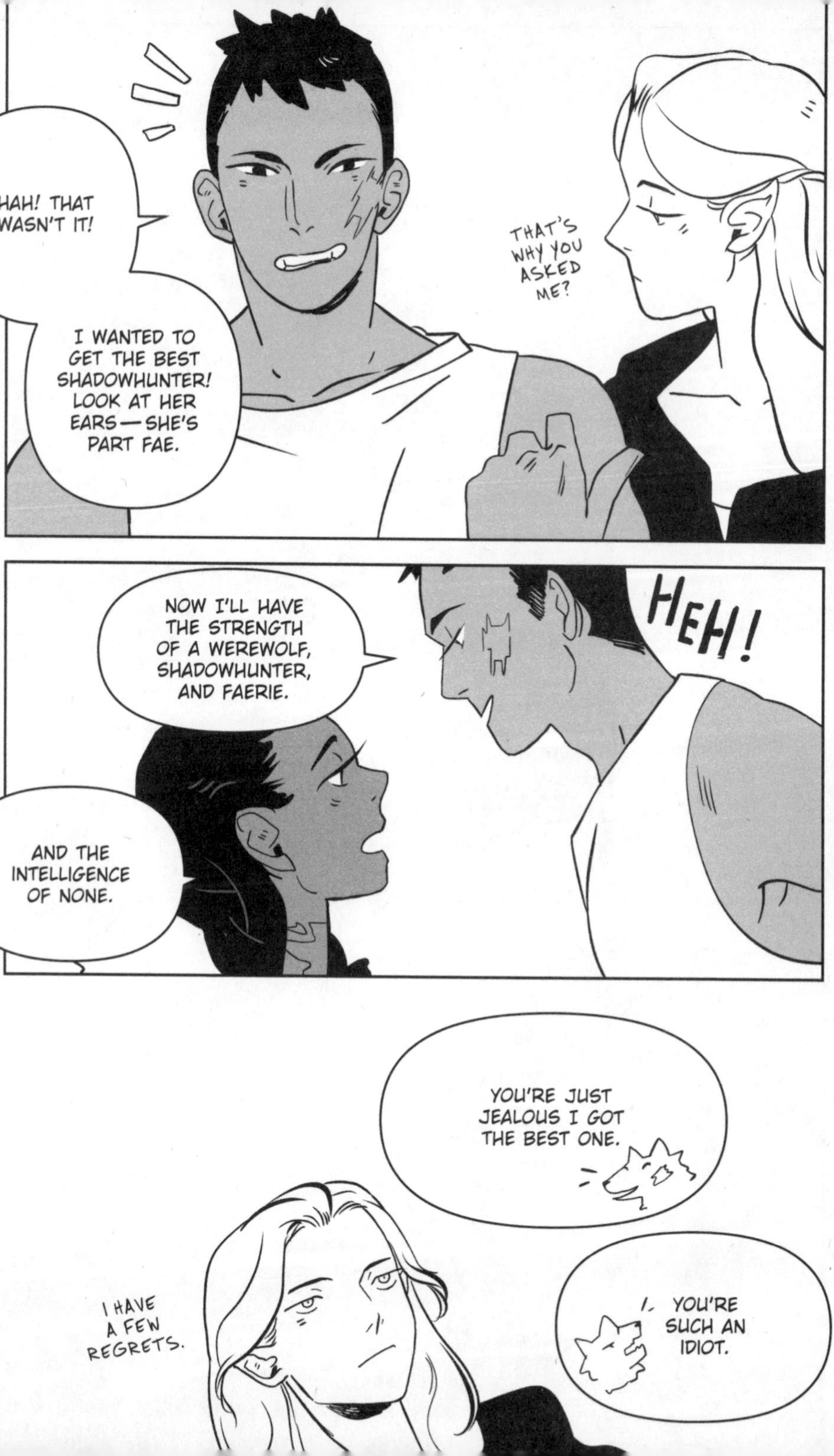
HAH! THAT WASN'T IT!
THAT'S WHY YOU ASKED ME?
I WANTED TO GET THE BEST SHADOWHUNTER! LOOK AT HER EARS—SHE'S PART FAE.
HEH!
NOW I'LL HAVE THE STRENGTH OF A WEREWOLF, SHADOWHUNTER, AND FAERIE.
AND THE INTELLIGENCE OF NONE.
YOU'RE JUST JEALOUS I GOT THE BEST ONE.
I HAVE A FEW REGRETS.
YOU'RE SUCH AN IDIOT.

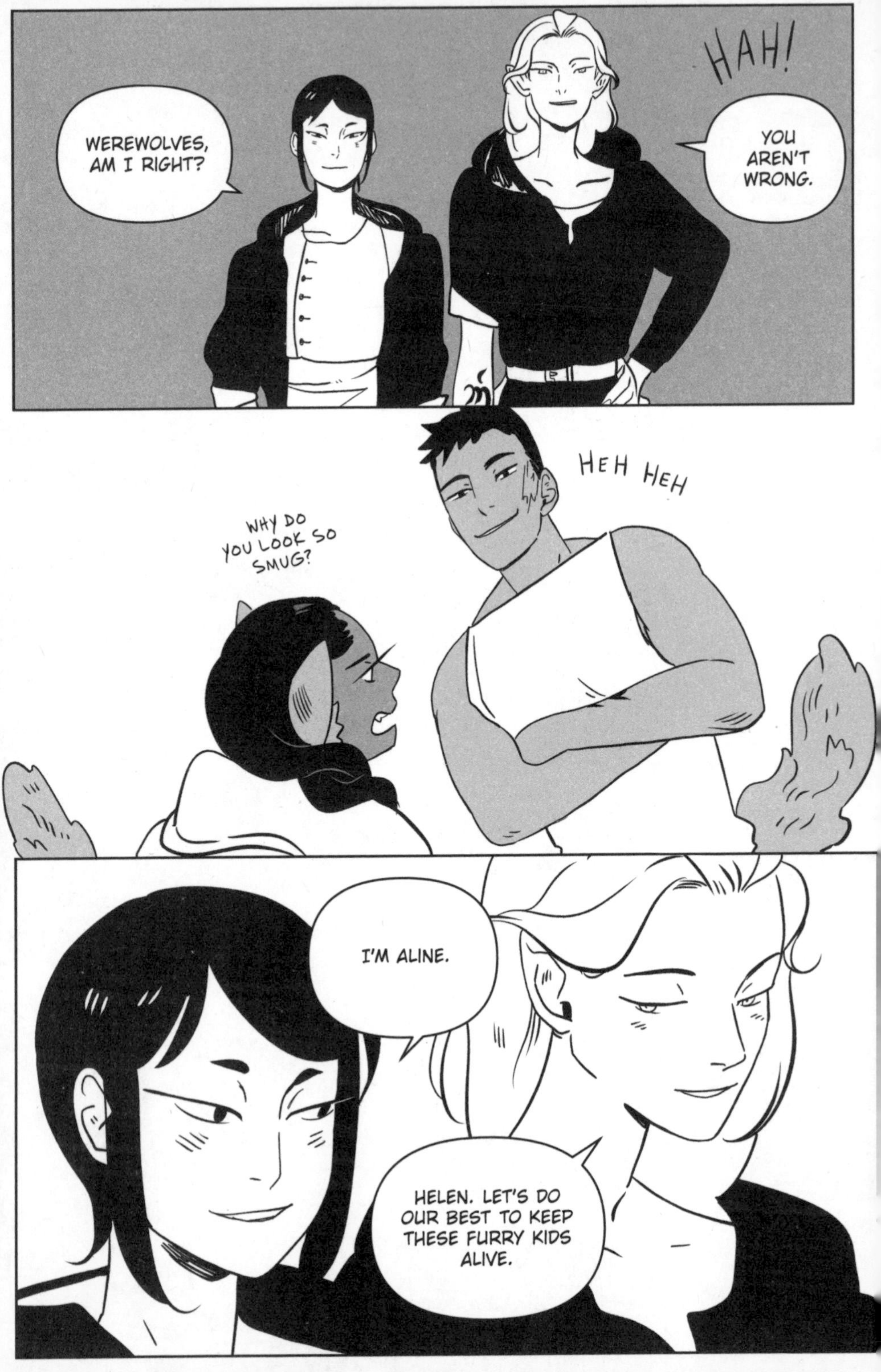
WEREWOLVES, AM I RIGHT?
HAH!
YOU AREN'T WRONG.
HEH HEH
WHY DO YOU LOOK SO SMUG?
I'M ALINE.
HELEN. LET'S DO OUR BEST TO KEEP THESE FURRY KIDS ALIVE.

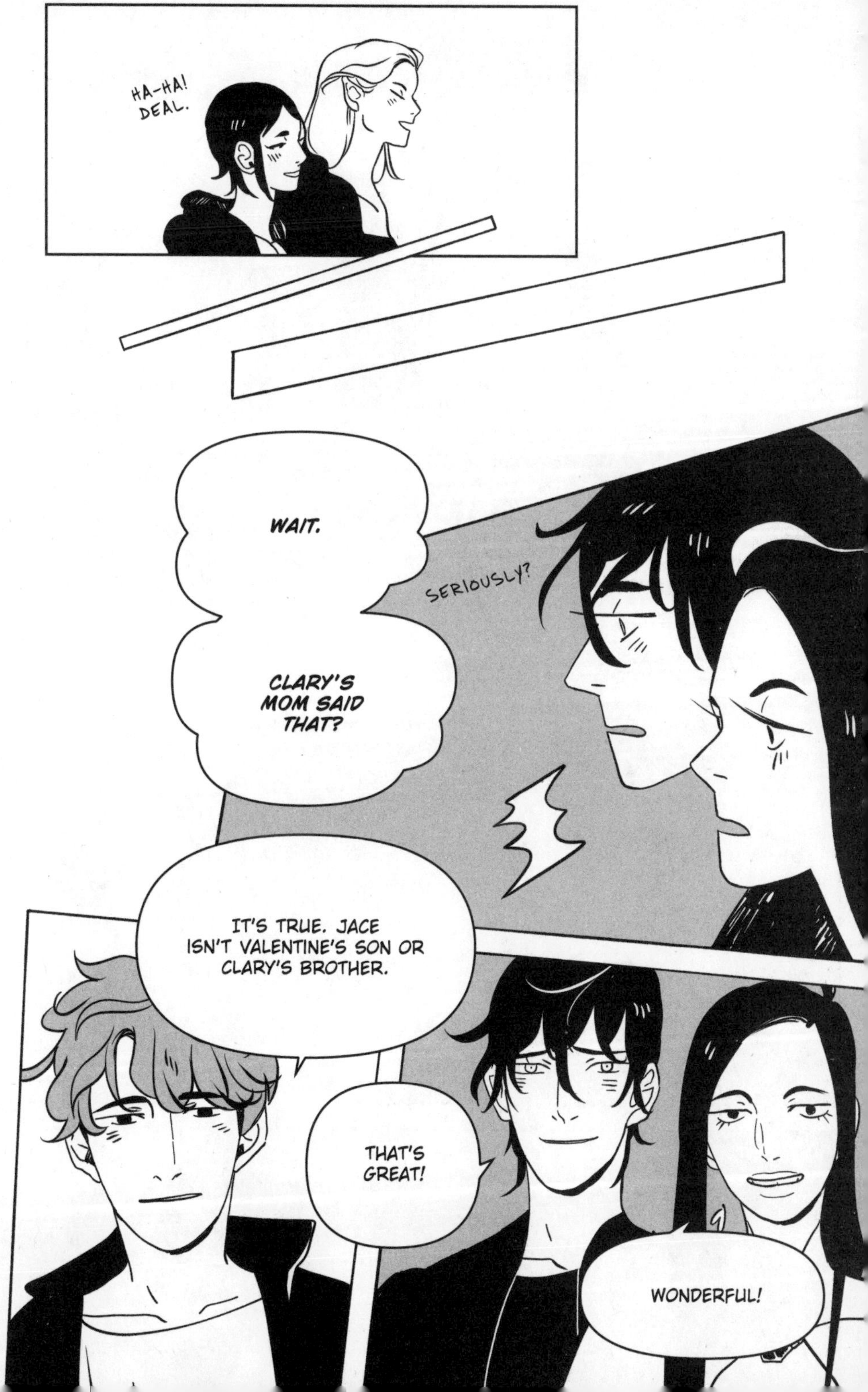
HA-HA! DEAL.
WAIT.
CLARY'S MOM SAID THAT?
SERIOUSLY?
IT'S TRUE. JACE ISN'T VALENTINE'S SON OR CLARY'S BROTHER.
THAT'S GREAT!
WONDERFUL!

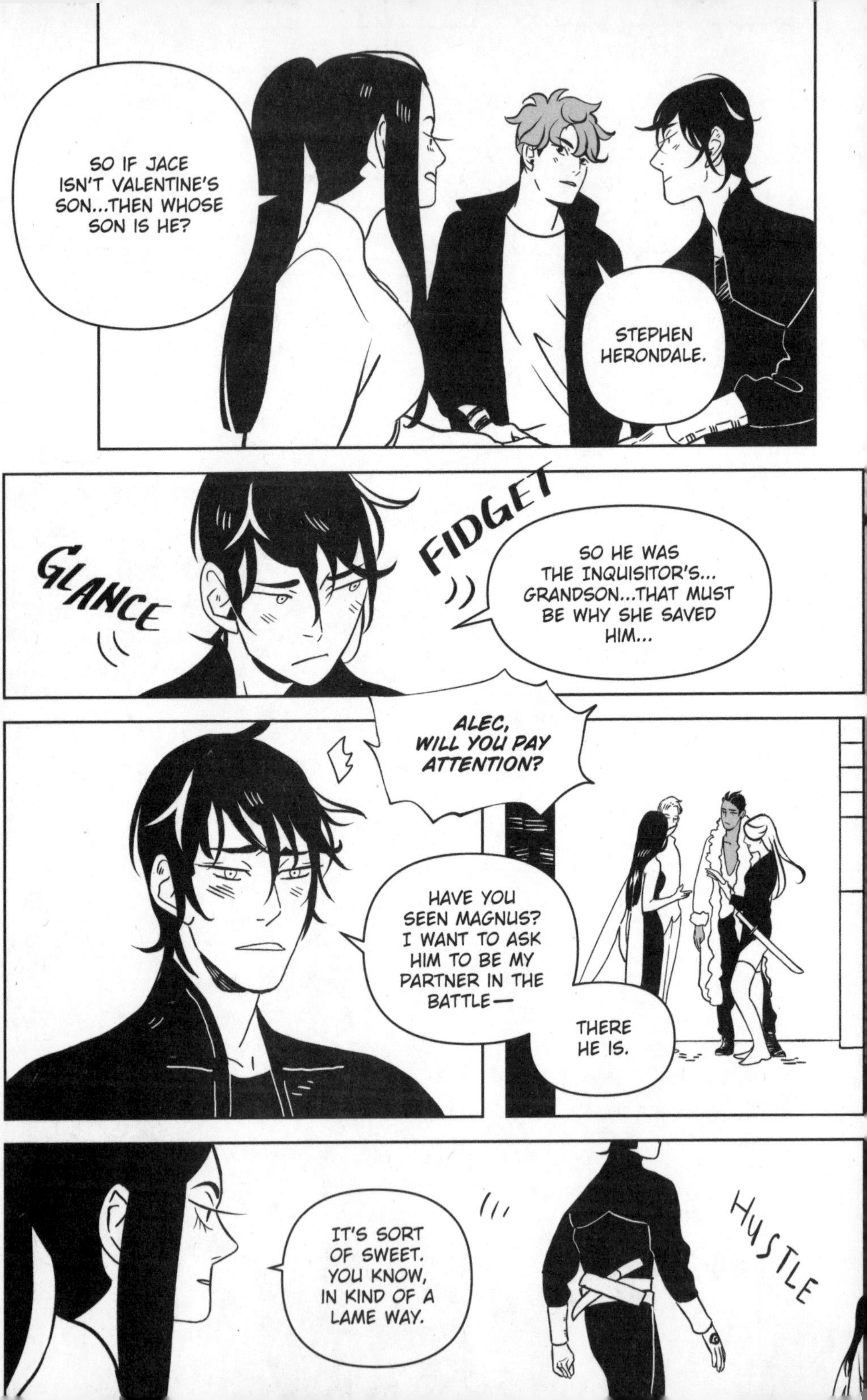
SO IF JACE ISN'T VALENTINE'S SON...THEN WHOSE SON IS HE?
STEPHEN HERONDALE.
GLANCE
FIDGET
SO HE WAS THE INQUISITOR'S... GRANDSON...THAT MUST BE WHY SHE SAVED HIM...
ALEC, WILL YOU PAY ATTENTION?
HAVE YOU SEEN MAGNUS? I WANT TO ASK HIM TO BE MY PARTNER IN THE BATTLE—
THERE HE IS.
IT'S SORT OF SWEET. YOU KNOW, IN KIND OF A LAME WAY.
HUSTLE

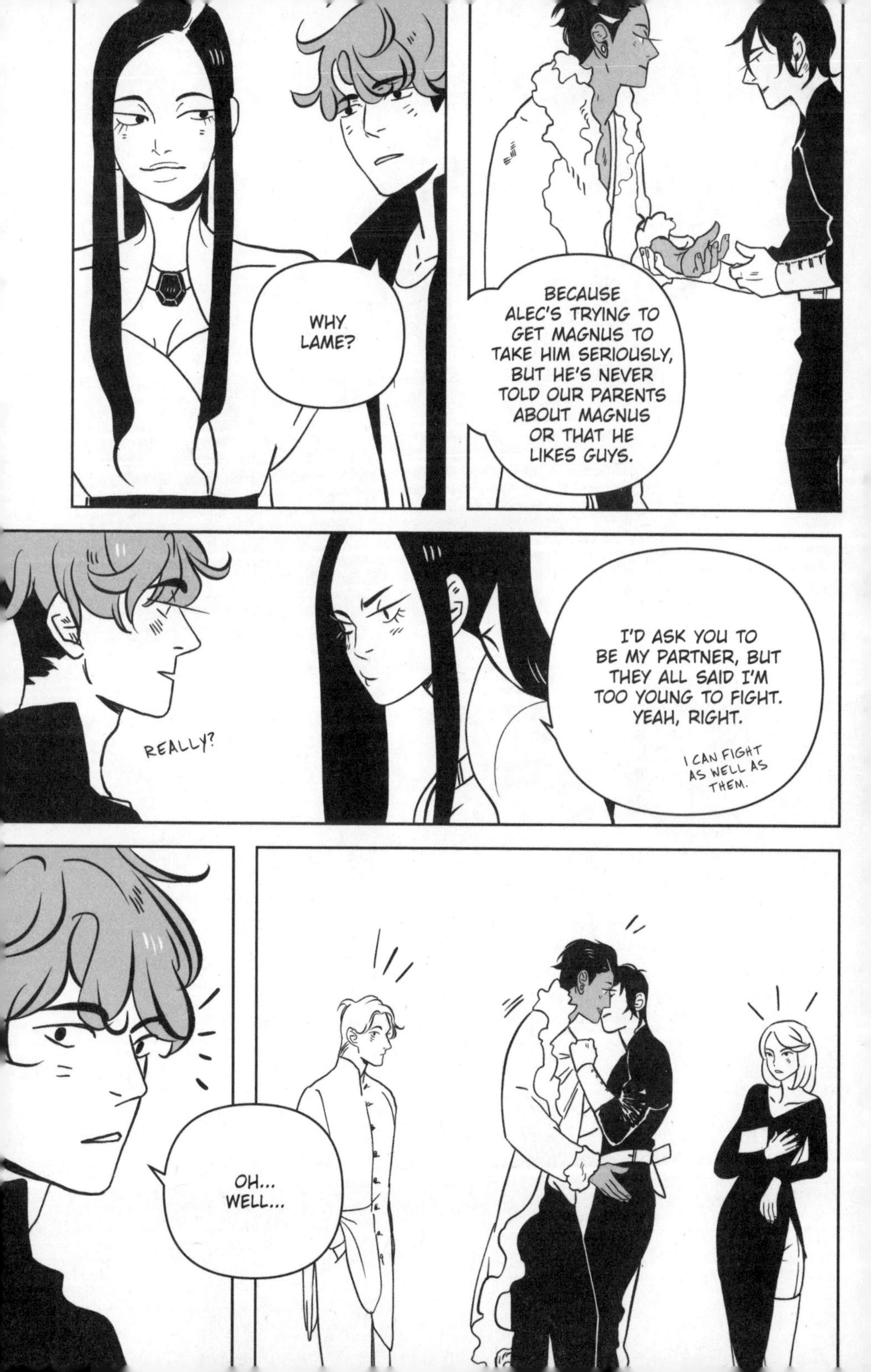
WHY LAME?
BECAUSE ALEC'S TRYING TO GET MAGNUS TO TAKE HIM SERIOUSLY, BUT HE'S NEVER TOLD OUR PARENTS ABOUT MAGNUS OR THAT HE LIKES GUYS.
I'D ASK YOU TO BE MY PARTNER, BUT THEY ALL SAID I'M TOO YOUNG TO FIGHT. YEAH, RIGHT.
I CAN FIGHT AS WELL AS THEM.
REALLY?
OH... WELL...

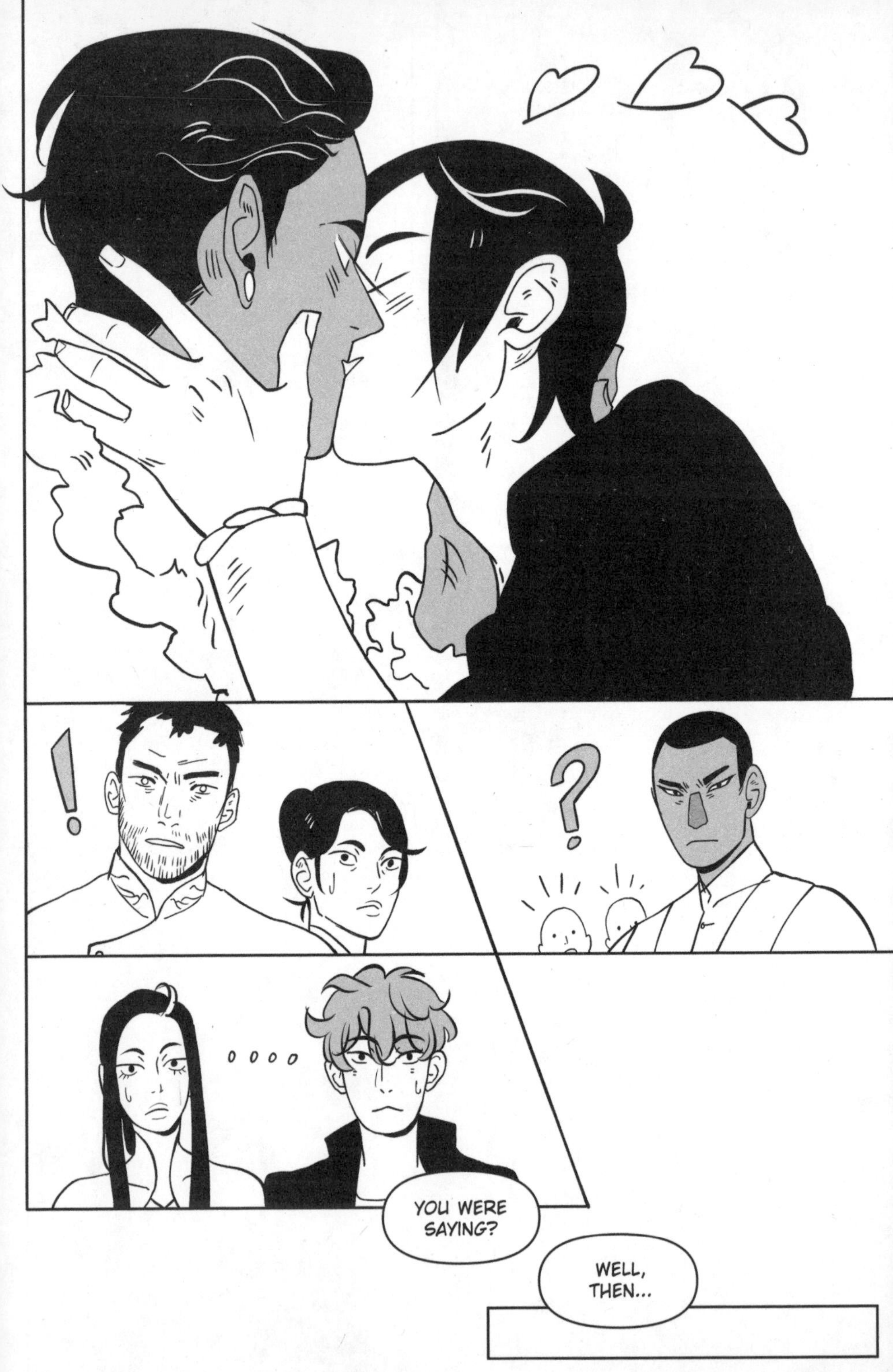
!
?
o o o o
YOU WERE SAYING?
WELL, THEN...

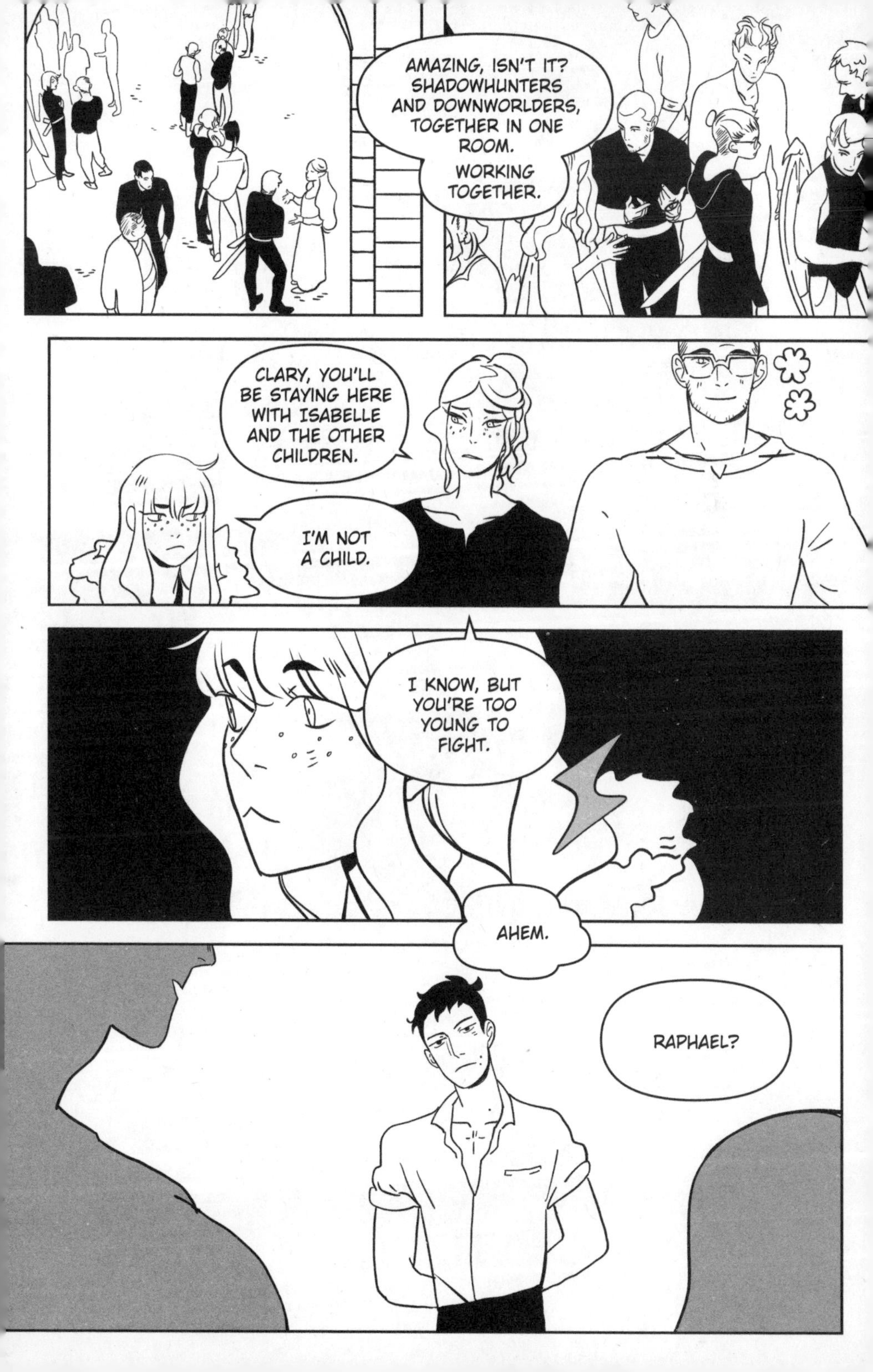
AMAZING, ISN'T IT? SHADOWHUNTERS AND DOWNWORLDERS, TOGETHER IN ONE ROOM.
WORKING TOGETHER.
CLARY, YOU'LL BE STAYING HERE WITH ISABELLE AND THE OTHER CHILDREN.
I'M NOT A CHILD.
I KNOW, BUT YOU'RE TOO YOUNG TO FIGHT.
AHEM.
RAPHAEL?

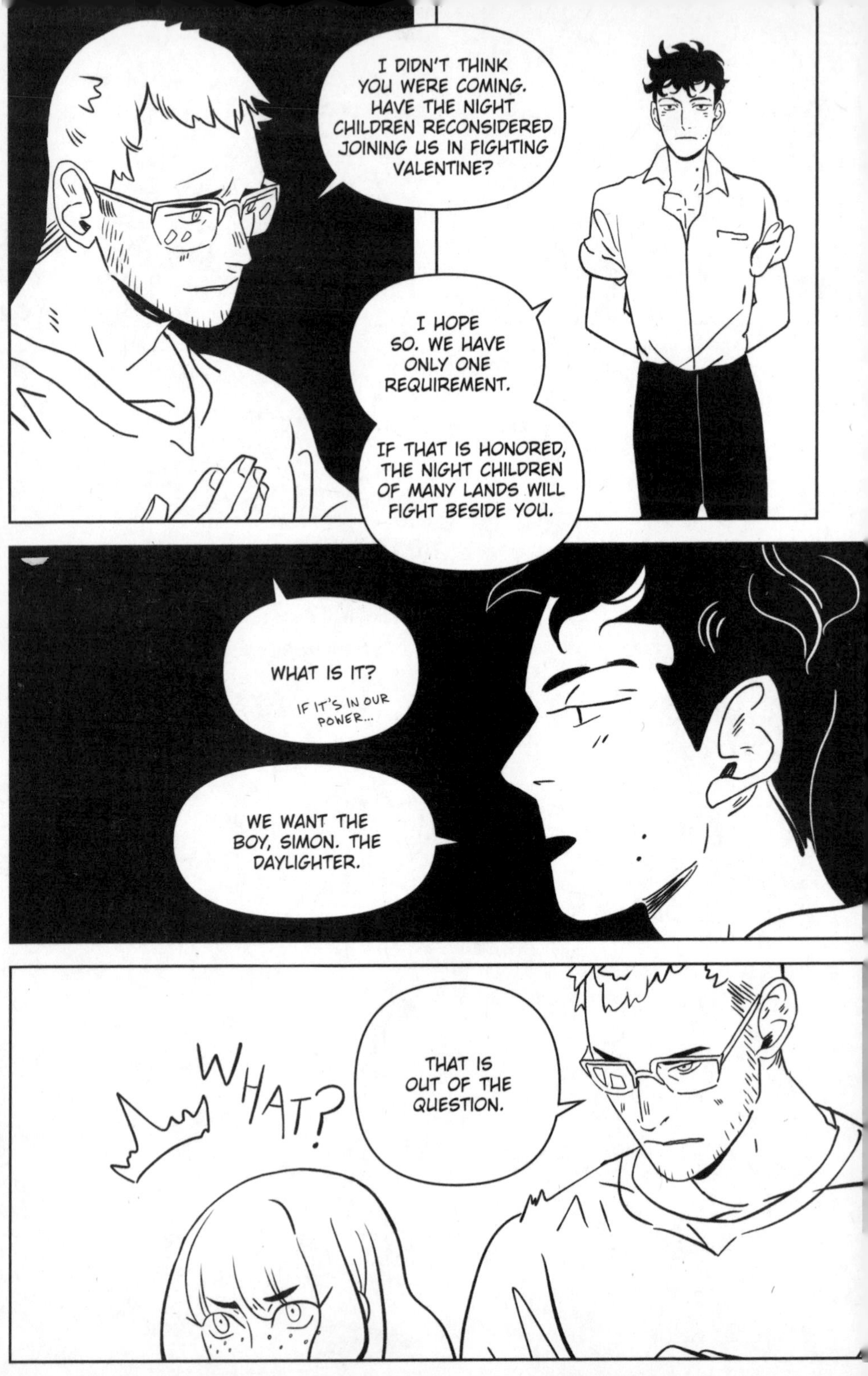
I DIDN'T THINK YOU WERE COMING. HAVE THE NIGHT CHILDREN RECONSIDERED JOINING US IN FIGHTING VALENTINE?
I HOPE SO. WE HAVE ONLY ONE REQUIREMENT.
IF THAT IS HONORED, THE NIGHT CHILDREN OF MANY LANDS WILL FIGHT BESIDE YOU.
WHAT IS IT?
IF IT'S IN OUR POWER...
WE WANT THE BOY, SIMON. THE DAYLIGHTER.
WHAT?
THAT IS OUT OF THE QUESTION.

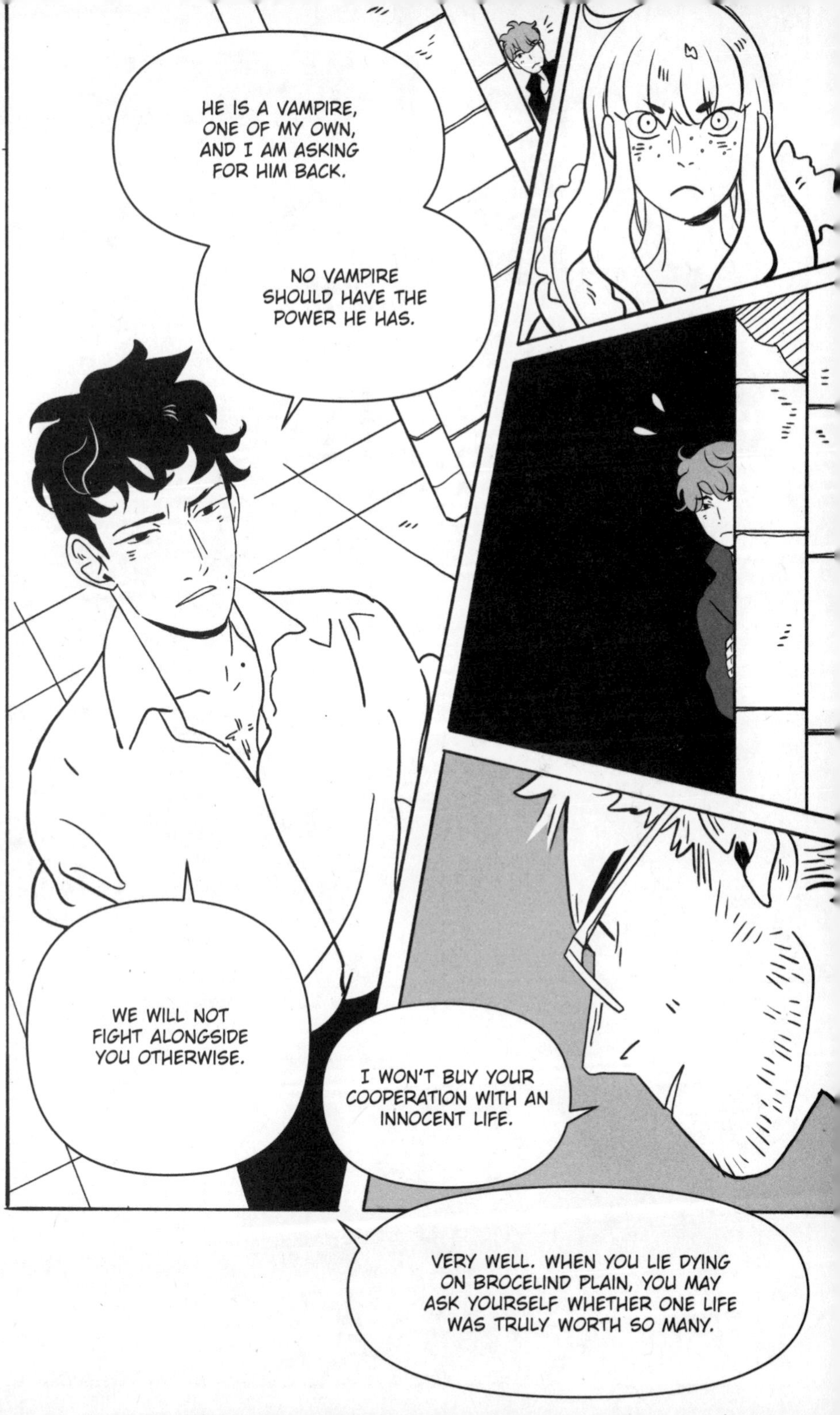
HE IS A VAMPIRE, ONE OF MY OWN, AND I AM ASKING FOR HIM BACK.
NO VAMPIRE SHOULD HAVE THE POWER HE HAS.
WE WILL NOT FIGHT ALONGSIDE YOU OTHERWISE.
I WON'T BUY YOUR COOPERATION WITH AN INNOCENT LIFE.
VERY WELL. WHEN YOU LIE DYING ON BROCELIND PLAIN, YOU MAY ASK YOURSELF WHETHER ONE LIFE WAS TRULY WORTH SO MANY.

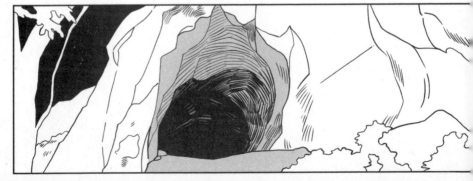

MURMUR

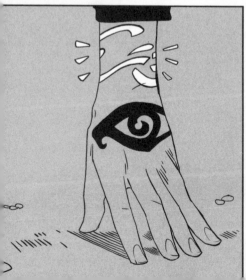

MURMUR

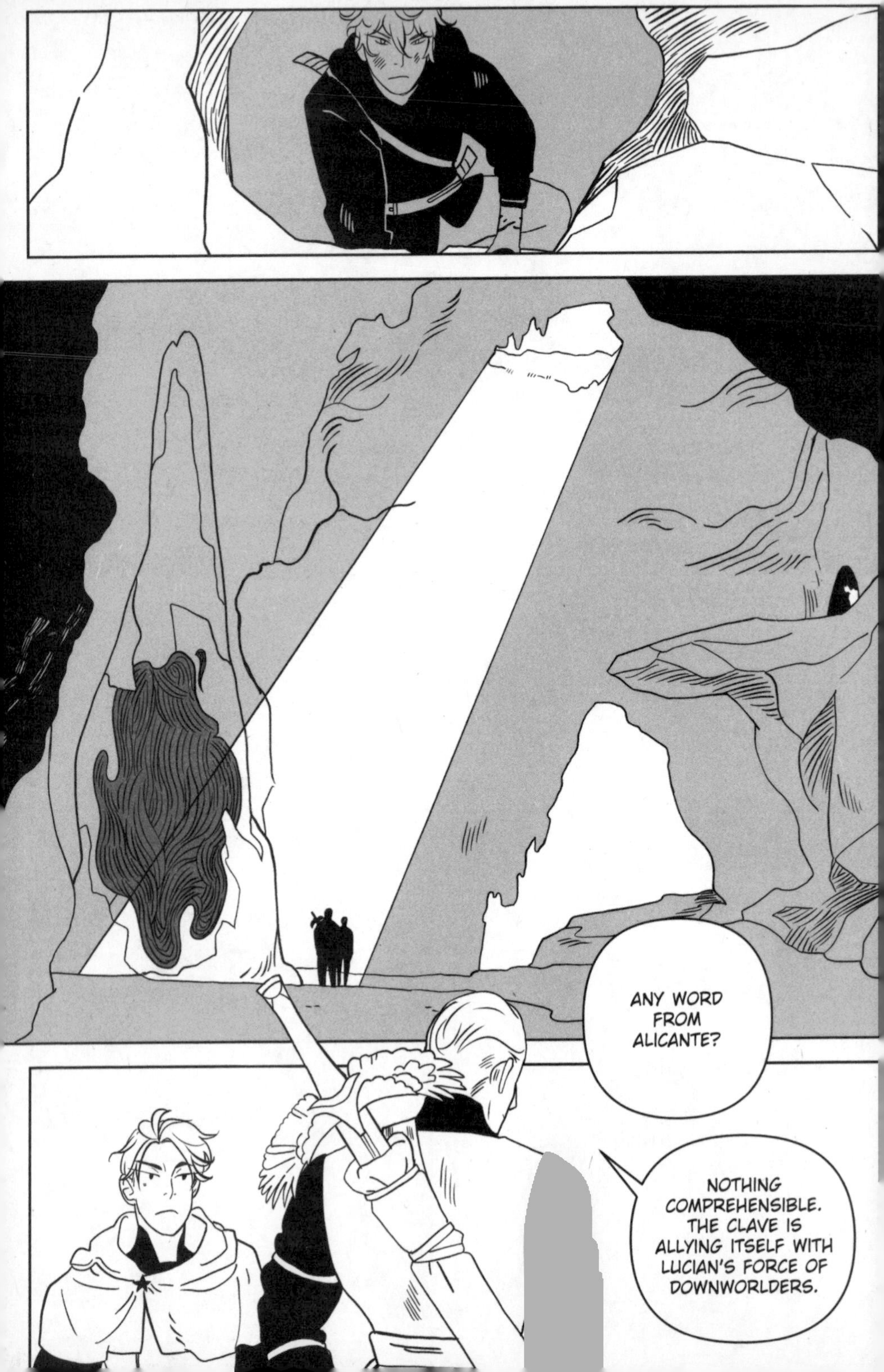
ANY WORD FROM ALICANTE?
NOTHING COMPREHENSIBLE. THE CLAVE IS ALLYING ITSELF WITH LUCIAN'S FORCE OF DOWNWORLDERS.

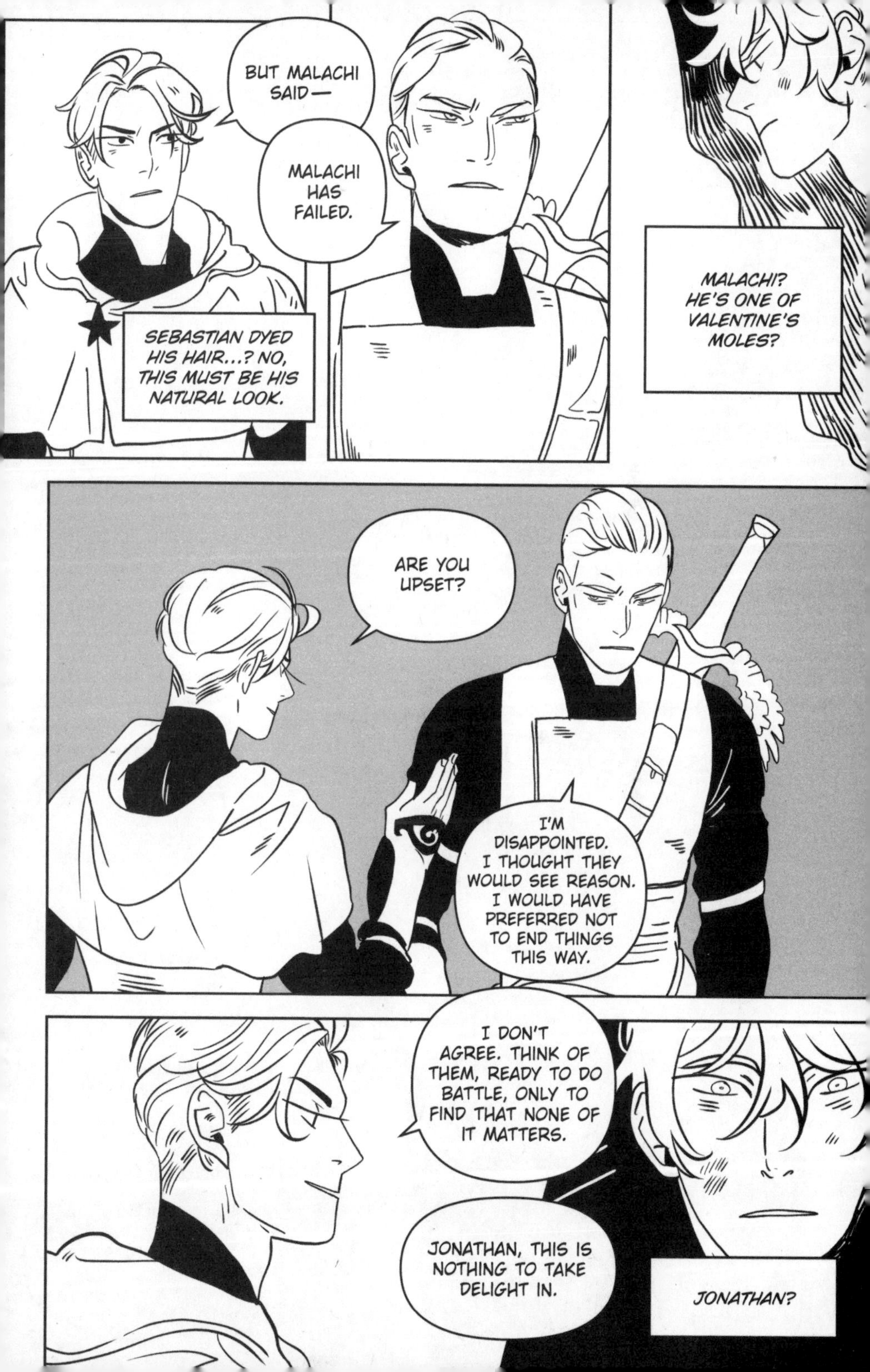
BUT MALACHI SAID—
MALACHI HAS FAILED.
SEBASTIAN DYED HIS HAIR...? NO, THIS MUST BE HIS NATURAL LOOK.
MALACHI? HE'S ONE OF VALENTINE'S MOLES?
ARE YOU UPSET?
I'M DISAPPOINTED. I THOUGHT THEY WOULD SEE REASON. I WOULD HAVE PREFERRED NOT TO END THINGS THIS WAY.
I DON'T AGREE. THINK OF THEM, READY TO DO BATTLE, ONLY TO FIND THAT NONE OF IT MATTERS.
JONATHAN, THIS IS NOTHING TO TAKE DELIGHT IN.
JONATHAN?

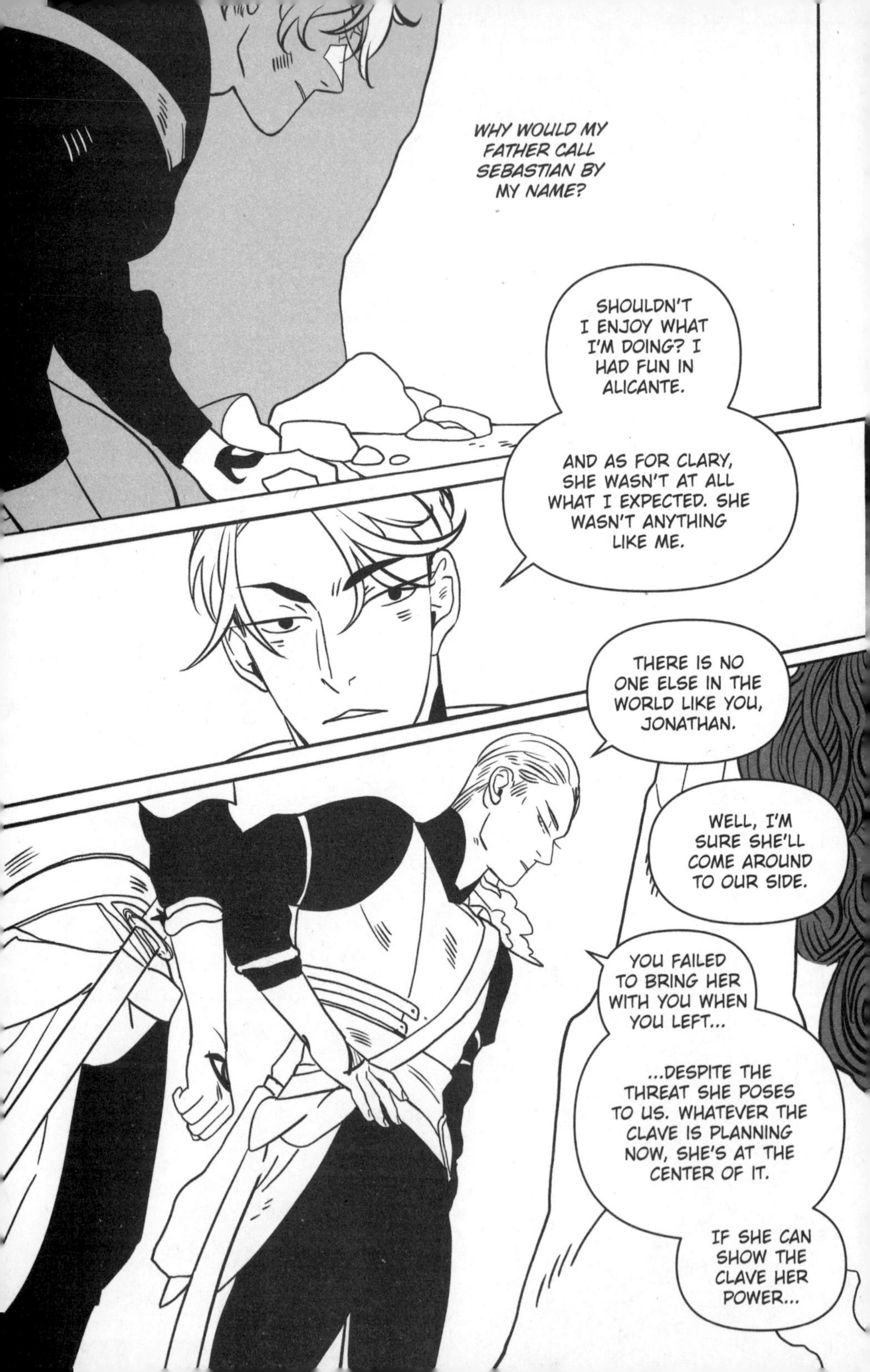
WHY WOULD MY FATHER CALL SEBASTIAN BY MY NAME?
SHOULDN'T I ENJOY WHAT I'M DOING? I HAD FUN IN ALICANTE.
AND AS FOR CLARY, SHE WASN'T AT ALL WHAT I EXPECTED. SHE WASN'T ANYTHING LIKE ME.
THERE IS NO ONE ELSE IN THE WORLD LIKE YOU, JONATHAN.
WELL, I'M SURE SHE'LL COME AROUND TO OUR SIDE.
YOU FAILED TO BRING HER WITH YOU WHEN YOU LEFT...
...DESPITE THE THREAT SHE POSES TO US. WHATEVER THE CLAVE IS PLANNING NOW, SHE'S AT THE CENTER OF IT.
IF SHE CAN SHOW THE CLAVE HER POWER...

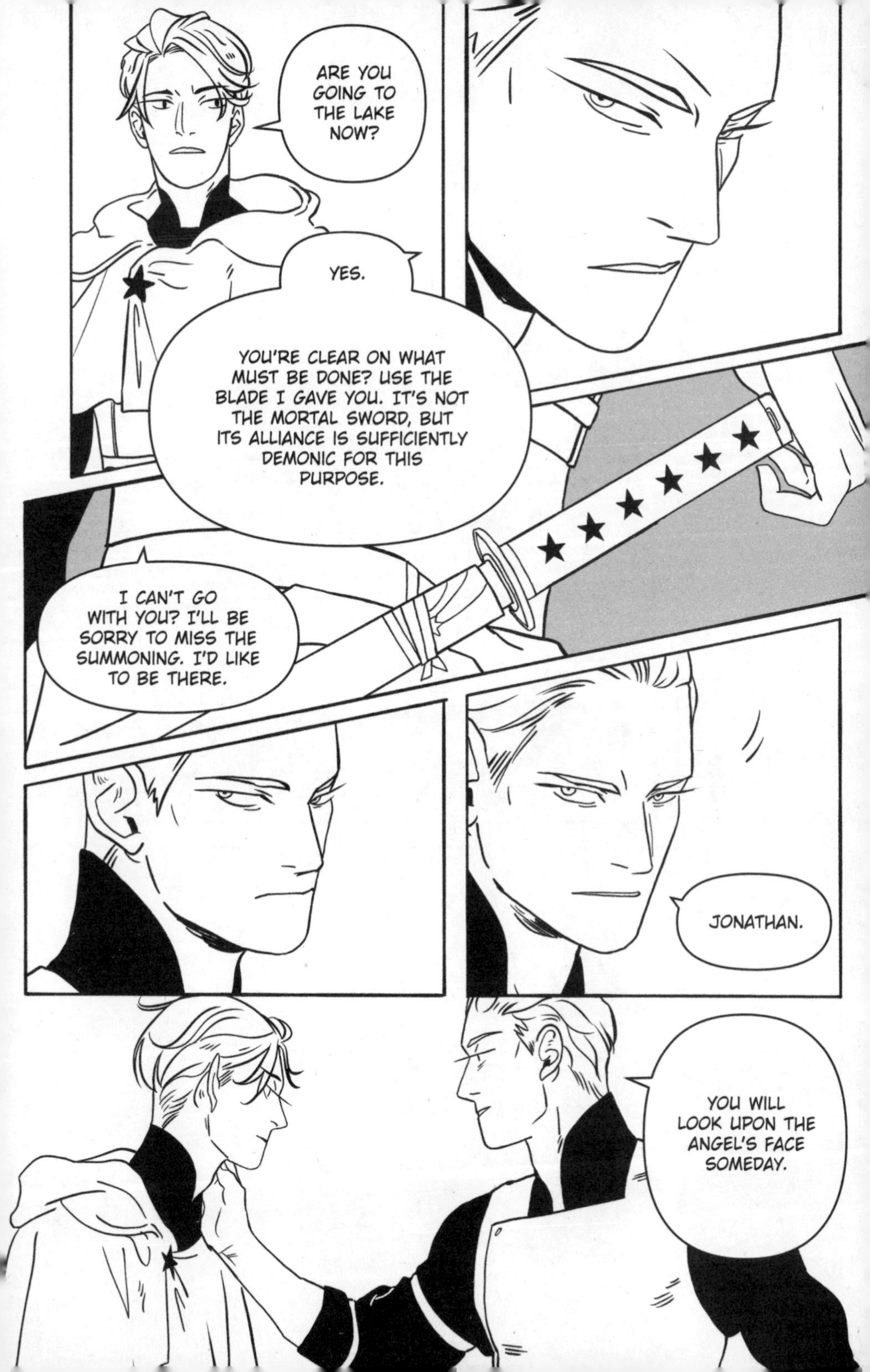
ARE YOU GOING TO THE LAKE NOW?
YES.
YOU'RE CLEAR ON WHAT MUST BE DONE? USE THE BLADE I GAVE YOU. IT'S NOT THE MORTAL SWORD, BUT ITS ALLIANCE IS SUFFICIENTLY DEMONIC FOR THIS PURPOSE.
I CAN'T GO WITH YOU? I'LL BE SORRY TO MISS THE SUMMONING. I'D LIKE TO BE THERE.
JONATHAN.
YOU WILL LOOK UPON THE ANGEL'S FACE SOMEDAY.

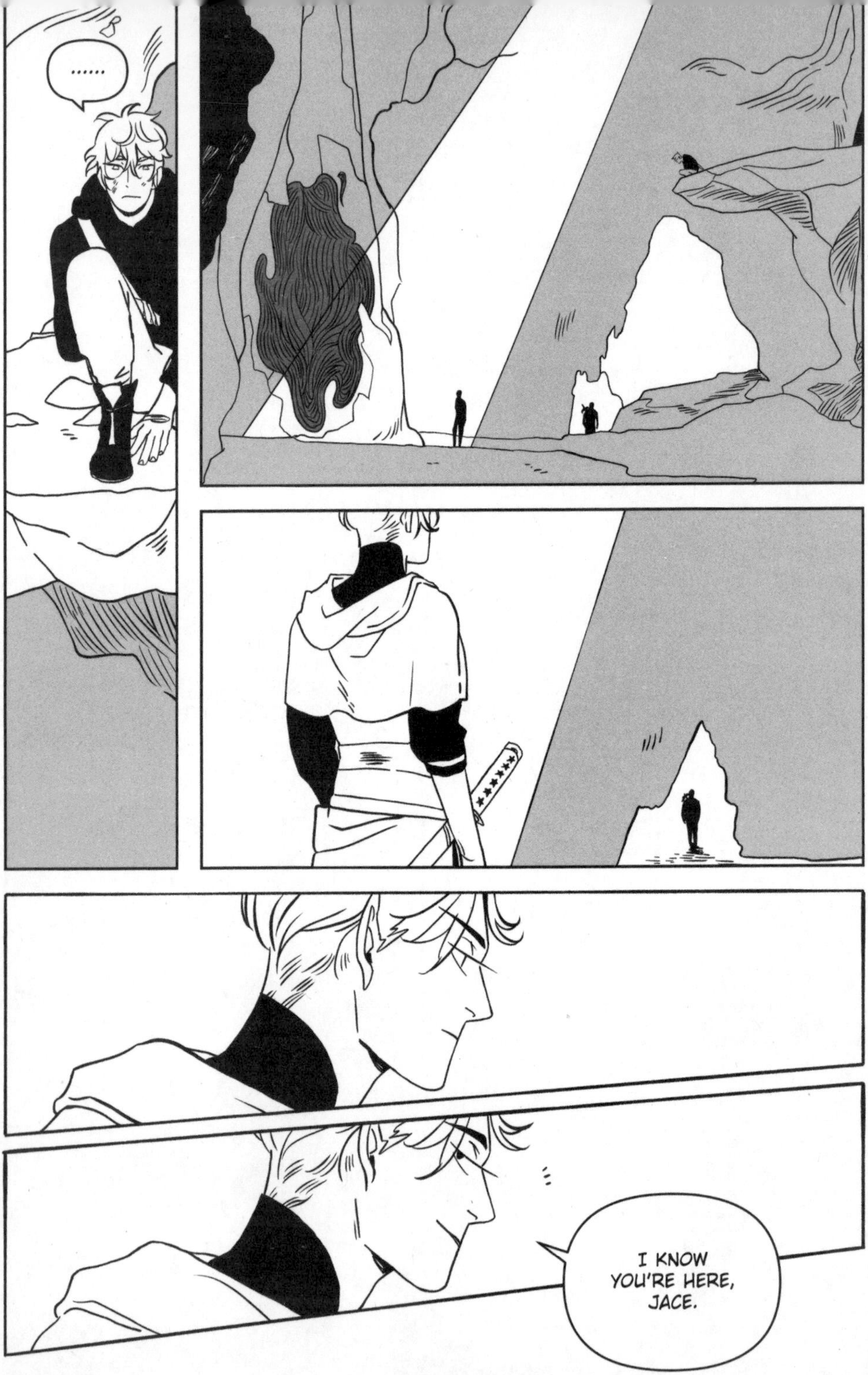

......
I KNOW YOU'RE HERE, JACE.

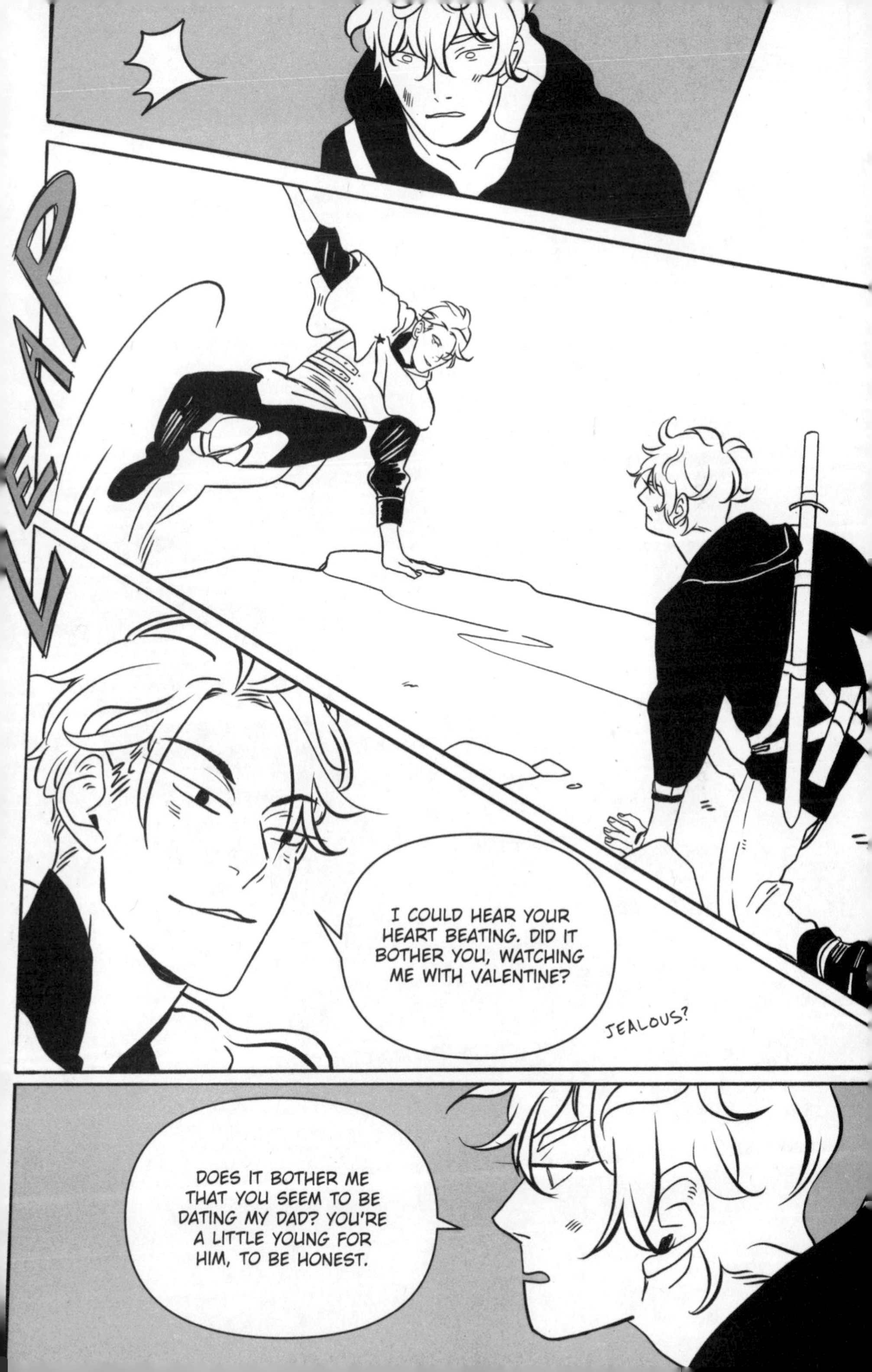
LEAP
I COULD HEAR YOUR HEART BEATING. DID IT BOTHER YOU, WATCHING ME WITH VALENTINE?
JEALOUS?
DOES IT BOTHER ME THAT YOU SEEM TO BE DATING MY DAD? YOU'RE A LITTLE YOUNG FOR HIM, TO BE HONEST.

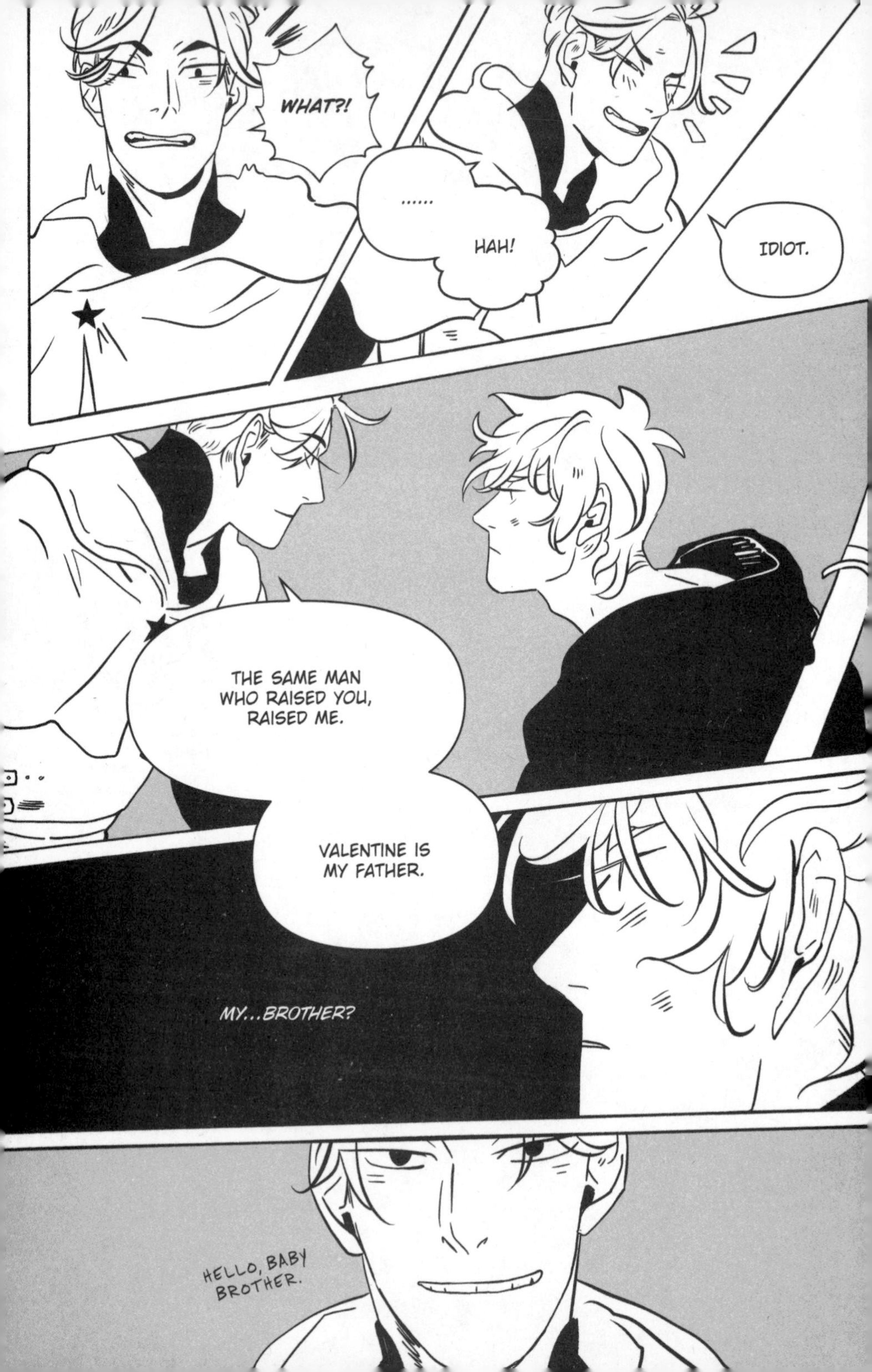
WHAT?!
......
HAH!
IDIOT.
THE SAME MAN WHO RAISED YOU, RAISED ME.
VALENTINE IS MY FATHER.
MY...BROTHER?
HELLO, BABY BROTHER.

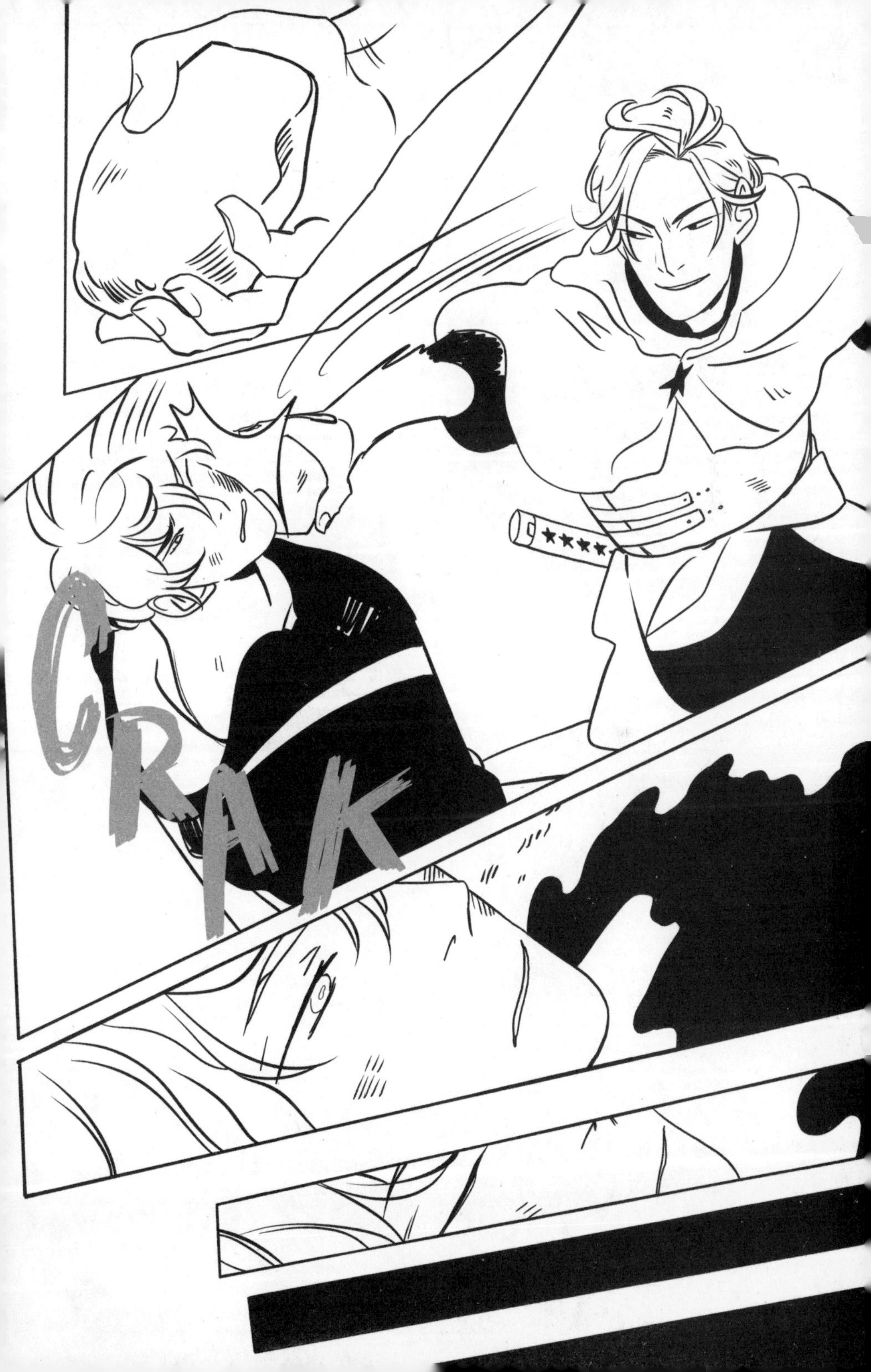
CRAK

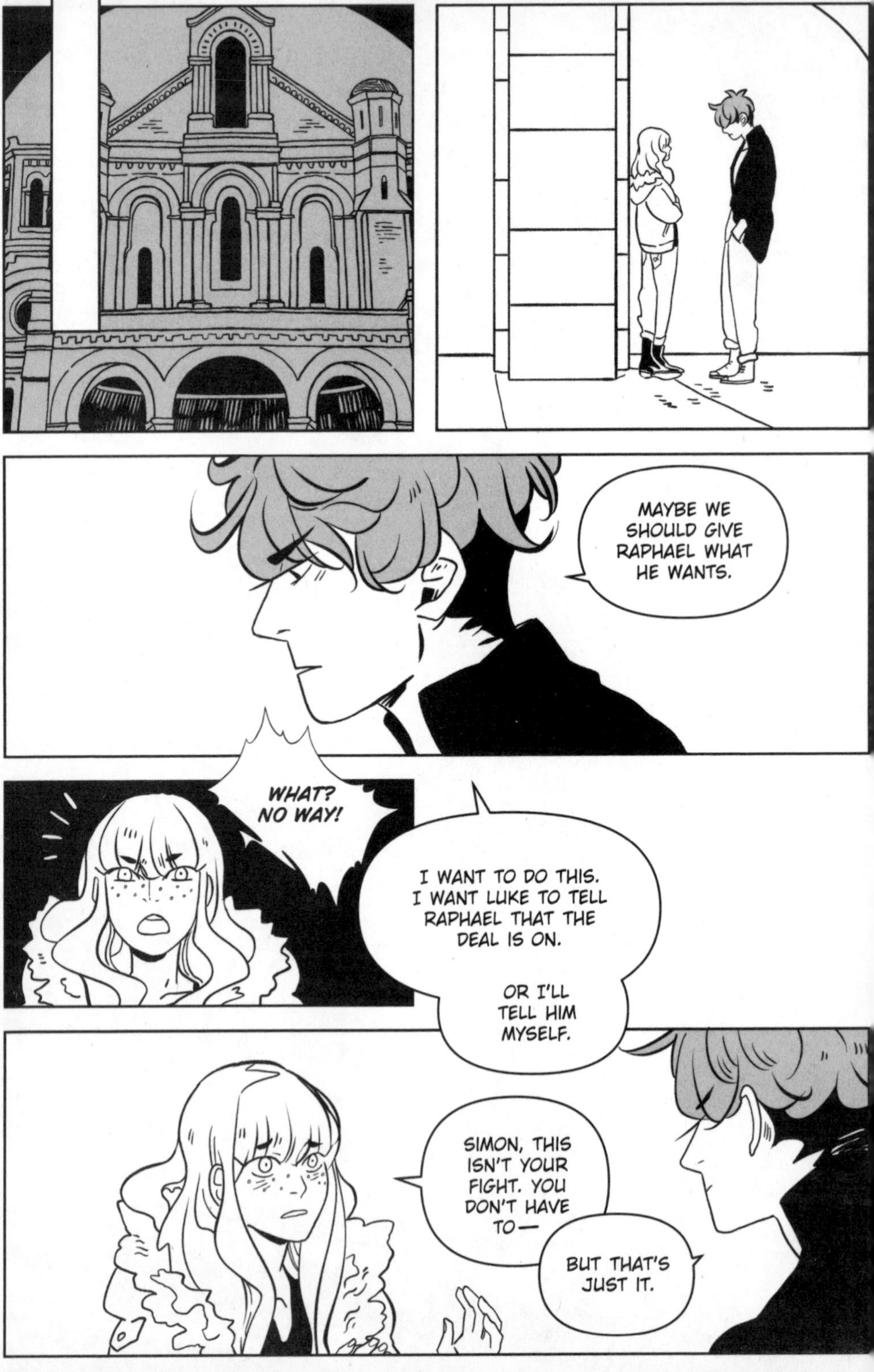

MAYBE WE SHOULD GIVE RAPHAEL WHAT HE WANTS.
WHAT? NO WAY!
I WANT TO DO THIS. I WANT LUKE TO TELL RAPHAEL THAT THE DEAL IS ON.
OR I'LL TELL HIM MYSELF.
SIMON, THIS ISN'T YOUR FIGHT. YOU DON'T HAVE TO—
BUT THAT'S JUST IT.

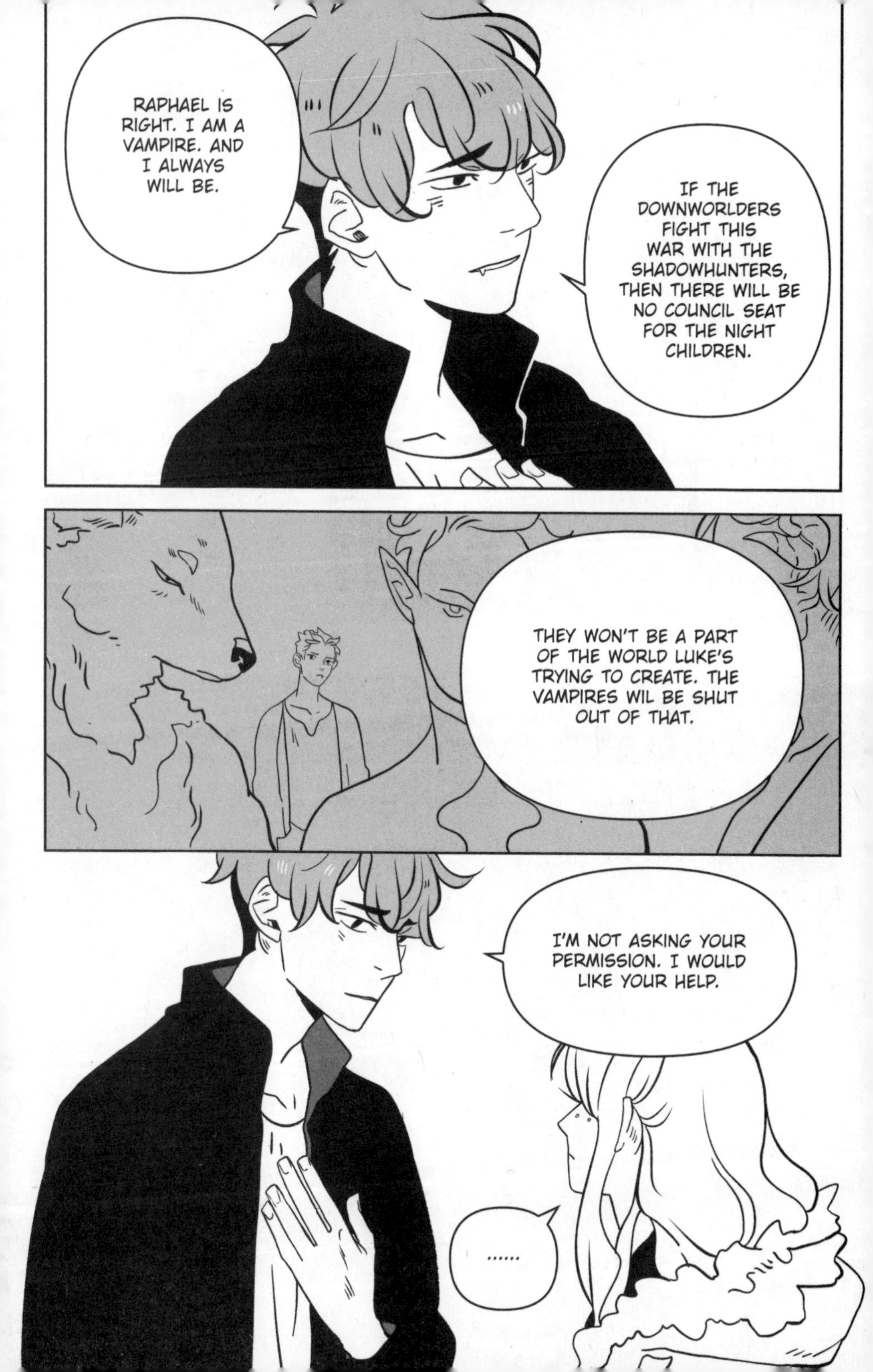
RAPHAEL IS RIGHT. I AM A VAMPIRE. AND I ALWAYS WILL BE.
IF THE DOWNWORLDERS FIGHT THIS WAR WITH THE SHADOWHUNTERS, THEN THERE WILL BE NO COUNCIL SEAT FOR THE NIGHT CHILDREN.
THEY WON'T BE A PART OF THE WORLD LUKE'S TRYING TO CREATE. THE VAMPIRES WIL BE SHUT OUT OF THAT.
I'M NOT ASKING YOUR PERMISSION. I WOULD LIKE YOUR HELP.
......

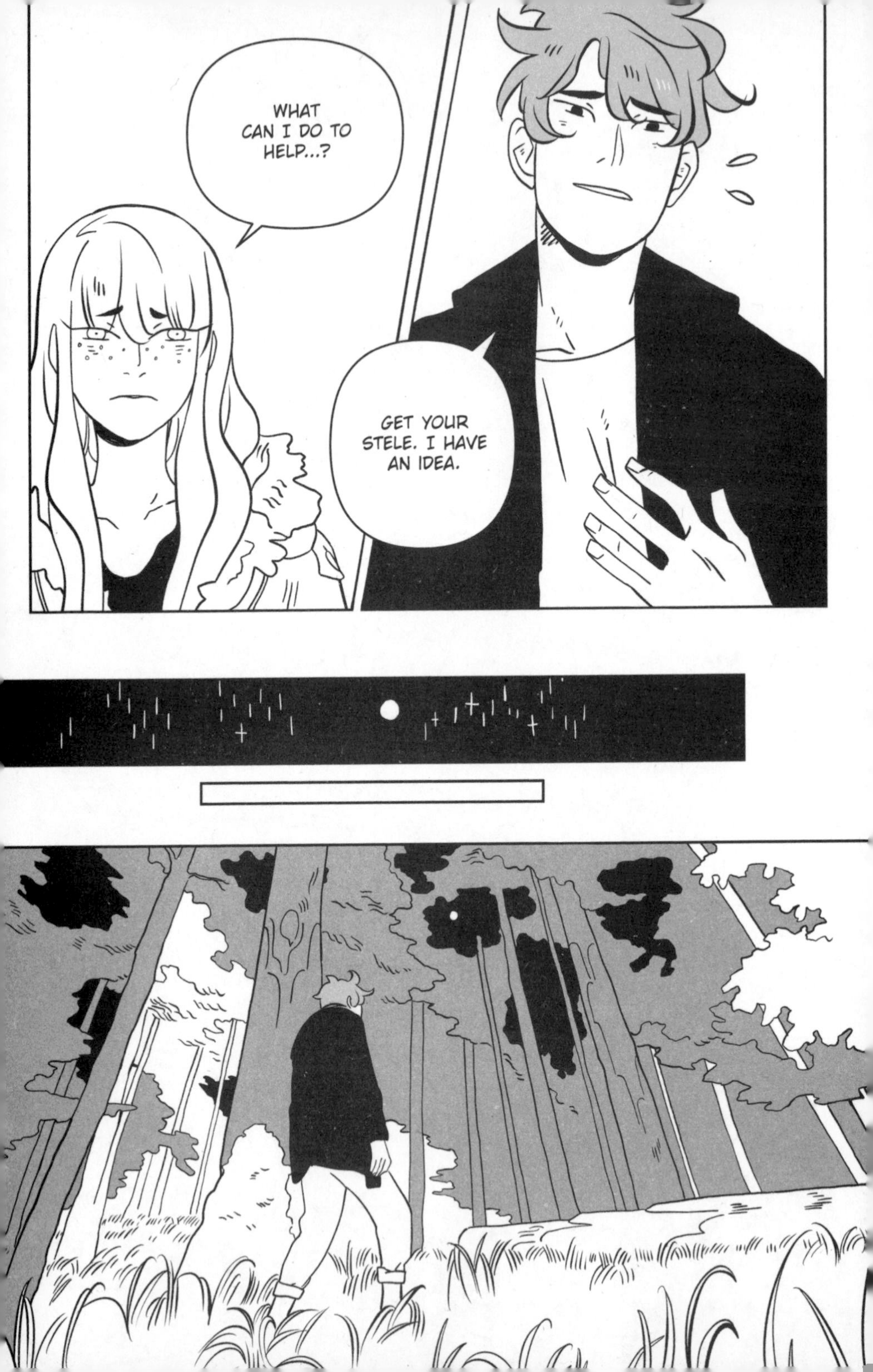
WHAT CAN I DO TO HELP...?
GET YOUR STELE. I HAVE AN IDEA.

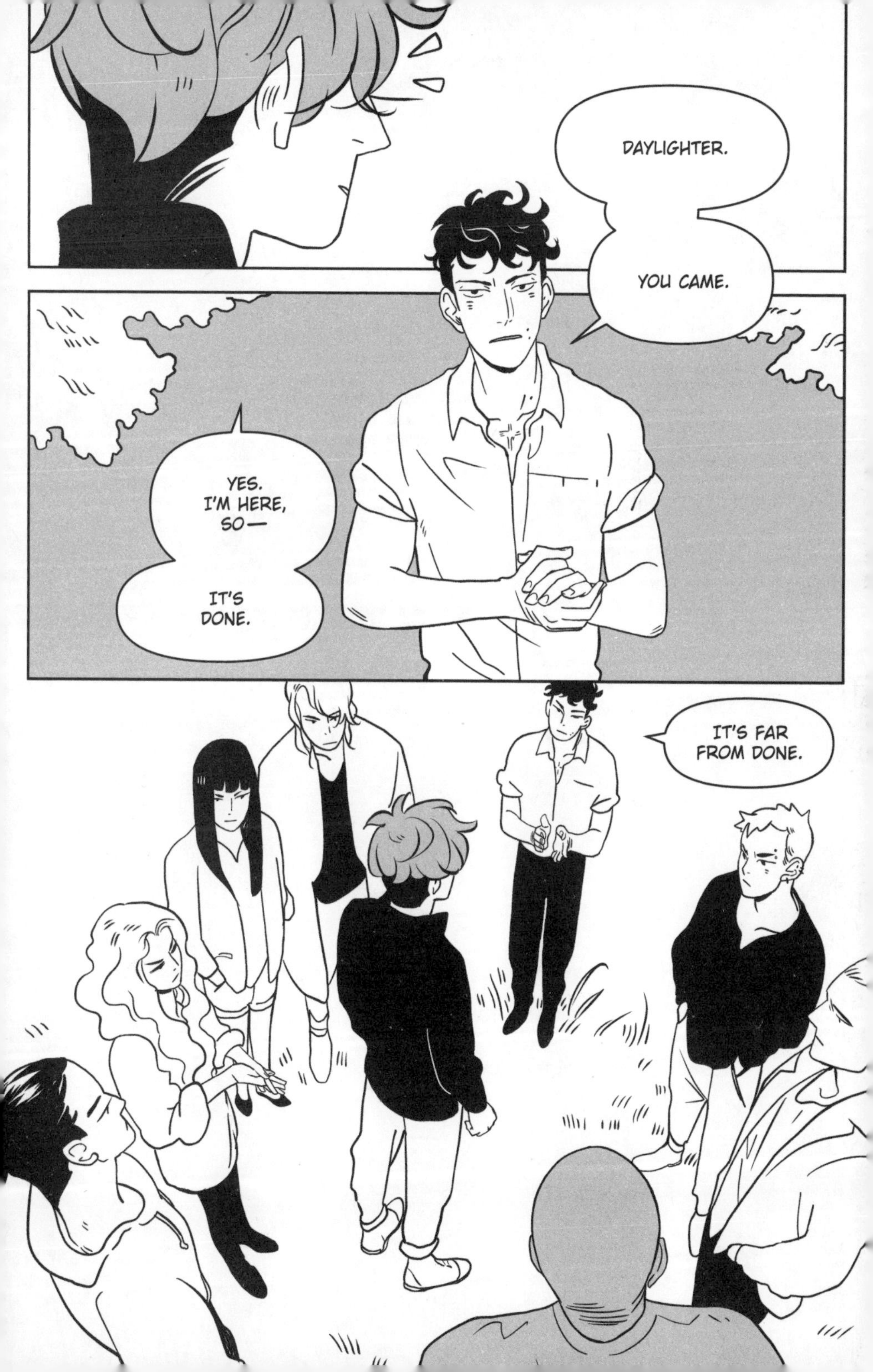
DAYLIGHTER.
YOU CAME.
YES. I'M HERE, SO—
IT'S DONE.
IT'S FAR FROM DONE.

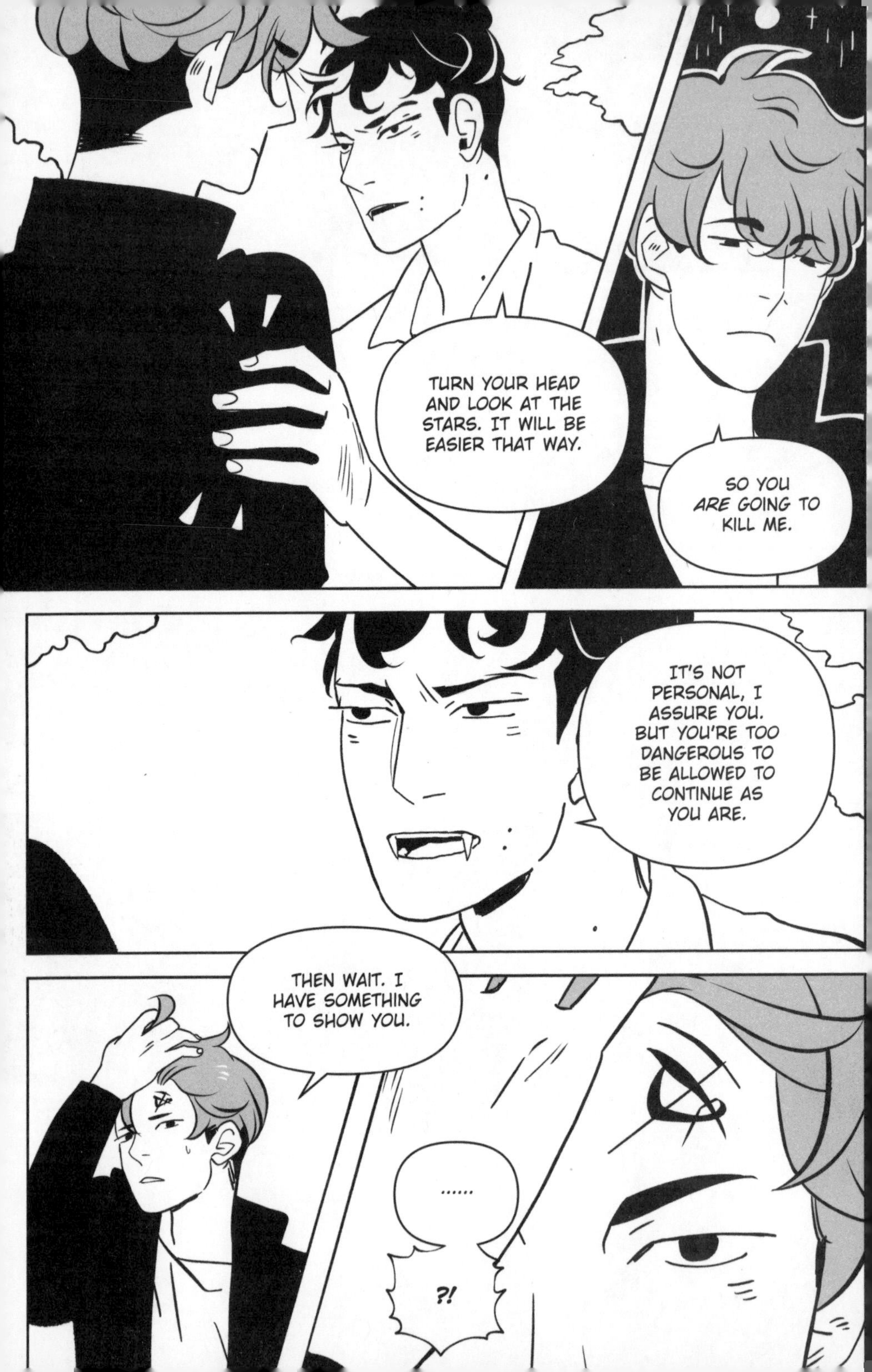
TURN YOUR HEAD AND LOOK AT THE STARS. IT WILL BE EASIER THAT WAY.
SO YOU ARE GOING TO KILL ME.
IT'S NOT PERSONAL, I ASSURE YOU. BUT YOU'RE TOO DANGEROUS TO BE ALLOWED TO CONTINUE AS YOU ARE.
THEN WAIT. I HAVE SOMETHING TO SHOW YOU.
......
?!

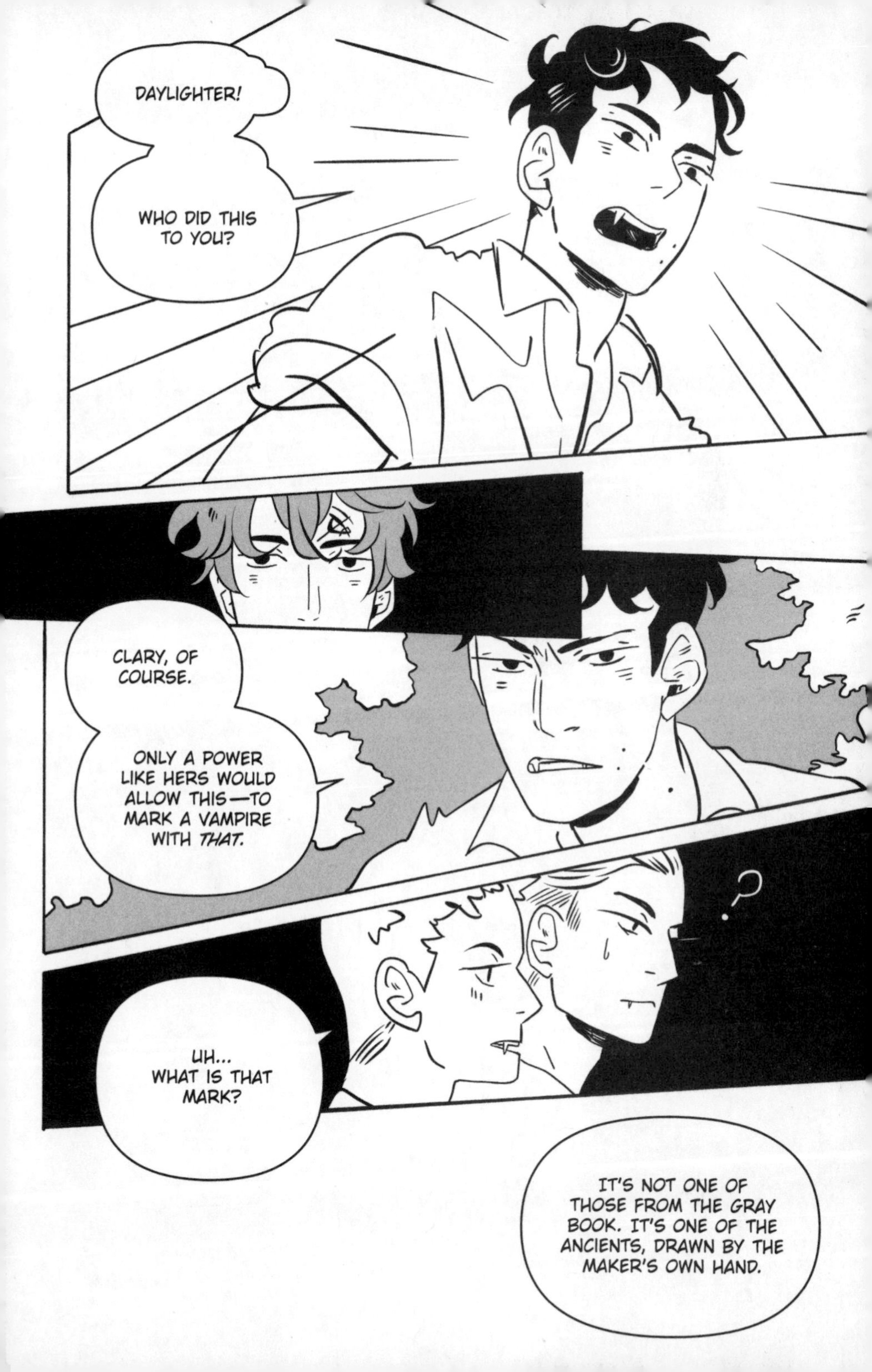
DAYLIGHTER!
WHO DID THIS TO YOU?
CLARY, OF COURSE.
ONLY A POWER LIKE HERS WOULD ALLOW THIS—TO MARK A VAMPIRE WITH *THAT*.
?
UH... WHAT IS THAT MARK?
IT'S NOT ONE OF THOSE FROM THE GRAY BOOK. IT'S ONE OF THE ANCIENTS, DRAWN BY THE MAKER'S OWN HAND.

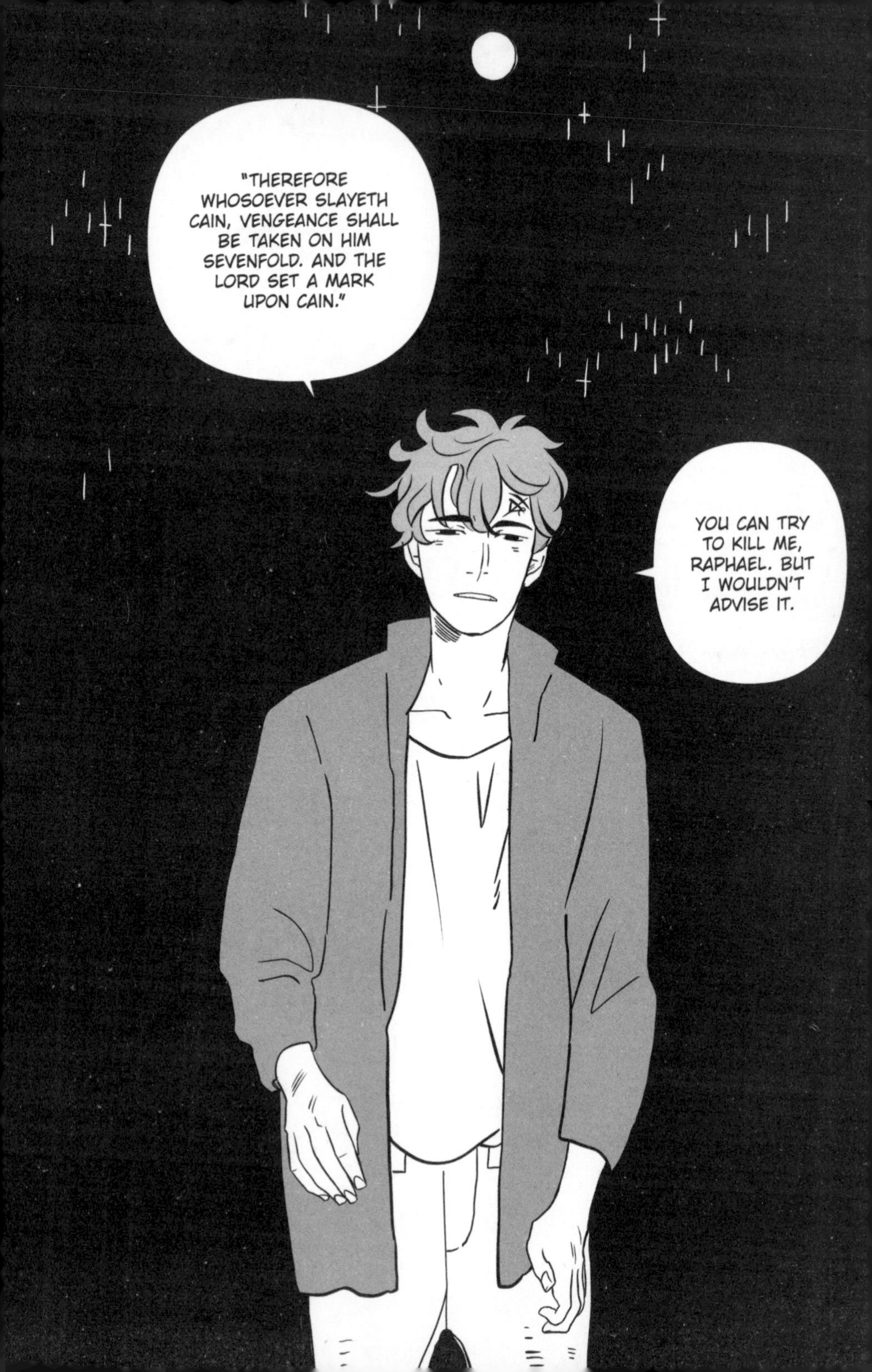
"THEREFORE WHOSOEVER SLAYETH CAIN, VENGEANCE SHALL BE TAKEN ON HIM SEVENFOLD. AND THE LORD SET A MARK UPON CAIN."
YOU CAN TRY TO KILL ME, RAPHAEL. BUT I WOULDN'T ADVISE IT.

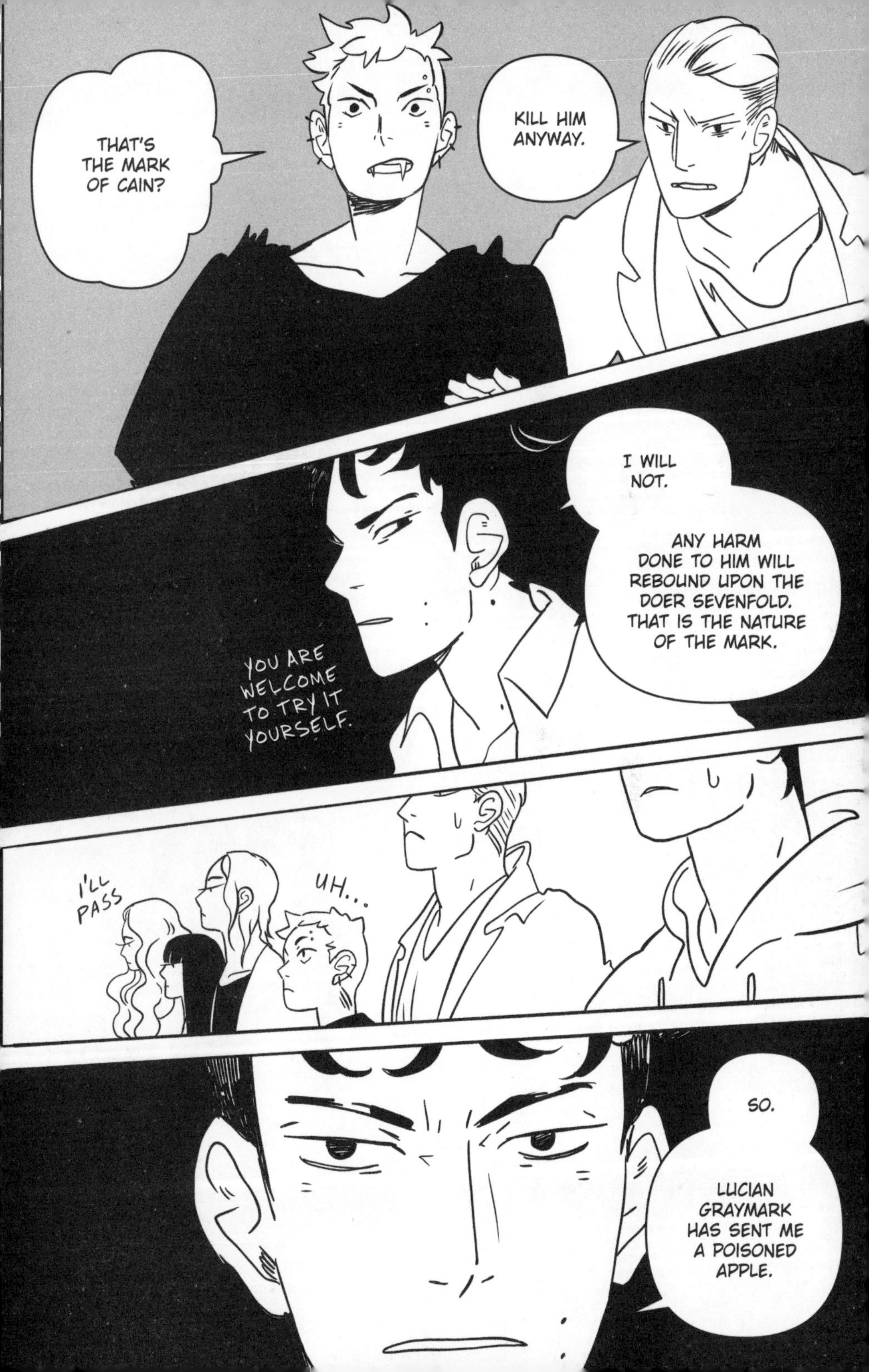
THAT'S THE MARK OF CAIN?
KILL HIM ANYWAY.
I WILL NOT.
ANY HARM DONE TO HIM WILL REBOUND UPON THE DOER SEVENFOLD. THAT IS THE NATURE OF THE MARK.
YOU ARE WELCOME TO TRY IT YOURSELF.
I'LL PASS
UH...
SO.
LUCIAN GRAYMARK HAS SENT ME A POISONED APPLE.

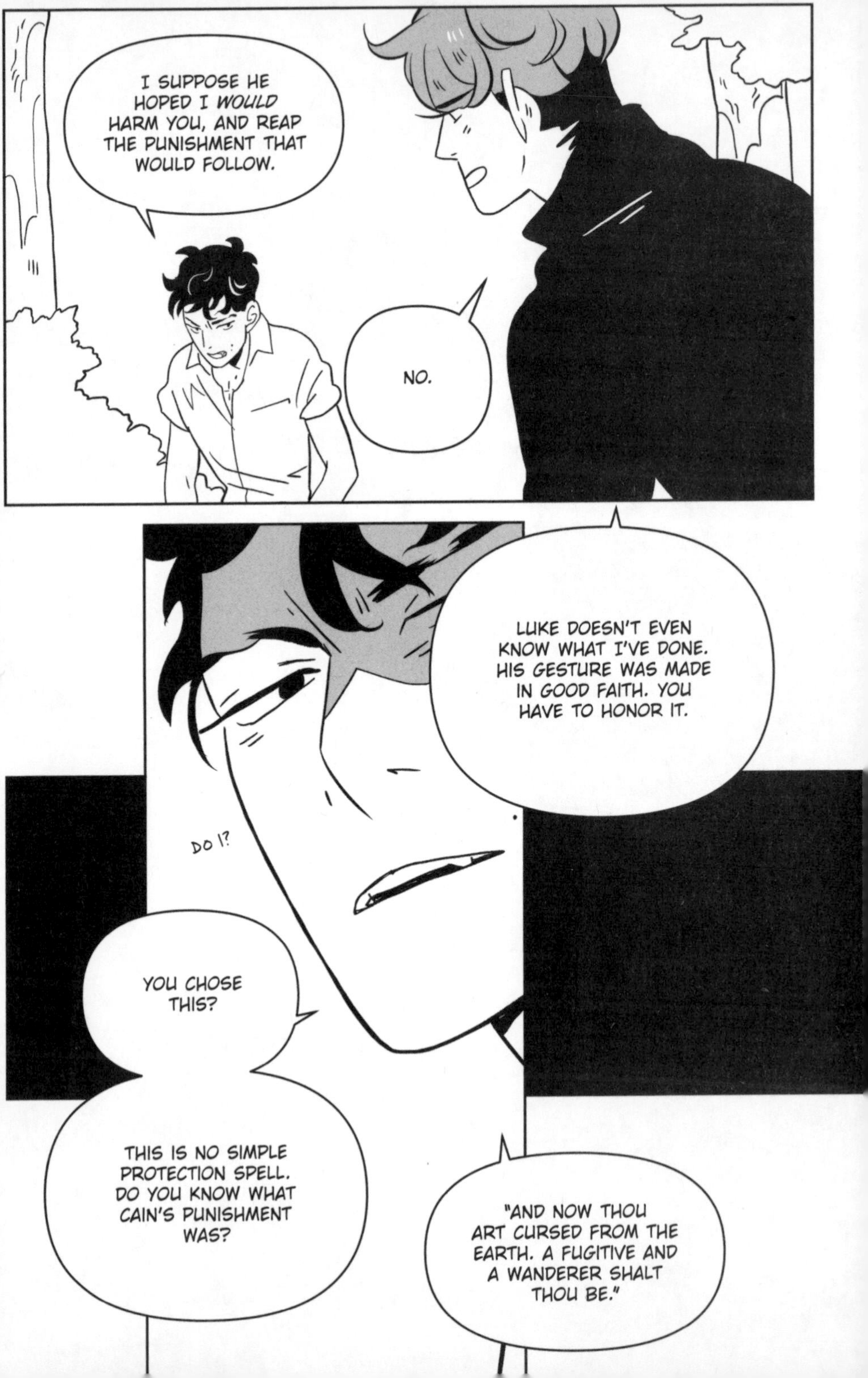
I SUPPOSE HE HOPED I *WOULD* HARM YOU, AND REAP THE PUNISHMENT THAT WOULD FOLLOW.
NO.
LUKE DOESN'T EVEN KNOW WHAT I'VE DONE. HIS GESTURE WAS MADE IN GOOD FAITH. YOU HAVE TO HONOR IT.
DO I?
YOU CHOSE THIS?
THIS IS NO SIMPLE PROTECTION SPELL. DO YOU KNOW WHAT CAIN'S PUNISHMENT WAS?
"AND NOW THOU ART CURSED FROM THE EARTH. A FUGITIVE AND A WANDERER SHALT THOU BE."

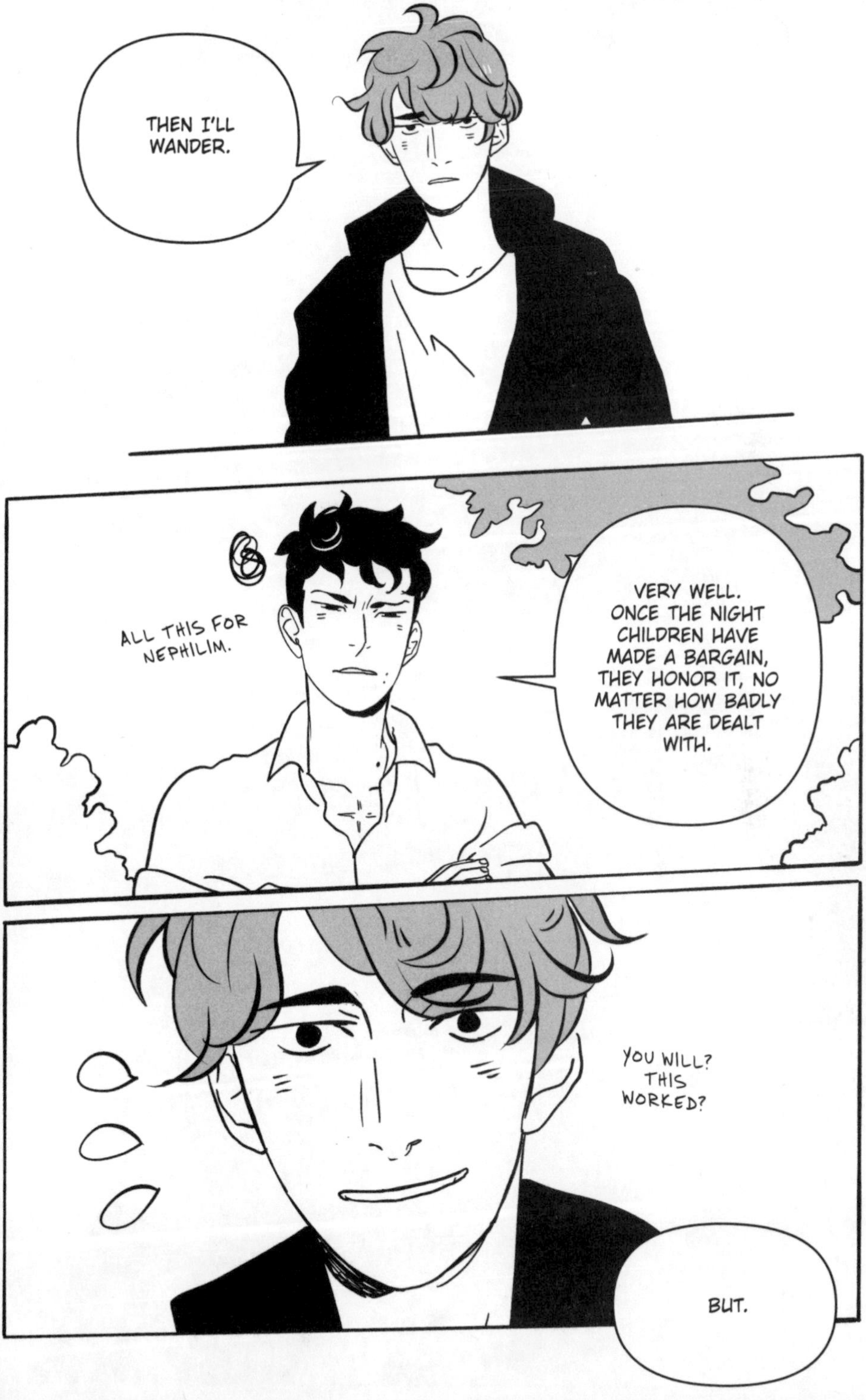
THEN I'LL WANDER.
ALL THIS FOR NEPHILIM.
VERY WELL. ONCE THE NIGHT CHILDREN HAVE MADE A BARGAIN, THEY HONOR IT, NO MATTER HOW BADLY THEY ARE DEALT WITH.
YOU WILL? THIS WORKED?
BUT.

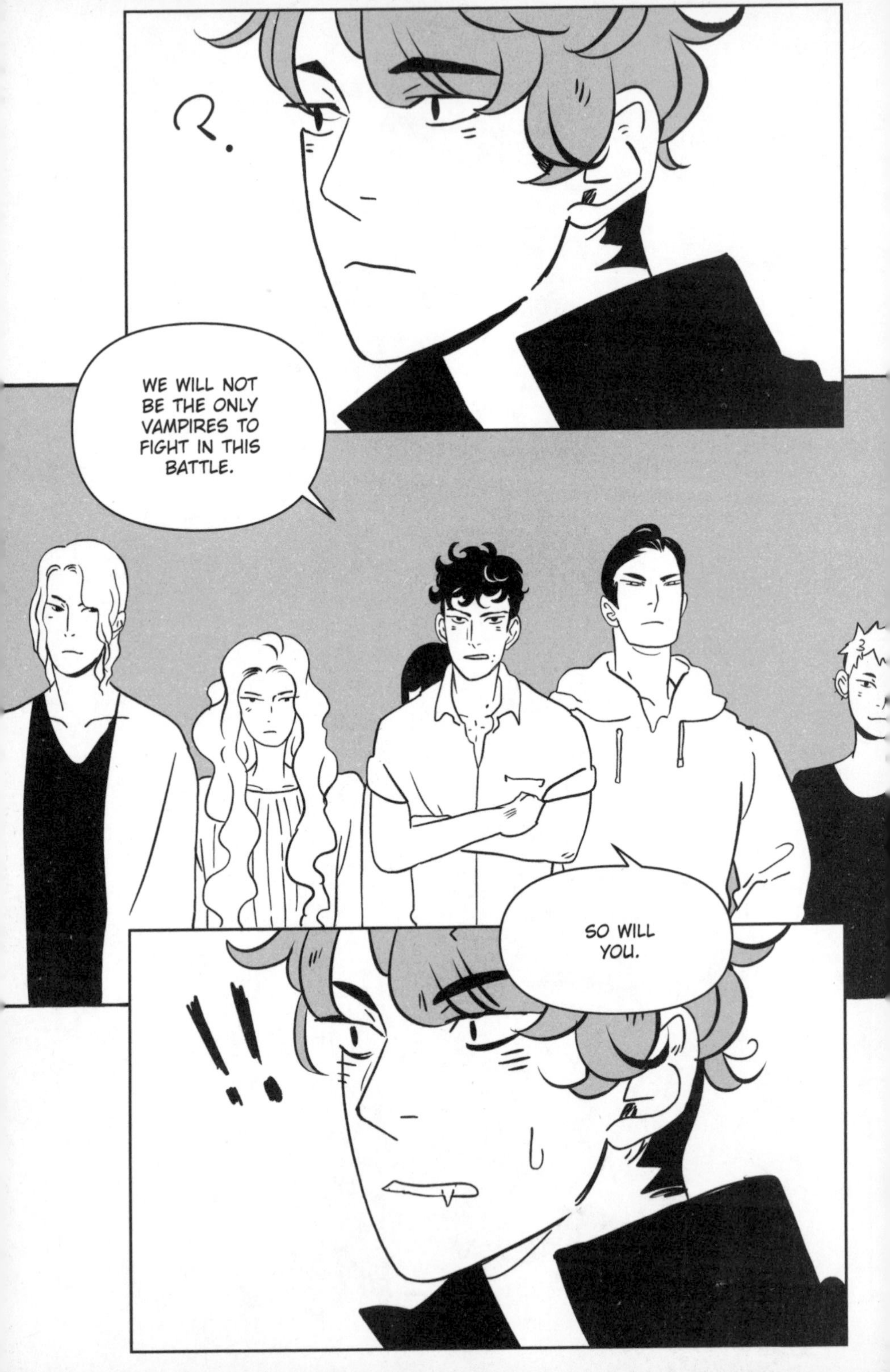
?..
WE WILL NOT BE THE ONLY VAMPIRES TO FIGHT IN THIS BATTLE.
SO WILL YOU.
!!..

THE MORTAL INSTRUMENTS

THE GRAPHIC NOVEL

THE MORTAL INSTRUMENTS
THE GRAPHIC NOVEL

CHAPTER 35

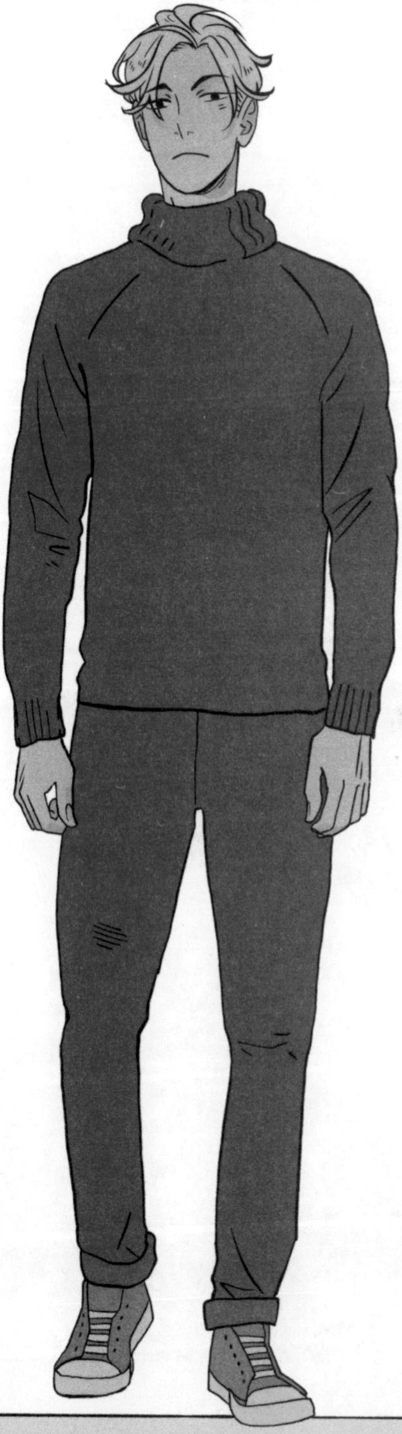

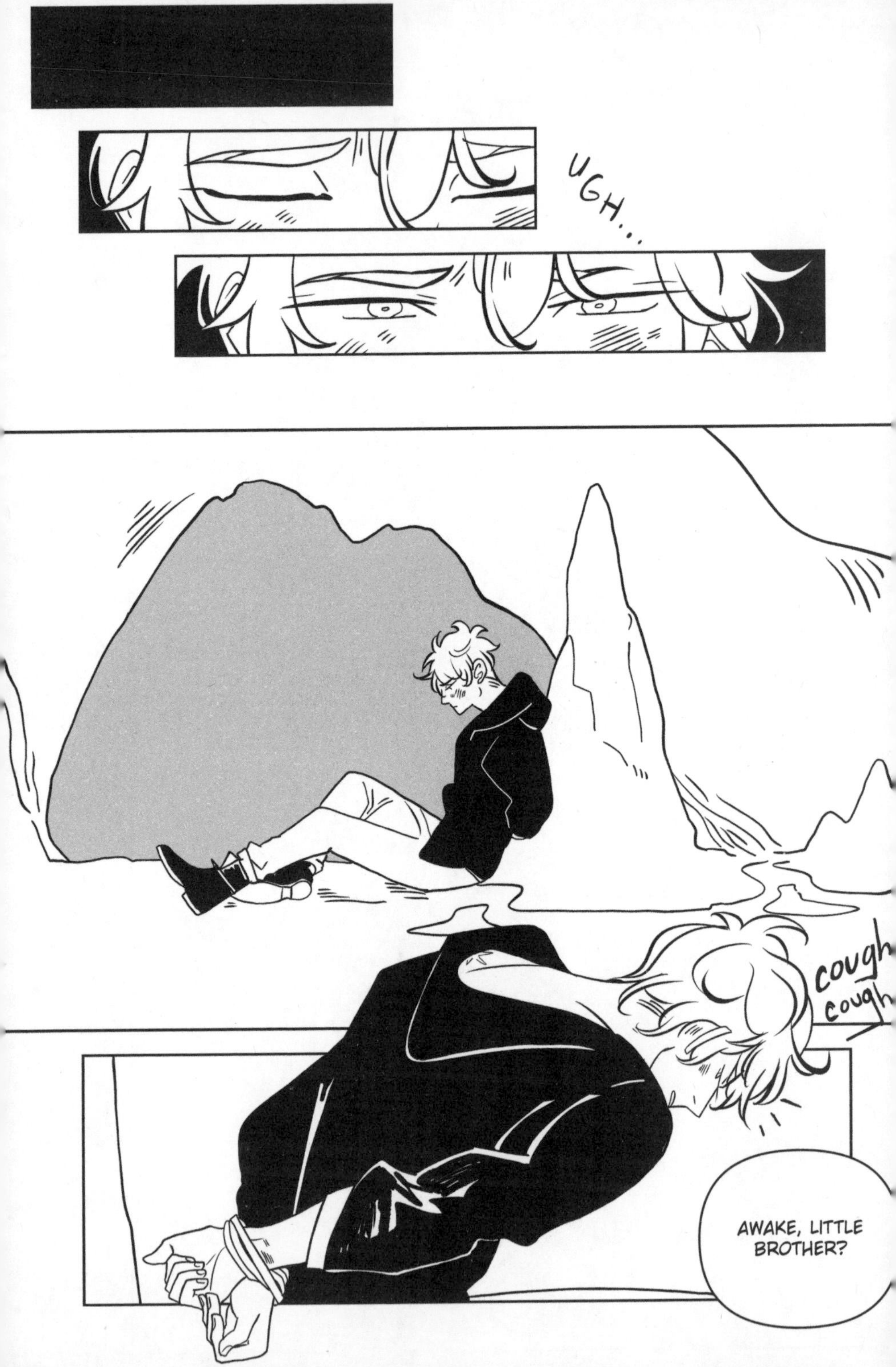
UGH...
cough
cough
AWAKE, LITTLE BROTHER?

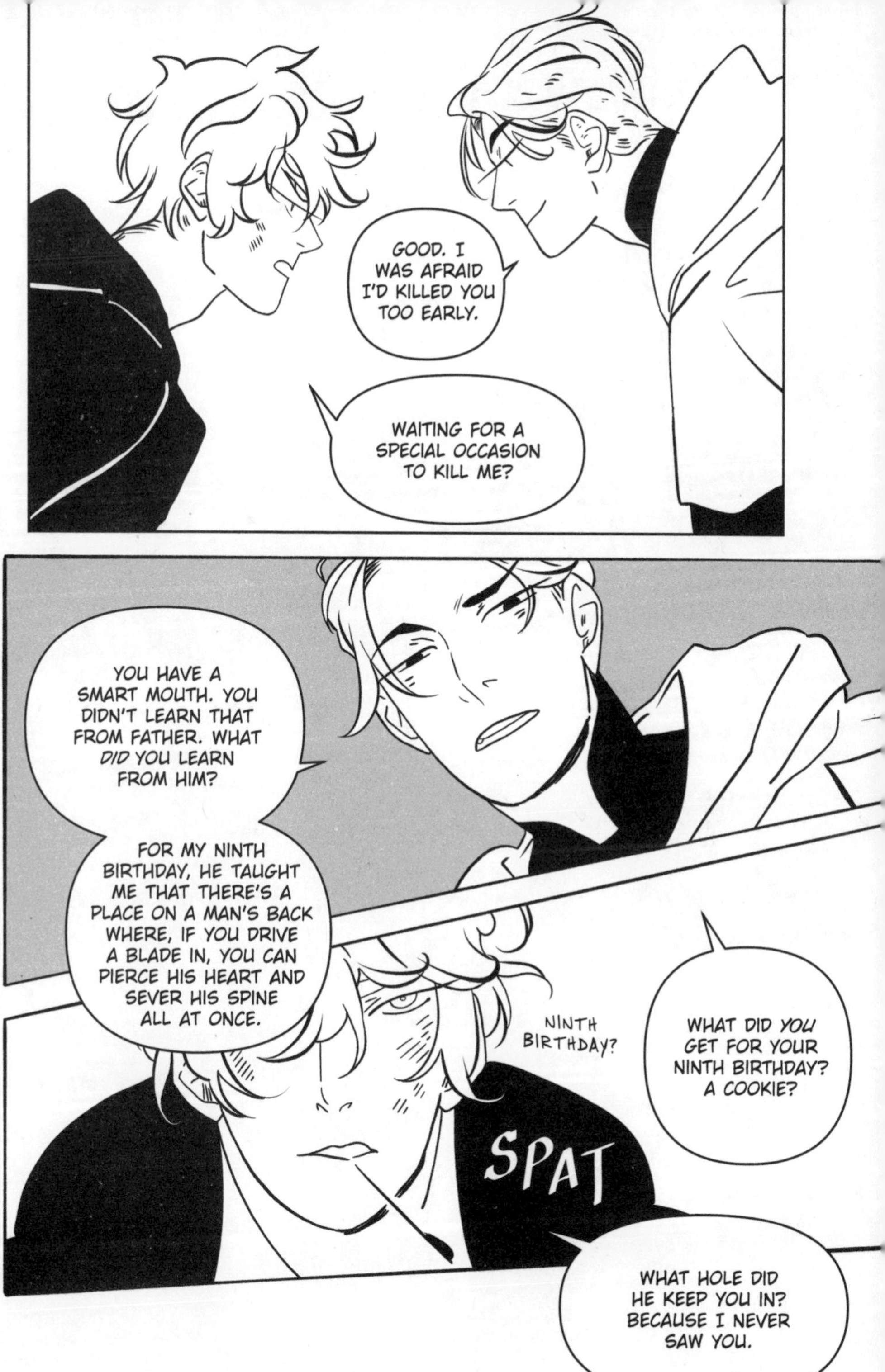
GOOD. I WAS AFRAID I'D KILLED YOU TOO EARLY.
WAITING FOR A SPECIAL OCCASION TO KILL ME?
YOU HAVE A SMART MOUTH. YOU DIDN'T LEARN THAT FROM FATHER. WHAT *DID* YOU LEARN FROM HIM?
FOR MY NINTH BIRTHDAY, HE TAUGHT ME THAT THERE'S A PLACE ON A MAN'S BACK WHERE, IF YOU DRIVE A BLADE IN, YOU CAN PIERCE HIS HEART AND SEVER HIS SPINE ALL AT ONCE.
NINTH BIRTHDAY?
WHAT DID *YOU* GET FOR YOUR NINTH BIRTHDAY? A COOKIE?
SPAT
WHAT HOLE DID HE KEEP YOU IN? BECAUSE I NEVER SAW YOU.

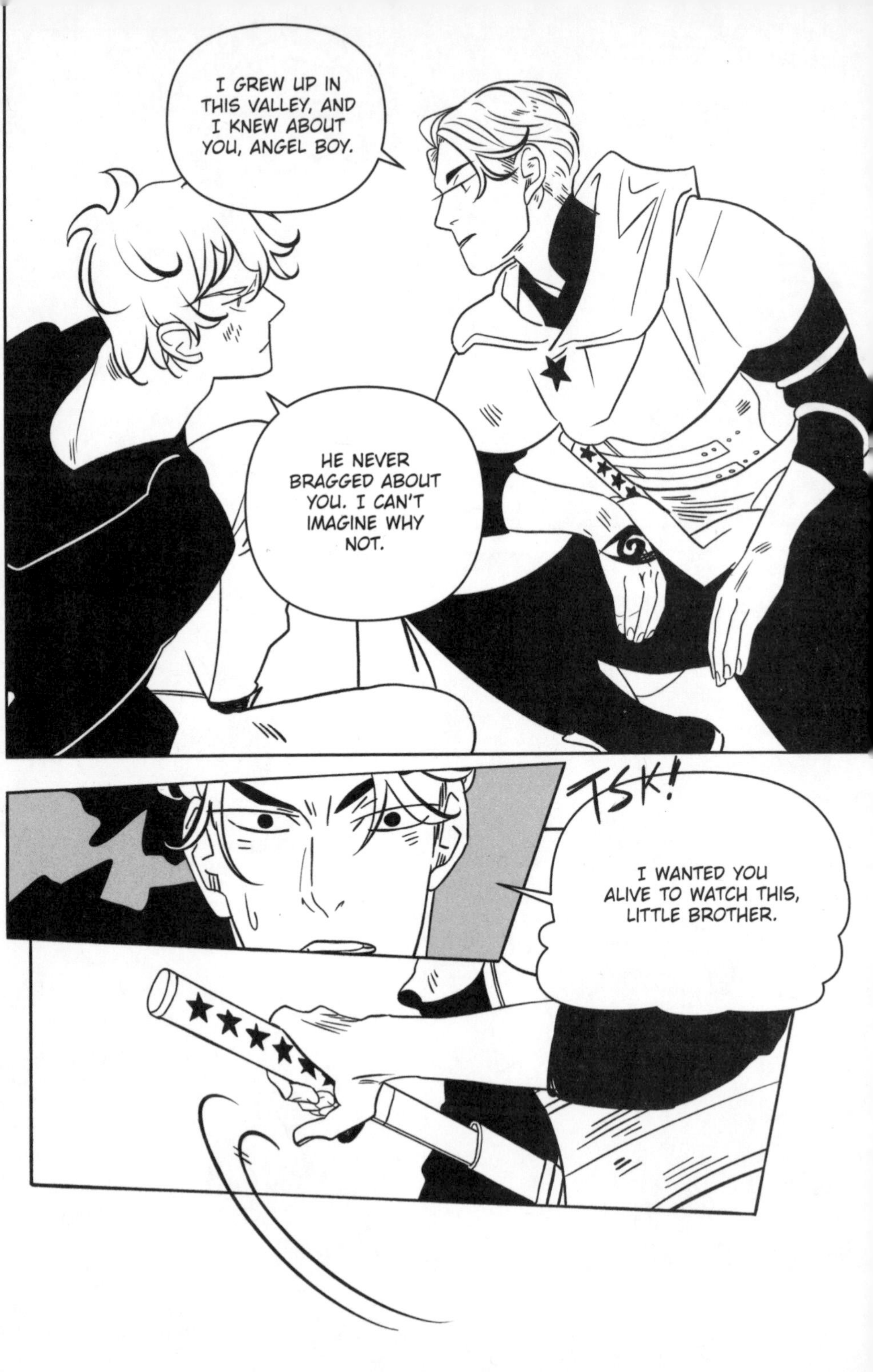
I GREW UP IN THIS VALLEY, AND I KNEW ABOUT YOU, ANGEL BOY.
HE NEVER BRAGGED ABOUT YOU. I CAN'T IMAGINE WHY NOT.
TSK!
I WANTED YOU ALIVE TO WATCH THIS, LITTLE BROTHER.

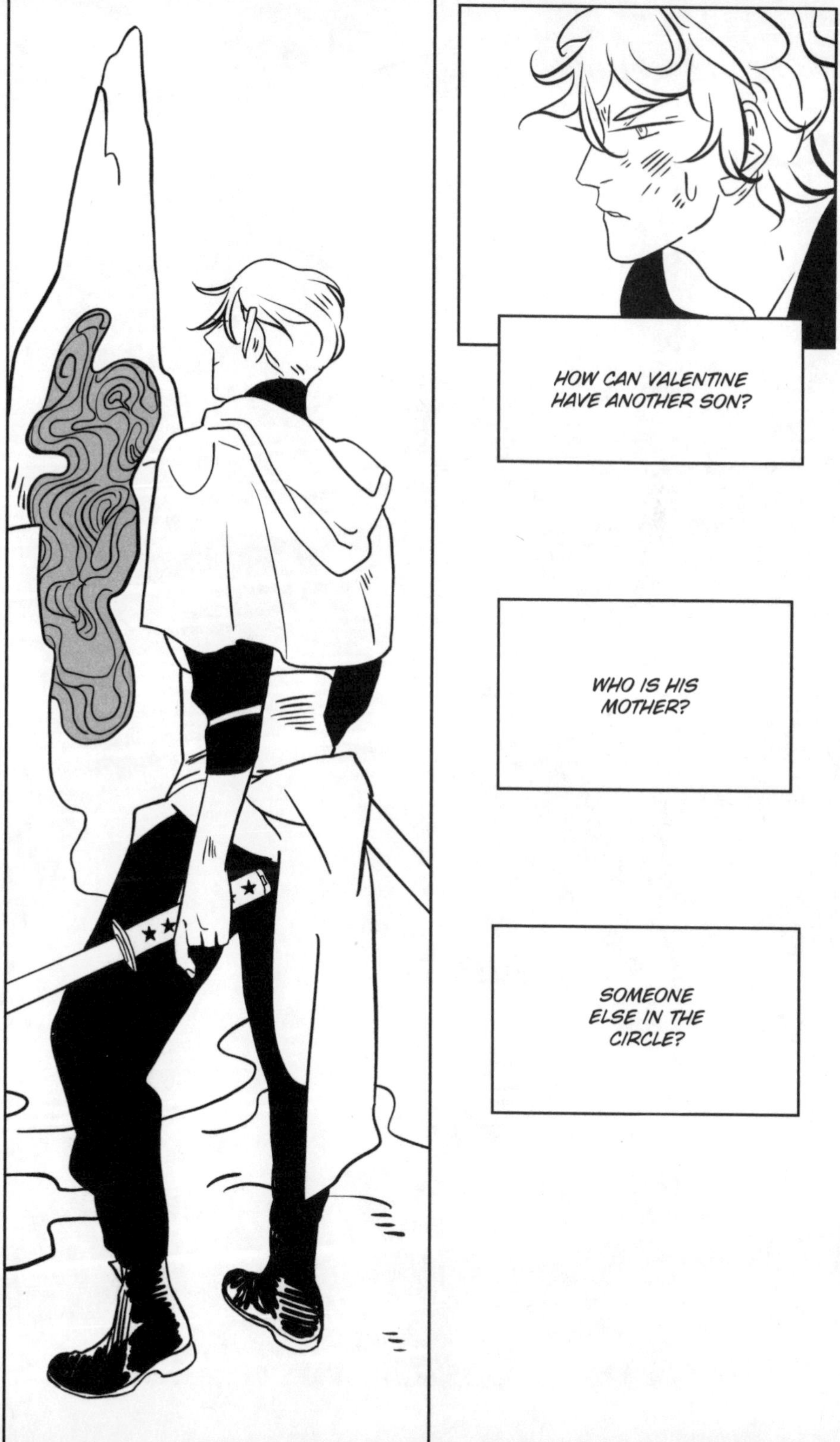
HOW CAN VALENTINE HAVE ANOTHER SON?
WHO IS HIS MOTHER?
SOMEONE ELSE IN THE CIRCLE?

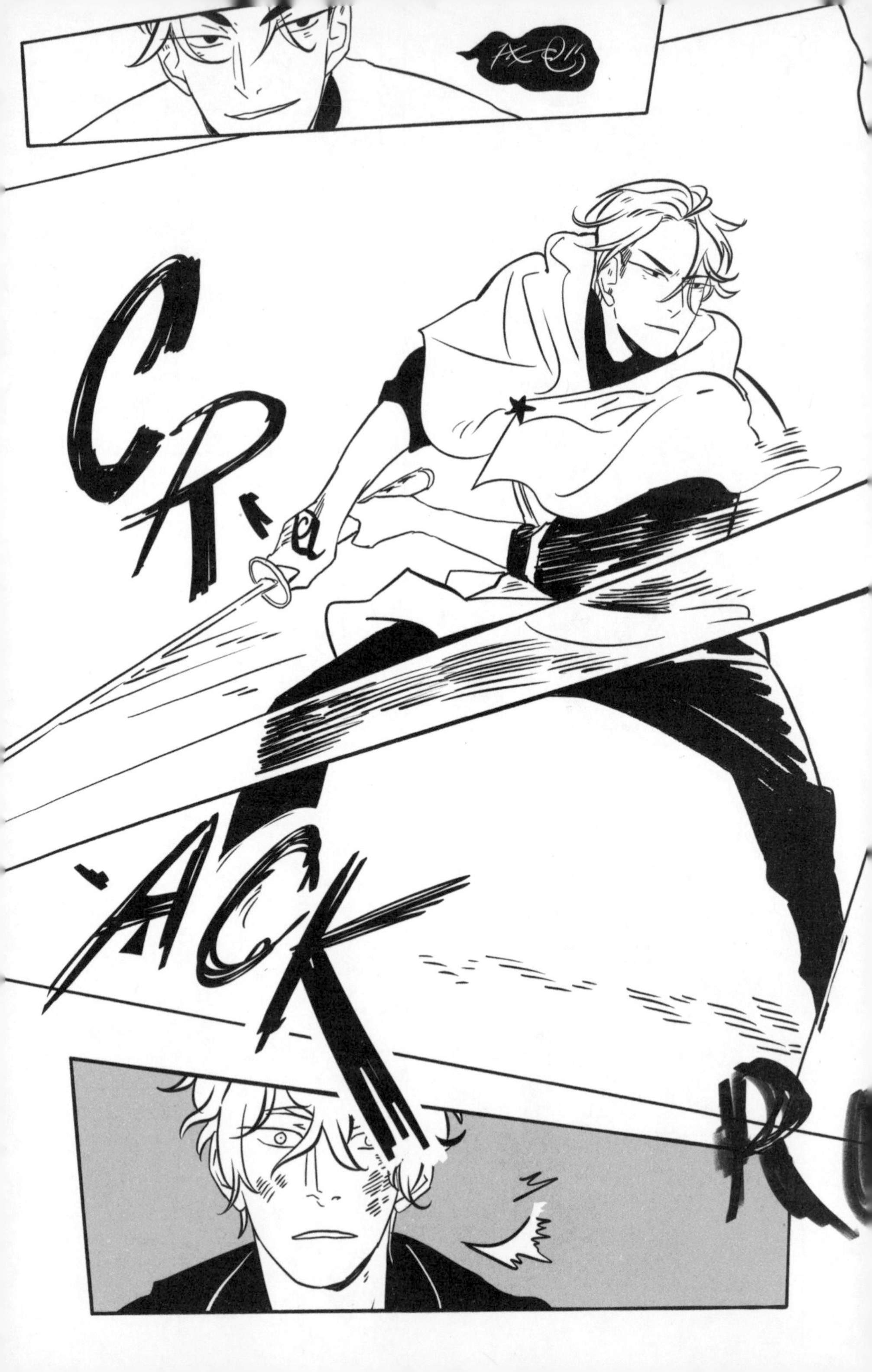
CRACK

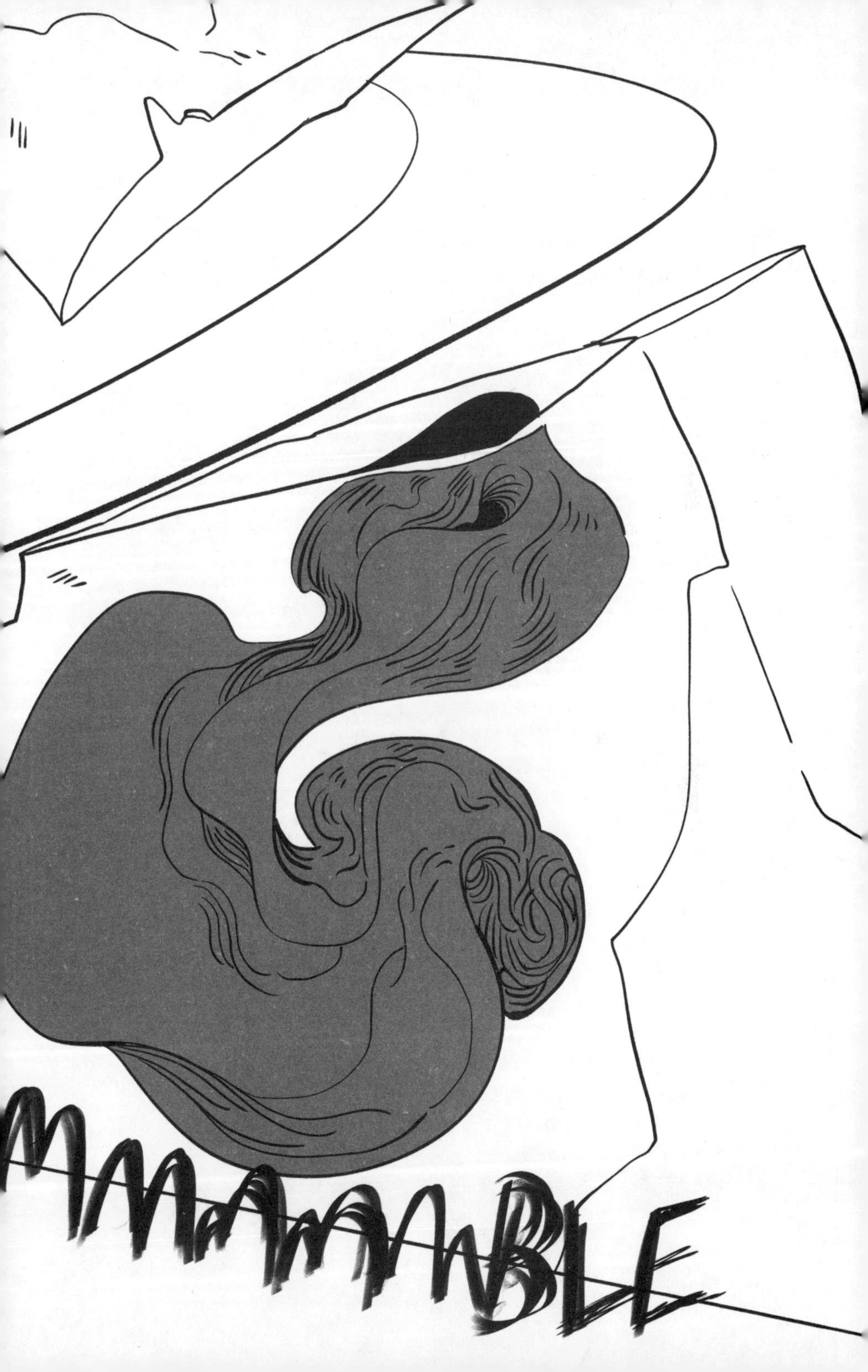
MMMMMBLE

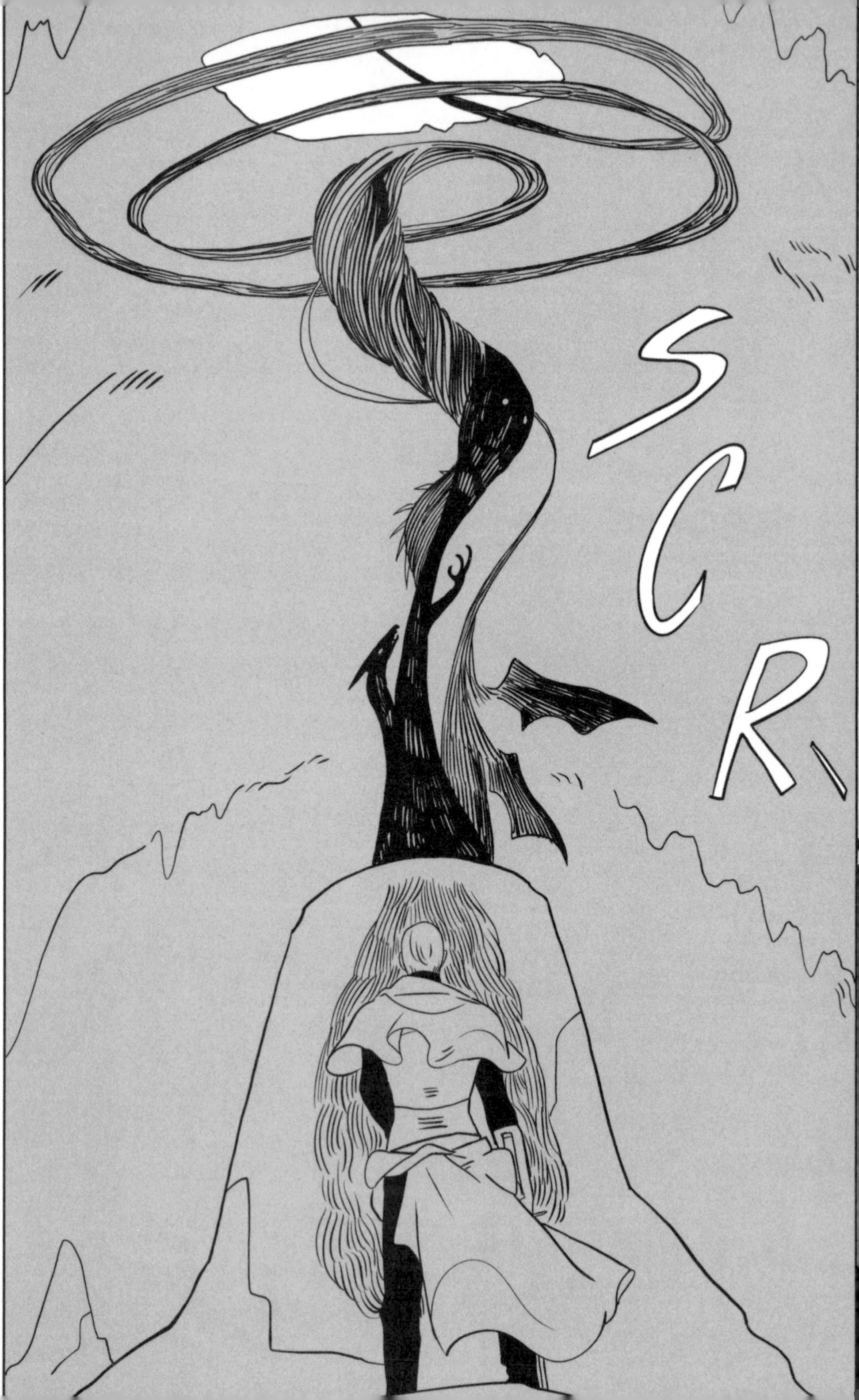
SCR

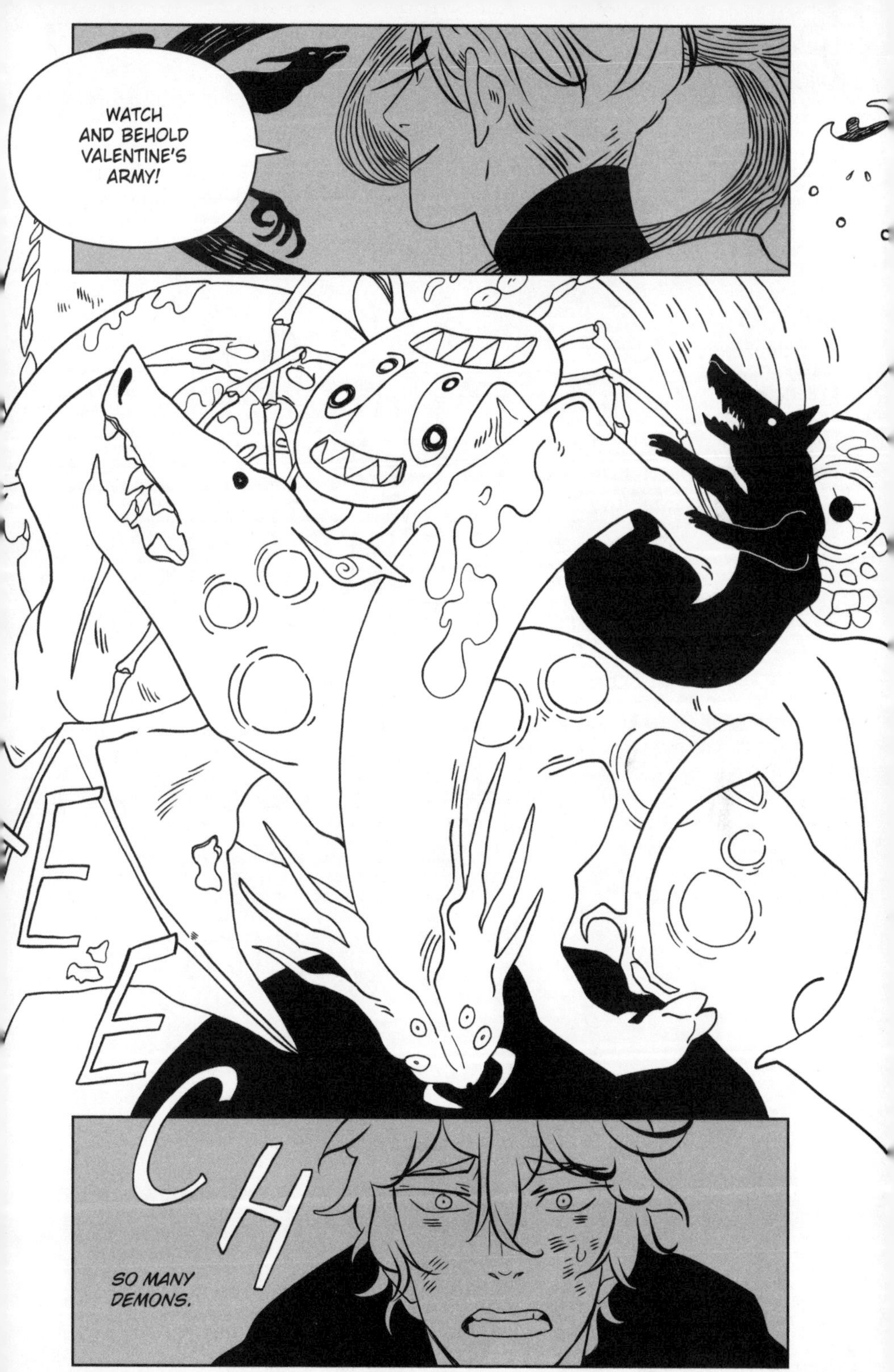
WATCH AND BEHOLD VALENTINE'S ARMY!
EEECH
SO MANY DEMONS.

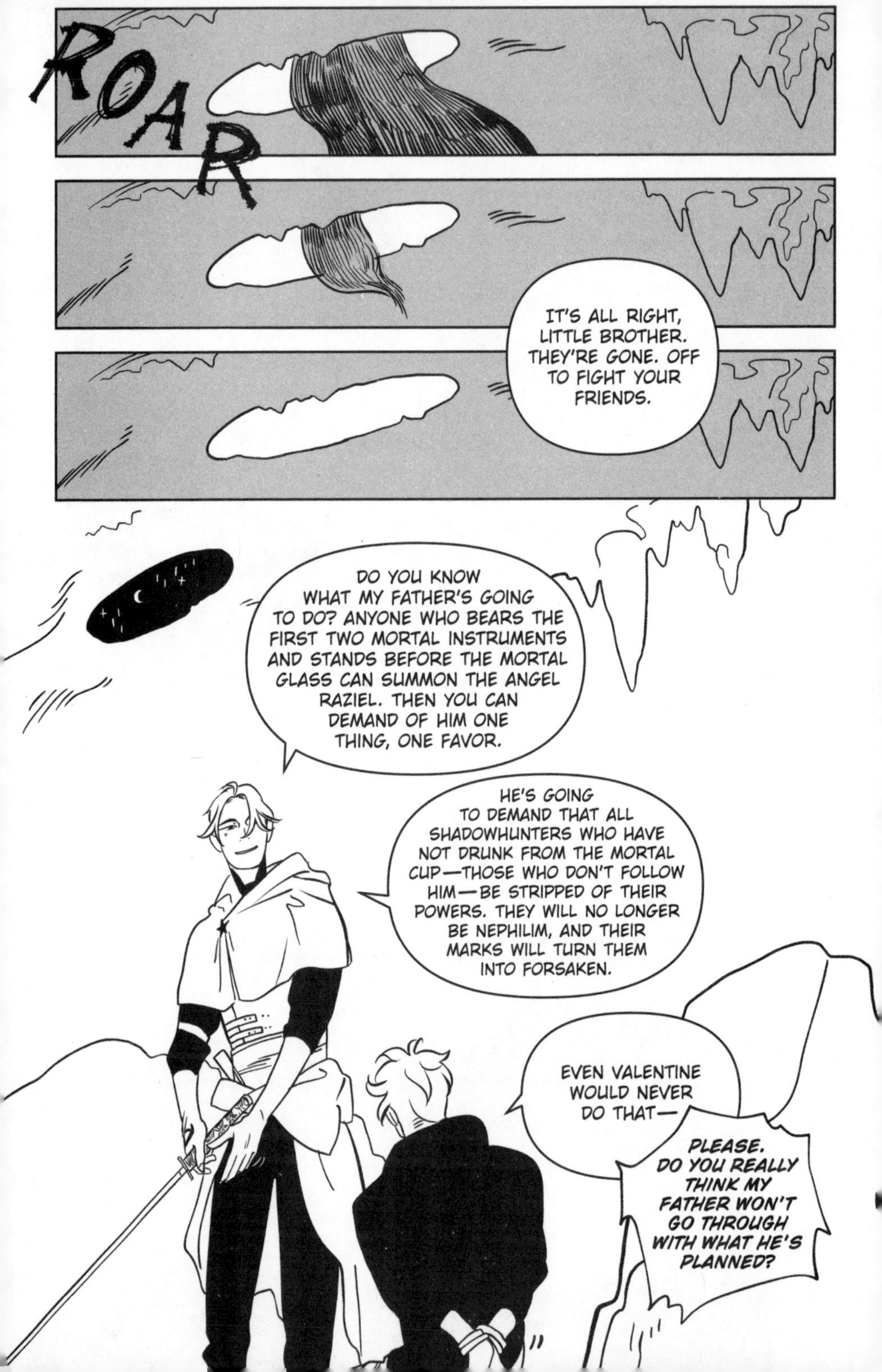
ROAR
IT'S ALL RIGHT, LITTLE BROTHER. THEY'RE GONE. OFF TO FIGHT YOUR FRIENDS.
DO YOU KNOW WHAT MY FATHER'S GOING TO DO? ANYONE WHO BEARS THE FIRST TWO MORTAL INSTRUMENTS AND STANDS BEFORE THE MORTAL GLASS CAN SUMMON THE ANGEL RAZIEL. THEN YOU CAN DEMAND OF HIM ONE THING, ONE FAVOR.
HE'S GOING TO DEMAND THAT ALL SHADOWHUNTERS WHO HAVE NOT DRUNK FROM THE MORTAL CUP—THOSE WHO DON'T FOLLOW HIM—BE STRIPPED OF THEIR POWERS. THEY WILL NO LONGER BE NEPHILIM, AND THEIR MARKS WILL TURN THEM INTO FORSAKEN.
EVEN VALENTINE WOULD NEVER DO THAT—
PLEASE. DO YOU REALLY THINK MY FATHER WON'T GO THROUGH WITH WHAT HE'S PLANNED?

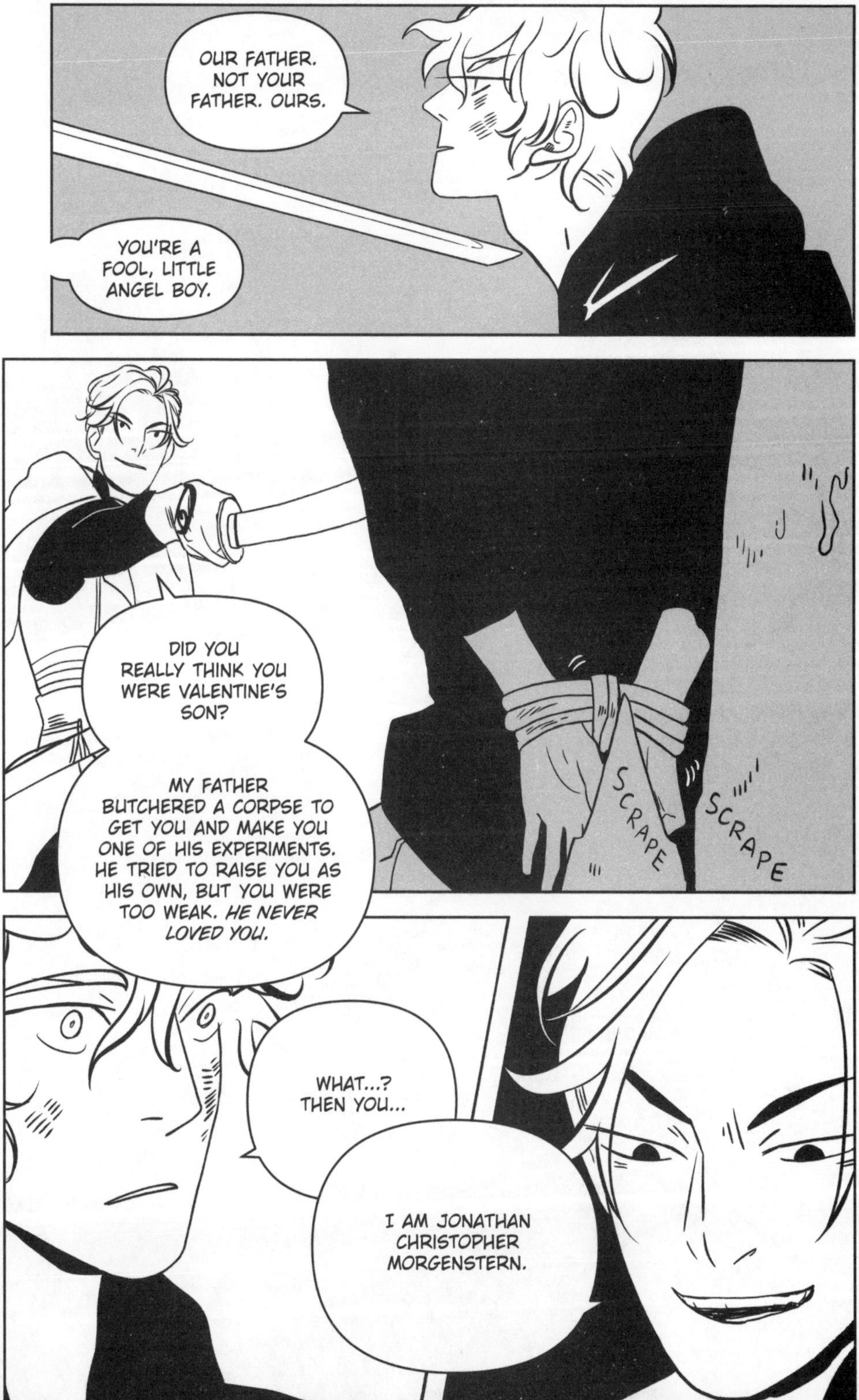
OUR FATHER. NOT YOUR FATHER. OURS.
YOU'RE A FOOL, LITTLE ANGEL BOY.
DID YOU REALLY THINK YOU WERE VALENTINE'S SON?
MY FATHER BUTCHERED A CORPSE TO GET YOU AND MAKE YOU ONE OF HIS EXPERIMENTS. HE TRIED TO RAISE YOU AS HIS OWN, BUT YOU WERE TOO WEAK. *HE NEVER LOVED YOU.*
SCRAPE
SCRAPE
WHAT...? THEN YOU...
I AM JONATHAN CHRISTOPHER MORGENSTERN.

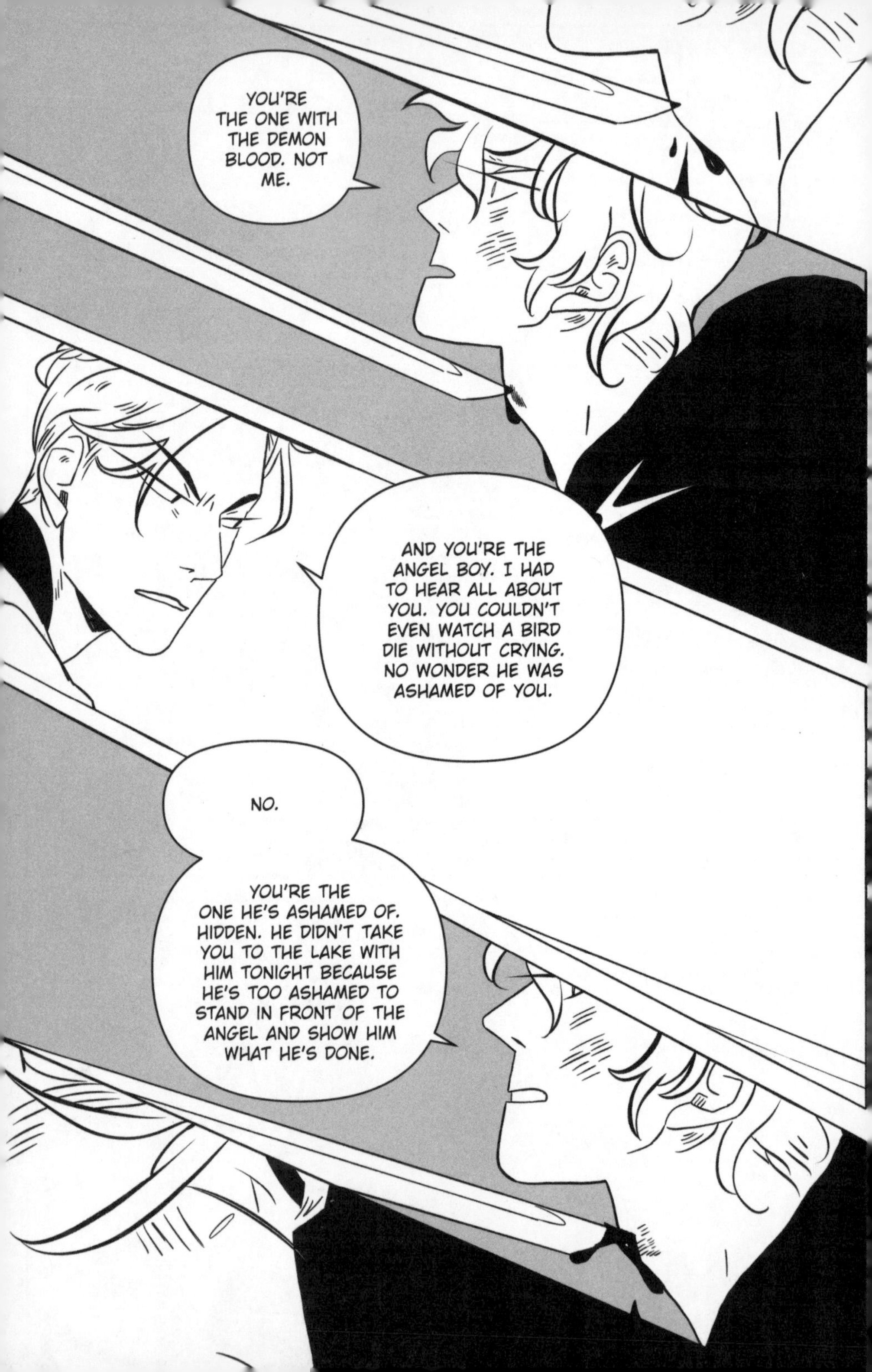
YOU'RE THE ONE WITH THE DEMON BLOOD. NOT ME.
AND YOU'RE THE ANGEL BOY. I HAD TO HEAR ALL ABOUT YOU. YOU COULDN'T EVEN WATCH A BIRD DIE WITHOUT CRYING. NO WONDER HE WAS ASHAMED OF YOU.
NO.
YOU'RE THE ONE HE'S ASHAMED OF. HIDDEN. HE DIDN'T TAKE YOU TO THE LAKE WITH HIM TONIGHT BECAUSE HE'S TOO ASHAMED TO STAND IN FRONT OF THE ANGEL AND SHOW HIM WHAT HE'S DONE.

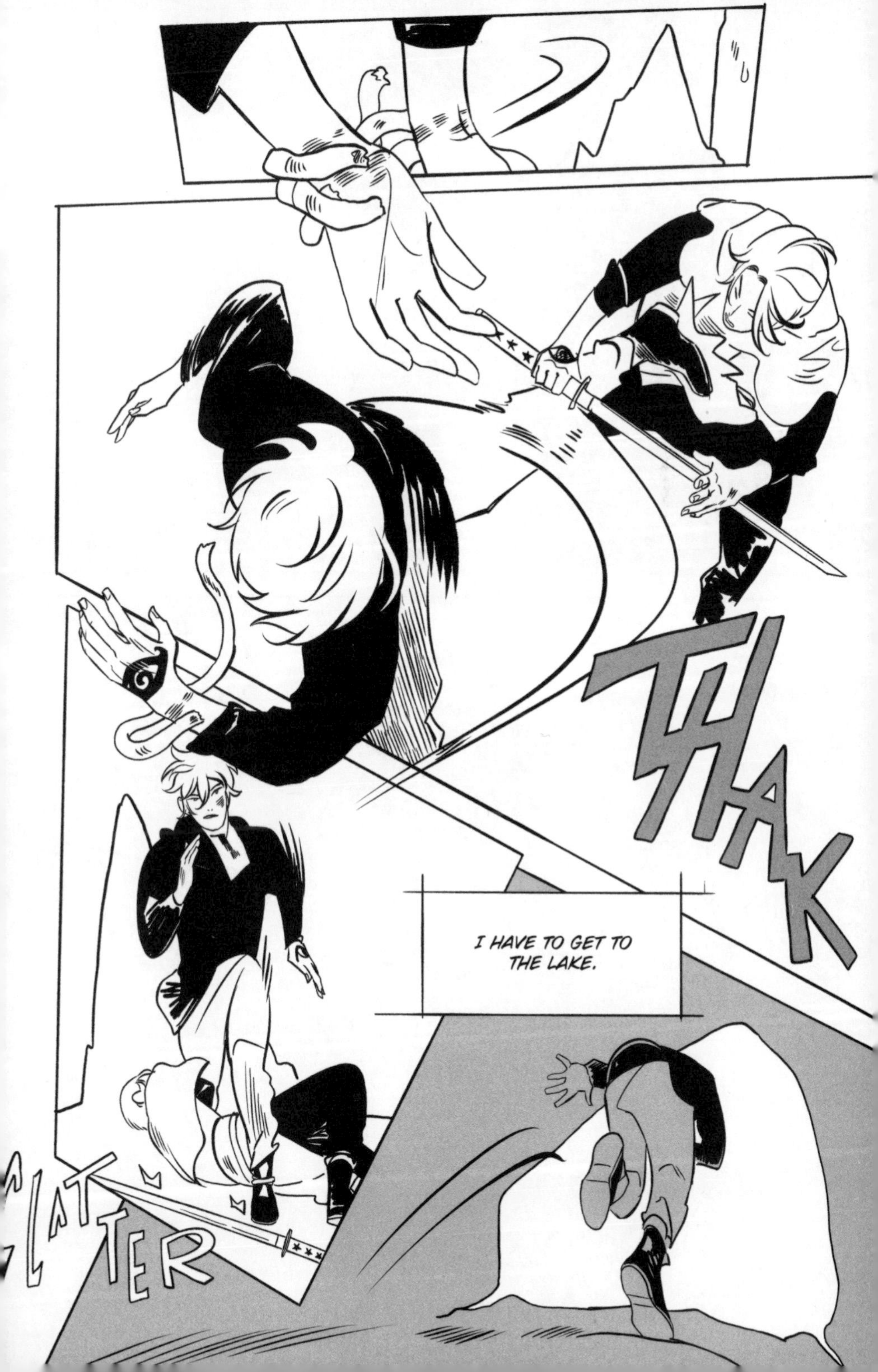

THAK
I HAVE TO GET TO THE LAKE.
CLATTER

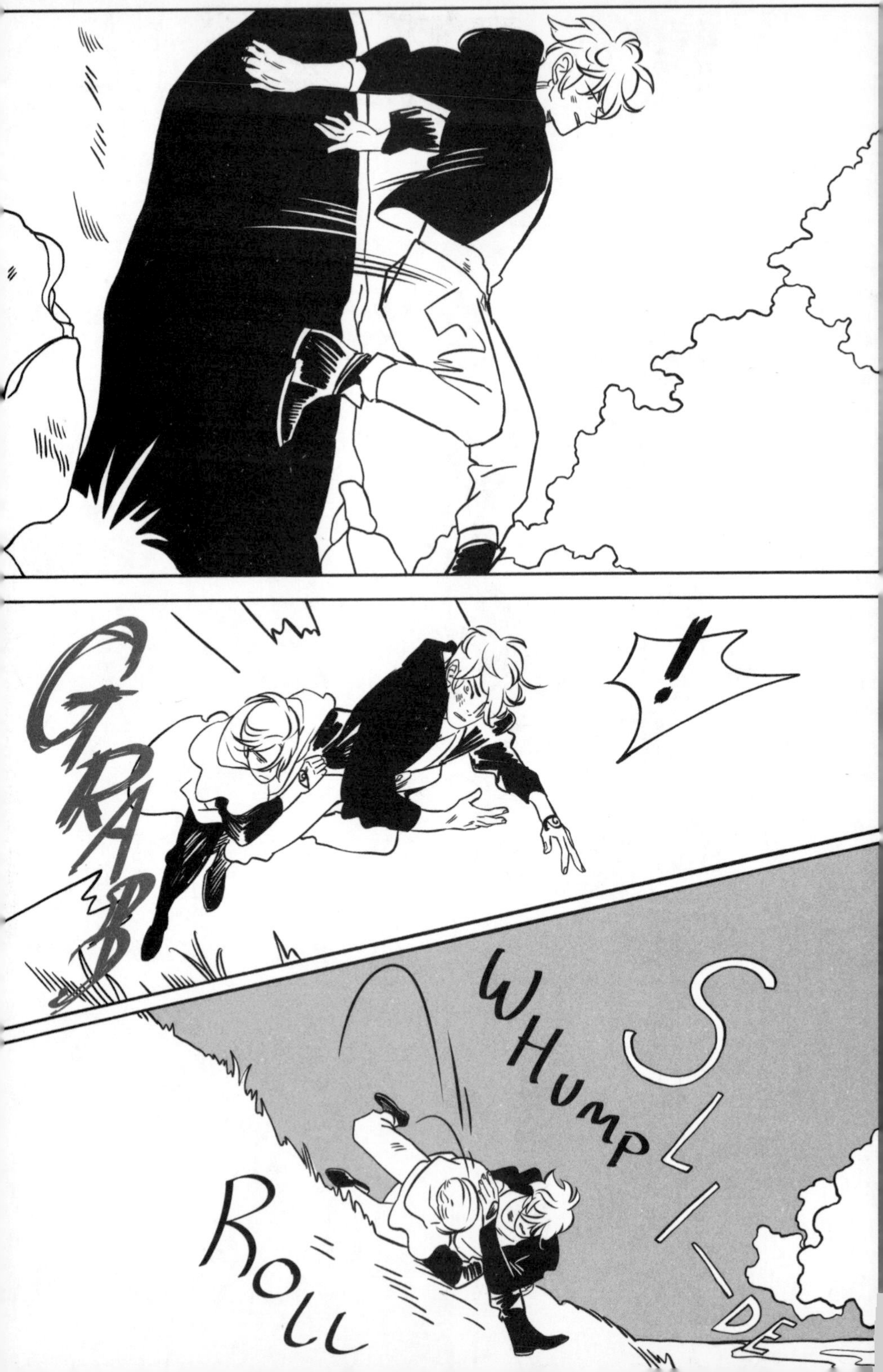
GRAB
!
WHUMP
SLIDE
ROLL

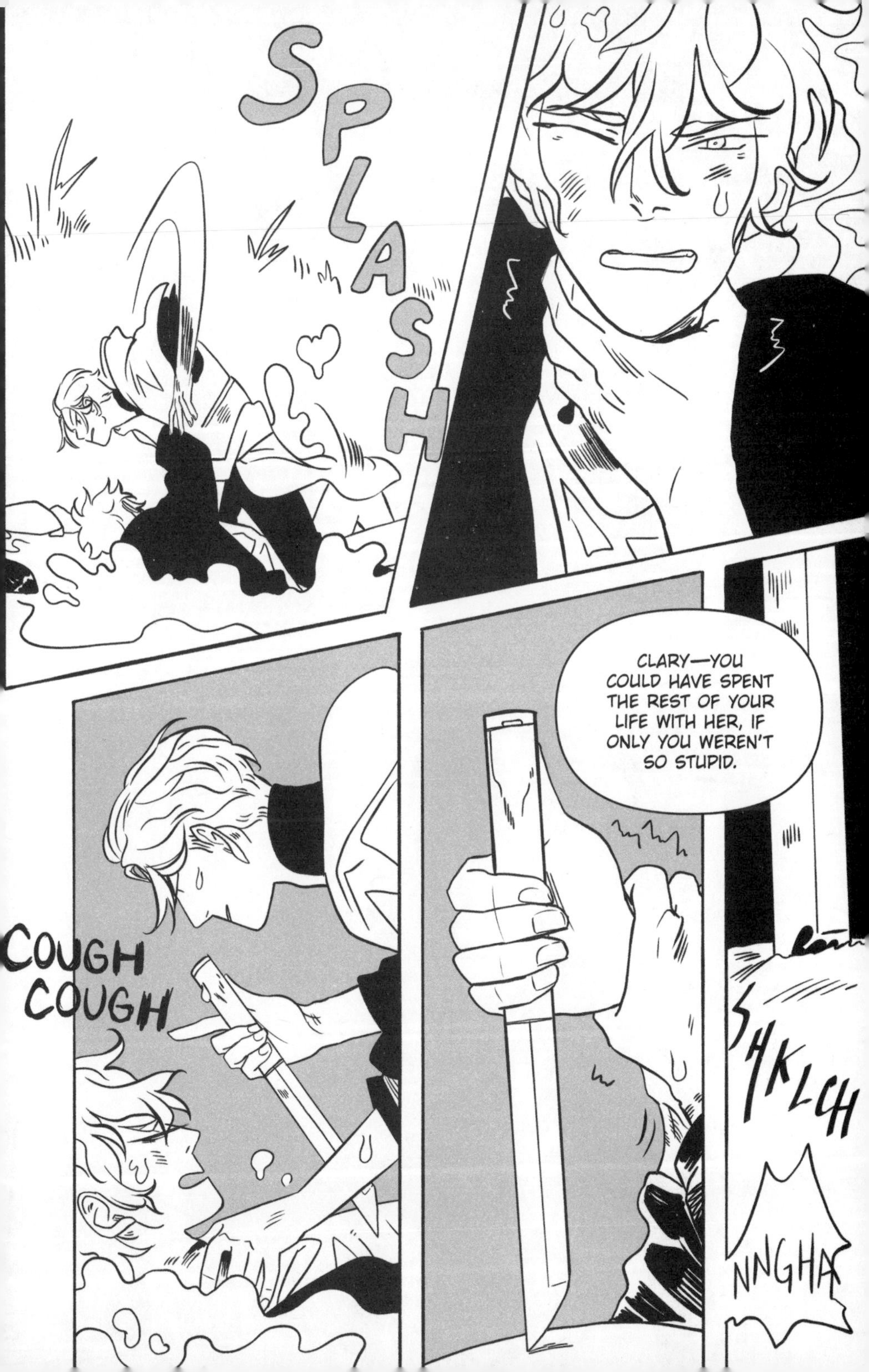
SPLASH
CLARY—YOU COULD HAVE SPENT THE REST OF YOUR LIFE WITH HER, IF ONLY YOU WEREN'T SO STUPID.
COUGH COUGH
SHKLCH
NNGHA

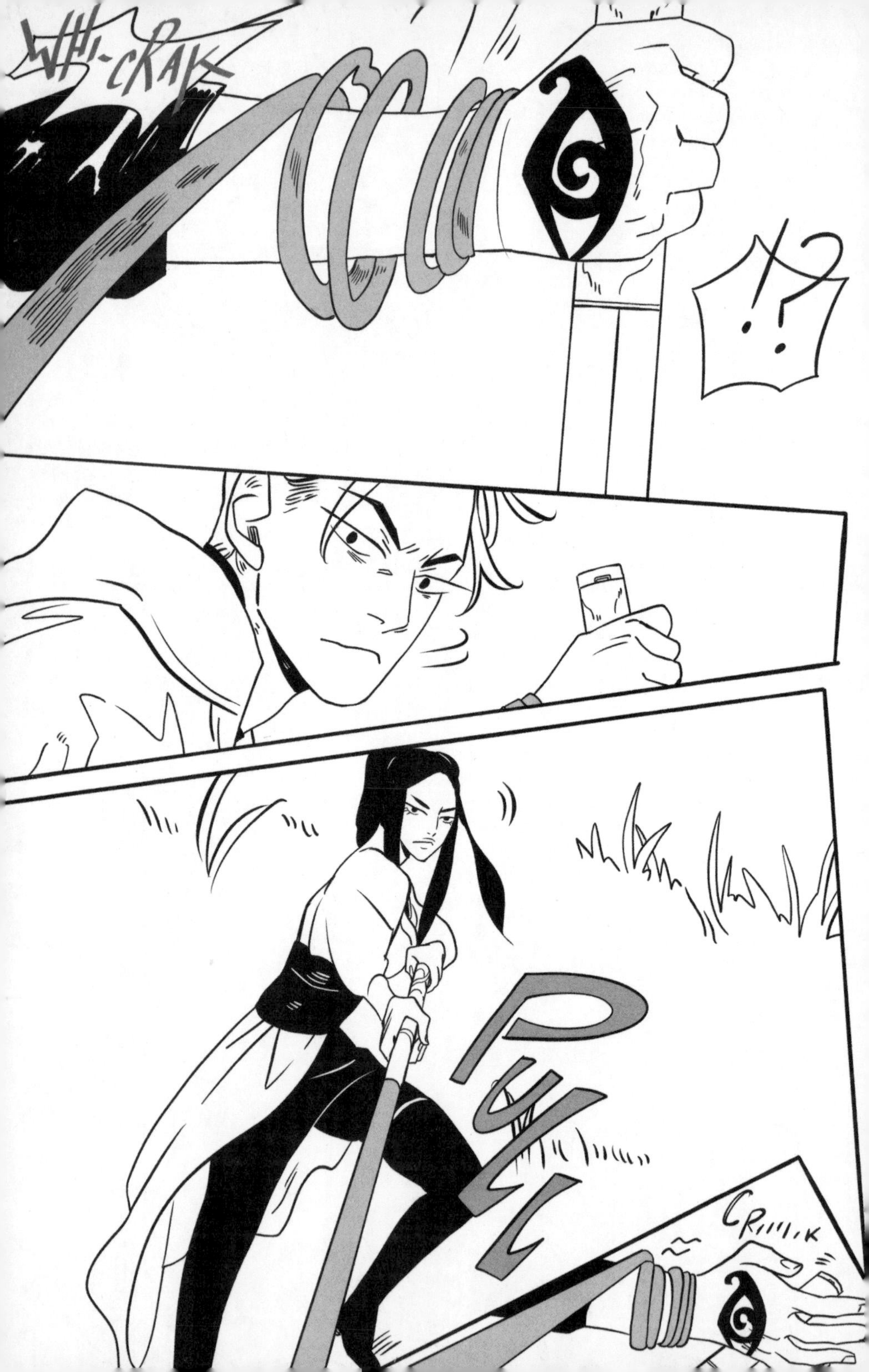
WHI-CRAK
!?
PULL
CRIIIIK

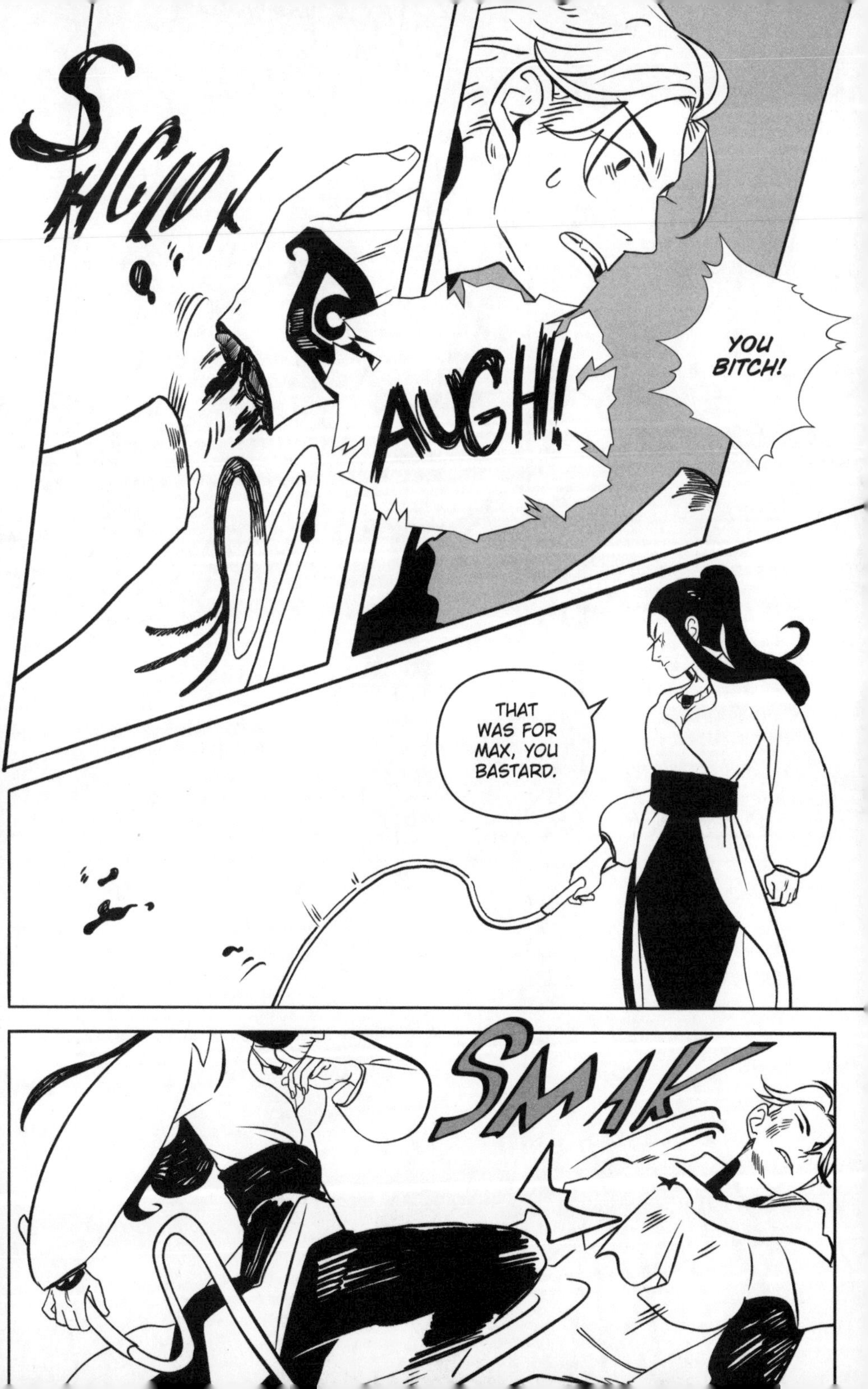
SHCLOK
AUGH!
YOU BITCH!
THAT WAS FOR MAX, YOU BASTARD.
SMAK

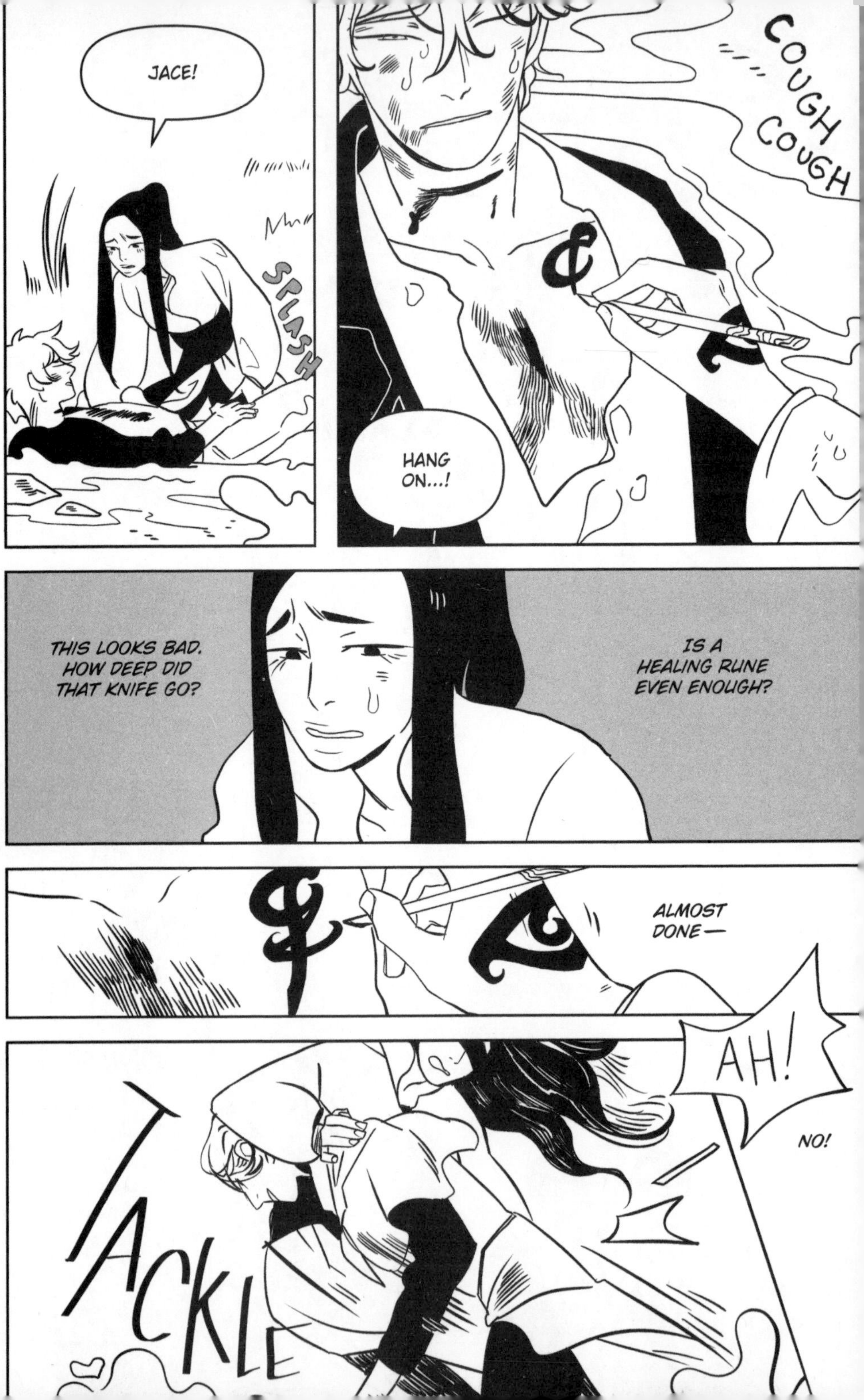
JACE!
SPLASH
COUGH COUGH
HANG ON...!
THIS LOOKS BAD. HOW DEEP DID THAT KNIFE GO?
IS A HEALING RUNE EVEN ENOUGH?
ALMOST DONE—
AH!
NO!
TACKLE

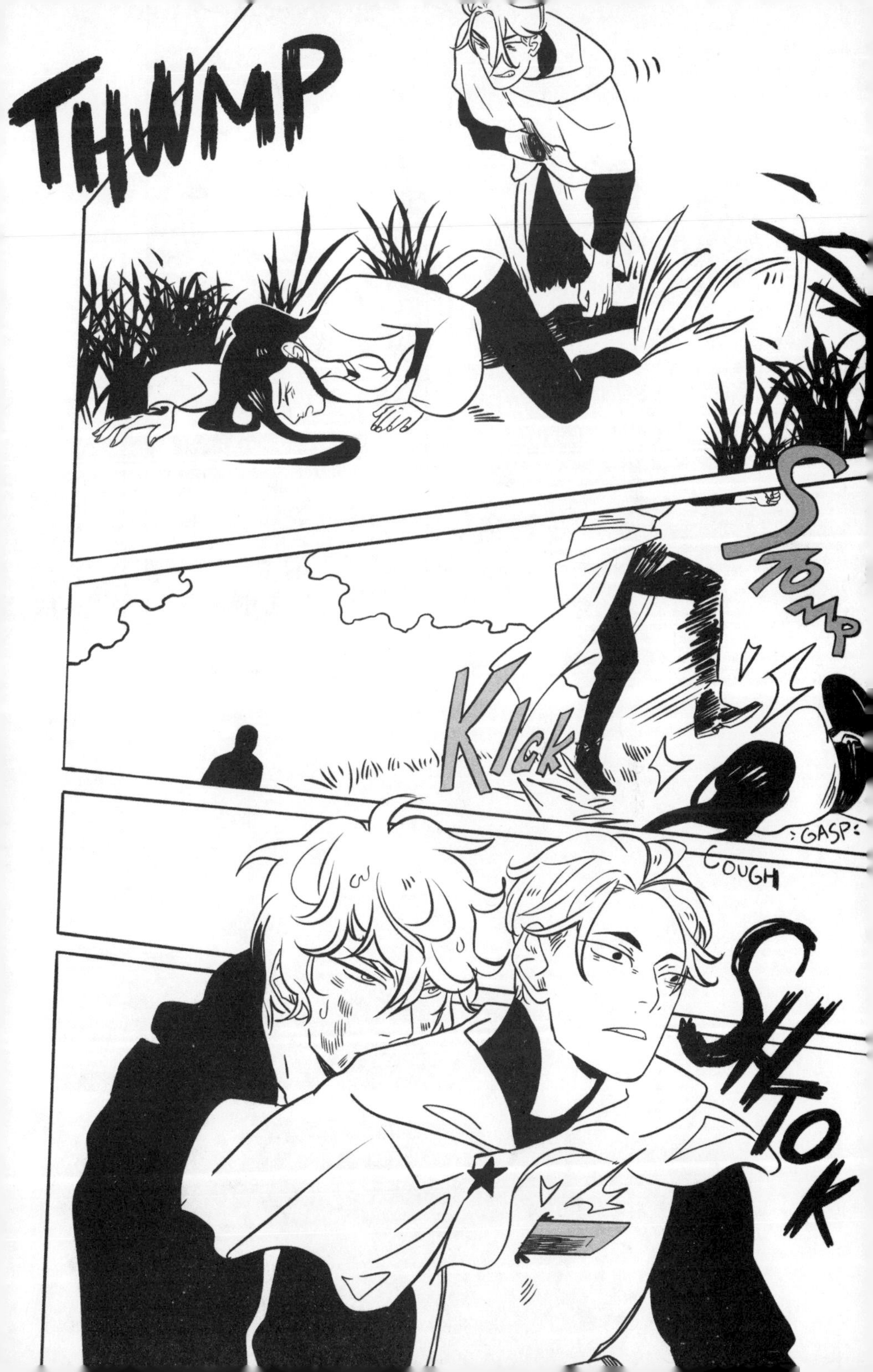
THUMP
STOMP
KICK
:GASP:
COUGH
SHTOK

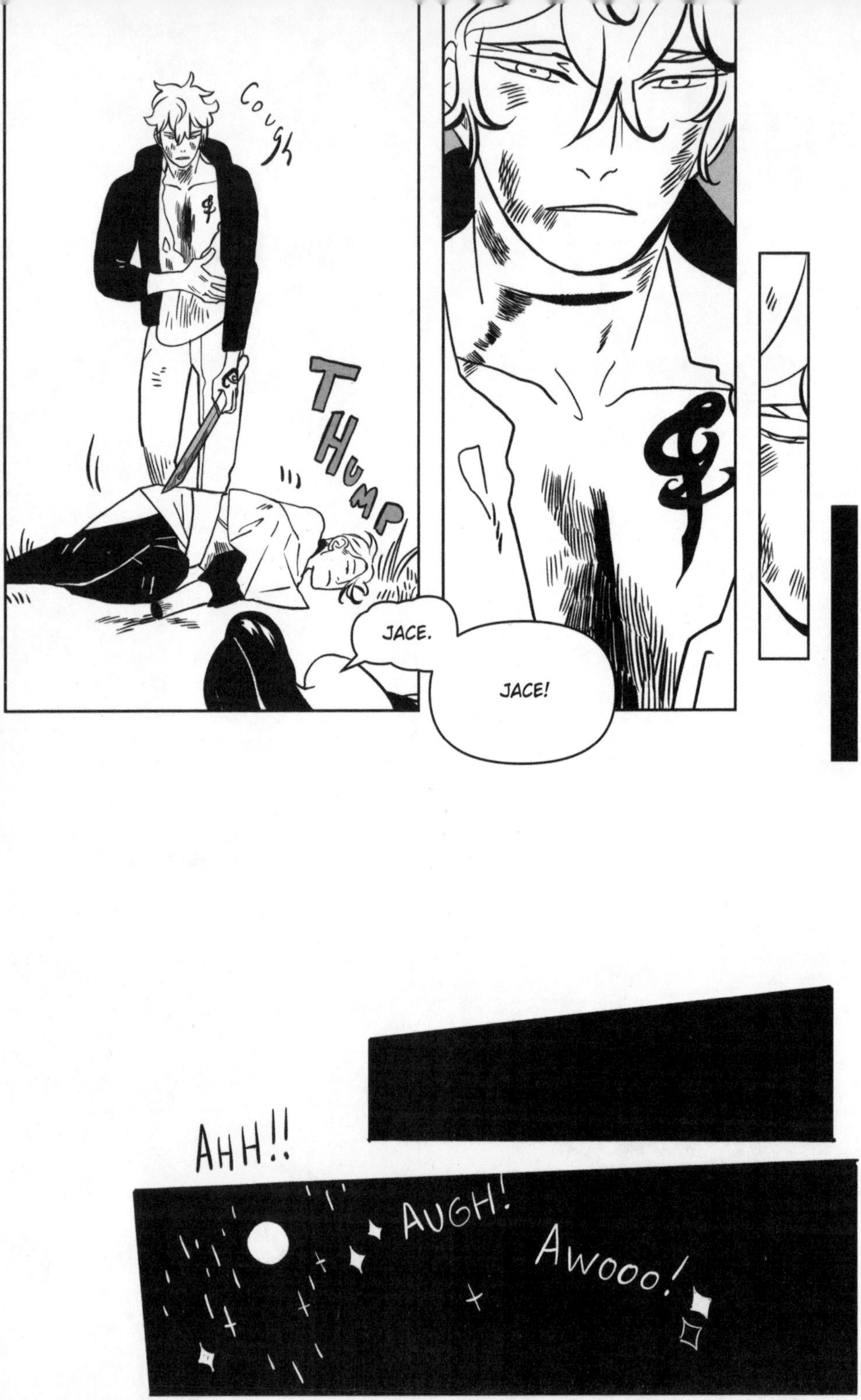
Cough
THUMP
JACE.
JACE!
AHH!!
AUGH!
Awooo!

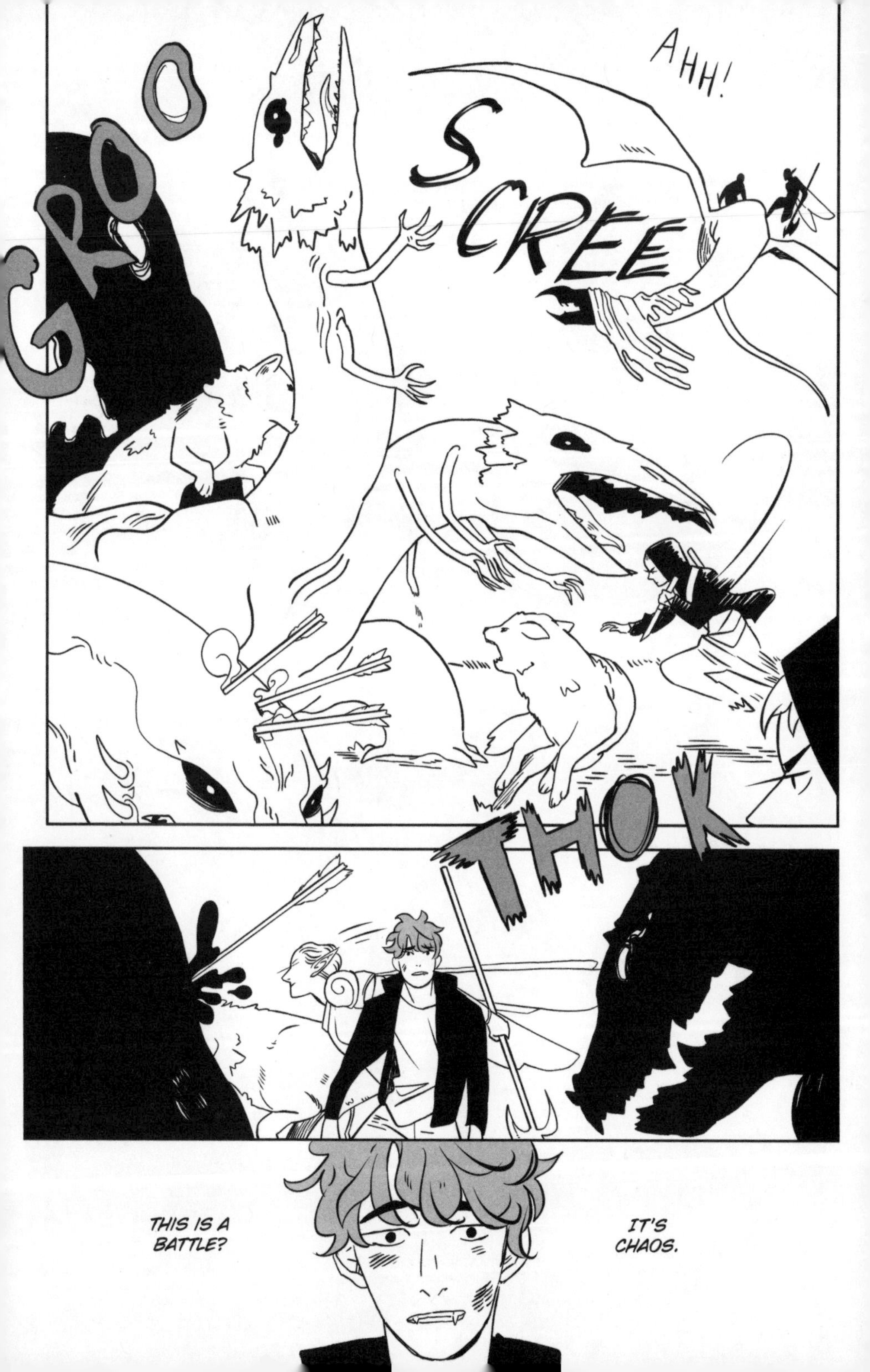
GROOO
AHH!
SCREE
THOK
THIS IS A BATTLE?
IT'S CHAOS.

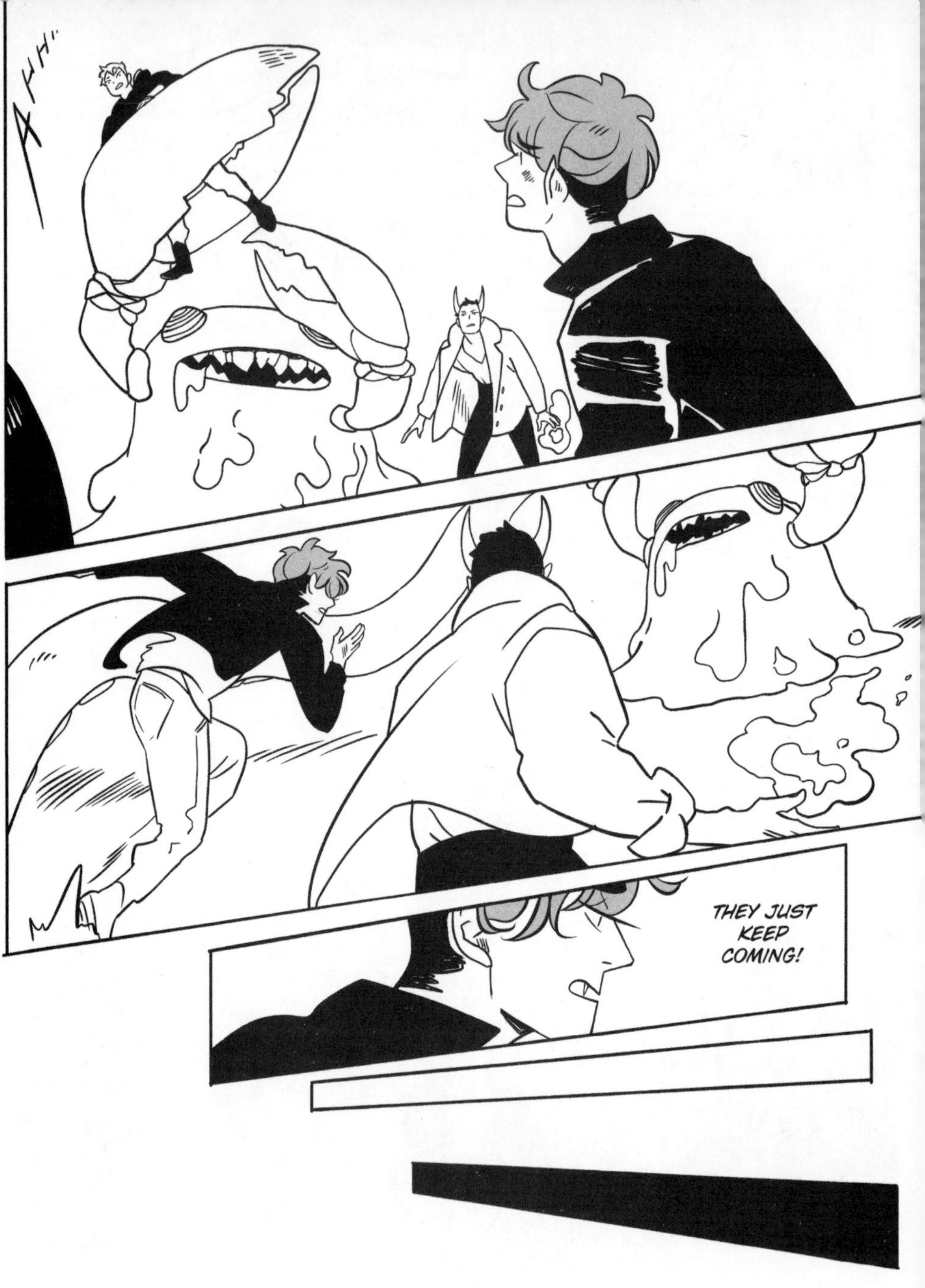
AHH..
THEY JUST KEEP COMING!

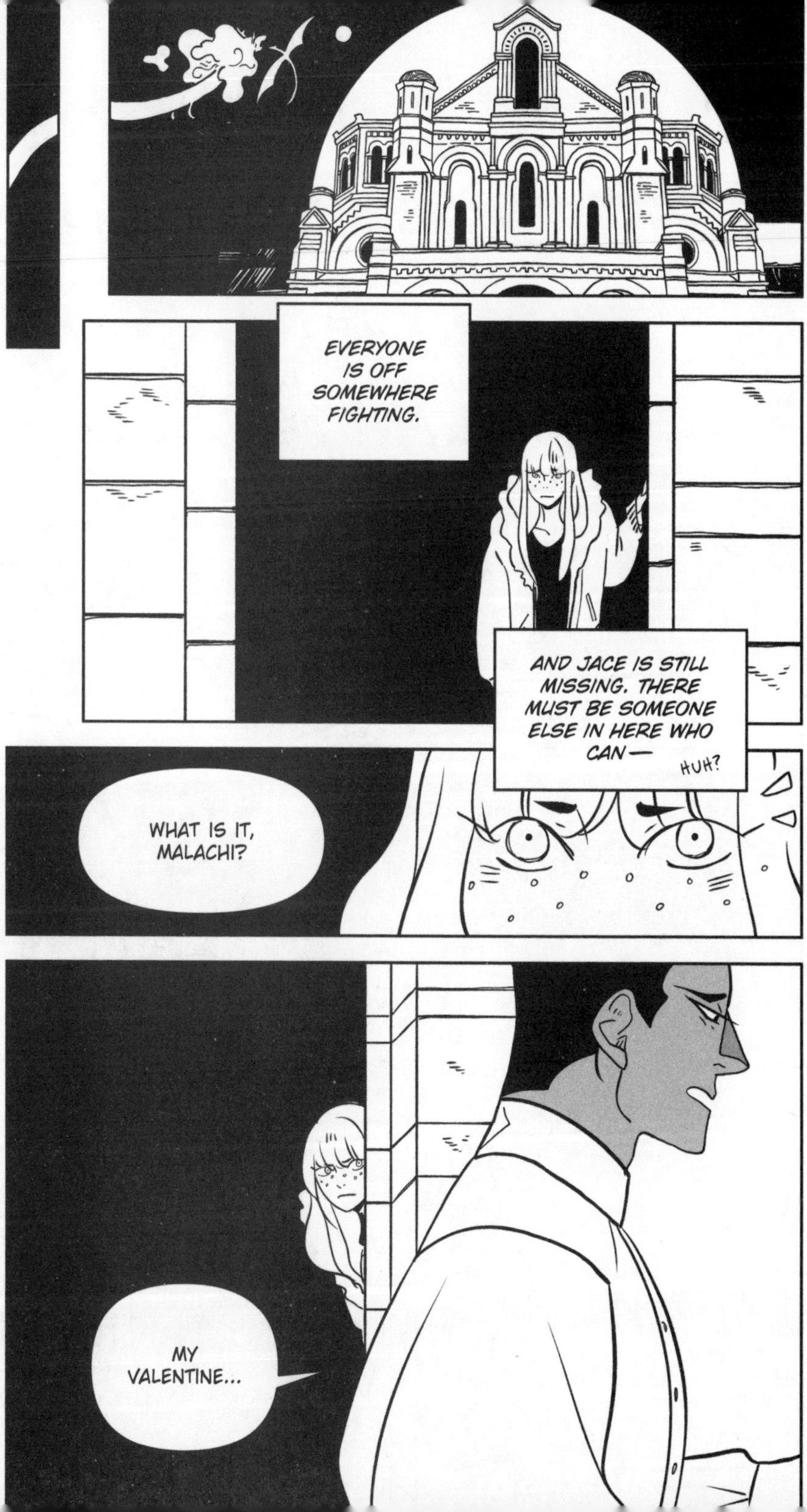
EVERYONE IS OFF SOMEWHERE FIGHTING.
AND JACE IS STILL MISSING. THERE MUST BE SOMEONE ELSE IN HERE WHO CAN—
HUH?
WHAT IS IT, MALACHI?
MY VALENTINE...

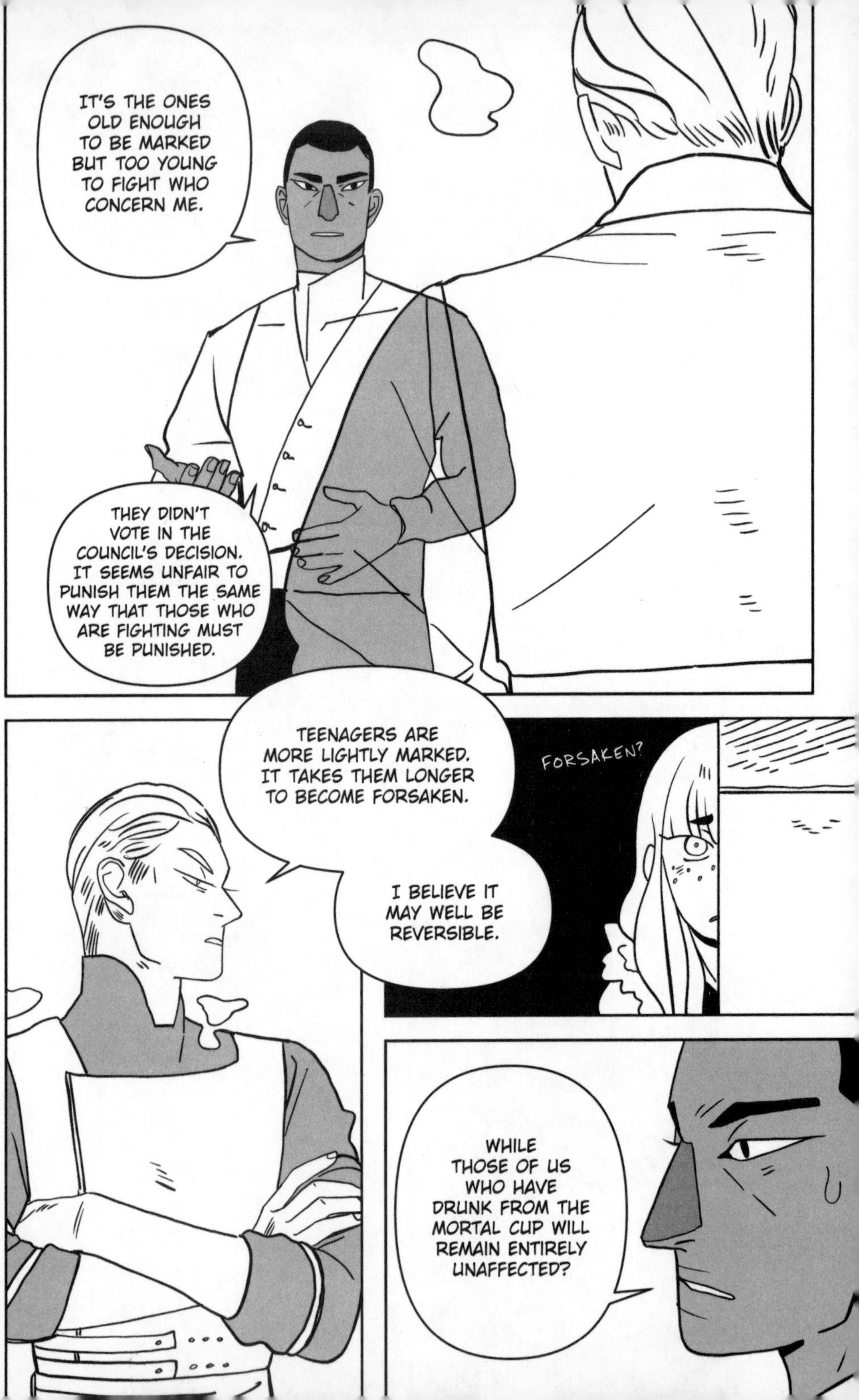
IT'S THE ONES OLD ENOUGH TO BE MARKED BUT TOO YOUNG TO FIGHT WHO CONCERN ME.
THEY DIDN'T VOTE IN THE COUNCIL'S DECISION. IT SEEMS UNFAIR TO PUNISH THEM THE SAME WAY THAT THOSE WHO ARE FIGHTING MUST BE PUNISHED.
TEENAGERS ARE MORE LIGHTLY MARKED. IT TAKES THEM LONGER TO BECOME FORSAKEN.
I BELIEVE IT MAY WELL BE REVERSIBLE.
FORSAKEN?
WHILE THOSE OF US WHO HAVE DRUNK FROM THE MORTAL CUP WILL REMAIN ENTIRELY UNAFFECTED?

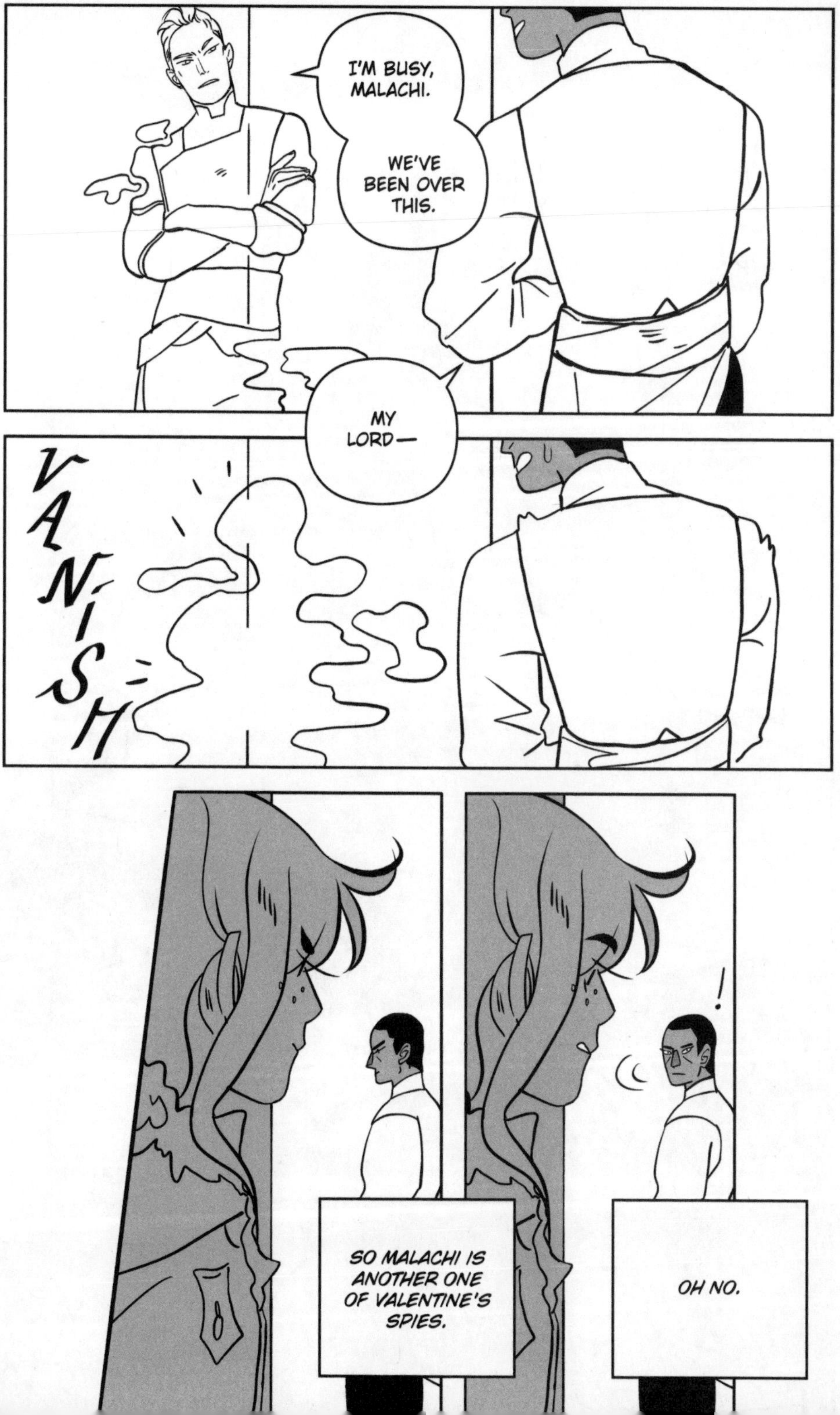
I'M BUSY, MALACHI.
WE'VE BEEN OVER THIS.
MY LORD—
VANISH
!
SO MALACHI IS ANOTHER ONE OF VALENTINE'S SPIES.
OH NO.

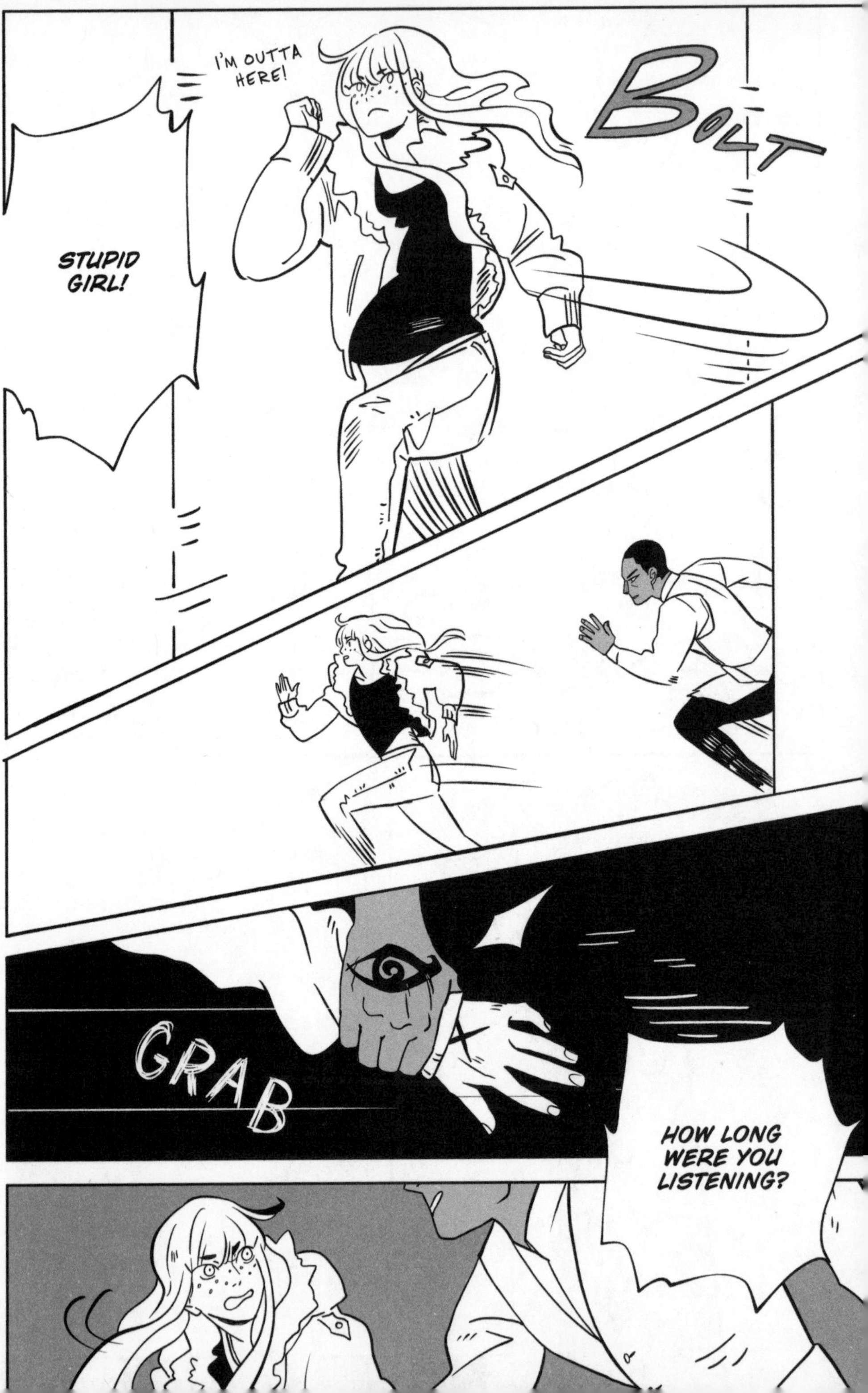
I'M OUTTA HERE!
BOLT
STUPID GIRL!
GRAB
HOW LONG WERE YOU LISTENING?

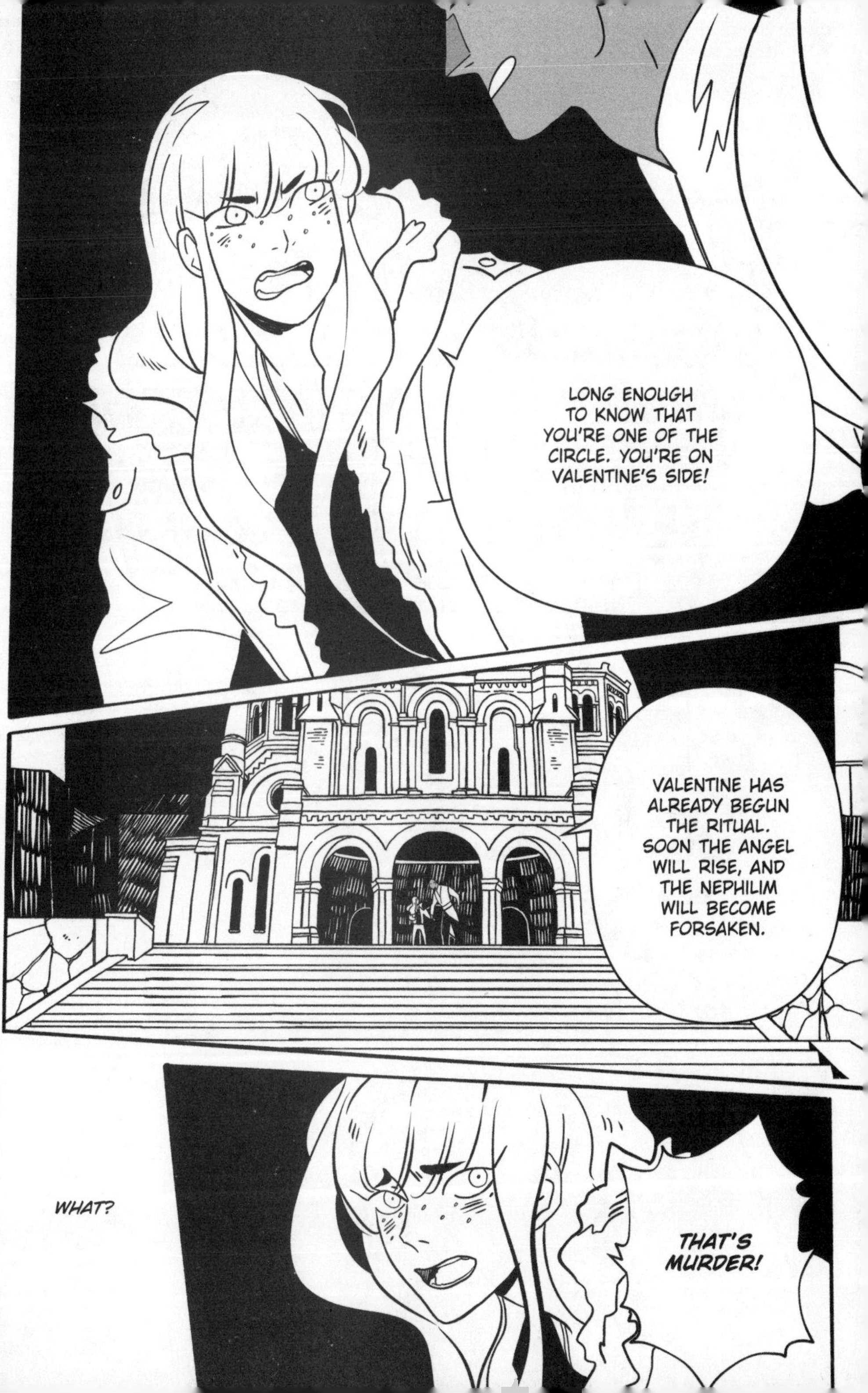
LONG ENOUGH TO KNOW THAT YOU'RE ONE OF THE CIRCLE. YOU'RE ON VALENTINE'S SIDE!
VALENTINE HAS ALREADY BEGUN THE RITUAL. SOON THE ANGEL WILL RISE, AND THE NEPHILIM WILL BECOME FORSAKEN.
WHAT?
THAT'S MURDER!

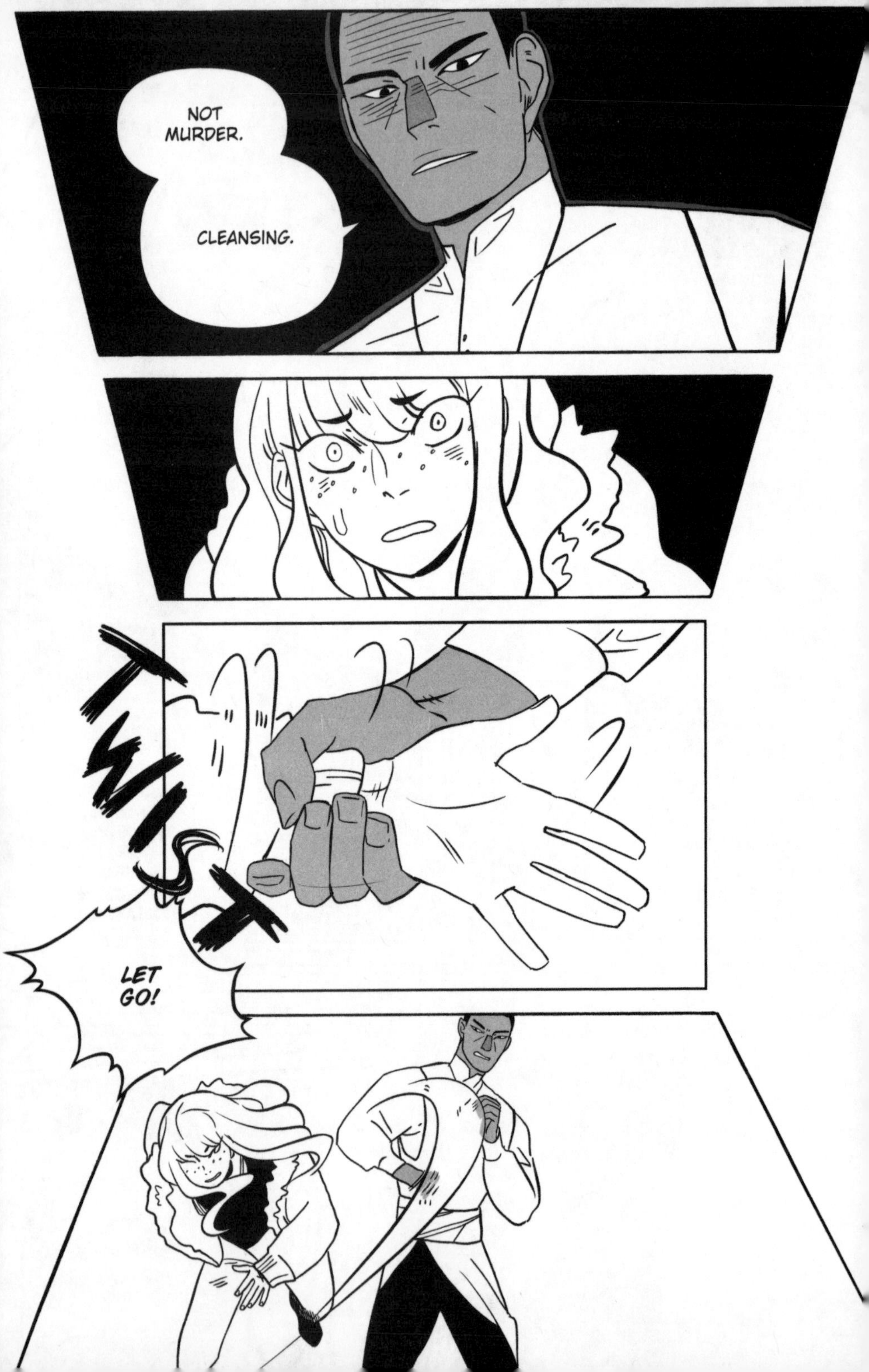
NOT MURDER.
CLEANSING.
TWIST
LET GO!

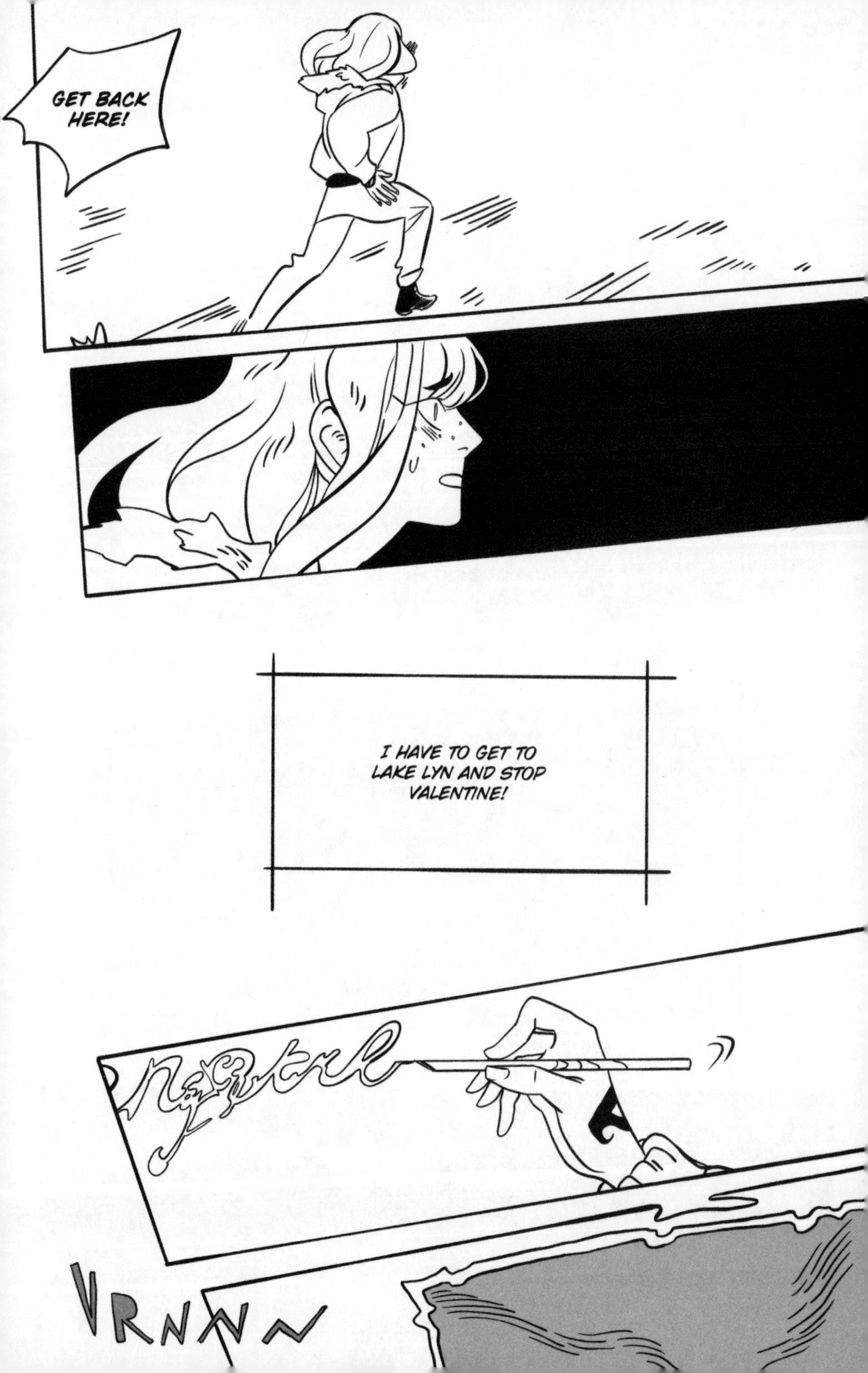
GET BACK HERE!
I HAVE TO GET TO LAKE LYN AND STOP VALENTINE!
VRNNNN

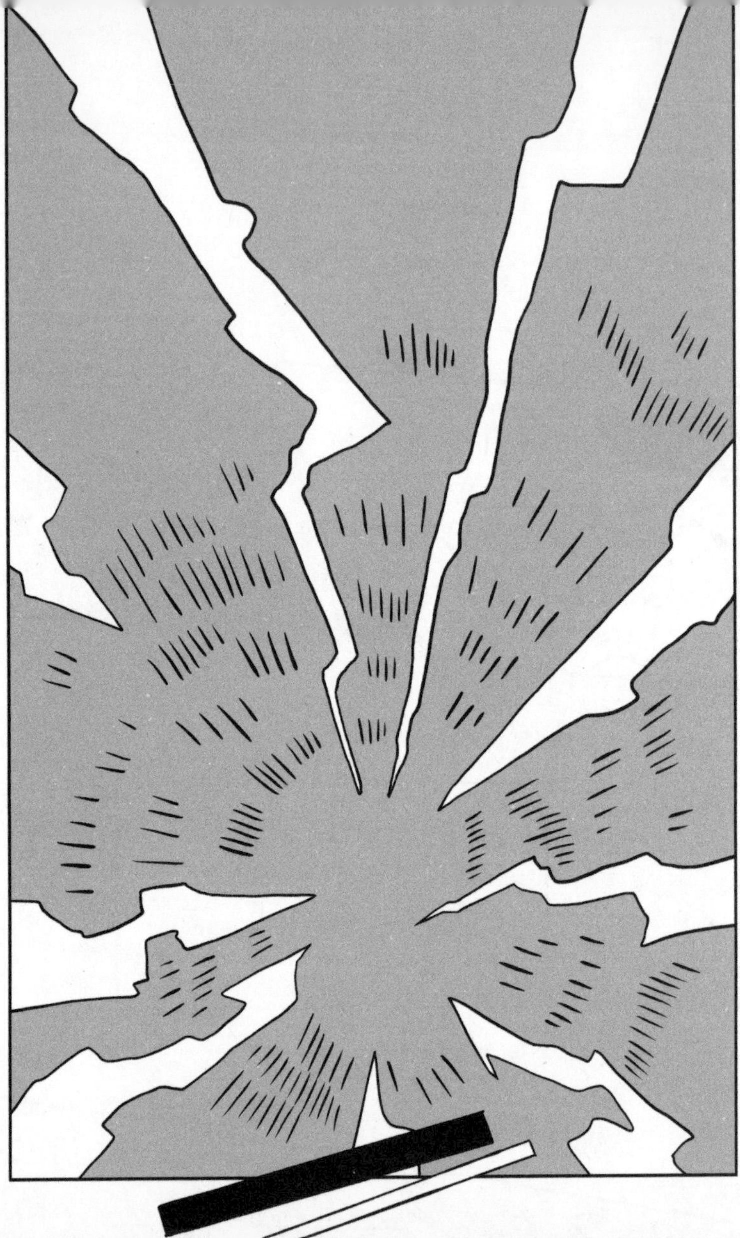

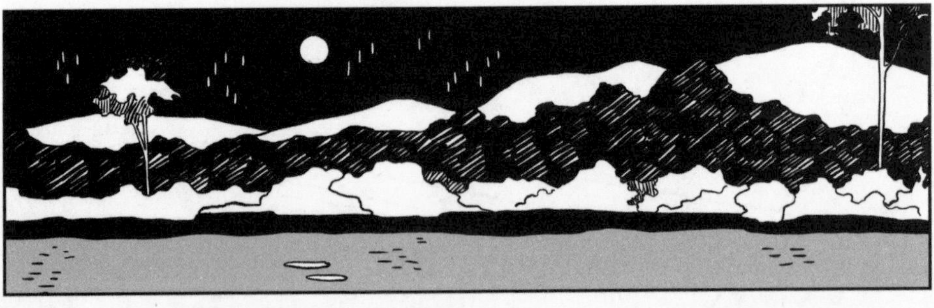

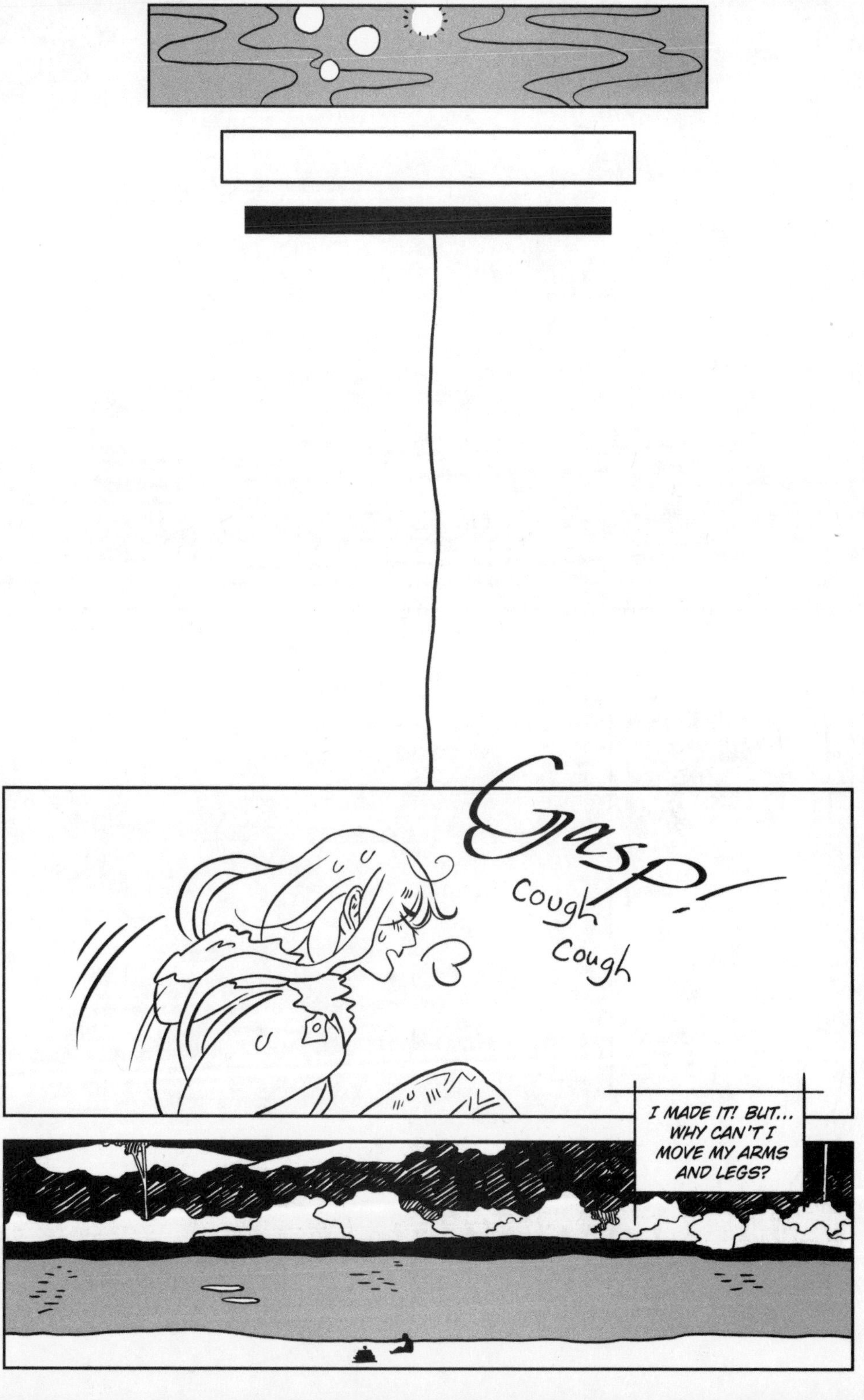
Gasp!
cough
cough
I MADE IT! BUT... WHY CAN'T I MOVE MY ARMS AND LEGS?

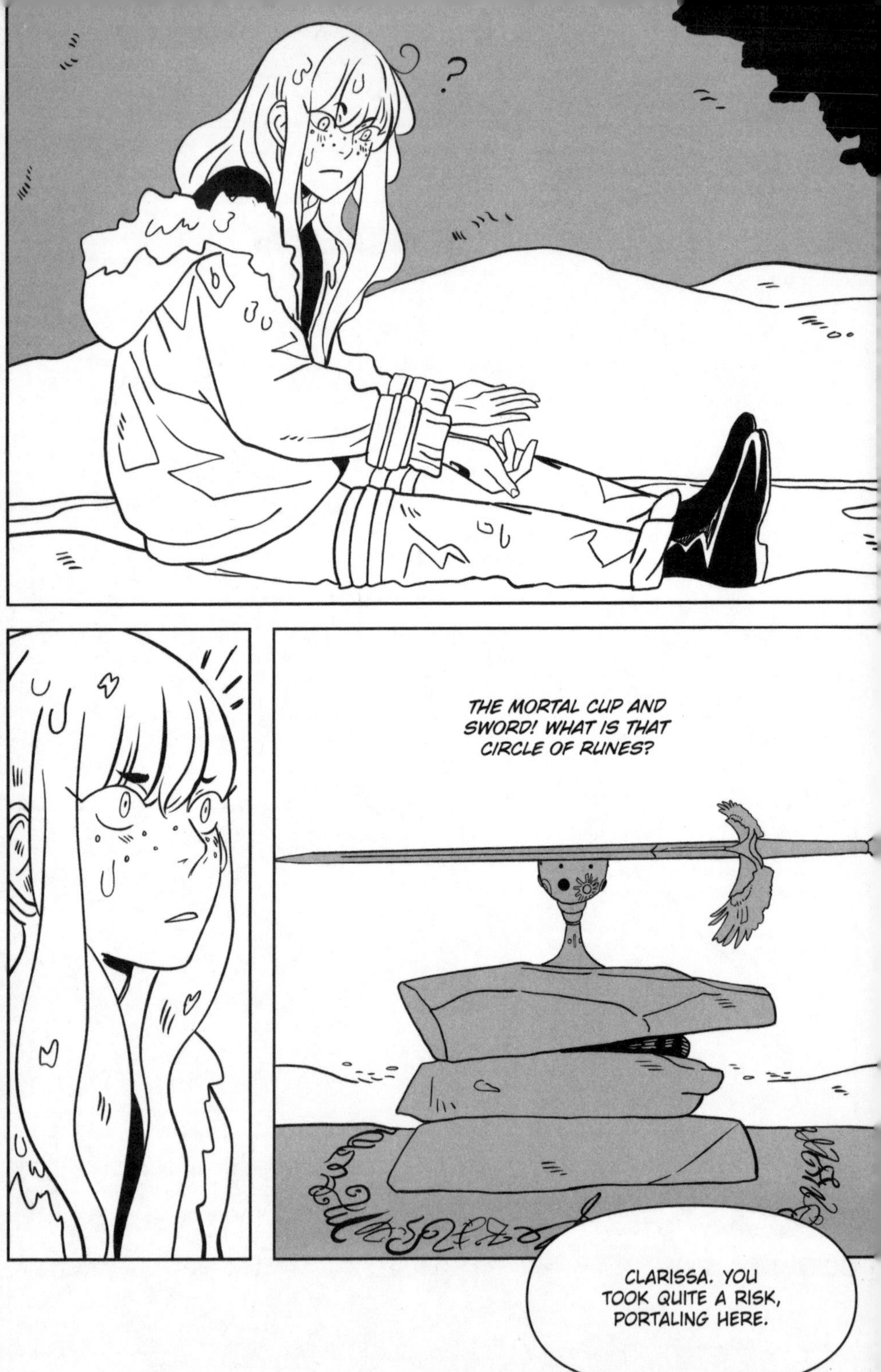
?
THE MORTAL CUP AND SWORD! WHAT IS THAT CIRCLE OF RUNES?
CLARISSA. YOU TOOK QUITE A RISK, PORTALING HERE.

THE MORTAL INSTRUMENTS

THE GRAPHIC NOVEL

THE MORTAL INSTRUMENTS

THE GRAPHIC NOVEL

Chapter 36

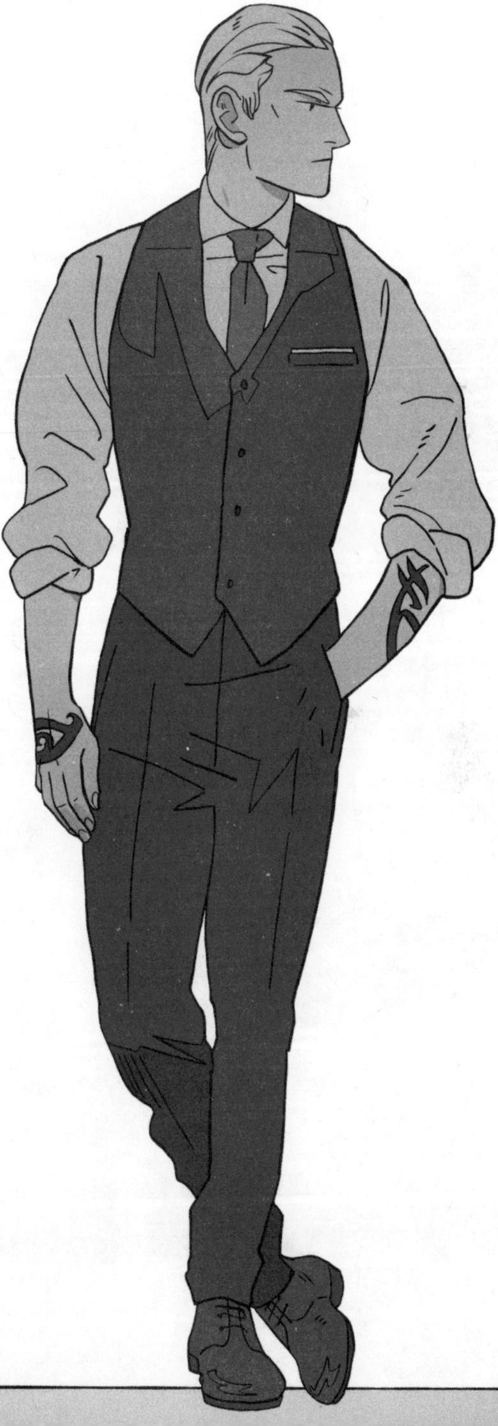

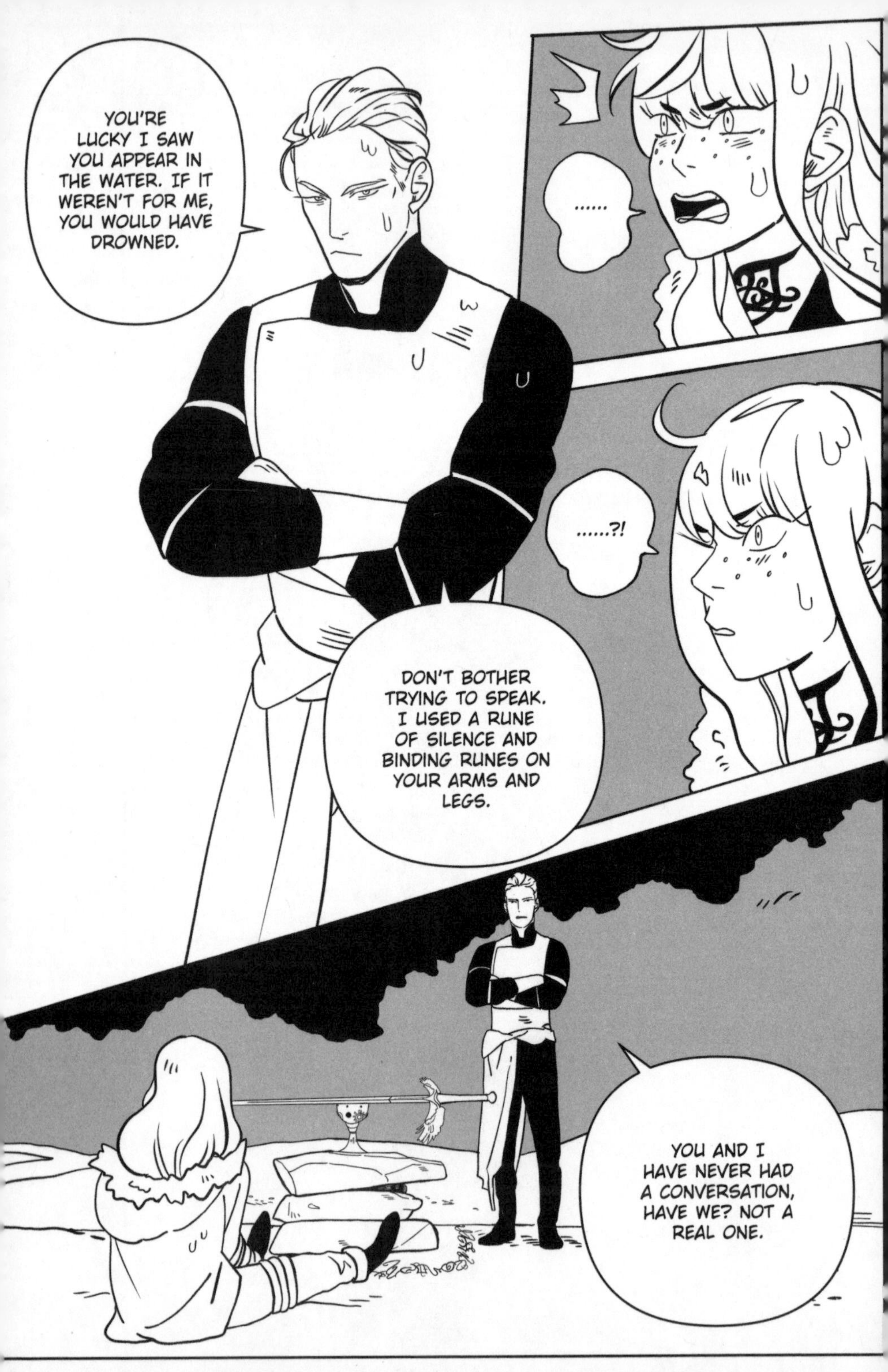
YOU'RE LUCKY I SAW YOU APPEAR IN THE WATER. IF IT WEREN'T FOR ME, YOU WOULD HAVE DROWNED.
......
......?!
DON'T BOTHER TRYING TO SPEAK. I USED A RUNE OF SILENCE AND BINDING RUNES ON YOUR ARMS AND LEGS.
YOU AND I HAVE NEVER HAD A CONVERSATION, HAVE WE? NOT A REAL ONE.

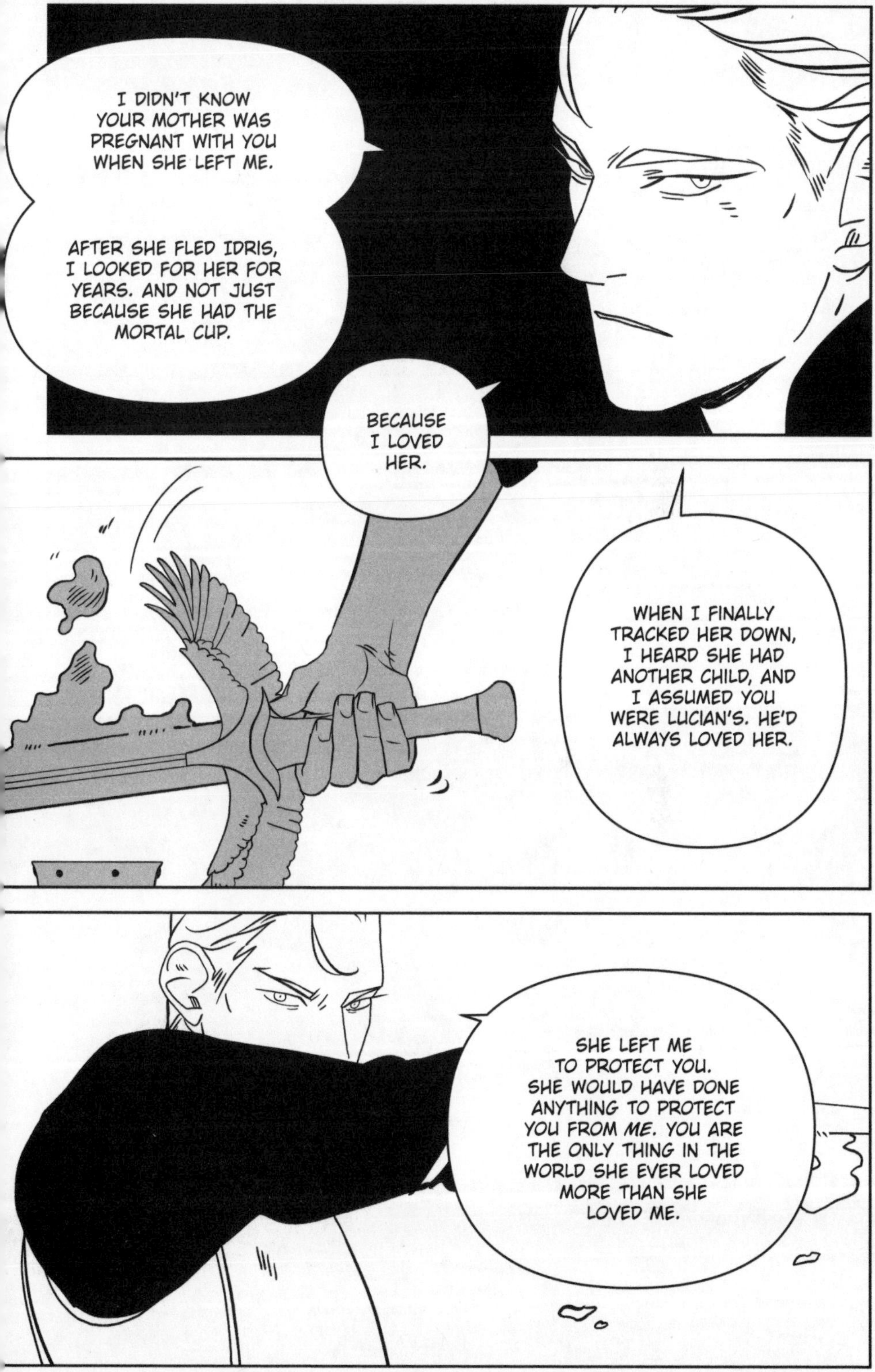
I DIDN'T KNOW YOUR MOTHER WAS PREGNANT WITH YOU WHEN SHE LEFT ME.
AFTER SHE FLED IDRIS, I LOOKED FOR HER FOR YEARS. AND NOT JUST BECAUSE SHE HAD THE MORTAL CUP.
BECAUSE I LOVED HER.
WHEN I FINALLY TRACKED HER DOWN, I HEARD SHE HAD ANOTHER CHILD, AND I ASSUMED YOU WERE LUCIAN'S. HE'D ALWAYS LOVED HER.
SHE LEFT ME TO PROTECT YOU. SHE WOULD HAVE DONE ANYTHING TO PROTECT YOU FROM *ME*. YOU ARE THE ONLY THING IN THE WORLD SHE EVER LOVED MORE THAN SHE LOVED ME.

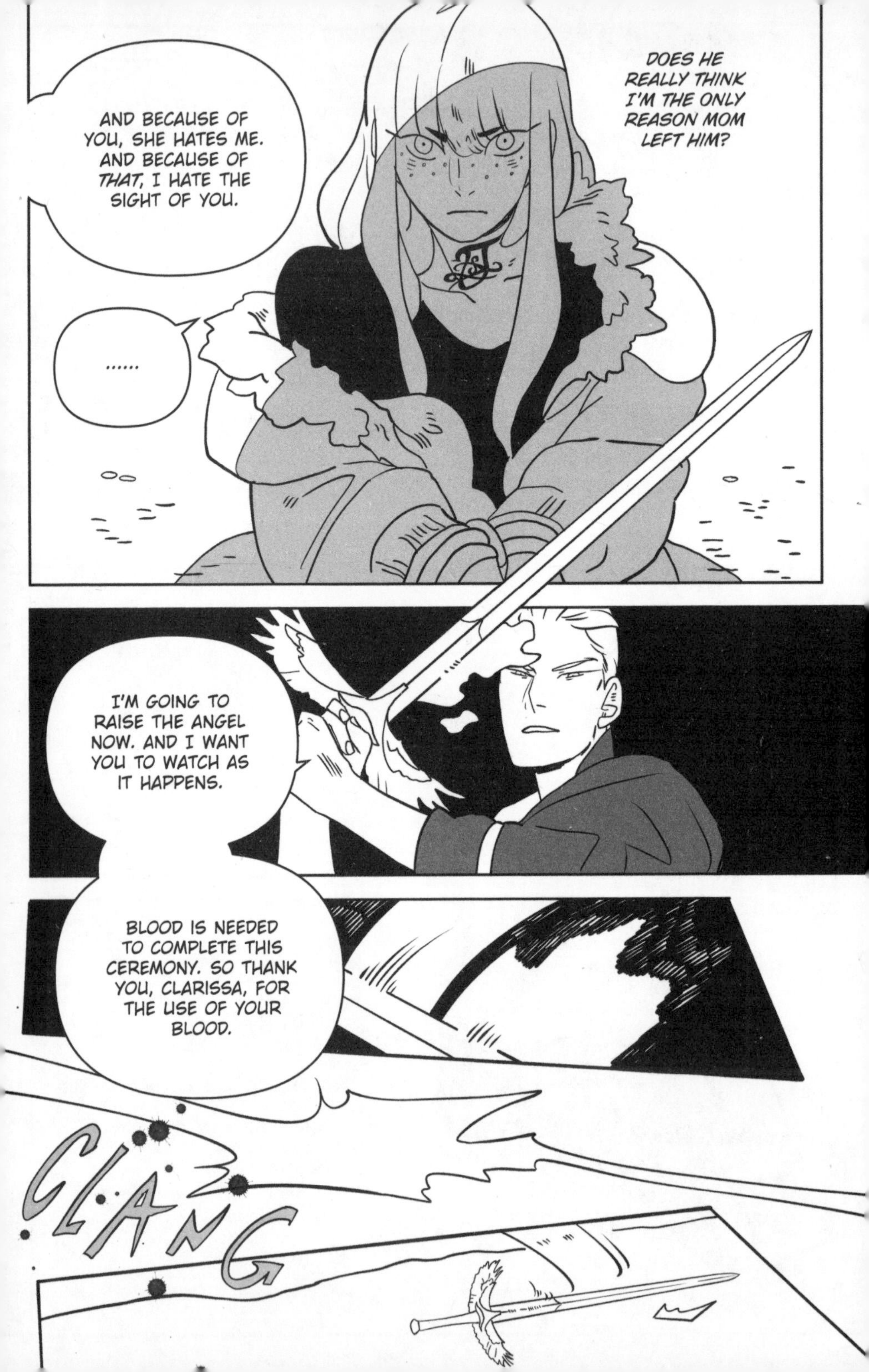
AND BECAUSE OF YOU, SHE HATES ME. AND BECAUSE OF *THAT*, I HATE THE SIGHT OF YOU.
DOES HE REALLY THINK I'M THE ONLY REASON MOM LEFT HIM?
......
I'M GOING TO RAISE THE ANGEL NOW. AND I WANT YOU TO WATCH AS IT HAPPENS.
BLOOD IS NEEDED TO COMPLETE THIS CEREMONY. SO THANK YOU, CLARISSA, FOR THE USE OF YOUR BLOOD.
CLANG

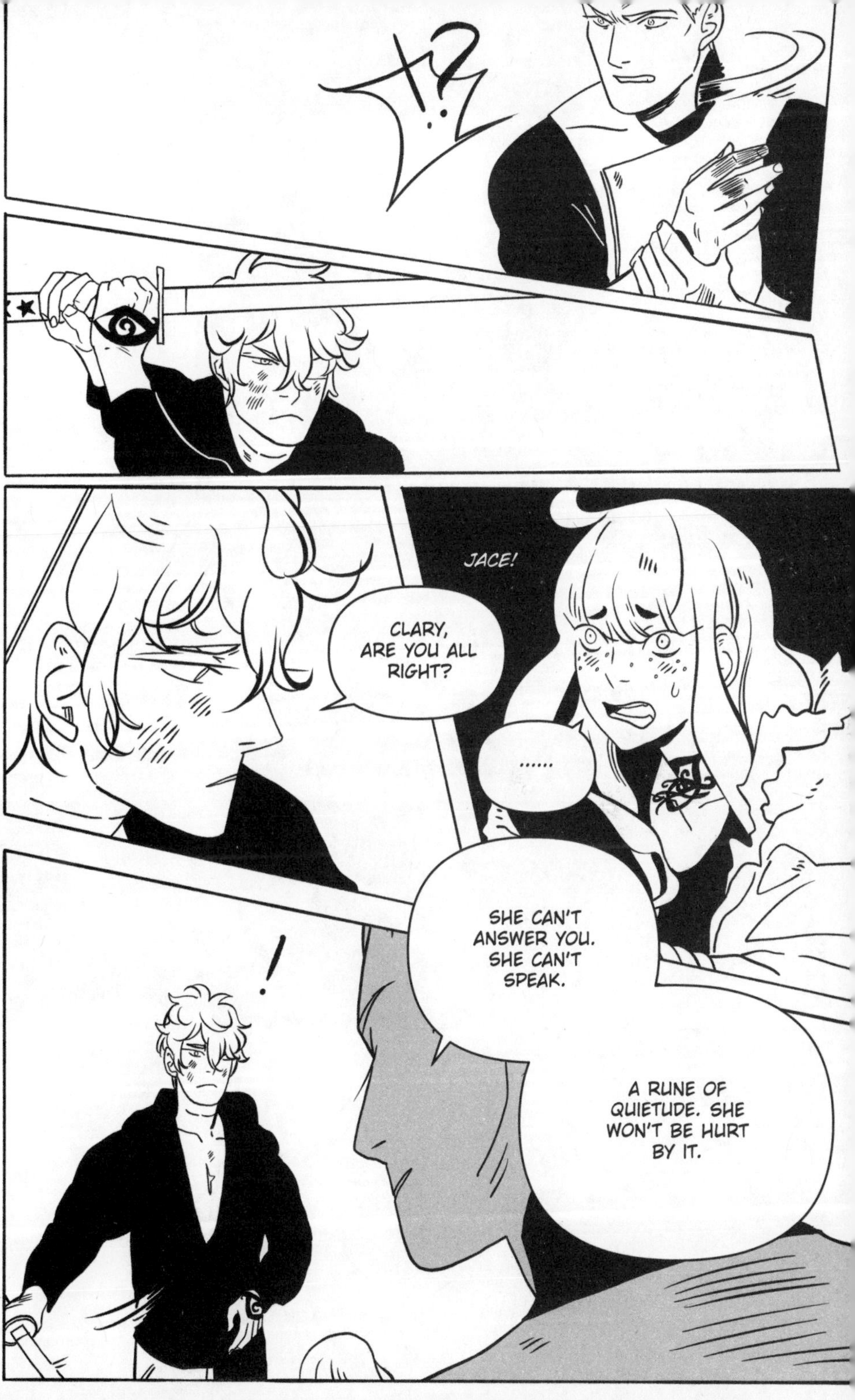
!?
JACE!
CLARY, ARE YOU ALL RIGHT?
......
!
SHE CAN'T ANSWER YOU. SHE CAN'T SPEAK.
A RUNE OF QUIETUDE. SHE WON'T BE HURT BY IT.

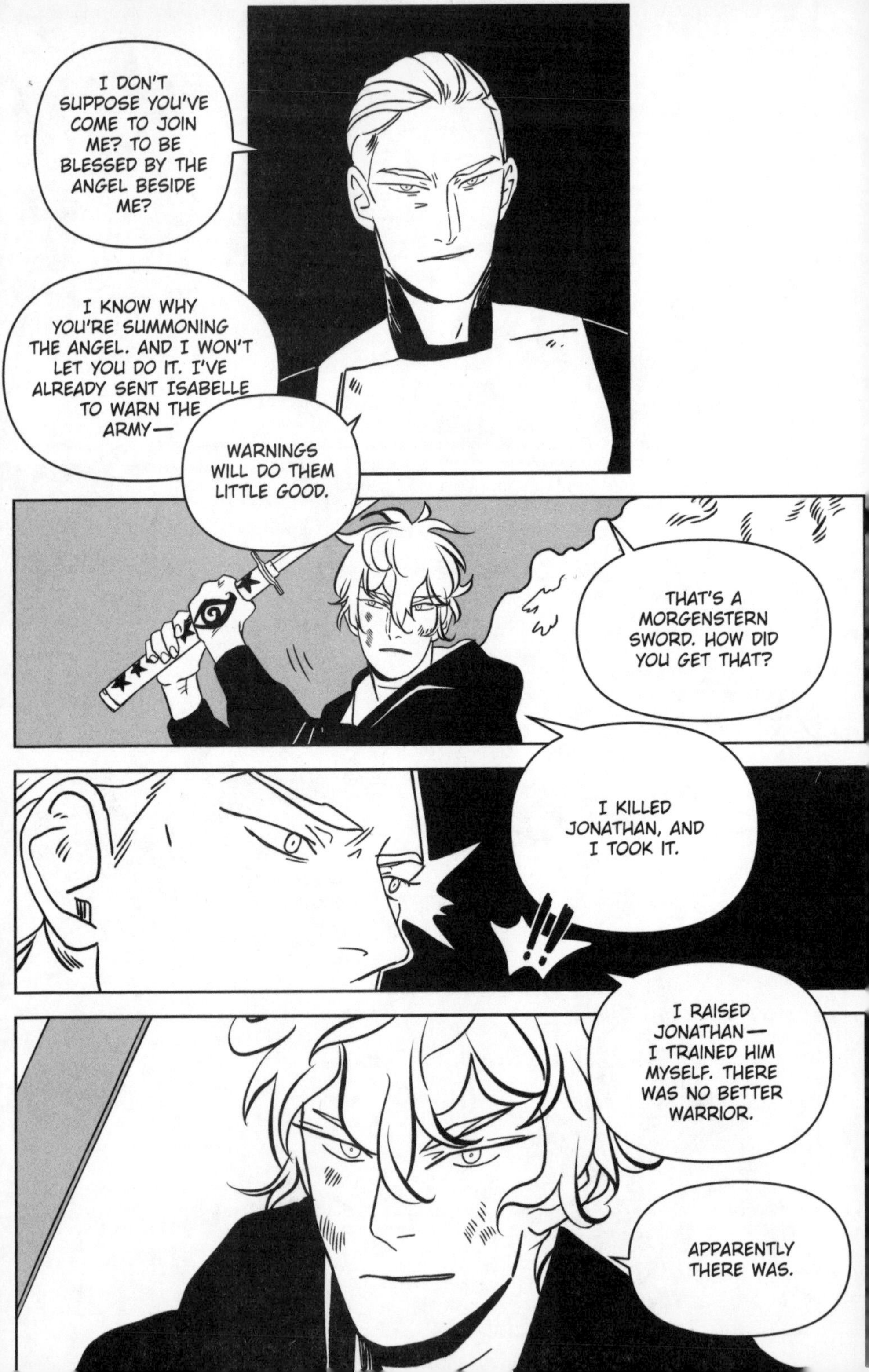
I DON'T SUPPOSE YOU'VE COME TO JOIN ME? TO BE BLESSED BY THE ANGEL BESIDE ME?
I KNOW WHY YOU'RE SUMMONING THE ANGEL. AND I WON'T LET YOU DO IT. I'VE ALREADY SENT ISABELLE TO WARN THE ARMY—
WARNINGS WILL DO THEM LITTLE GOOD.
THAT'S A MORGENSTERN SWORD. HOW DID YOU GET THAT?
I KILLED JONATHAN, AND I TOOK IT.
!!
I RAISED JONATHAN— I TRAINED HIM MYSELF. THERE WAS NO BETTER WARRIOR.
APPARENTLY THERE WAS.

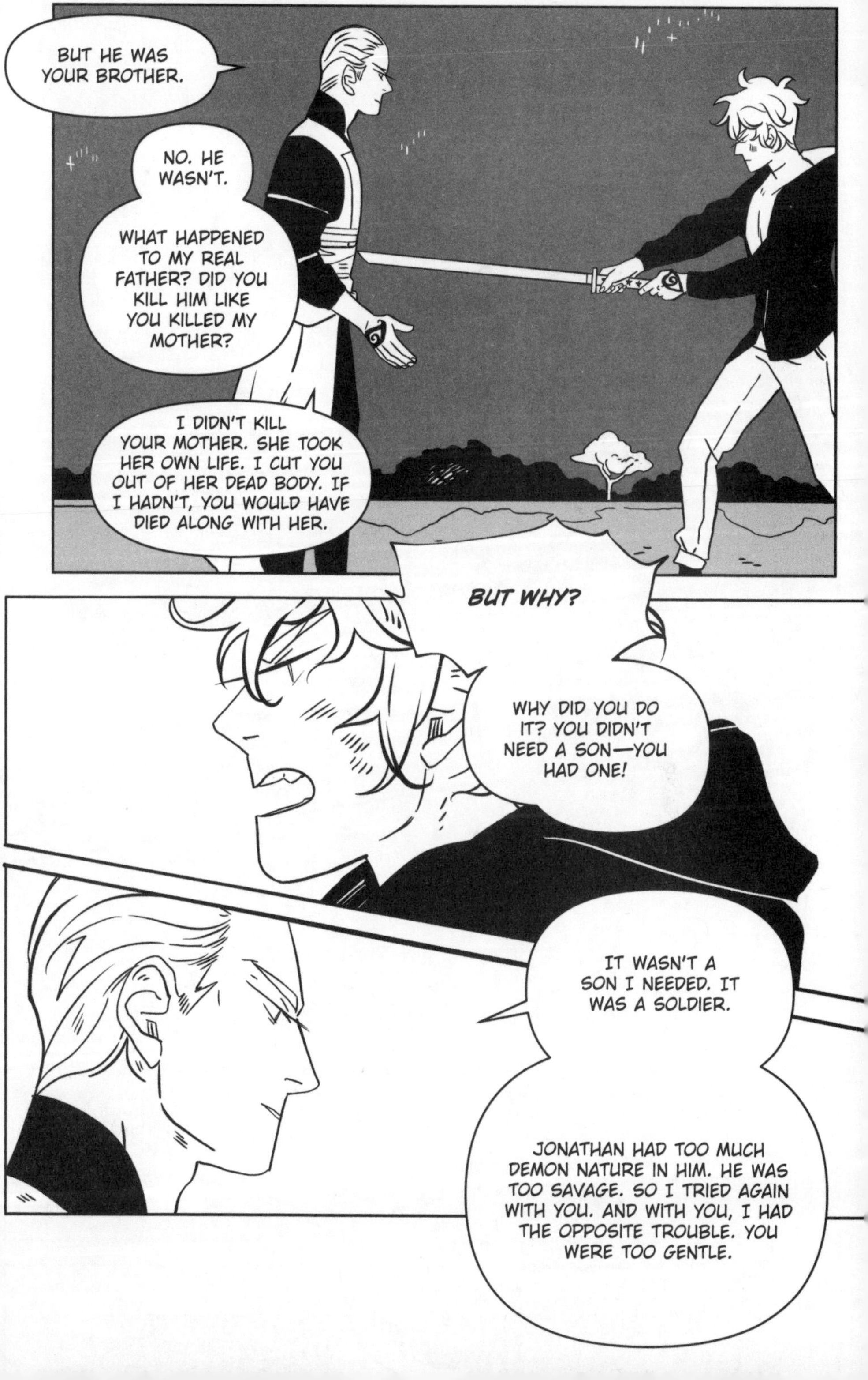
BUT HE WAS YOUR BROTHER.
NO. HE WASN'T.
WHAT HAPPENED TO MY REAL FATHER? DID YOU KILL HIM LIKE YOU KILLED MY MOTHER?
I DIDN'T KILL YOUR MOTHER. SHE TOOK HER OWN LIFE. I CUT YOU OUT OF HER DEAD BODY. IF I HADN'T, YOU WOULD HAVE DIED ALONG WITH HER.
BUT WHY?
WHY DID YOU DO IT? YOU DIDN'T NEED A SON—YOU HAD ONE!
IT WASN'T A SON I NEEDED. IT WAS A SOLDIER.
JONATHAN HAD TOO MUCH DEMON NATURE IN HIM. HE WAS TOO SAVAGE. SO I TRIED AGAIN WITH YOU. AND WITH YOU, I HAD THE OPPOSITE TROUBLE. YOU WERE TOO GENTLE.

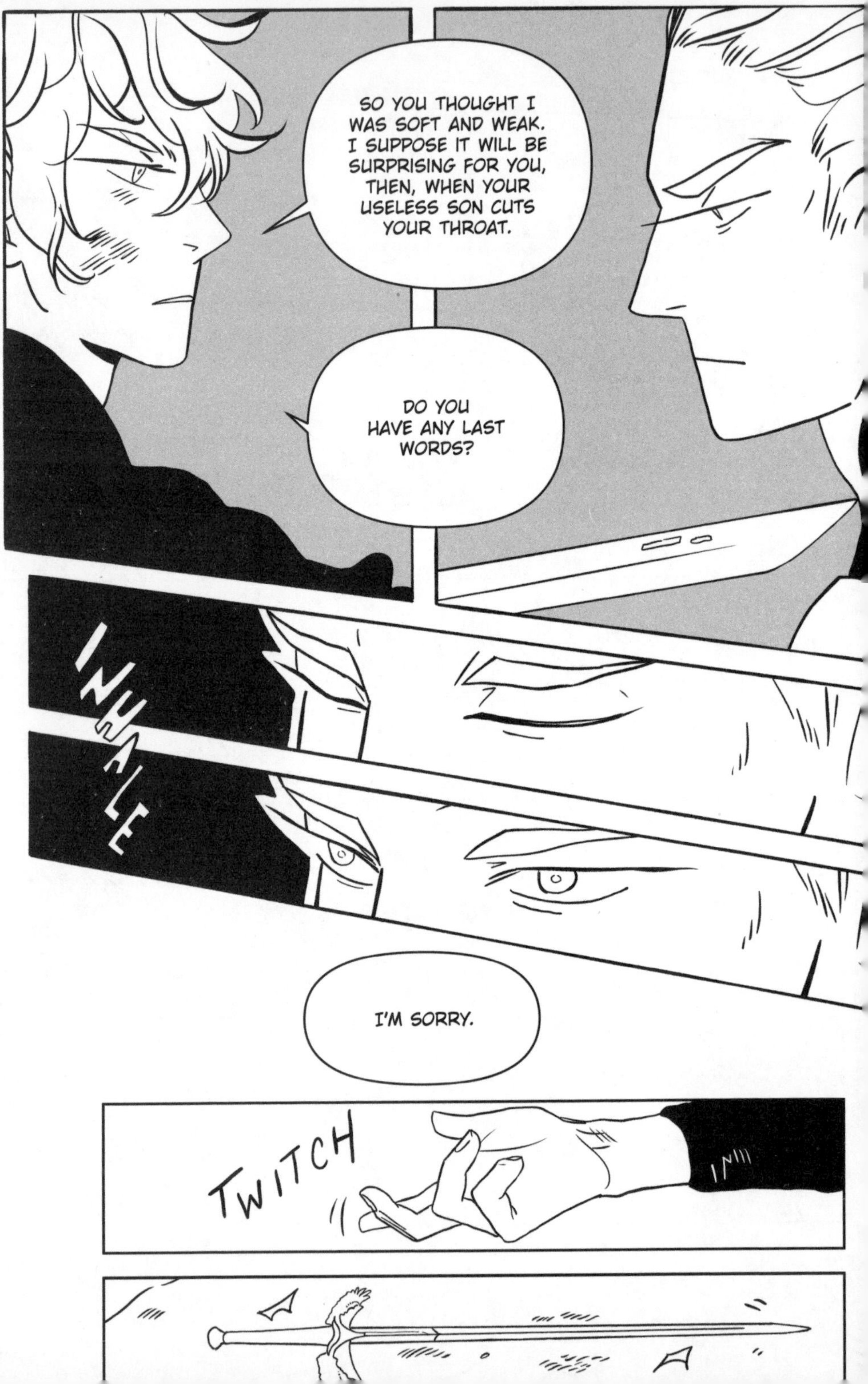
SO YOU THOUGHT I WAS SOFT AND WEAK. I SUPPOSE IT WILL BE SURPRISING FOR YOU, THEN, WHEN YOUR USELESS SON CUTS YOUR THROAT.
DO YOU HAVE ANY LAST WORDS?
INHALE
I'M SORRY.
TWITCH

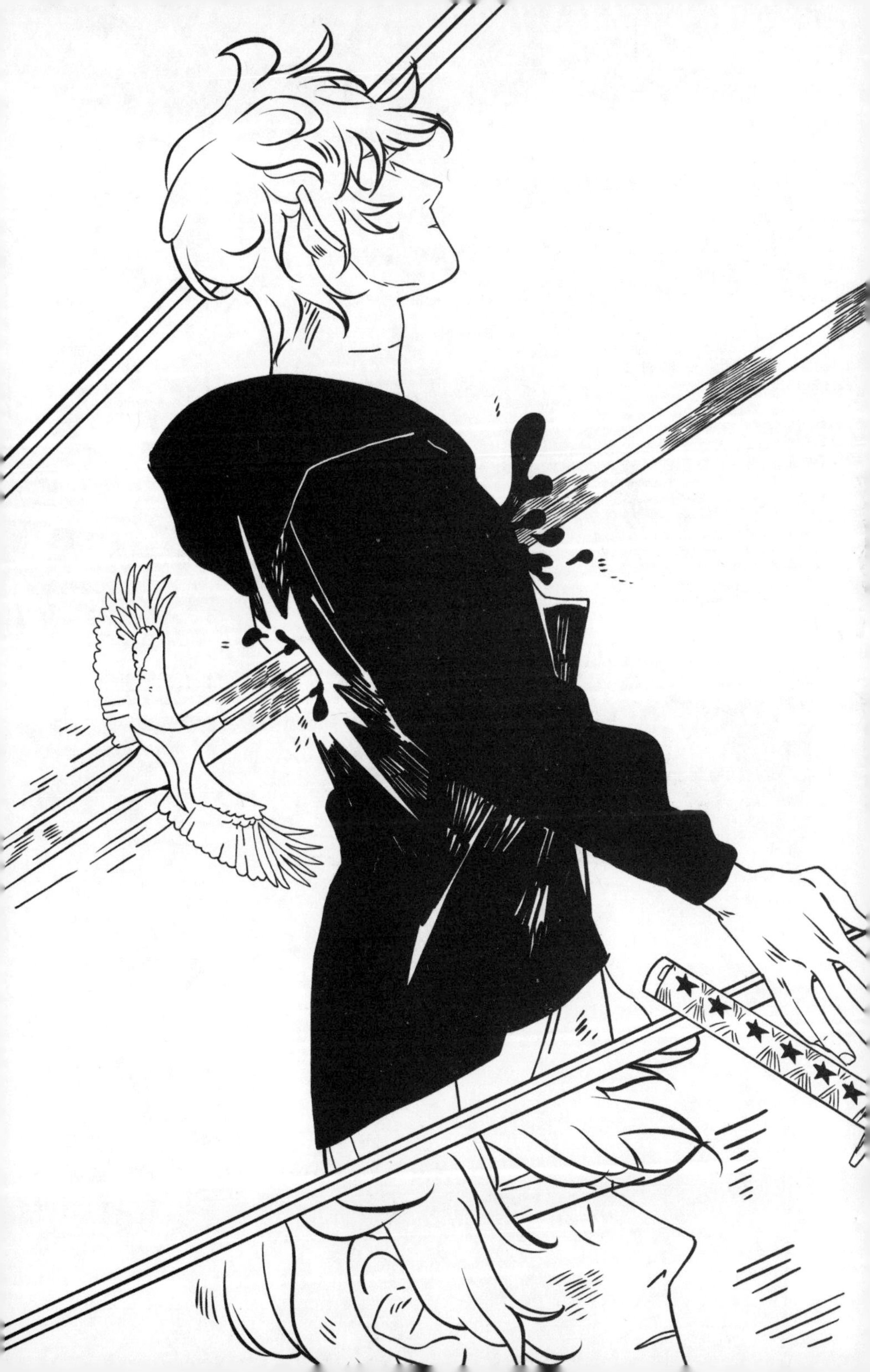

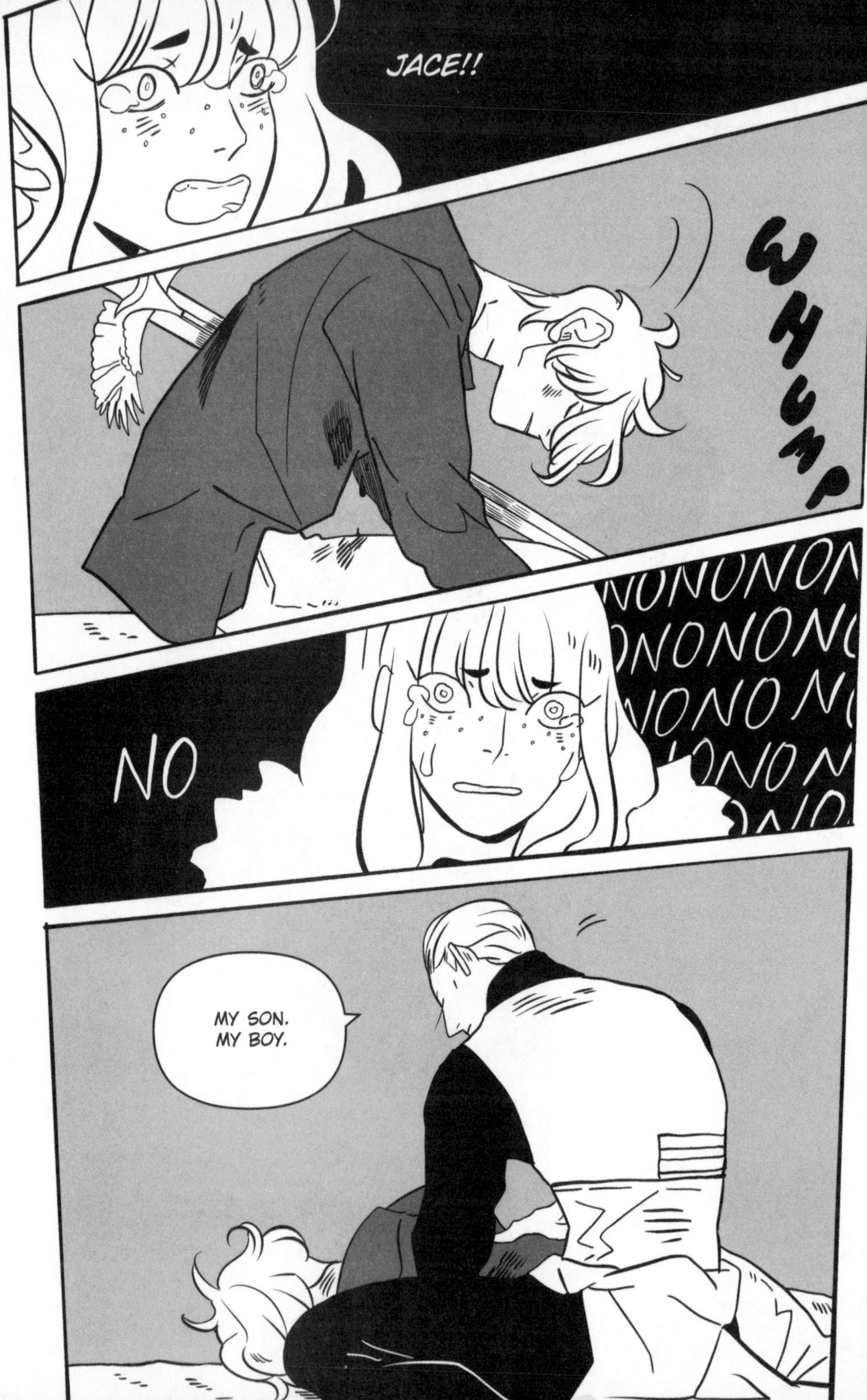
JACE!!
WHUMP
NO
NONONONONONONONONONONONONONONONONONO
MY SON.
MY BOY.

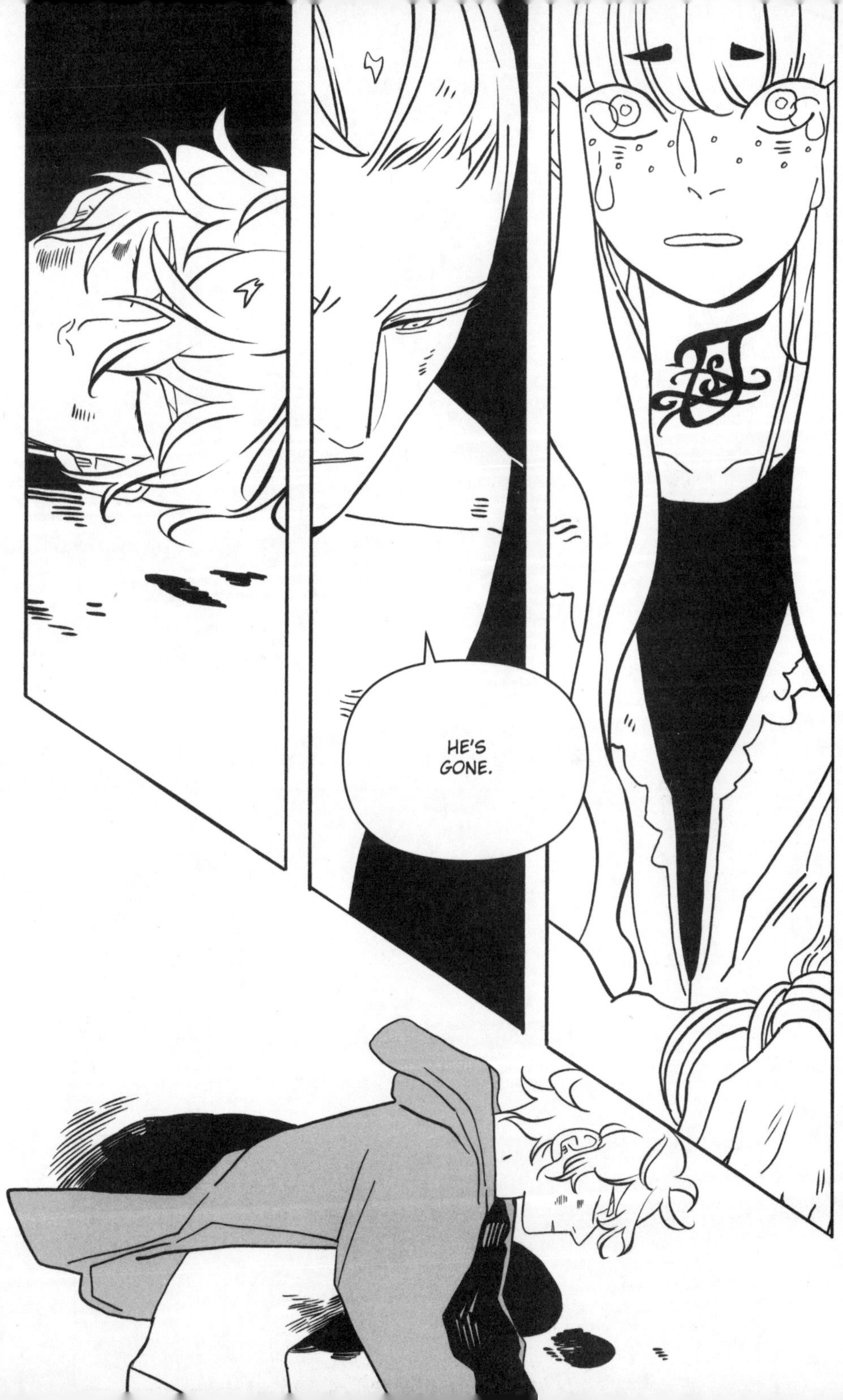
HE'S GONE.

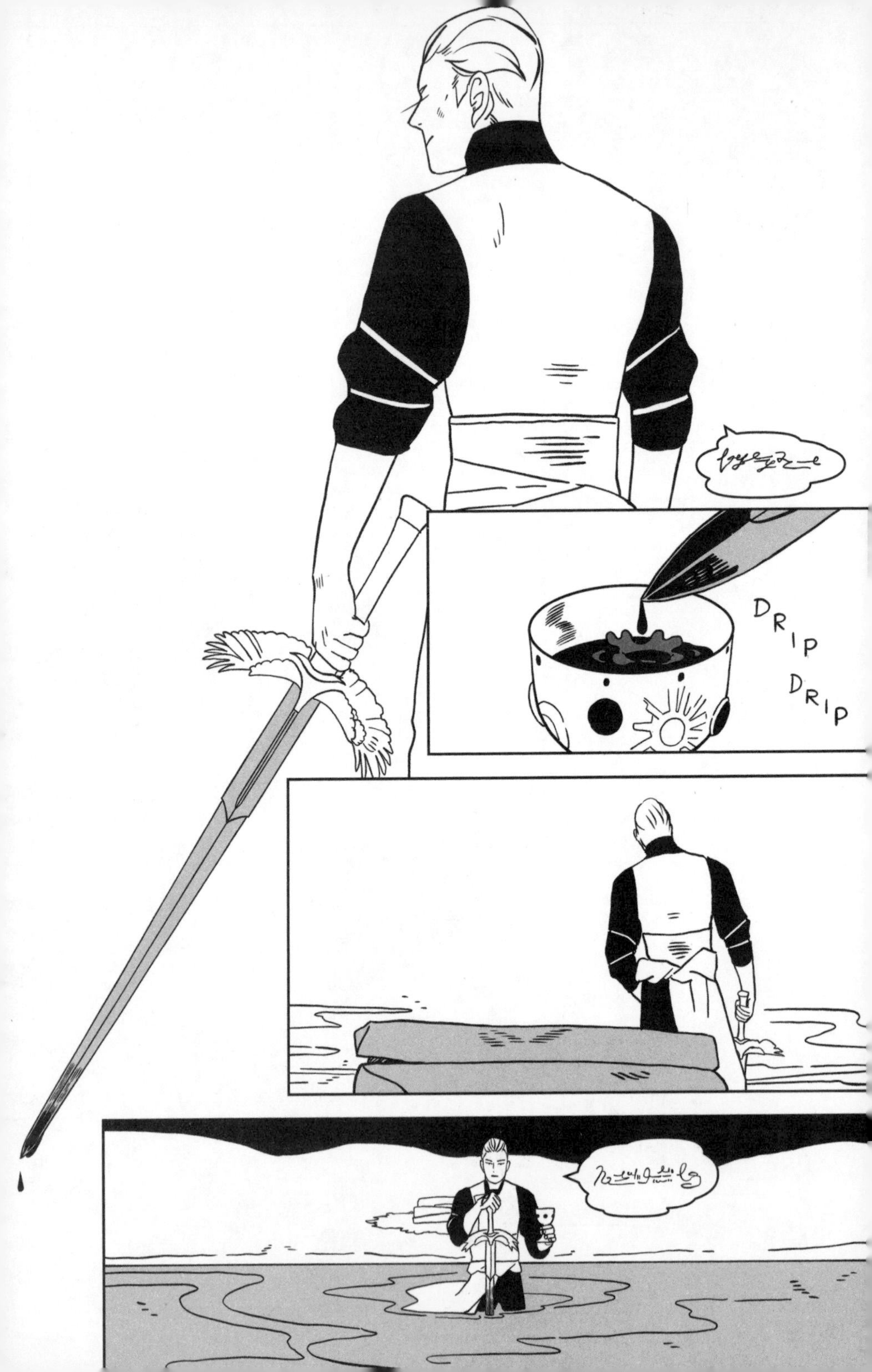
DRIP
DRIP

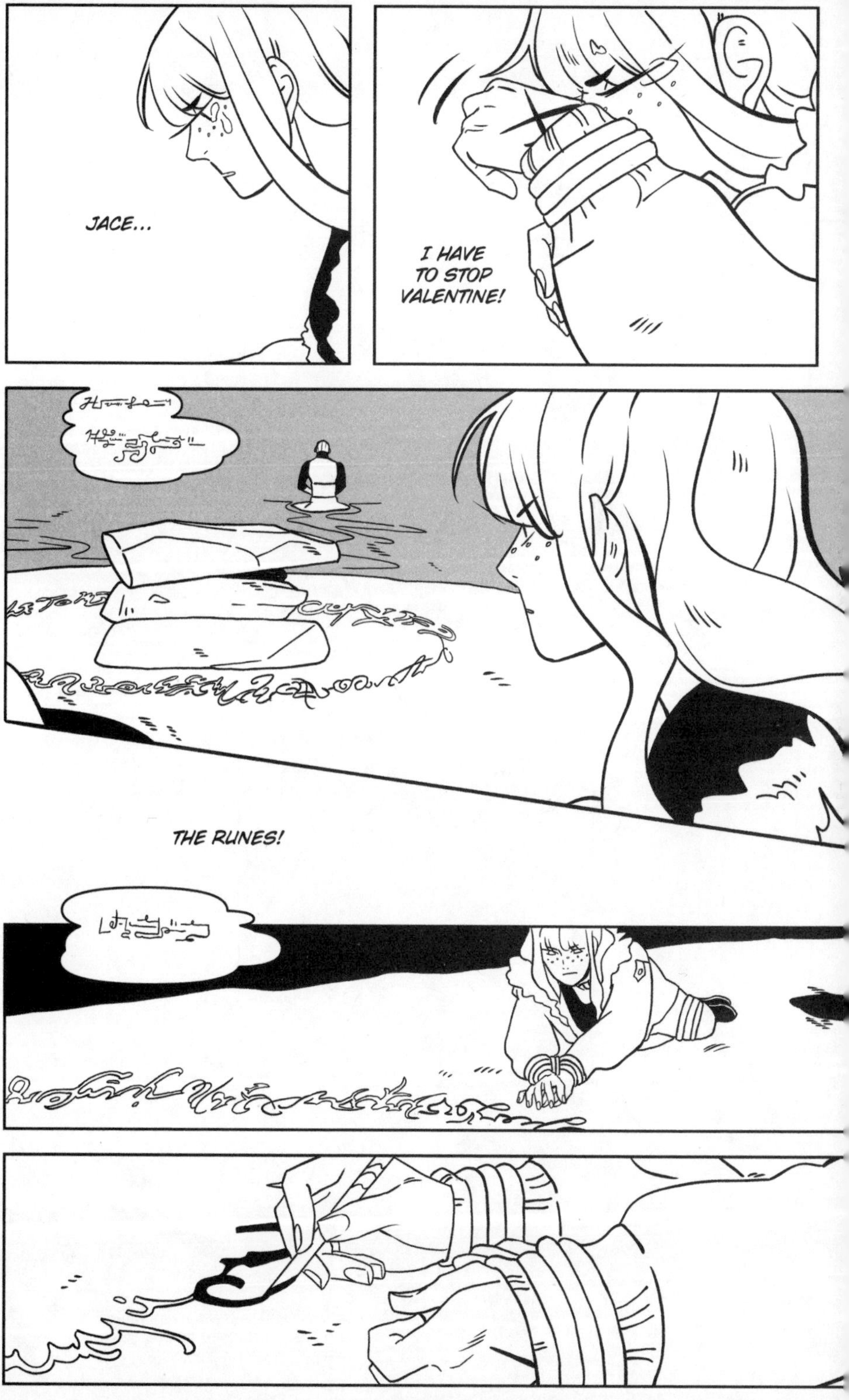
JACE...
I HAVE TO STOP VALENTINE!
THE RUNES!

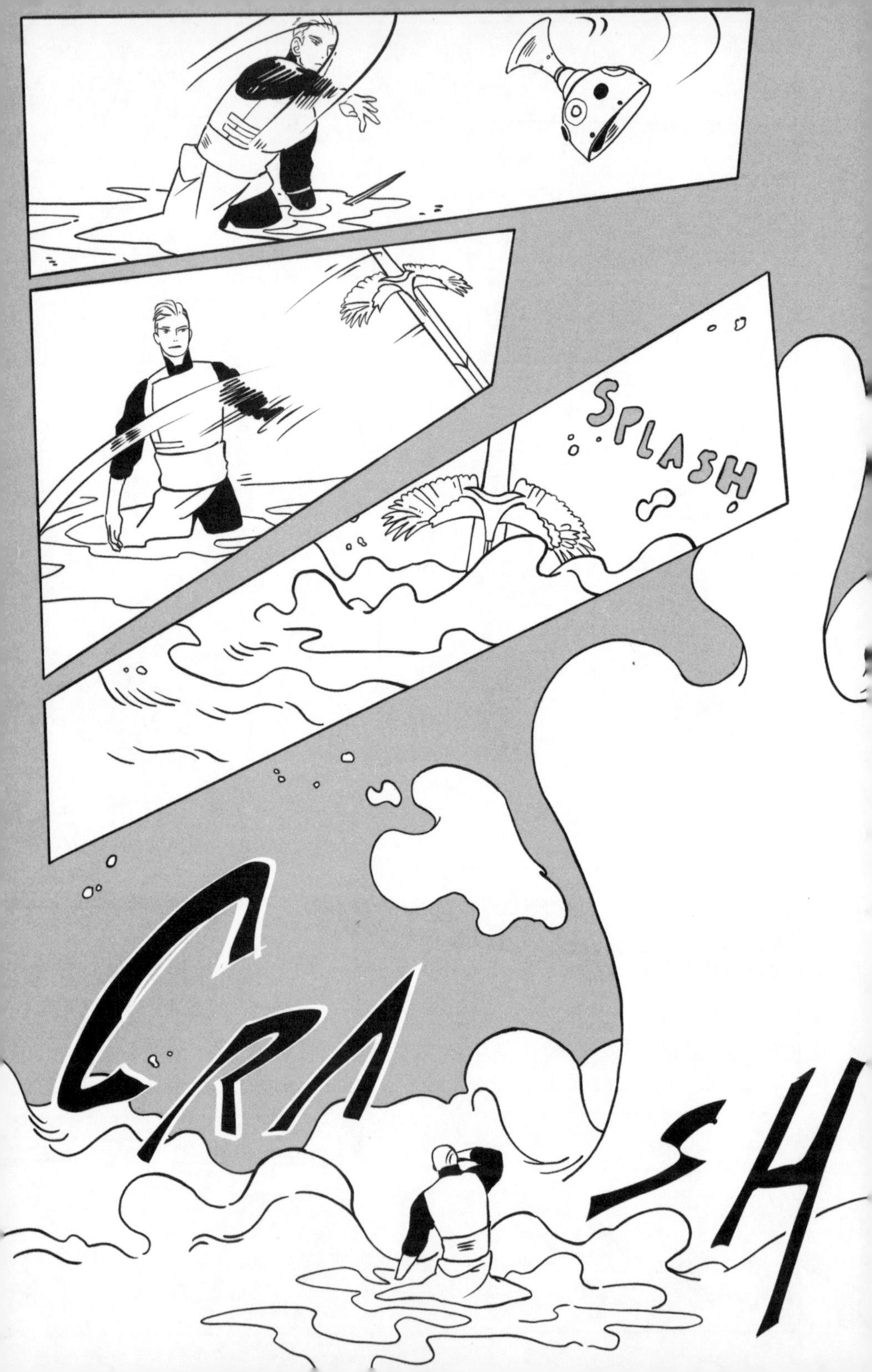
SPLASH
CRASH

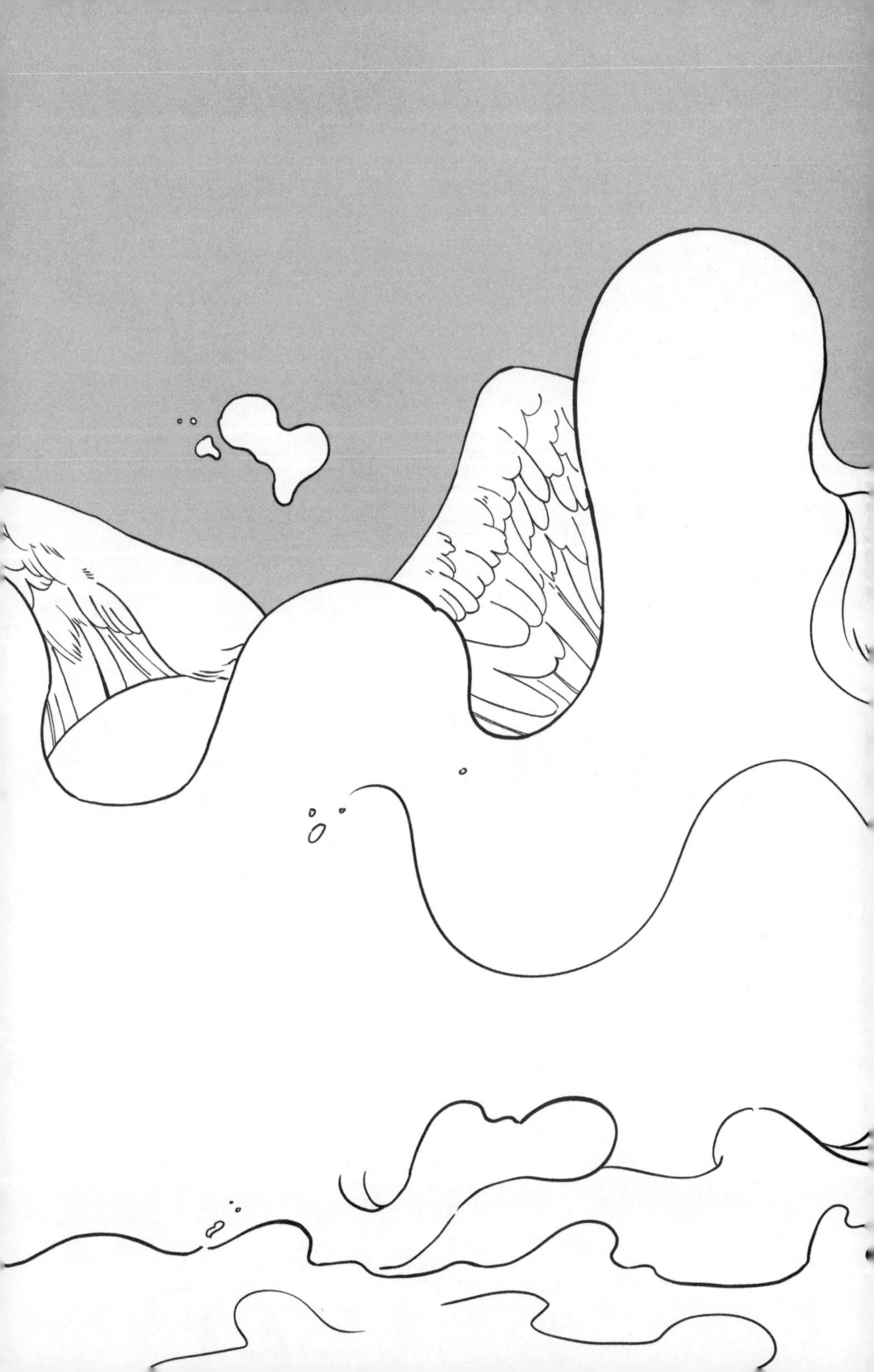

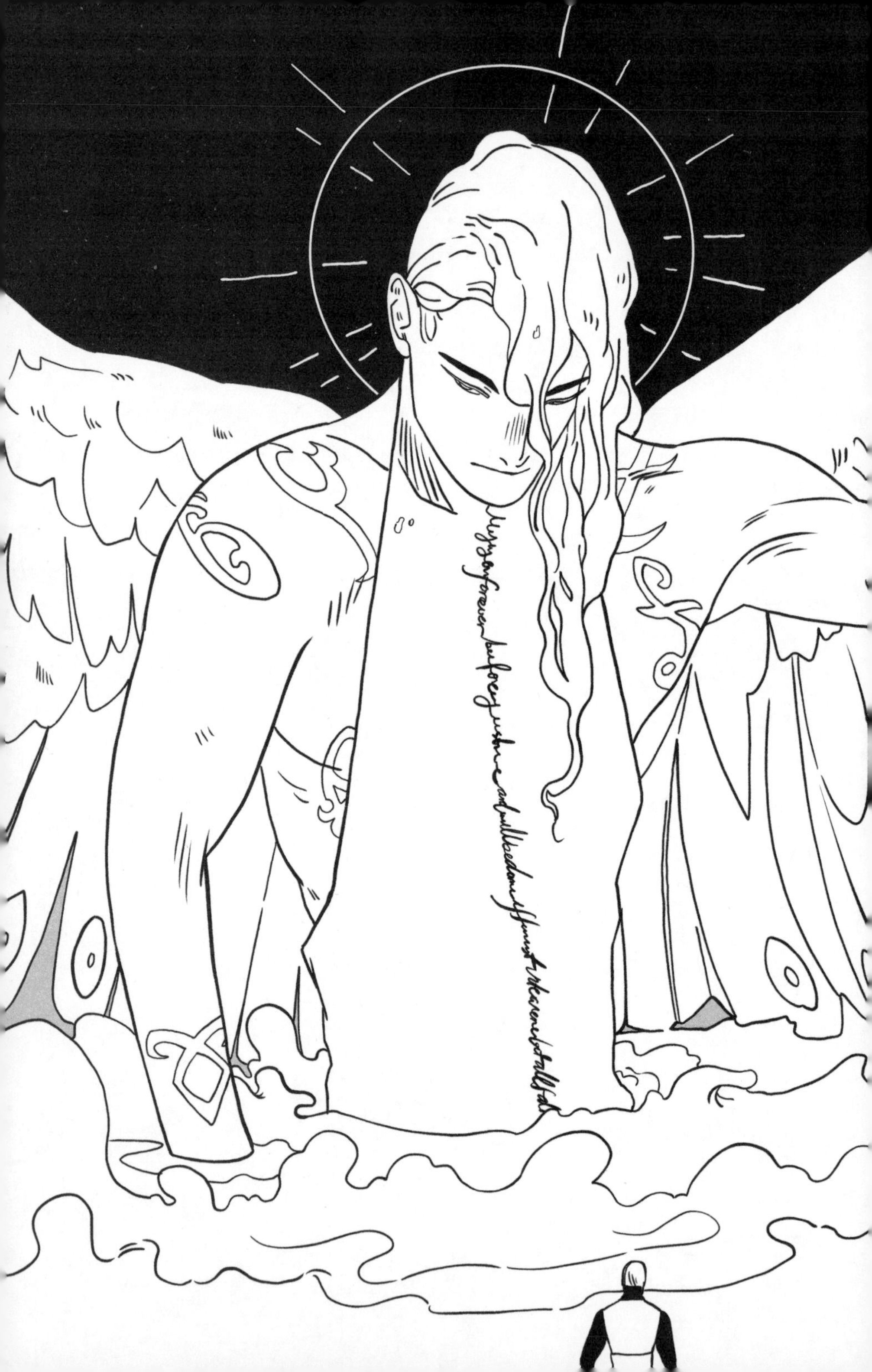

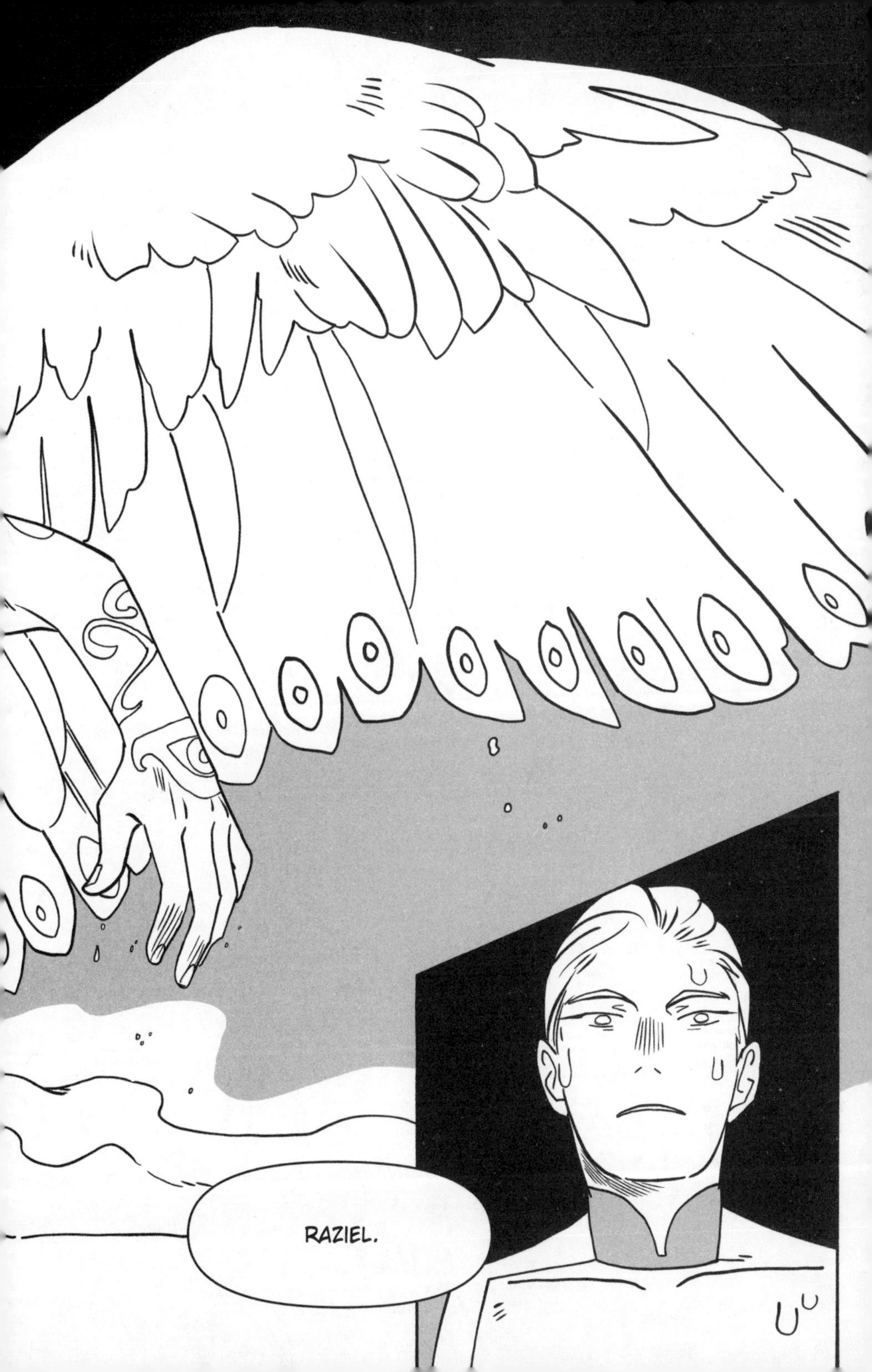
RAZIEL.

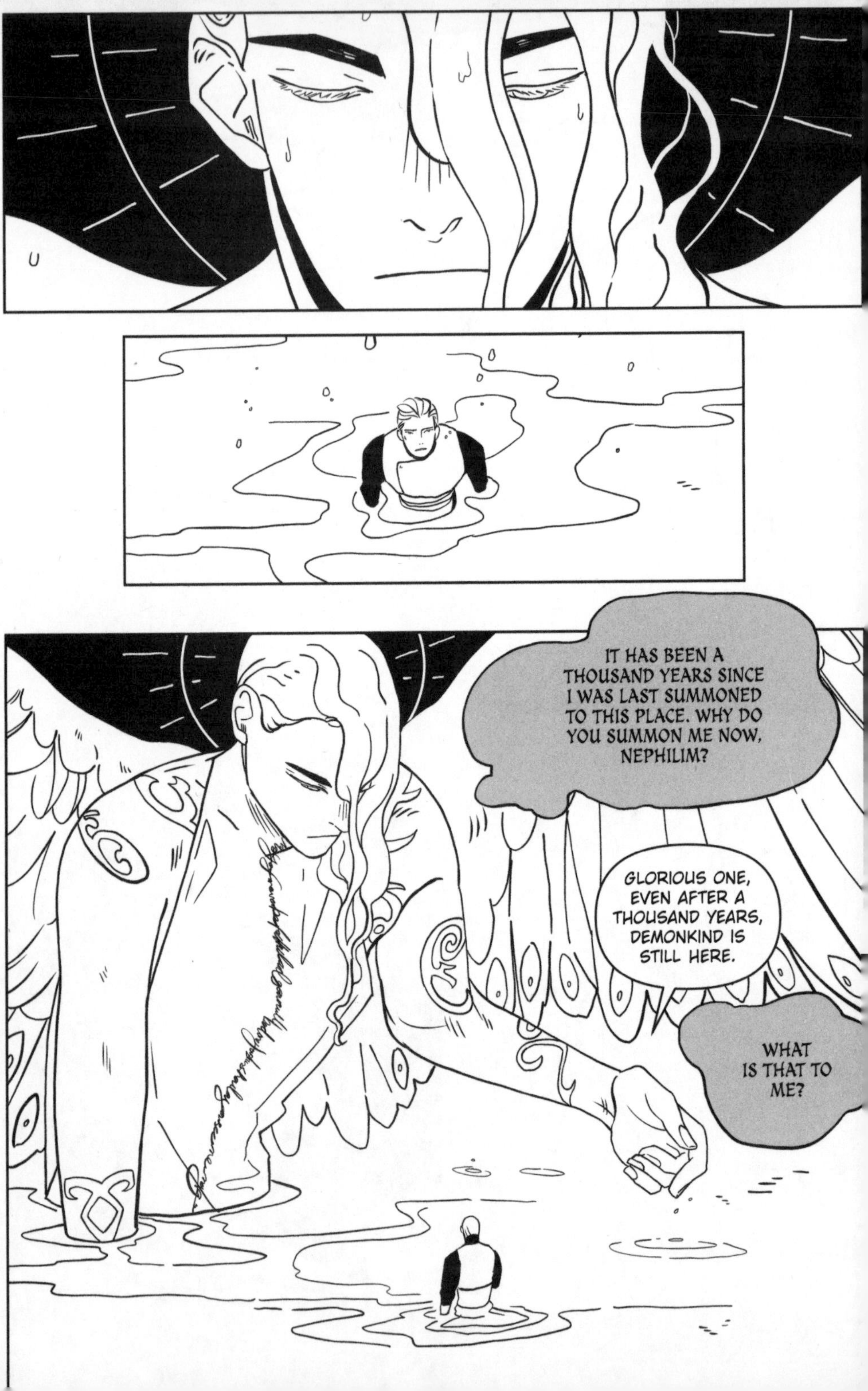
IT HAS BEEN A THOUSAND YEARS SINCE I WAS LAST SUMMONED TO THIS PLACE. WHY DO YOU SUMMON ME NOW, NEPHILIM?
GLORIOUS ONE, EVEN AFTER A THOUSAND YEARS, DEMONKIND IS STILL HERE.
WHAT IS THAT TO ME?

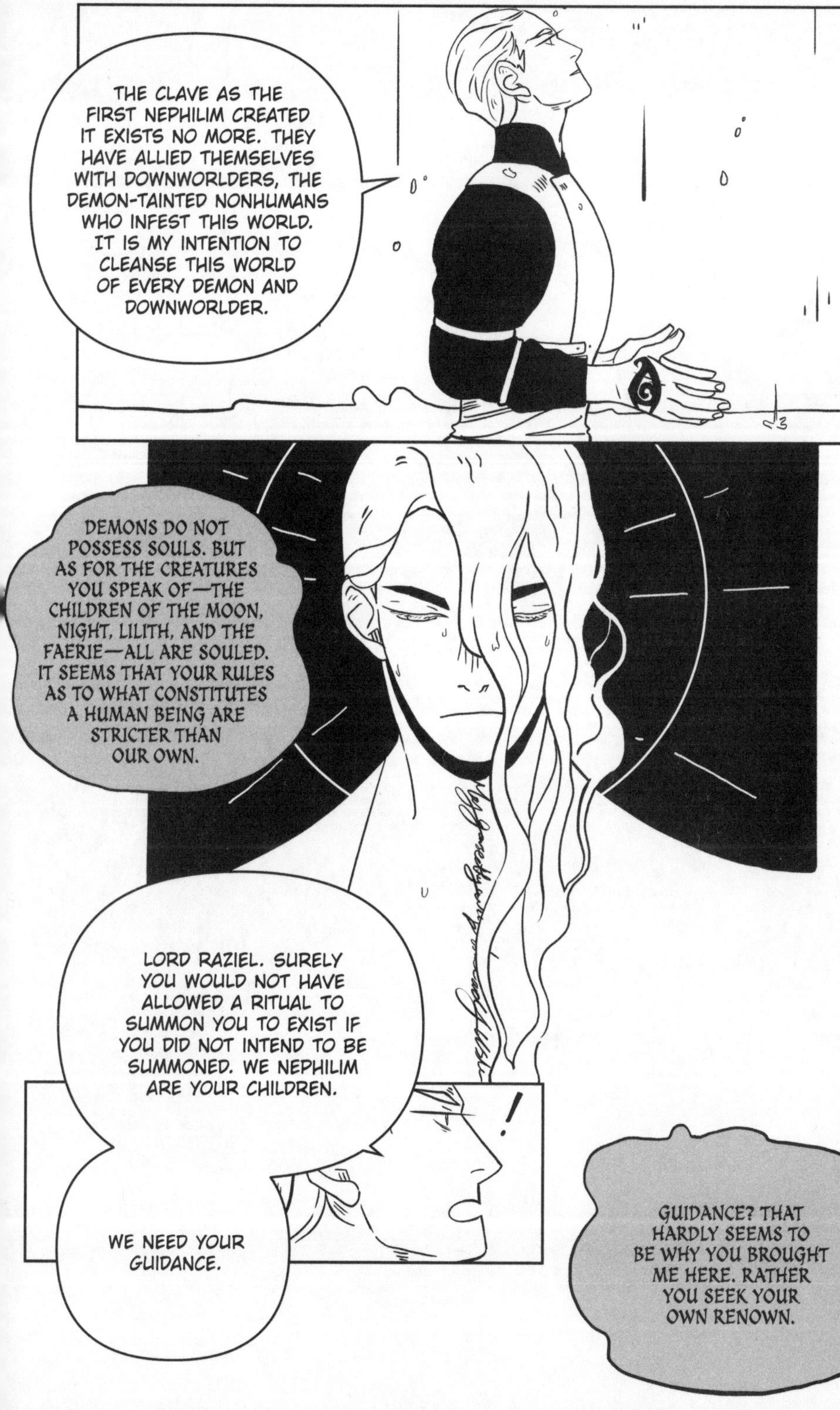
THE CLAVE AS THE FIRST NEPHILIM CREATED IT EXISTS NO MORE. THEY HAVE ALLIED THEMSELVES WITH DOWNWORLDERS, THE DEMON-TAINTED NONHUMANS WHO INFEST THIS WORLD. IT IS MY INTENTION TO CLEANSE THIS WORLD OF EVERY DEMON AND DOWNWORLDER.
DEMONS DO NOT POSSESS SOULS. BUT AS FOR THE CREATURES YOU SPEAK OF—THE CHILDREN OF THE MOON, NIGHT, LILITH, AND THE FAERIE—ALL ARE SOULED. IT SEEMS THAT YOUR RULES AS TO WHAT CONSTITUTES A HUMAN BEING ARE STRICTER THAN OUR OWN.
LORD RAZIEL. SURELY YOU WOULD NOT HAVE ALLOWED A RITUAL TO SUMMON YOU TO EXIST IF YOU DID NOT INTEND TO BE SUMMONED. WE NEPHILIM ARE YOUR CHILDREN.
!
WE NEED YOUR GUIDANCE.
GUIDANCE? THAT HARDLY SEEMS TO BE WHY YOU BROUGHT ME HERE. RATHER YOU SEEK YOUR OWN RENOWN.

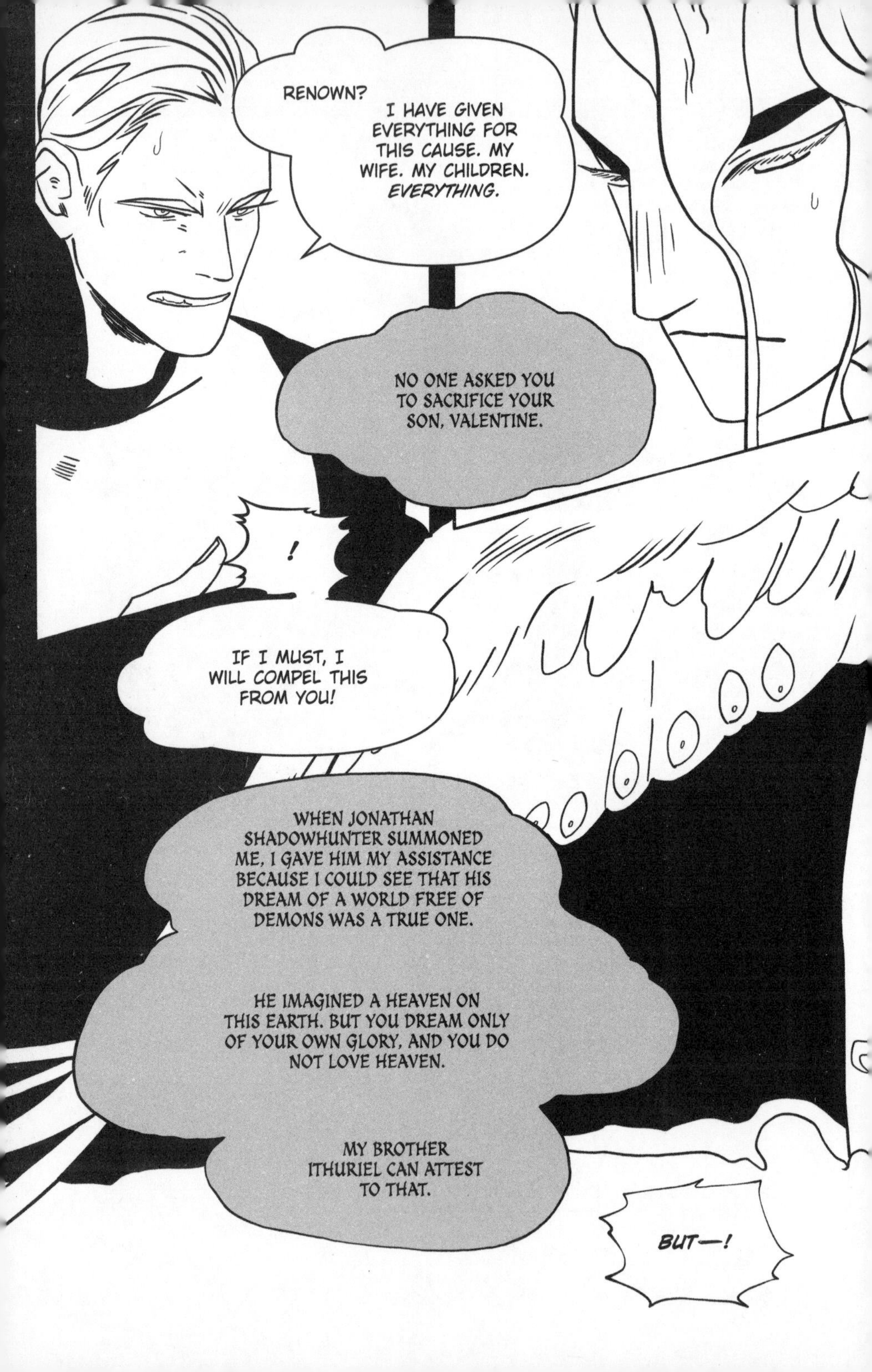
RENOWN? I HAVE GIVEN EVERYTHING FOR THIS CAUSE. MY WIFE. MY CHILDREN. *EVERYTHING.*
NO ONE ASKED YOU TO SACRIFICE YOUR SON, VALENTINE.
!
IF I MUST, I WILL COMPEL THIS FROM YOU!
WHEN JONATHAN SHADOWHUNTER SUMMONED ME, I GAVE HIM MY ASSISTANCE BECAUSE I COULD SEE THAT HIS DREAM OF A WORLD FREE OF DEMONS WAS A TRUE ONE.
HE IMAGINED A HEAVEN ON THIS EARTH. BUT YOU DREAM ONLY OF YOUR OWN GLORY, AND YOU DO NOT LOVE HEAVEN.
MY BROTHER ITHURIEL CAN ATTEST TO THAT.
BUT—!

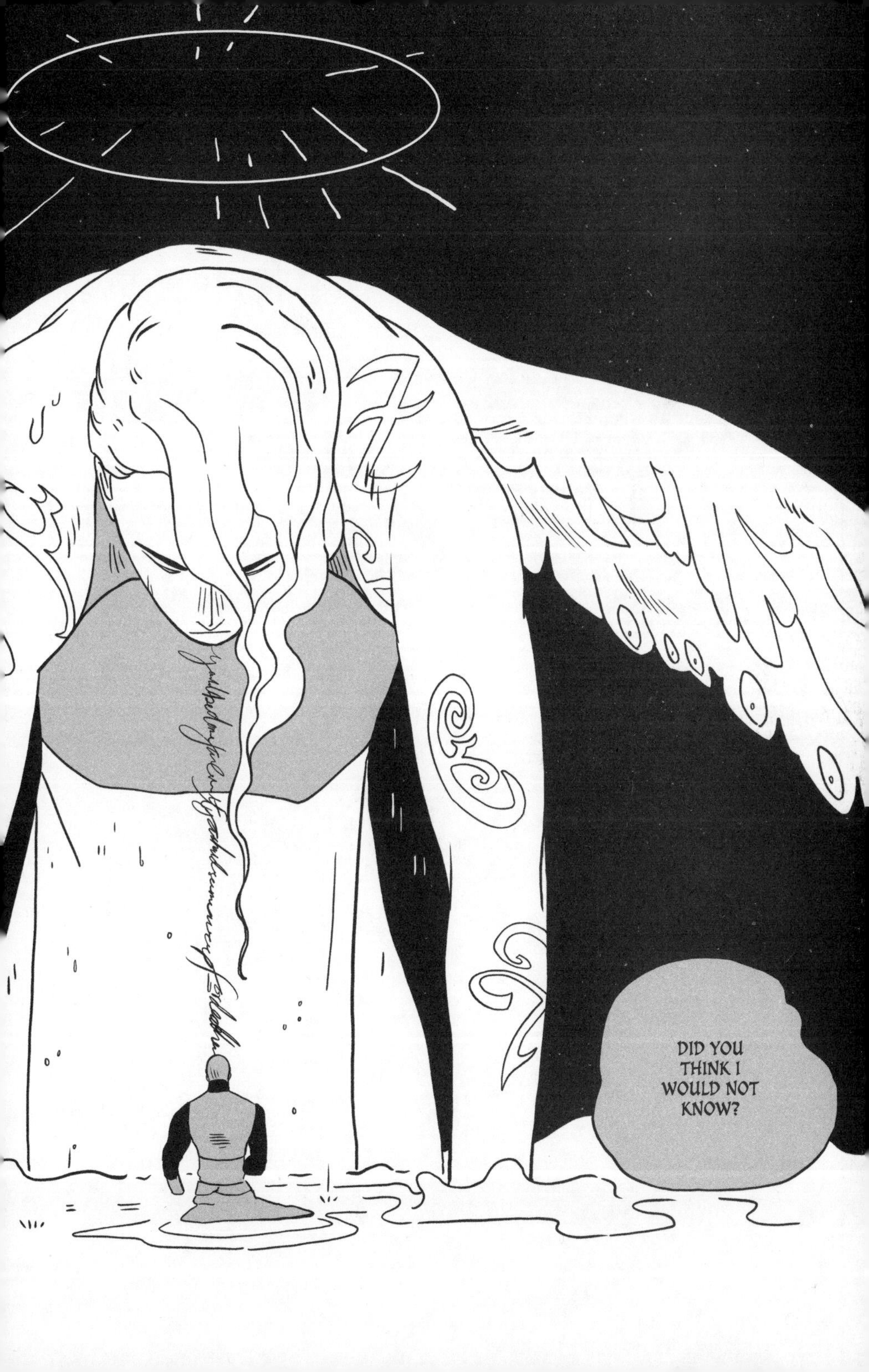
DID YOU THINK I WOULD NOT KNOW?

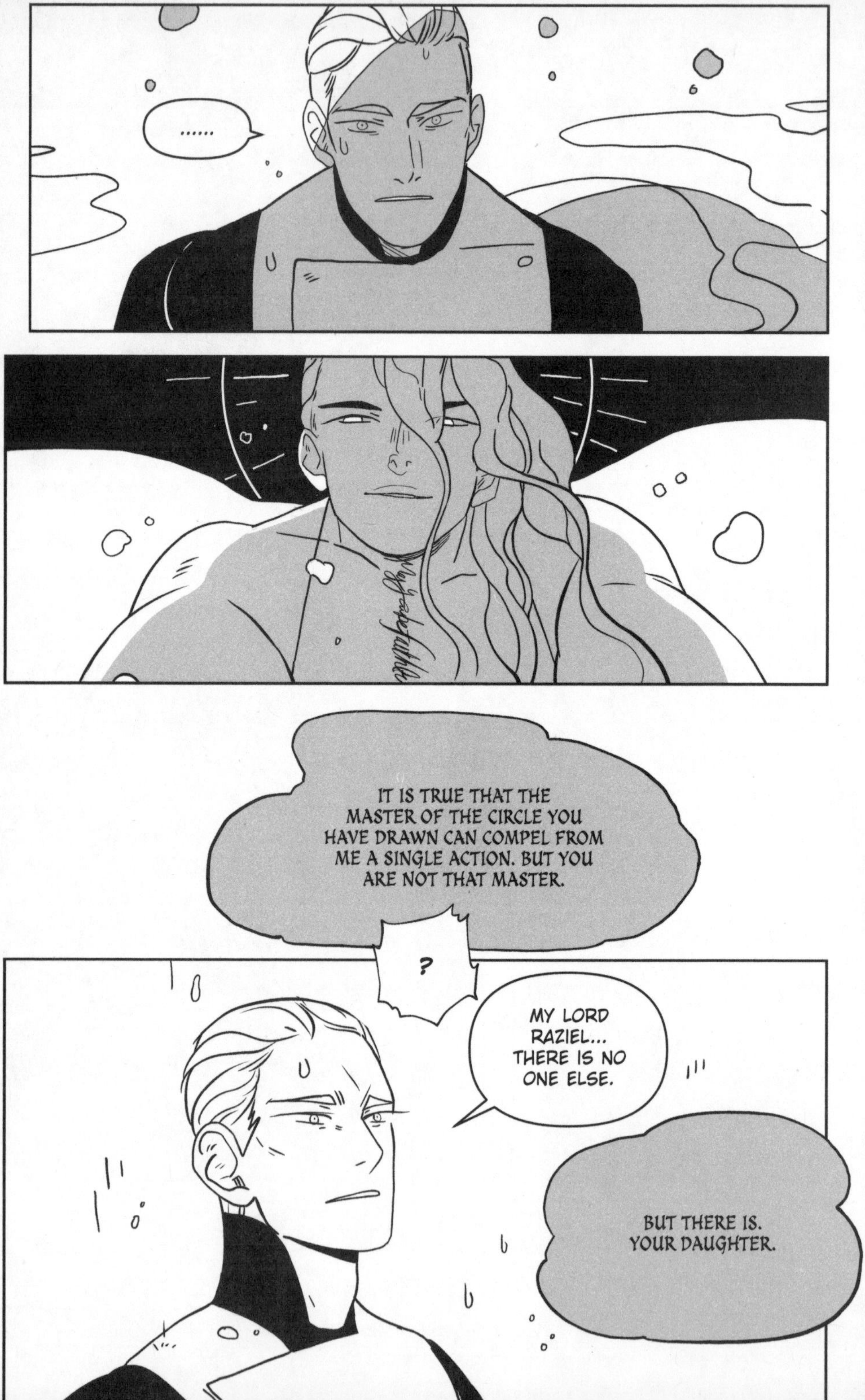
......
IT IS TRUE THAT THE MASTER OF THE CIRCLE YOU HAVE DRAWN CAN COMPEL FROM ME A SINGLE ACTION. BUT YOU ARE NOT THAT MASTER.
?
MY LORD RAZIEL... THERE IS NO ONE ELSE.
BUT THERE IS. YOUR DAUGHTER.

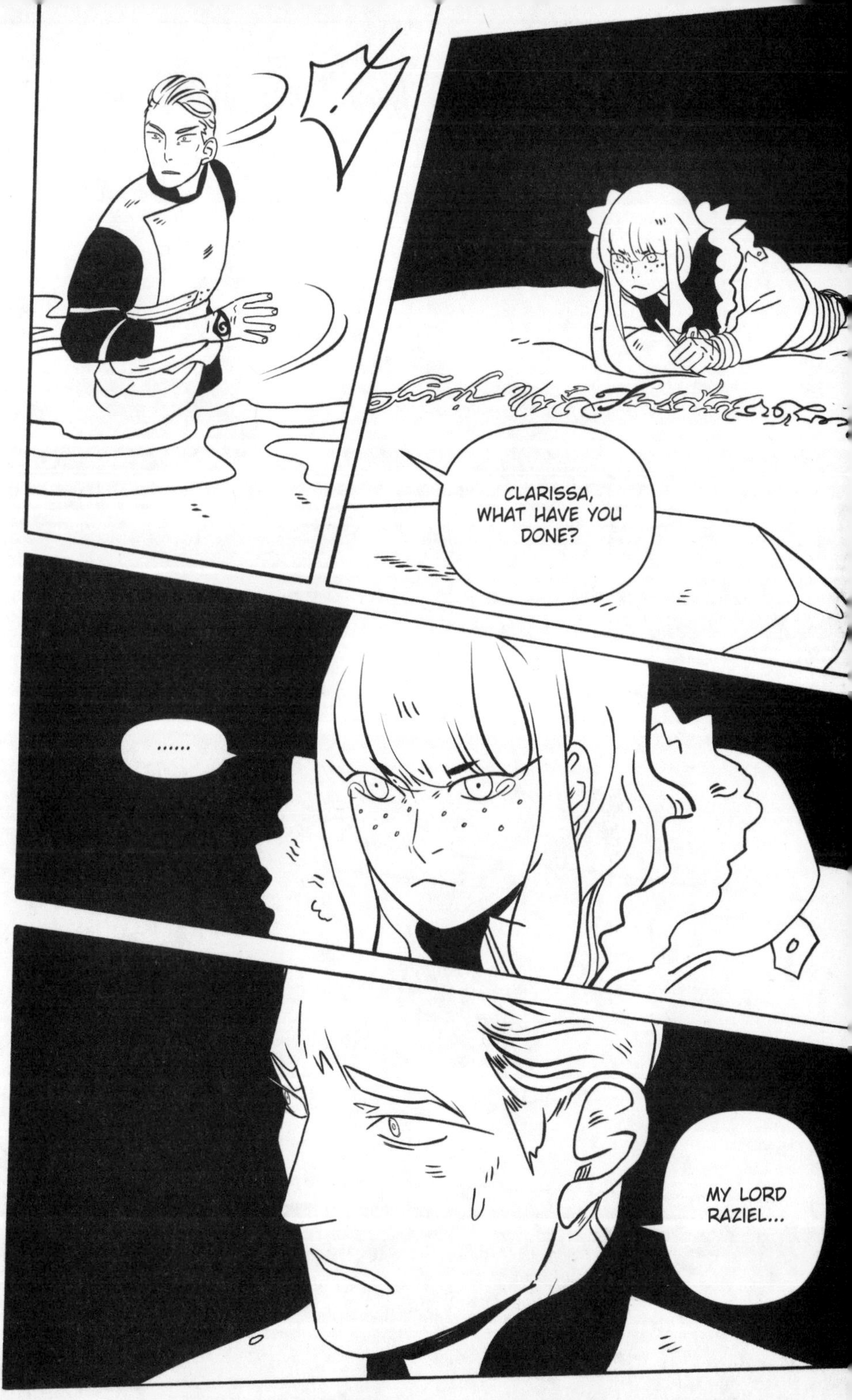
CLARISSA, WHAT HAVE YOU DONE?
......
MY LORD RAZIEL...

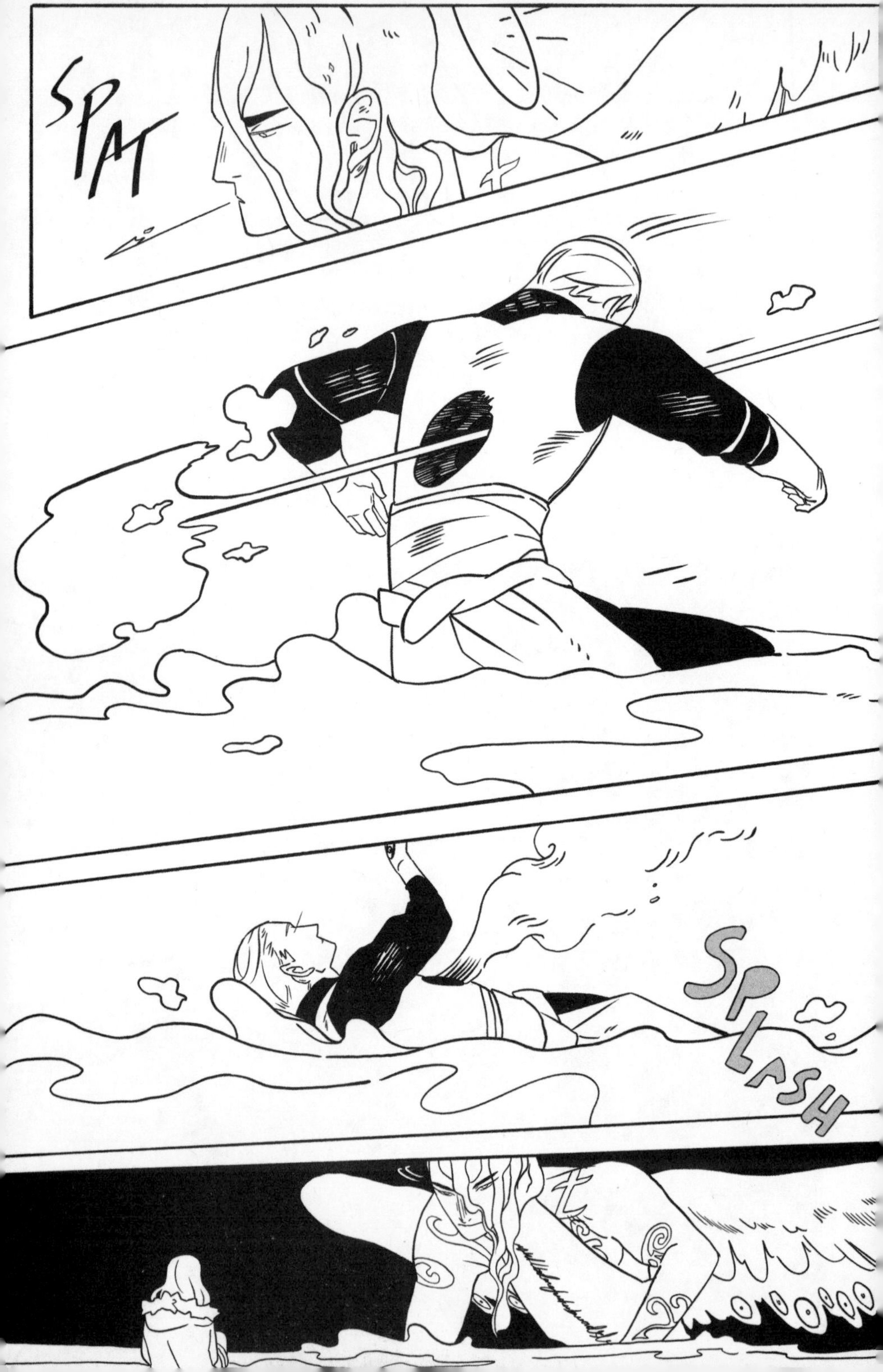
SPAT
SPLASH

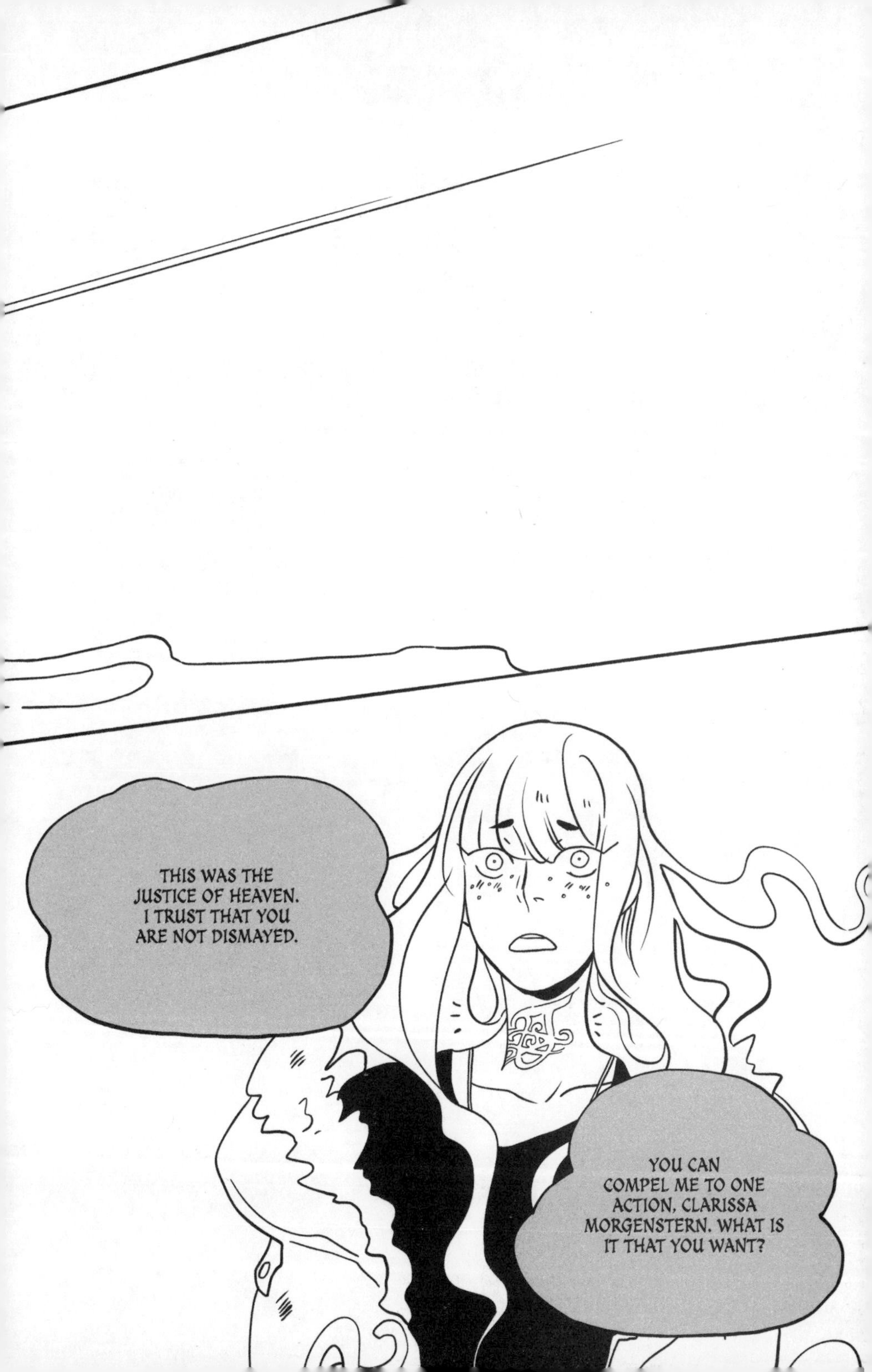
THIS WAS THE JUSTICE OF HEAVEN. I TRUST THAT YOU ARE NOT DISMAYED.
YOU CAN COMPEL ME TO ONE ACTION, CLARISSA MORGENSTERN. WHAT IS IT THAT YOU WANT?

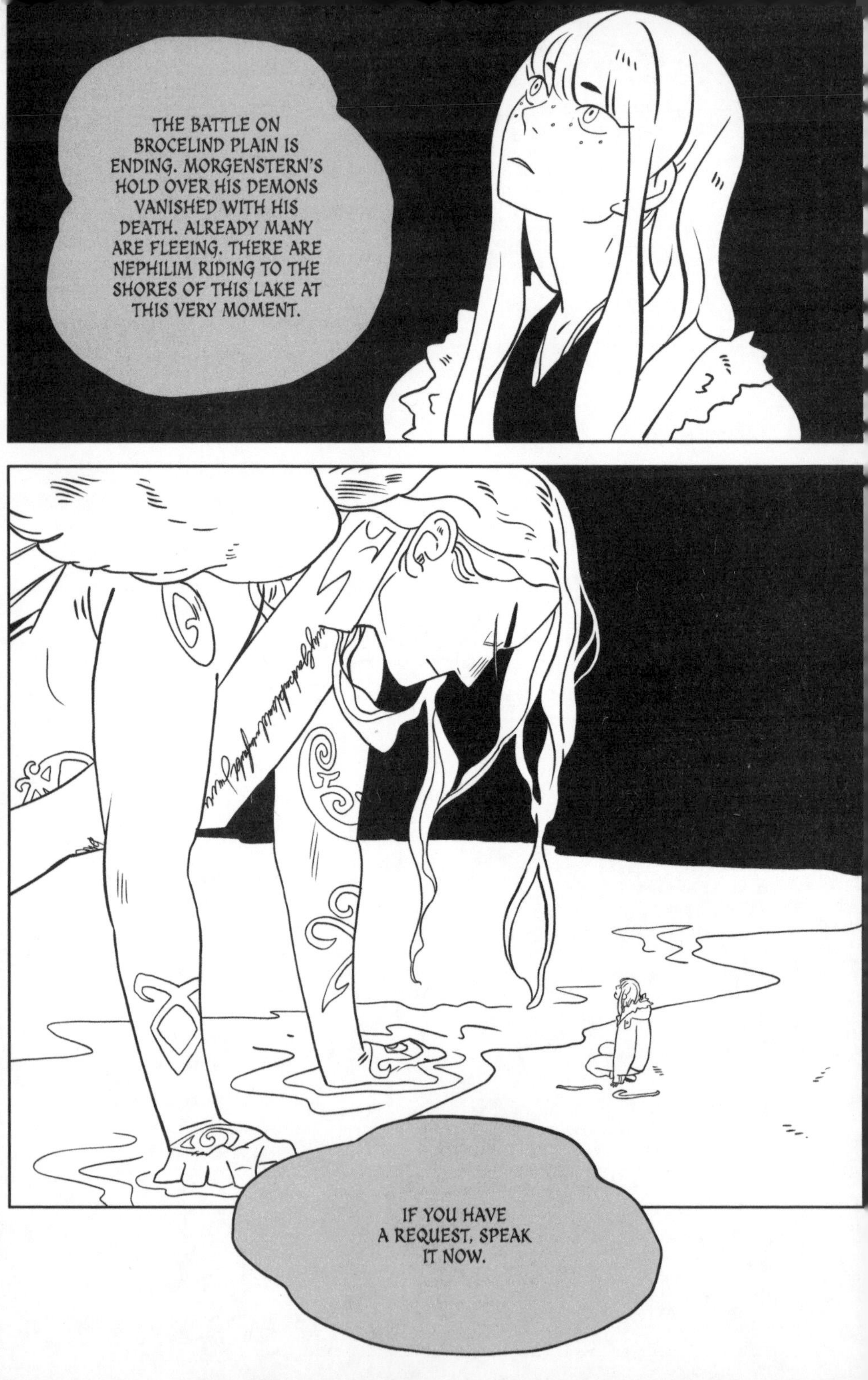
THE BATTLE ON BROCELIND PLAIN IS ENDING. MORGENSTERN'S HOLD OVER HIS DEMONS VANISHED WITH HIS DEATH. ALREADY MANY ARE FLEEING. THERE ARE NEPHILIM RIDING TO THE SHORES OF THIS LAKE AT THIS VERY MOMENT.
IF YOU HAVE A REQUEST, SPEAK IT NOW.

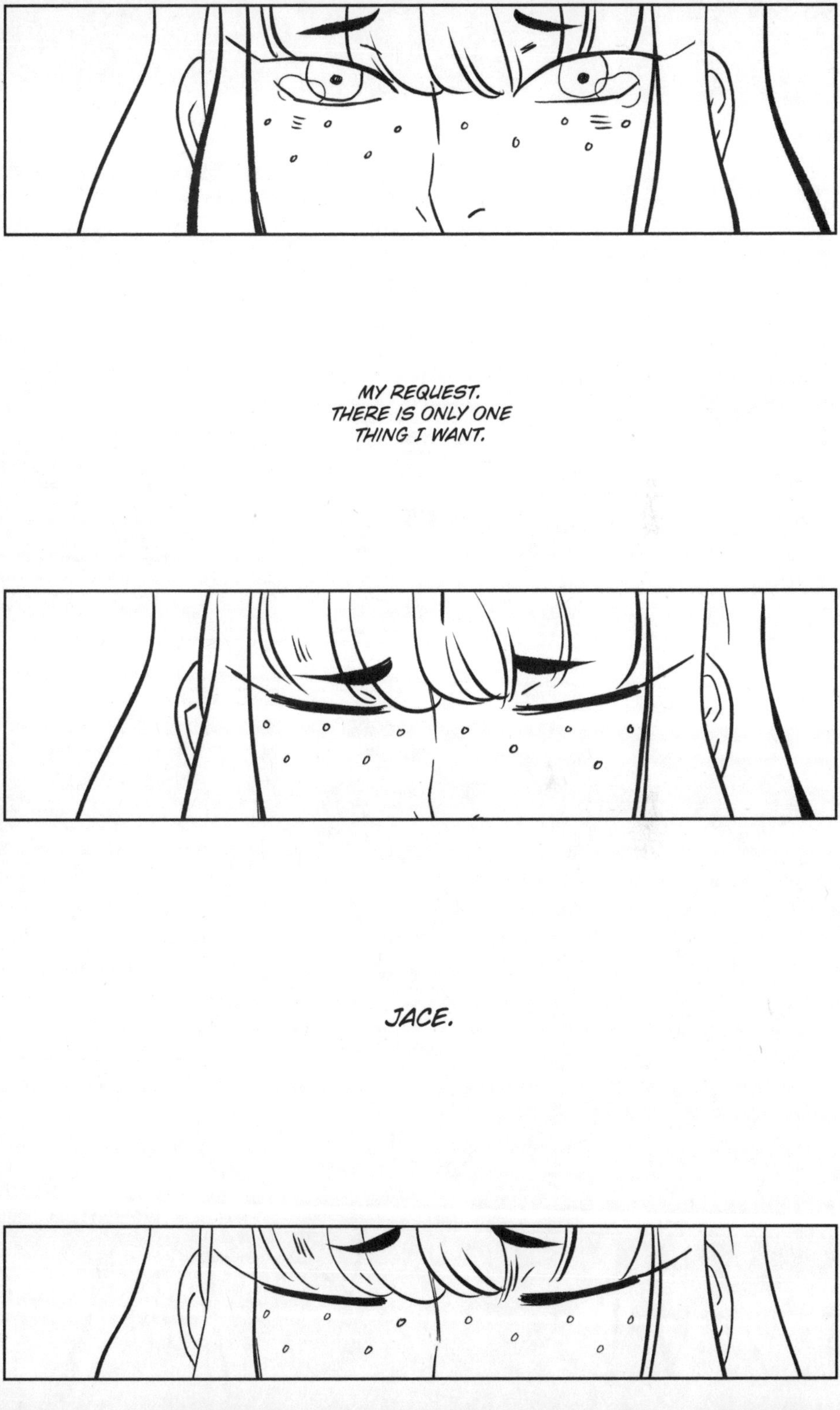
MY REQUEST. THERE IS ONLY ONE THING I WANT.
JACE.

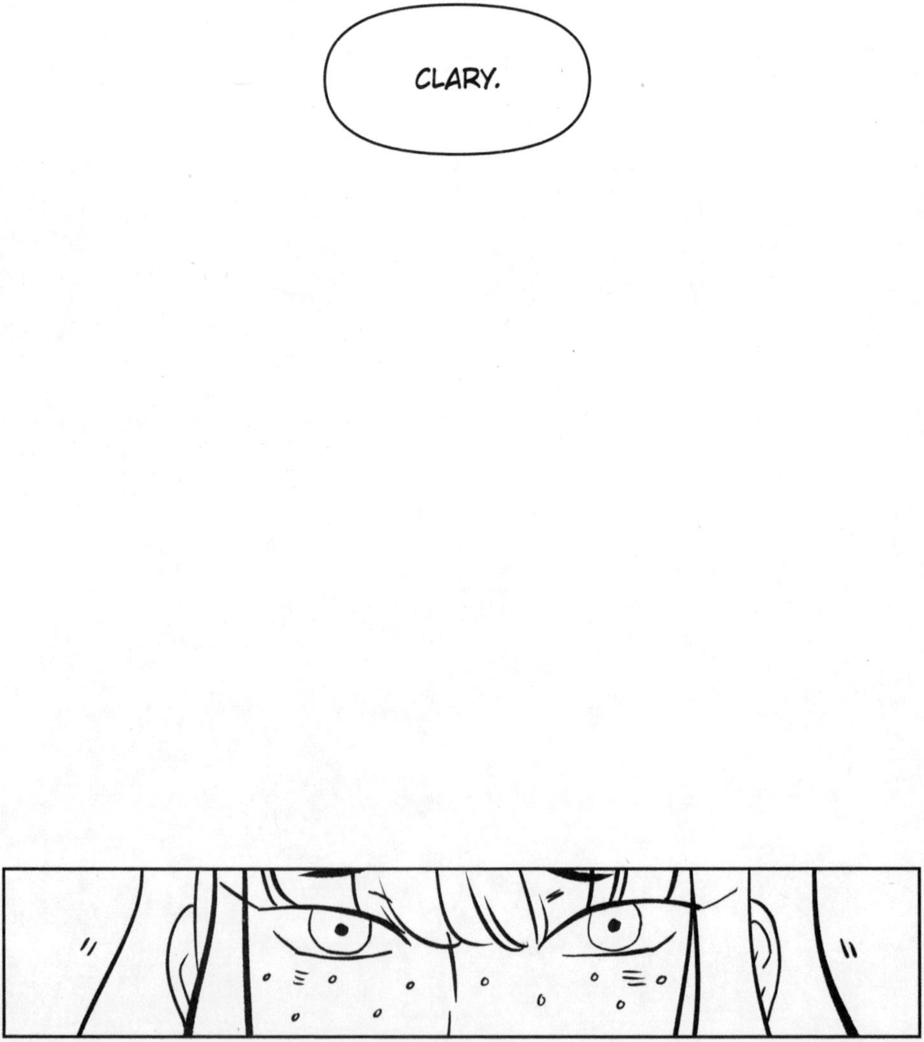
CLARY.

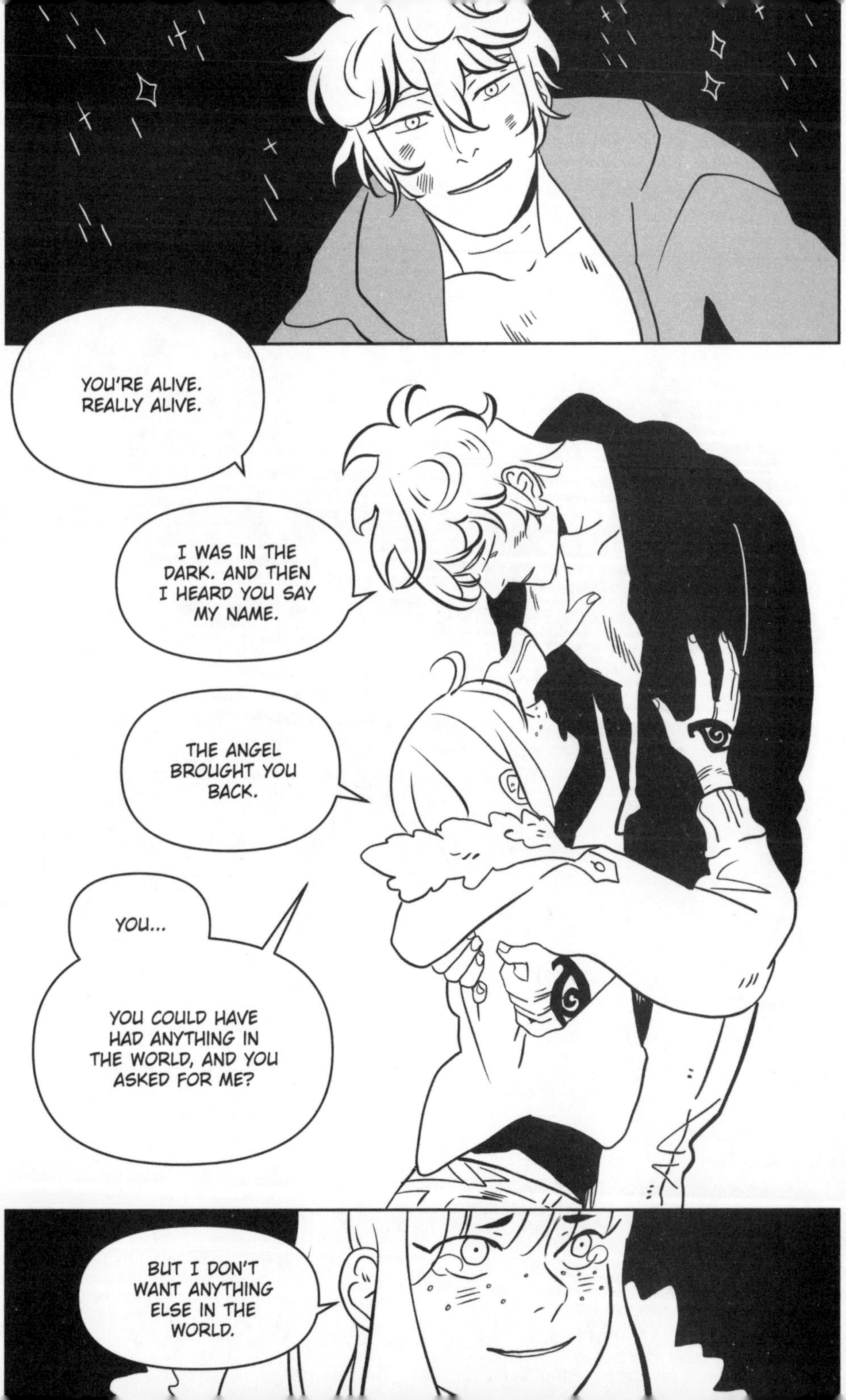
YOU'RE ALIVE. REALLY ALIVE.
I WAS IN THE DARK. AND THEN I HEARD YOU SAY MY NAME.
THE ANGEL BROUGHT YOU BACK.
YOU...
YOU COULD HAVE HAD ANYTHING IN THE WORLD, AND YOU ASKED FOR ME?
BUT I DON'T WANT ANYTHING ELSE IN THE WORLD.

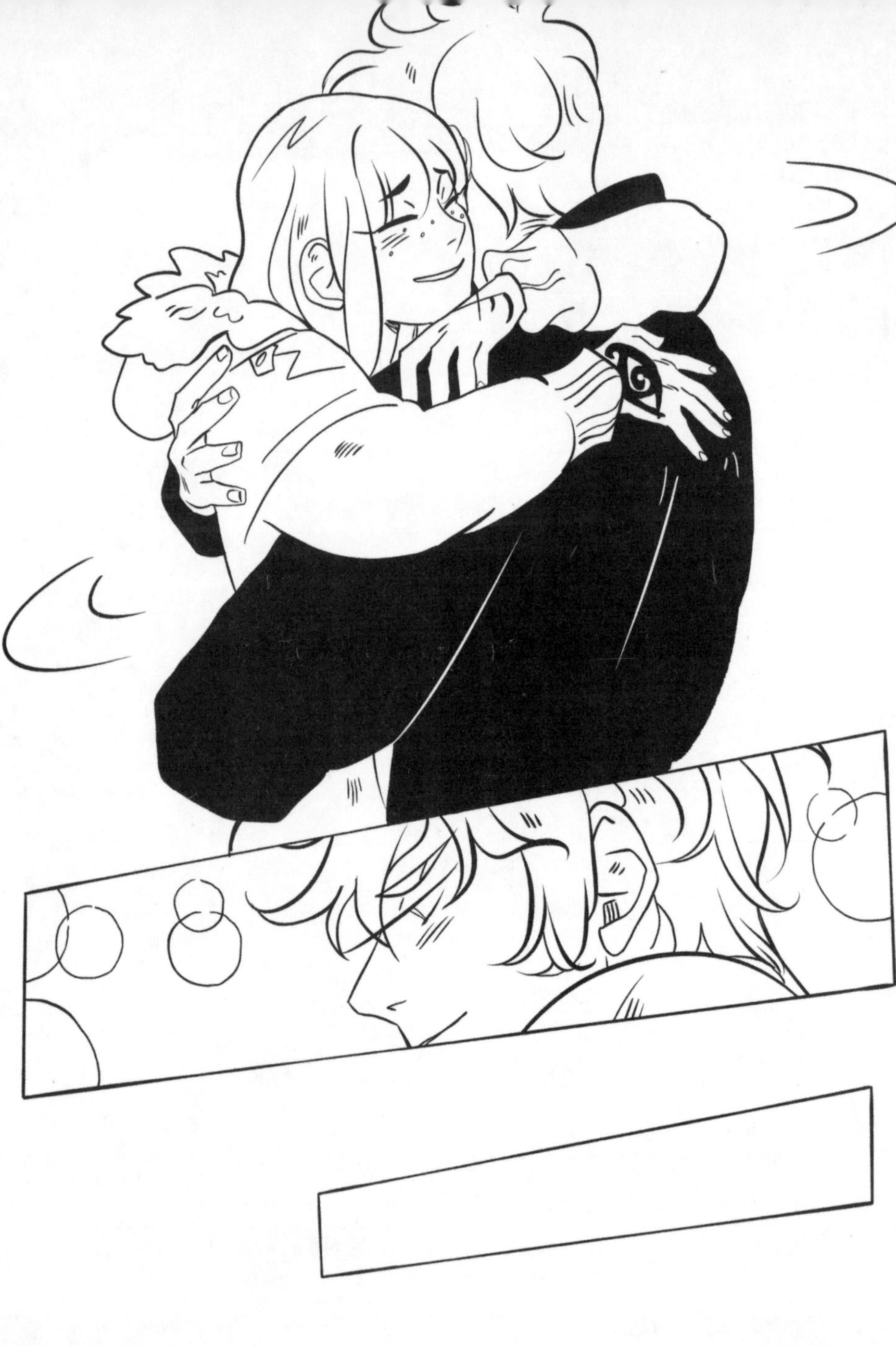

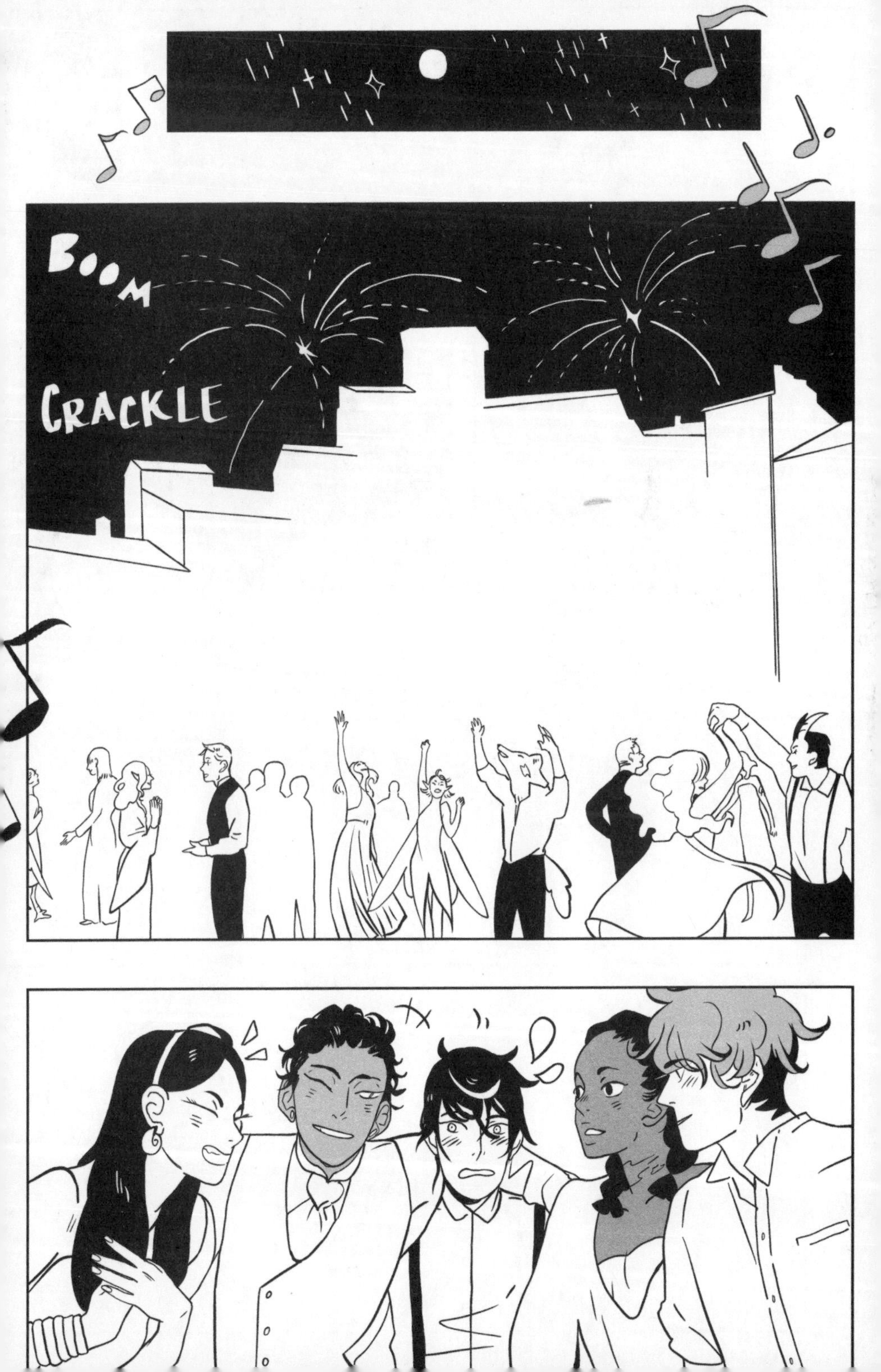
BOOM
CRACKLE

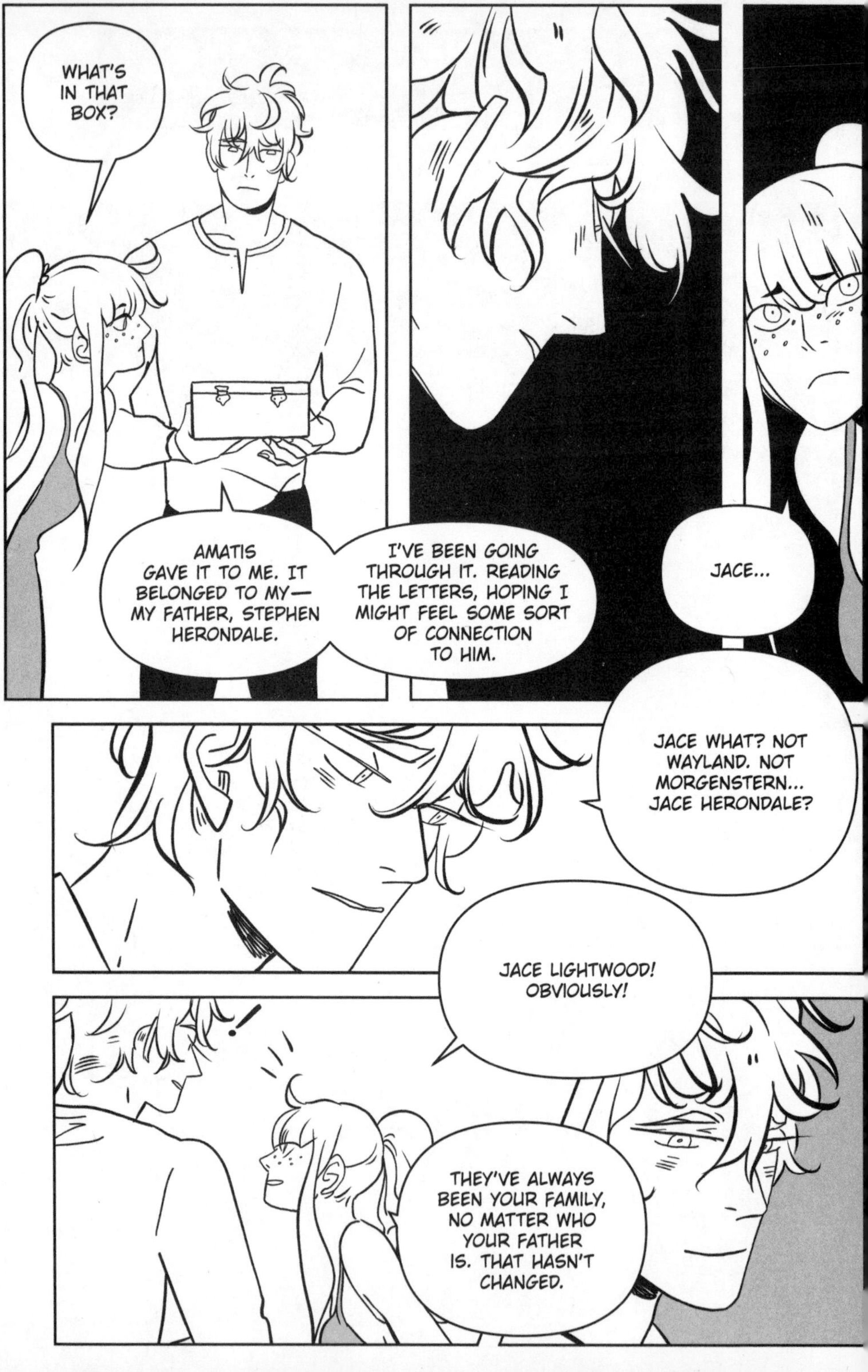
WHAT'S IN THAT BOX?
AMATIS GAVE IT TO ME. IT BELONGED TO MY— MY FATHER, STEPHEN HERONDALE.
I'VE BEEN GOING THROUGH IT. READING THE LETTERS, HOPING I MIGHT FEEL SOME SORT OF CONNECTION TO HIM.
JACE...
JACE WHAT? NOT WAYLAND. NOT MORGENSTERN... JACE HERONDALE?
JACE LIGHTWOOD! OBVIOUSLY!
!
THEY'VE ALWAYS BEEN YOUR FAMILY, NO MATTER WHO YOUR FATHER IS. THAT HASN'T CHANGED.

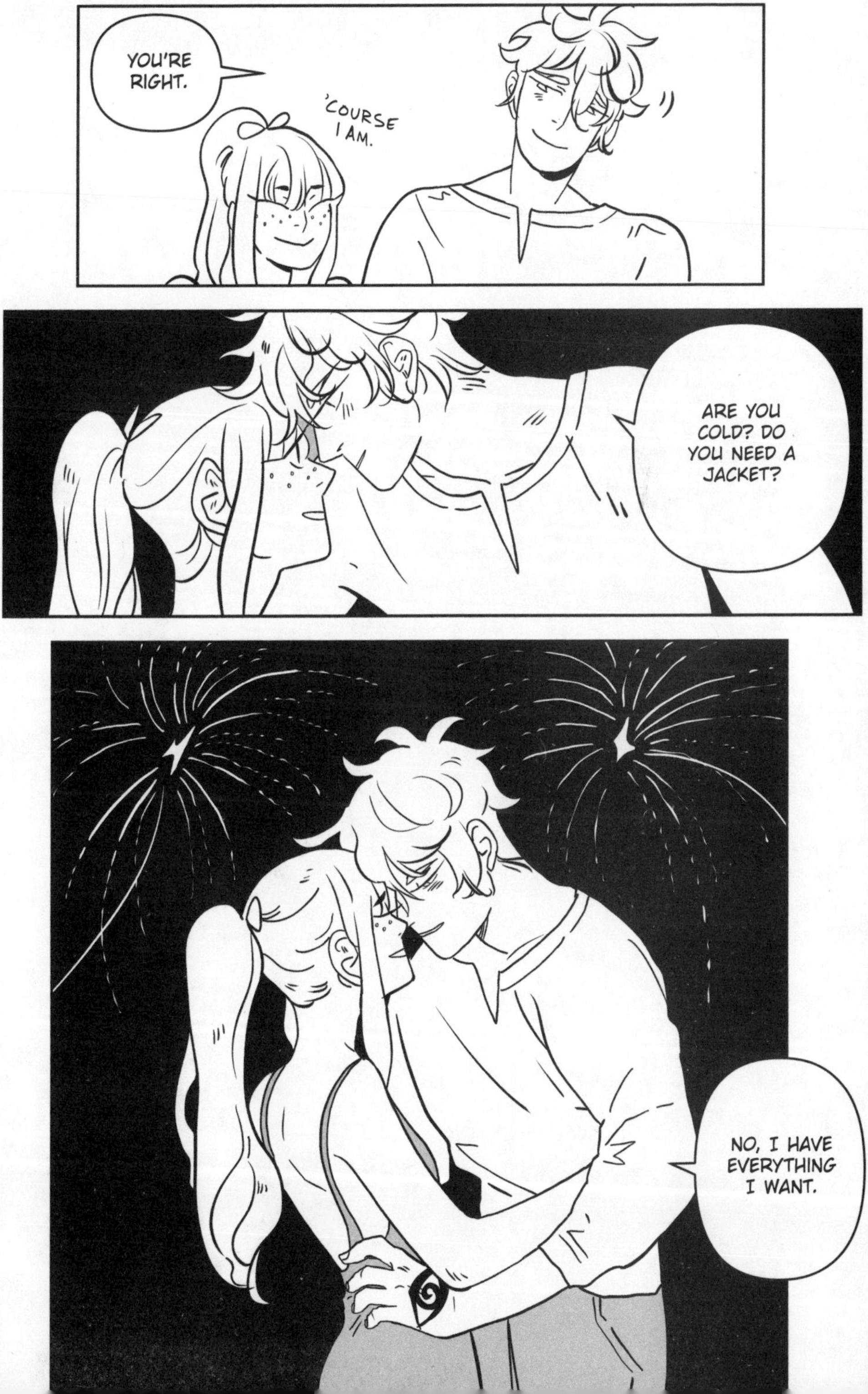

YOU'RE RIGHT.
'COURSE I AM.
ARE YOU COLD? DO YOU NEED A JACKET?
NO, I HAVE EVERYTHING I WANT.

To be continued in the seventh volume of

The MORTAL INSTRUMENTS
THE GRAPHIC NOVEL